Martin Denny's *Hypnotíque*, Liberty Records, Inc. Album cover credits: color photography: Garrett-Howard.

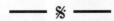

— ✂ —

Publishers/Editors: V. Vale/Andrea Juno
Production Manager: Elizabeth Borowski
Staff Photographers: Robert Waldman, Olivier Robert
Production Staff: Mindaugis Bagdon, Matthew Connors, Tim Dufour, Monique Gerard, Don Ed Hardy, Caroline Hébert, Mason Jones, Erica Olsen, Catherine Reuther, Mary Ricci, Jordana Rosenberg, Jennifer Sharpe, Suzanne Stackle, Christine Sulewski
Book Design: Andrea Juno
Communications Director: Christopher Trela
Chief Consultant: Ken Werner
Special Thanks to: David S. Kahn, Brad Bunnin, Craig A. Newman, Jorie Rose, Eugene H. Winick
Publicist/Foreign Rights: Ira Silverberg, NYC, Tel.: 212-226-6580

BOOKSTORE DISTRIBUTION: Subco, PO Box 168 or 265 So. 5th St, Monroe OR 97456. (503) 847-5274 or (800) 274-7826. FAX: (503) 847-6018.
NON BOOKSTORE DISTRIBUTION: Last Gasp, 2180 Bryant, SF CA 94110. (415) 824-6636.
U.K. DISTRIBUTION: Airlift, 26 Eden Grove, London N7 8EL, UK (071) 607-5792.

Send SASE for catalog: RE/SEARCH PUBLICATIONS
20 Romolo #B
San Francisco, CA 94133
(415) 362-1465

Printed in Hong Kong by Colorcraft Ltd.
Type service bureau: Pinnacle Type, San Francisco
Photostat service: Northern Lights, San Francisco

10 9 8 7 6 5 4 3 2 1

Front Cover Albums:
Limbo Party by Ivy Pete and his Limbo Maniacs, Somerset SF 17600, Alshire International, Inc.
Mallet Mischief, Vol.2 by Harry Breuer & His Quintet, (originally released by Audio-Fidelity Publishing Co.), Eleventh Avenue Theatricals.
The Plastic Cow Goes Moooooog by Michael Melvoin, originally released by Dot Records.
　　　Album cover credits: art direction & cover illustration: Honeya Thompson.
The Cats Meow by The Harmonicats, Mercury Records.

Back Cover Photo (of Lypsinka): Robert Waldman

— ✂ —

CONTENTS

Incredibly Strange Music explores the sonic territory of vinyl recordings (mostly c.1950-1980) largely neglected by the music criticism establishment. Classical, opera, jazz, blues, rock and international music have their specialized critics and publications, but many amazing recordings seem to have escaped critical attention. Often transcending notions involving technical expertise and "good taste," these records defied categories and genres; as a consequence they "fell into the cracks" and are unlikely to be reissued on CD. In record stores they were classified under: easy listening, promotional, novelty/comedy, religious, soundtracks, spoken word, children, celebrity, as well as instrumental headings like accordion and organ (however, whistling, harmonica, and theremin records could be anywhere).

When high-fidelity stereo was first introduced, it immediately inspired an enthusiastic audience for imaginative stereo recordings—many of which are celebrated in this book. During these "golden years" (1955-1965), a huge buying public supported labels like Omega, Audio Fidelity, Command, and RCA Victor's *Stereo Action* series, enabling them to explore the frontiers of sound effects, percussion and "foreign" music toward the goal of providing amazing entertainment. Many of these LPs had gorgeous, colorful covers which were themselves (framable) works of art. An incredible spectrum of genre-busting and experimental records were produced.

In the '50s when people began settling into boring suburban housing tracts, there sprang up a deep longing for the *exotic*. In the early twentieth century, Hawaiian music had inspired a ukelele and steel guitar craze, and after World War II, servicemen reminiscing about their days in the Pacific eagerly embraced the "tiki culture" fad (backyard luaus, tiki bars, hula hoops, Hawaiian shirts, and the hula dancing rage taken up by housewives). At a time when sexuality was most repressed and hypocritical, the phallic symbol of the tiki was planted in backyards by thousands of all-American families. "Import" dance crazes such as the mambo, the cha-cha, the merengue, the belly dance, and the bossa nova also leaked sexuality into our puritanical American society. Just as a dream cloaked in symbols can reveal what we have unconsciously suppressed, so music can expose unsurfaced longings and desires and thus grant unexpected insights into our culture.

In general, the recordings discussed in this book were dismissed and disparaged as unworthy of serious preservation and study by music critics and educational institutions, as they catered to mass appetites or mercenary aspirations (e.g., fad recordings such as the short-lived sitar-with-rock trend; recordings using mock-barnyard sounds like Andre Williams' "Greasy Chicken"; promotional records intended to sell carpeting or air-

Les Baxter's *Space Escapade*, Capitol Records.

conditioners; or records by ex-drug addicts telling how they found god). A lot of the "B" sides of rockabilly or R&B vocal singles were wild, devil-may-care improvisations done in one take just to fill out the record, yet they expressed amazing, potent creativity. In such recordings, technical flaws serve to counter the ideal of *artificial perfection* marketed in many domains by this society; in music, studio-perfect recording techniques often disguise a fundamental lack of *inspiration,* animal vitality, magic and wit—the surprise factors that infuse life into "art."

Most of this ephemeral music that never had a defined place in musical "history" existed in a shadowy area between categories. It was a direct expression of the society and the trends at the time—simply by being untethered from any self-consciousness of its "artistic" status as music. For example, some of it was unabashedly and un-ashamedly self-promotional—done strictly as a marketing gimmick, or to capitalize on fads such as the James Bond movie craze of the early '60s. The heresy that much of this music falls under is: it had a *practical* purpose. Art criticism is *appalled* by any practical usage of art; consequently, highbrow art critics have usually snubbed their noses at recordings like *Music to Read By, How to Strip for Your Husband,* and even the highly collectible *Rhapsody of Steel* (a promotional record produced by U.S. Steel).

Just as many of the films discussed in our previous book (*Incredibly Strange Films)* transcended their original commercial purposes, so many of these recordings became a conduit for something more than the sum of their parts. Almost *because* they were free from "artistic" self-consciousness, they could express something unique which with the passing of time can be viewed as important and revelatory. Society often distances itself from creative work through the imposition of convenient categories, and here it's interesting to note that a lot of the music found in "easy listening" record bins is *not* easy—instead of being calming and tranquilizing, it contains contagious rhythms that stop conversation and compel listeners to get up and dance!

In search of amazing endangered records as well as insights as to their genesis, we interviewed not just original musical innovators (who once experienced fame), but trailblazing *collectors* who, without benefit of discography or reference guide, went out into backwater flea markets and thrift stores to search through that which society has

Music to Make Automobiles By . . . , Volkswagen of America.

discarded. Experiencing the thrill and adventure of the hunt, they made their selections and then listened for hours to ferret out exceptional recordings. Through their discriminating eye we view what they select and gain a deviant perspective; by their inspiring eloquence and love of their subject, the records take on fresh significance. These pioneers link one recording to another and create genres where none previously existed. The act of an individual creating their own categories and evaluations for *any* cultural field constitutes a dismantling of the status quo's control system which rules our lives and perceptions through implanted "aesthetics"—what society deems good or bad (highbrow or lowbrow). Nothing—especially *art*—exists in and of itself, but always in relation to its context. Each generation rediscovers and reappraises artistic or cultural phenomena as historical perspective changes. (Unfortunately, much of the music mentioned here *won't* be preserved for future rediscovery—it was never printed on sheet music, the master tapes have probably been lost, and when all of the vinyl albums wear out, it'll be gone forever!)

In an age of information overload, the mere act of wading through and deciphering society's discards becomes a political act. By the process of selection based on personal observation as to what gives them entertainment and pleasure, the collectors subvert the invisible, tight reins by which

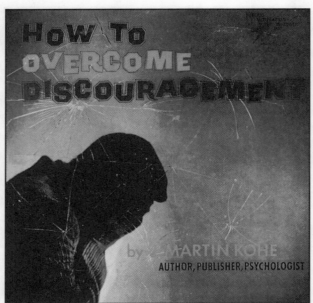

J. Martin Kohe's *How to Overcome Discouragement*,
Success Motivation ® Institute, Inc.

society controls us; additionally, they aid us in developing our *own* aesthetic about pop culture phenomena. When one hears their enthusiasm and their philosophical justifications, one also hears multiple levels of irony as well as nostalgic associations. Thus these records become more than a consumeristic product; they become a reflection of the collector's inner vision and express an alternate aesthetic philosophy. (Note: this kind of activity does not have to be restricted to *records*—we are in an age where *recycling* is of paramount importance. In this complex society which has produced so many permutations of "culture," there will always be new uncharted areas that are cheap and accessible to anyone possessed of a discriminating eye. Whether it be "exotica" music or "B" movies or '60s "adult" paperbacks, there will always be a realm that is overlooked and abandoned by society—that has escaped the eye of the academic, the critic and the antique dealer. The thrill of making an exciting "find" need not be tied to a high price tag.)

From the beginning, the very *existence* of recording technology encroached upon *live* music-making. At the turn of the century, millions of homes had a piano or at least a guitar; thousands of families and friends used to make music together in the evenings. Within a few years after radio swept the country (beginning in 1920), sheet music sales fell by 80%. In the '40s James Petrillo, the head of the Musicians Union, opposed the institution of the jukebox because he foresaw that it would put out of work tens of thousands of local bands that played roadhouse cafes all over the country—that prediction rapidly came true. The proliferation of mass media in general has supplanted a lot of the grassroots art that people created unselfconsciously to "amuse themselves": embroidery, Sunday painting (*that* phrase has vanished from the vocabulary), whittling, quilting, model-making, woodworking, street corner singing, *inventing* (in short, all the "hobbies"—another word fallen into disuse). Today, the creativity that used to be a *norm* of daily life has been confused with (and replaced by) unending acts of "selective" consumption manipulated by aggressive marketing strategists. Television-watching has become the number one "hobby" in America, with "shopping" a close second.

Society uses aesthetics in order to control us through our buying patterns, and to coerce us into buying higher-priced commodities. Even the concept of the "vacation" has been altered—today one of the hottest vacation attractions in America is a SuperMall in the Midwest! In fact, in vacation areas themselves, shopping is a major part of the experience. Most people's identities are based on what they buy; their value or sense of self-worth is linked to what they own, with a hierarchical judgment system that says that a Rolex or a BMW is "better" because the price is higher. We live in the age of the *pathological consumer* where an act of consumption characterizes virtually every possible "spare time" activity. Therefore, it's a subversive act to rediscover and value that which is cheap and readily available . . . what society has thrown out.

The pleasure which music can provide is very important to our well-being. In our Calvinist society with its Puritan underbelly, pleasure is a political statement and has always been a destabilizer of the power structure which has implanted an anti-pleasure work ethic. Inherent in our culture is the idea that if something is fun, it can't be art, or *important*. (Conversely, if it's boring, it must be high art!) Behind everything pleasurable a punishment lurks; even in a subculture where the term "high brow" has been replaced by the terms "cool" or "hip," there still remains a guilty underpinning that a record you love has to be esoteric or rare; you have to *earn* your pleasure—it can't be *easy*. To hearken back to Emma Goldman:

what's the point of a revolution if you can't dance to it?

This is not a completist's volume—countless examples of incredible music remain to be uncovered, such as from other countries. Even though the music discussed here may be fun, this is not to say that it's any more important than opera, rap, top 40 or any other genre of music. Music really is like *food* . . . some people may like their eggs over-easy, poached, or scrambled—but one doesn't assume a stance of "political correctness" based on personal preference. One cannot say that somebody who likes rap is more "cutting edge" or "cool" than someone who likes easy listening.

New technologies inspire creativity by providing new potential for experimentation, and today computer-interfaceable digital sound technology has made sampling, overdubbing and editing much more available and affordable. But there is an insidious trend in the recording industry to continue to market new formats (DAT, DCC, the recordable CD, etc) which render *extinct* decades of previous recordings. We're currently witnessing the death of record-playing technology, yet the CD is *not* a permanent medium. Early industry claims for the CD's "indestructibility" were ad agency falsifications (remember the TV commercial showing a CD being put into a dishwasher?). On the contrary, the CD is quite fragile, and the metallic oxide coatings are subject to the effects of atmospheric and environmental erosion—whereas the vinyl record has a proven longevity; it can last indefinitely if not played. The advantage of the CD remains its 70-minute playing time and the ability to play tracks selectively, but digital sound indisputably lacks the warmth and "living presence" of analog sound.

With all the media deluging us today, we have a plethora of information available in many different formats. Everything is out there, especially in the field of music where almost all styles exist simultaneously, and all the world's culture seems to be flashing before our stunned, TV-watching eyes. In earlier centuries, each tribe or country basically had only one regional type of music available to its citizens (e.g., Bulgarian folk choruses; Moroccan *djilala* music; Balinese gamelan) but in today's post-technological global village, *all* music is at our disposal, with exciting new recombinations and cross-pollinations asserting themselves. The blurring of the edges of media culture could be positive, adumbrating a hoped-for cooperation between diverse cultures in the years ahead.

It is important to maintain a fluid *multiplicity* of identity—any fixed identity tends to lead to cultural ossification and dogmas. (This was the fallacy of most undergrounds, including the hippies and the punks who imposed very strict codes regulating rigid styles of fashion and music.) All the world's culture is now simultaneously available, and this could be the foundation for limitless possibilities to arise in the future.

It is now almost possible to *have it all*. The treasures of "history" (formerly for only the wealthy ruling elite: books, films, art and music from around the world) are finally becoming accessible. Rare books are being reprinted in unprecedented numbers or can be obtained on xerox from inter-library loan. Just a few years ago only millionaires could own movies; now almost anyone can own hundreds of films on videotape. Thanks to advanced computer scanning technology it is even technically possible to own an exact textured copy of a "great" painting or sculpture, and we look forward to the day when every book in the world can be had *on-line* by anyone with a home computer. Because all this information is becoming freely available, there is no excuse for remaining culturally insular; the only barrier to virtually unlimited knowledge and insight remains one's "taste."

—Andrea Juno & V. Vale

Charles Camilleri's *Spectacular Accordions*, MGM Records.

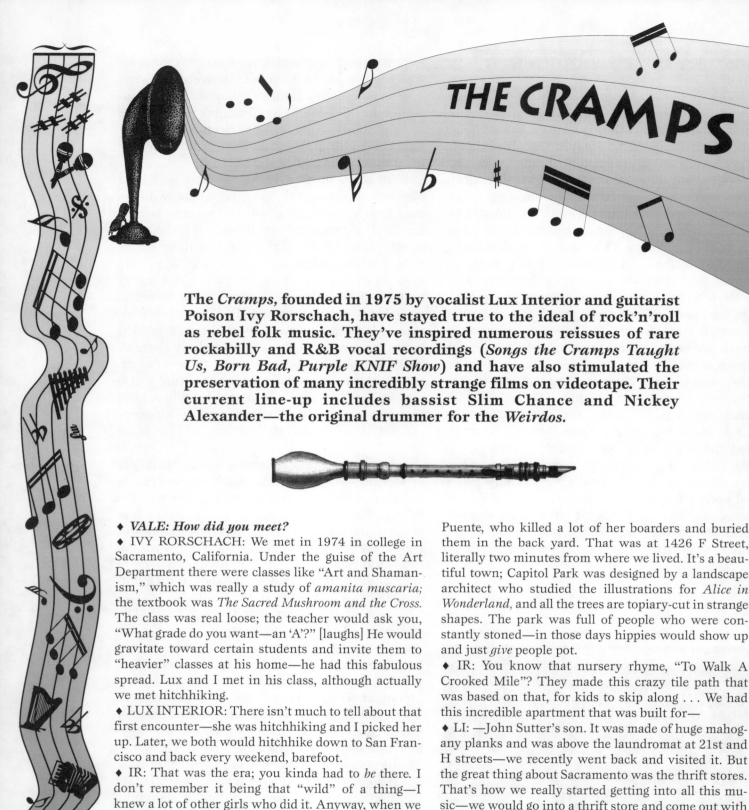

THE CRAMPS

The *Cramps,* founded in 1975 by vocalist Lux Interior and guitarist Poison Ivy Rorschach, have stayed true to the ideal of rock'n'roll as rebel folk music. They've inspired numerous reissues of rare rockabilly and R&B vocal recordings (*Songs the Cramps Taught Us, Born Bad, Purple KNIF Show*) and have also stimulated the preservation of many incredibly strange films on videotape. Their current line-up includes bassist Slim Chance and Nickey Alexander—the original drummer for the *Weirdos.*

♦ *VALE: How did you meet?*

♦ IVY RORSCHACH: We met in 1974 in college in Sacramento, California. Under the guise of the Art Department there were classes like "Art and Shamanism," which was really a study of *amanita muscaria;* the textbook was *The Sacred Mushroom and the Cross.* The class was real loose; the teacher would ask you, "What grade do you want—an 'A'?" [laughs] He would gravitate toward certain students and invite them to "heavier" classes at his home—he had this fabulous spread. Lux and I met in his class, although actually we met hitchhiking.

♦ LUX INTERIOR: There isn't much to tell about that first encounter—she was hitchhiking and I picked her up. Later, we both would hitchhike down to San Francisco and back every weekend, barefoot.

♦ IR: That was the era; you kinda had to *be* there. I don't remember it being that "wild" of a thing—I knew a lot of other girls who did it. Anyway, when we met hitchhiking, we talked and discovered we were going to see each other again in this teacher's class. Actually, the first kiss was in this instructor's house— we'd taken mushrooms, I think.

♦ *V: I visited Sacramento then and it seemed safe; that serial killer mentality wasn't there—*

♦ LI: But you *did* have serial killers! The Sacramento vampire, Richard Chase, was "working" at that time, as was that old lady with the rooming house, Dorothea

Puente, who killed a lot of her boarders and buried them in the back yard. That was at 1426 F Street, literally two minutes from where we lived. It's a beautiful town; Capitol Park was designed by a landscape architect who studied the illustrations for *Alice in Wonderland,* and all the trees are topiary-cut in strange shapes. The park was full of people who were constantly stoned—in those days hippies would show up and just *give* people pot.

♦ IR: You know that nursery rhyme, "To Walk A Crooked Mile"? They made this crazy tile path that was based on that, for kids to skip along . . . We had this incredible apartment that was built for—

♦ LI: —John Sutter's son. It was made of huge mahogany planks and was above the laundromat at 21st and H streets—we recently went back and visited it. But the great thing about Sacramento was the thrift stores. That's how we really started getting into all this music—we would go into a thrift store and come out with a stack of 45s a foot high. They might sell for $50 or $100 each today, but we'd be buying them for a *nickel.* If they were a dime we'd be outraged, and if they were a quarter we'd be ready to break windows!

♦ IR: It wasn't like we already knew about a certain kind of music and were seeking it out; our attitude was more, "Gee, I wonder what *this* is?" We loved just discovering music. Not long after we met, this guy "Ed" at the K Street Mall opened a collector's record

Ivy & Lux hang out in their record lair.   Photo: Lux Interior

store that had amazing record covers on the wall. Before that, we used to go to another record store on the K Street Mall that had cut-out records for a quarter, so we already were into buying records we didn't know anything about—we'd make decisions just based on the cover, etc.

At the time all these boring Northern California folk rock singers were moaning about their feelings . . . meanwhile, we're finding stuff way beyond that: people *screaming*, all nervous and crazy and horny!

Sacramento is a small town and there wasn't much to do, so we spent a lot of time talking to Ed, and he kinda educated us about music. I don't know if people understand what collecting was at that time. Now people know what "rockabilly" is from reissues, but back then there were no reissues, there was no clue as to what anything even *was*. We'd been given a few clues by Ed, plus another guy—

◆ LI: —who gave us a stack of *unplayed* 78s a foot high; fabulous records that would sell for $50 apiece now.

◆ IR: His rejects or duplicates—that's what started our record collection. I don't know why he turned us on to them, but that town was so small and friendly and there weren't many collectors, so things weren't so competitive.

◆ LI: At that time the only clue we had was if the label said "BMI" instead of "ASCAP." If it said "ASCAP" it could not be rock'n'roll, because they wouldn't publish that. With few exceptions, ASCAPs were all bad records.

◆ IR: Also, we'd ask: does the name of the artist sound like it could be cool—you know, not "Hugo Winterhalter." You'd get burned a lot of times, but when you didn't—it was such *heaven* finding songs that way. We'll never experience that again because thrift stores are too picked over; now it's more down to seeking out things you've heard of. But at the time it was just this *discovering.*

◆ LI: Ivy actually went out and got a *job* at a Goodwill so she could be there when the truck pulled in. Sometimes we would sit outside these stores in our car half-asleep waiting for the truck, hoping there would be these golden records.

◆ IR: I said there was no competition but there actually was a little bit. The job stunk—it was like a *real* job, so I quit.

◆ LI: Once we went into a junk store near where we

Lux digs a tape on the stupendous Trophonic Helmetphones.

Photo: Lux Interior

lived and got an unplayed copy of "Let It Roll" by SID KING & THE FIVE STRINGS and "Let the Jukebox Keep on Playing" by CARL PERKINS—his first record which is now selling for a hundred bucks. I remember saying, "Let's try out some of these and see what they sound like; they're only a nickel." And they were *really* wild. At the time all these boring Northern California folk rock singers were moaning about their feelings; nothing was going on that could be called rock'n'roll. Meanwhile, we're finding this stuff that was way beyond that: people *screaming,* all nervous and crazy and horny and everything.

♦ IR: We were mainly looking for records by vocal groups. I had never heard this music before so it wasn't nostalgia for me—it was a whole new world. And it was incredibly strange music: otherworldly, unearthly. As for rockabilly, even the people who collected vocal groups weren't into that.

♦ *ANDREA JUNO: It must have been a thrill: to explore this uncharted, totally unlabeled world—*

♦ IR: At the time all the other collectors we knew were middle-aged men only into doowop and vocal groups, because they had experienced it the first time around. There was no one our age at all. Again, I don't think this could have happened in a bigger town, but in Sacramento people who weren't that socially similar

could still be friends.

The other thing we were into that no one else was interested in was '60s garage band music—what people would now call *Pebbles* music [after the reissue series of LPs]. That was music of our era, but I only knew the hits—whereas actually there was a ton of garage band music that was really obscure. So we were obsessed with getting that kind of music, and going to see groups like Alice Cooper and T-Rex [laughs]—that didn't seem incongruous to us at all. In fact, through record collecting I was finding out that T-Rex was influenced by HOWLIN' WOLF—I was making connections like that. With other people, record collecting seemed like more of a nostalgia thing, but somehow for us it was different—we were gonna *use* it.

♦ *V: How did you get into performing?*

♦ IR: I had played guitar since I was a kid, but not like disciplined. First I learned from my brother, then I was kinda self-taught. When I met Lux, he said he'd sung in his little brother's garage bands but not seriously. I was amazed, because he was so into music; he had this incredible record collection of bands (like The Pretty Things) I'd never heard of. I was surprised that he wasn't already in a band—that it was just fandom.

♦ LI: Not too long after I met Ivy we moved to Ohio, where I was from, on the way to moving to New York. In Sacramento, if you didn't wear a white t-shirt and jeans, you were considered some kind of *egomaniac:* "You weren't common, man!" We left that environment and went to Ohio where all the local bands were playing dressed head to toe in sequins and rhinestones. It was absolutely nothing like Sacramento.

♦ IR: Sacramento started out like a real cool scene, like a flash hippie crazy renaissance—"Be everything you can be!"

♦ LI: In the beginning it was very glamorous—

♦ IR: We used to go to rock'n'roll concerts and the crowd would look like a Fellini movie—everybody just dressed up wild. You could tell that every person there had taken all day to get ready, and the band was just one more decoration. But then Sacramento became downright macho; it seemed like every male had a beard and dressed like a farmer, and every woman looked like an "earth mother." You started hearing the same music on the radio—Crosby Stills & Nash and the Grateful Dead—and the same songs, not even their newest material.

Sacramento became really oppressive—it got to the point where people would yell out of their car windows at us for how we looked. After *Transformer* came out we were real excited about going to see Lou Reed—we got tickets for the second row! But the show got canceled—

♦ LI: —it turned out they only *sold* two rows of tickets! We asked ourselves, "What are we *doing* here?"

♦ IR: At the time Lux looked a lot like Alice Cooper—people actually thought he was this tall woman. We worked it out that he wouldn't speak, and we'd get

Ivy just in from the pool listens to cool sounds on the Zenith Cobramatic.   Photo: Lux Interior

invited out: "Hey, you girls want to come to a party?" Lux wouldn't say anything but he'd have long hair and be wearing high heels and thrift store fox stoles and makeup, and we'd be like two girls. Or the other thing: I was real skinny, I was into Marc Bolan and I had curly hair just like his, so we'd be like this skinny boy with this weird tall woman. But that's what we had to do to amuse ourselves, because we wouldn't spend money except on records; we'd barely spend it on food.

After we moved to Akron, our record collecting escalated because the really good music had never *come* to Sacramento; it never was that kind of industrial cultural center. Where you really found those records was the Midwest. Akron was a rubber industry town and Cleveland was steel industry, so this was where Southerners, black and white, had migrated. You could find tons of original records that had only been released in some small region of the South. And there were no collectors in Ohio then. Ohio's weird, because like DEVO said, there are like spuds and a few quirky outsiders, and the place made the crazy people even crazier. So even though it was repressed in some ways, there was kind of a cool underworld there.

♦ LI: In Ohio we'd always go places where all the white people would say, "Oh, man, don't go *there*—are you kidding? You'll never get out *alive!*"

♦ IR: Like where we *lived*. [laughs]

♦ LI: We lived in Ohio for two years and not one person visited us. We knew a whole mess of people, but they wouldn't go to a "mixed" neighborhood. And the blacks were just as stereotyped; they had raccoon tails hanging from the aerial of their car and Zodiac bumper-stickers, you name it—

♦ IR: This was the '70s.

♦ LI: It really was like two different civilizations living next to each other. But we'd go into black neighborhoods looking for records and they didn't have any problem with us. We went to one woman's store that had a million dolls in it, all decayed, with cobwebs everywhere. We thought, "This is weird; let's go in and ask her if she has any records." We always did that, because that's how you find stuff—you have to talk to people. And she said, "I got my mother's records at home." We said, "What kind of records are they?" and she said, "They're really *good* records." It wasn't till we got there that we found out her mother was a blues singer. And the records in her basement were unbelievable. We went down there and were drinking—

♦ IR: Boone's Farm peach wine. Her name was Mickey and she was real pretty and like plump. This was the mid-'70s, and she was wearing purple hot pants with a matching purple vest that went down to the ankles, with boots—she looked wild. She was getting us drunk, coming on heavy to *him*—but it didn't matter. We were just having fun drinking her peach wine and listening to these records and she was having a sloppy good time. She reminded me of GYPSY ROSE LEE, whose autobiography I had read. And this basement was cool, with Christmas lights, original Maxfield Parrish prints, and that kind of furniture that has cow hooves—

We used to go to rock'n'roll concerts and the crowd would look like a Fellini movie—everybody just dressed up wild. You could tell that every person there had taken all day to get ready, and the band was just one more decoration.

♦ LI: —or cow horns. And there were no square corners in her house; she had put chicken wire in all the corners, and then put plaster over the chicken wire—

♦ IR: Rounded all the corners, like a cave—

♦ LI: We went down to the basement and started playing these 78s. She had ten stacks of 'em, each about a foot high—unbelievably rare, impossibly good stuff: '20s blues, Mamie Smith, Clara Smith. And she sold them to us for 20 cents apiece.

We met some weird people in Ohio. There was a record collector named Les Cottrell who's single-handedly responsible for cataloging every release on Capitol and Imperial Records. He was a King Kong collector and there were a million King Kong dolls hanging from the ceiling of his beautiful Victorian house in the

middle of Akron. We'd go to junk stores all over northeastern Ohio and buy records and bring 'em to him. We'd trade him 20 Fabian records for some really amazing rockabilly record.

♦ IR: We became record scouts for him. He was a major dealer, and had customers coming from Germany and other places.

♦ LI: He would *make* records, too. If he had a $200 record that you couldn't afford, he would make you a 45 with a lathe on his table—

♦ IR: You know those smelly blue records—they're not like modern acetates, but they smell weird and they're dark blue.

♦ LI: You hold them up to the light and they look purple.

Even in Sacramento we thought we'd have a band; it was partly musical inspiration, partly people making fun of us. We'd think, "Someday they'll *pay* to see us!"

♦ *AJ: You used to be able to go into these little booths at train stations and make a 45—*

♦ LI: These were better quality—heavier. People used to have these to record birthday parties of their kids and things like that.

♦ IR: Les Cottrell was a major record dealer, but no one in collector circles knows him now. What happened to him—foul play? It seems peculiar that someone of that stature could just *disappear*.

He educated us, too. We weren't as much into instrumentals and he'd say, "You know, the thing I'm really into is instrumentals," and he would play the things that *he* loved and they were just incredible. He was a weird beatnik guy—really strange cat.

♦ IR: Before we left California we also met RONNIE WEISER. We went to L.A. and called him up and said, "We wanna come to your store" and he said, "I don't have a store." Somehow we scammed to go to his house, and he played us a bunch of records.

♦ LI: That's where we bought our first CHARLIE FEATHERS record—

♦ IR: On Weiser's own Rollin' Rock label: "That Certain Female" b/w "She Set Me Free."

♦ *AJ: So you started the band because you loved the music so much?*

♦ IR: Even in Sacramento we thought we'd have a band; it was partly musical inspiration, partly people making fun of us. We'd think, "Someday they'll *pay* to see us!" I suspect that anyone who's been made fun of for being outwardly artistic has thought: "Someday,

you're gonna be throwing *money* at me and applauding me!" We actually started the band in Akron; we had the name and I was teaching Lux guitar. We'd written songs already; we'd bought our own P.A. system because we thought that's what bands did.

In Sacramento a homeless person walked up to us on K Street and said, "You know what you are? You're beautiful monsters." We loved that—that was just what we felt like. We felt like kings and queens in our world; we had *made* our own world because there wasn't another one for us.

♦ *AJ: In a recent Details article, you're quoted as saying, "Even when circumstances dictate that we furnish our pad with papier-maché and stuff from the street, we'll always live in the manner of the King and Queen of Siam."*

♦ IR: We used to get our furniture off the street. We would live from day to day ("I wonder how we're going to eat?") but people thought we were rich. We didn't spend anything on furnishings—

♦ LI: We paid $3.50 for this lamp here; kings and queens don't have lamps that beautiful.

♦ IR: I remember thinking that we had found the Holy Grail. Here was this fabulous, magical world and we were going to be a channel for this magic because *we* knew about it. The only thing was: we weren't accomplished musicians—

♦ LI: We didn't know anything about it.

♦ IR: But we didn't let that stop us. I think what enabled us to actually execute this fantasy was our isolation, which protected us from the criticism most people would encounter—people saying, "You can't do that. You're crazy. Do you know how many bands there are in the world?" Nobody stopped us, there was nothing in our path. We just charged ahead on this

Born Bad, Volume 2, Born Bad Records.
CD cover credits: cover: Autist Inc., layout: Mad Mick.

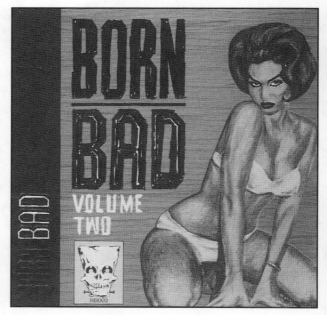

crazy flaming vision.

◆ LI: Since we always lived in "mixed" neighborhoods we didn't have a lot of friends. I notice that "friends" can do this to you: you have ideas of doing something bigger than your current situation and they don't like that. I think "friends" hold a lot of people *back!*

◆ IR: Besides *not* having those kind of friends, we had each other. We never put each other down, we just said, "Yeah, yeah—and then you could do *that!*" Do you know "So Young" by CLYDE STACEY? That song makes me think of Charlie Starkweather and Caril Fugate and their whole killin' spree. See, me and Lux coulda been like Charlie and Caril or Bonnie and Clyde, but we had this little band instead. They went on killing sprees, but somehow we ended up with a healthy outlet.

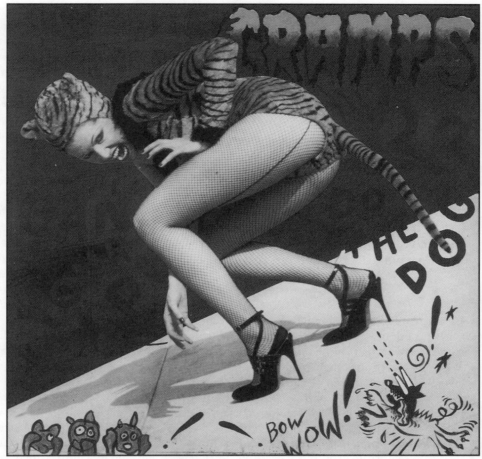

The Cramps' *Can Your Pussy Do the Dog?*, New Rose Records. Album cover credits: front cover artwork: Lux.

◆ LI: We were sitting in Sacramento in our crummy rusted-out '61 Chevy station wagon and saw this tiny article in *Rolling Stone* that said, "Sun Records Warehouse still exists in Memphis. You can buy these records at Select-o-Hits, run by Sam Phillips' brother, for 20 cents apiece or 6 for a dollar!" We thought, "Hmm," loaded up our station wagon and drove straight to Memphis. Fifty miles outside of Memphis our car fell apart, but we managed to get there and spend our last money on records. At the Select-o-Hits warehouse, records were stacked up to the ceiling. You could buy BILLY LEE RILEY & THE LITTLE GREEN MEN doing "Red Hot" for whatever a sixth of a dollar is—amazing. We have almost every SUN rockabilly single ever made, about 190 of them (although we didn't get the blues ones; they were already gone).

◆ IR: There was another reason we wanted to get out of Sacramento—

◆ LI: My name at that time was Vip Vop, and this particular cop didn't like that. Besides being the hippie psychic capital of the world at the foot of Mount Shasta with the abominable snowman and everything, Sacramento also had the most uptight police force; it was considered an all-American city, so they got the money to "try out" all this really intense riot gear for use in other places. I had VIP VOP (an old Isley Broth-

ers song) on my driver's license and every time I got stopped by the cops they would hassle me: "Vip Vop— I oughta give you a ticket just for *that!*"

◆ IR: It was a good thing, because that was the catalyst to finally leave. We got to Select-o-Hits and the sad thing was, a lot of collectors who'd been there had smashed 78s and other records to make *theirs* more valuable. They would buy what they could afford to get and then smash the duplicates!

◆ LI: That's a common collector practice. Bob Hite, who was in Canned Heat, went into the Record Rendezvous in Cleveland, the store where Leo Mintz and Alan Freed coined the term "rock'n'roll." In the attic there were a million great 78s. Hite went in there and bought all the ones he wanted and broke the rest of 'em!

◆ *V: He admits doing that?*

◆ LI: He doesn't admit it, but the people at the store told us he did it. Some of these collector types have the old thumb-up-the-ass; they're really messed-up people.

◆ IR: There weren't nearly as many collectors then as there are now. The records at Select-o-Hits were bought up mostly by foreigners. You had to already know about the old Sun records for sale; you had to say, "I want to go back into the warehouse," because the front of the building was just a regular record store.

◆ *V: Did you make any more pilgrimages on*

this trip?

♦ LI: No, we didn't have enough money. I had to call and get some money from my parents because our car was falling apart. All the money we got from them we spent on records.

♦ IR: It was the middle of winter, too—January. The entire state of Texas was ice. I remember we went at 15 miles an hour across Texas; the car was skidding—

In Sacramento a homeless person walked up to us on K Street and said, "You know what you are? You're beautiful monsters." We loved that— that was just what we felt like.

♦ LI: We were so loaded down with records that if we hit a little bump the car went *bang!* There was no spring left; it was just riding on the axle.

♦ IR: We haven't gone on any real record-buying vacations—for years that was our dream. We thought it would be great to have no particular destination . . . if you see a sign for "Pop 1280" you go, "Let's check it out!"

♦ *AJ: The last remaining area is easy listening—*

♦ IR: We're really into exotic easy listening. Surf's rare now, but some hot rod music still can be gotten cheap.

♦ *V: Tell us about some strange records you've found—*

♦ LI: There are a lot of great slow instrumentals on the B side of rockabilly singles, and some of them sound like MARTIN DENNY in a way, but weirder because it was just the band having fun—they figured no one would ever listen to 'em. That's a whole genre I never see any reissues of. And that *is* incredibly strange music, because it was all these hillbillies on speed!

♦ IR: A lot of people who collect rockabilly think those B sides aren't any good. But it's a whole other world.

♦ LI: They sound like what a stripper would have stripped to in the '50s. It's considered schlock, but eventually even *that* will become something: a genre.

♦ *V: When you were discovering rockabilly, the genre wasn't as defined as it is today.*

♦ LI: For years people claimed that rock'n'roll was just black music, and that's *all* there is to it. But when rockabilly started, it was the first real white rock'n'roll—not Frankie Avalon or some kind of pop manufactured rock. It was a real folk object from real folk. And while black people were buying rockabilly, white people were buying LITTLE RICHARD records. You really have to laugh when people squawk about how rock'n'roll is destroying our sons and daughters, when it was the first time there was any kind of integration in this country. There were a million kids

in white suburbia buying records by blacks, and they didn't have any idea that they should *not* be buying these "nigger records"—all they knew is: "This is *great!*" That was probably the first time there was no *thought* given to: "Oh, but it's by a black person . . ."

♦ IR: I think rockabilly was a quantum leap in culture—something happened in the evolution of people's minds. Like that rockabilly vocal style that's so emotional—it's hyper-emotionalism, hyper-surrealism. It had to have been more than just previous musical precedents leading up to it. Maybe it was the atom bomb: "Let's do it now because we might get blown up!" In the '50s everybody was *bigger than life* about everything. Their cars, their clothes, their vocal performances were all bigger than life. SONNY BURGESS had red hair, wore a red suit, red shoes—

♦ LI: —and played a red guitar.

♦ IR: These people had lifestyles that went with everything in their music. You hear about how there was such stupid music in the '50s, how there was an all-time low hit parade and people were so robot-like and gung-ho America. But that kind of thing probably provokes the most flamboyant outer fringes to rebel, because things were so dull in some ways, so sickeningly goody-goody.

♦ LI: Rock'n'roll wasn't intellectual, it had nothing to do with snobbery, but it *was* a way that cool people could find other cool people. The people originally doing rockabilly were serious *rebels* making underground music—the wildest stuff never became famous. Now a lot of modern "rockabilly" bands try to mimic the mannerisms of that time, but to try to duplicate a hiccup is missing the point. This insane emotional expression came from *within;* it was a completely unfettered expression of passion. And it should inspire you to live an unfettered life—*that* should be what it makes you want to do!

I will never understand the "rockabilly revival" a few years ago, when all these groups were singing about hubcaps and soda shops and stuff like that—this was *never* in rockabilly! They were just singin' wild; you talk about being outta control—ANDY STARR sings lyrics like, "Give me a woman; any kind of woman will do!"

♦ IR: The *Cramps* covered that. It reminds me of Henry Lee Lucas [alleged serial killer].

♦ *AJ: Wasn't he from a state where you could get married at 12 or 14?*

♦ IR: The Southern states. Everyone flipped out about Jerry Lee Lewis marrying his 13-year-old cousin, but that wasn't uncommon. It's a shame he was persecuted.

♦ LI: The English specialize in persecuting people for being human. These were real people singing things that they really thought. It's the difference between the Rolling Stones and the Beatles singing "I wanna hold your hand." These rockabillies wanted to do much *more* than hold your hand!

♦ IR: And they were real men, even if it was LARRY COLLINS who was 14 singing about real men's passions, not kid stuff. Most rockabilly lyrics freely express sex as a positive thing, like "I want that." Whereas in the '60s a lot of garage bands were puttin' the girls down or bitchin' about how it had gone wrong. It's weird that today the popular music vocalists, even if they're singing about sex or love, are wallowing in their feelings, not glorifying something outside themselves. It's "I feel like this" rather than "Wow—look at her!" Whereas a lot of '50s rock'n'roll is just *celebrating* things—celebrating a girl, not making sure that the world understands how "I feel."

♦ LI: It's funny how certain rock critics don't really understand what they're writing about. We've known a few people who go down to Memphis to get the story on this or that rockabilly guy and end up almost getting raped, or running out of the room . . . and write about what a jerk he is, 'cause they don't understand that he is a *real* person, with real thoughts that are different from yours, and it's just folk music.

♦ IR: If you invite one of them to stay at your house, it's like inviting a wild man from the jungle and expecting him to behave. If you play with fire, expect to get burned!

♦ LI: Somebody sent us a picture of HASIL ADKINS. It's really something to see him perform—have you ever seen a videotape or seen him live? He's a one-man band and he does all that stuff himself—outta control.

We felt like kings and queens in our world; we had *made* our own world because there wasn't another one for us.

♦ *AJ: Have you ever met any of your heroes?*

♦ IR: No . . . I've heard people say about an artist, "You know, I've met them and they're really like *this*— they're not really like you think." I don't agree; I like to think that what you hear is what they're really like: "I'm making a record and now I can be *me!*" And whatever it is people say they're like—well, that's just them trying to get by in the social world without getting arrested!

We met ERSEL HICKEY who did "Bluebirds Over the Mountain" b/w "Hangin' Around"—a rockabilly record. He's a real sweet guy.

♦ LI: That record is typical in that the hit side is "Bluebirds Over the Mountain" which is more of a pop song, but the B side "Hangin' Around" is much better: "You say that you love me/That's why I keep hangin' around."

Las Vegas Grind! Vol. 3, Strip Records.

♦ IR: He should have been content performing on a certain level. But he had played with the Beach Boys once ('cause they do "Bluebirds Over the Mountain") and his management had him thinking he was bigger than he really was—

♦ LI: They were telling him, "Rockabilly's big now— you gotta hold out for the *arenas!*"

♦ IR: I idolize LINK WRAY and wanted to meet him but I've never gone up to him . . . I just admired him from afar, 'cuz he's hot shit. We did meet RONNIE DAWSON who did the original "Rockin Bones" and "Action-Packed." He's a great performer and is still young—he was probably 15 when he recorded those songs. He was called The Blonde Bomber—

♦ LI: —the most beautiful boy you've ever seen; he had white hair and was really skinny and tall—

♦ IR: What do you mean? He's tiny . . . shorter than me!

♦ LI: *Really?*

♦ IR: He's 5'5"; a sawed-off Texan guy from Dallas. He still looks great; he has this brush-cut crewcut. He's an incredible guitarist (something you wouldn't know from his older rockabilly) and he's young enough to start a whole other career. We had him open for a show we did at the Town & Country in London—he's a real vivacious guy, kinda hyper.

♦ LI: His record "Action-Packed" goes, "Cause I'm action-packed; hear me?" Between all the lines he keeps going, "Hear me?" to make sure you're listening. A lot of times these old guys put out a new album and it's miserable, but he has a new album out that's great.

We were supposed to interview SCREAMING JAY HAWKINS for a magazine published by *Penthouse, Rip* (before it went heavy metal). We were all excited but he didn't do it; we found out that he was just trying to get this girl he was living with into *Penthouse.* Then we

saw him at the Ritz in New York; there were only two other people in the audience besides us. We did a radio show with him once that started at midnight and was four hours long. He showed up in all his regalia, with the bone in his nose (full makeup and everything) for a *radio* show!

♦ IR: He brought his head-on-a-stick. Lux took a 3-D photo of him—

♦ **V: You have a 3-D camera?**

♦ IR: Many. Everywhere we go, Lux takes beautiful photos of the incredibly strange world of 3-D. It's amazing that 3-D is not more popular—it's laughed at as a quirk from another era. But there's nothing like it.

♦ LI: People say, "3-D's *weird;* you have to look through a viewer or put on special glasses." But to experience stereo, you have to sit between the two speakers—so I guess we should go back to mono! It's funny; I always think Ivy and I are living 30 years into the future, but we get this bad rap that we're old-fashioned. Yet we constantly buy magazines, looking for something cool to happen—

♦ IR: —that's futuristic. This attitude toward 3-D is like saying you're old-fashioned because you're into Tesla.

♦ LI: I think that these days, you're considered old-fashioned if you remember anything that happened prior to two weeks ago!

We weren't accomplished musicians, but we didn't let that stop us. I think what enabled us to actually execute this fantasy was our isolation, which protected us from the criticism most people would encounter—people saying, "You can't do that. You're crazy. Do you know how many bands there are in the world?"

♦ **V: When the VCR revolution happened, you weren't conservative; you immediately got into it—**

♦ LI: We've got over 4,000 films on videotape—all incredibly strange movies, too. There's a network of people all over the country discovering films in warehouses; they'll rent them, project them onto a sheet and videotape them. All these movies that were *almost* lost are now being saved because of videotape. And some of them are right up there with *Gone with the Wind!* [laughs] They're made by real people, and they can give you a look into somebody's *very* unusual life.

♦ **AJ: People think we're so advanced about sexuality or drugs now, but you look at some of these old films and go, "Ohmigod . . ."**

♦ LI: I don't understand where people's *know-it-all* attitude comes from. I try hard and I can't get *near* knowin' it all. We've spent all our time and money to do this, yet I constantly think, "I don't know nothin'." I do think there's a general feeling of "I'm so sophisticated, I better not get up. If I move either way, it could be wrong, so I better not even move."

♦ **AJ: It's this illusionary belief that culture is evolving—**

♦ LI: Yes, that's the big problem: the idea that if it's new, it's worthwhile—

♦ IR: Not realizing that this is the Dark Ages . . . and that culture doesn't evolve linearly, anyway.

♦ LI: It's unbelievable: the incredible things that have happened just in the past few years that people don't know about. Things that happened from the '50s on have already been lost, just as much as something that happened 500 years ago.

♦ IR: A lot of the music or movies we're talking about were never a part of mainstream culture when they came out—they were fringe and underground. We're trying to make a more enlightened culture by getting into them, because everything great from *any* era has been repressed. Even scientific discoveries from the late 1800s were not taken seriously at the time.

♦ LI: We've only been writing things down for a few thousand years. Yet people think you're "old-fashioned" if you're interested in something from the recent past.

♦ IR: Movies, even more than music, are keys to what a culture was really like. Well, a 1962 high-budget movie isn't, but a low-budget movie is: it's the only way you'll know how people *really* talked or dressed . . . because they didn't get actors and they didn't write dialogue. So you had people wearing clothes out of their closets, talking like they really talked, and behaving like they really behaved—there it is, right on film. And it's only going to be in some really cheap movie.

♦ **AJ: You've said that rockabilly springs from real experience, not out of self-conscious notions about what art is, or what glamour is. It's the same with a lot of neglected films; when I interviewed Doris Wishman, she had no idea why I should take her seriously—**

♦ IR: We saw a showing of *Nude on the Moon* and *Double Agent 73,* which stars Chesty Morgan. Then Doris Wishman came up to speak, and she was so mean. One person asked, "What's Chesty Morgan doing now?" and she replied, "Who knows? Who *cares?!*"

♦ LI: When she walked up, everyone applauded. Then she said [abruptly], "Okay—*what?*" Some guy had the gall to ask, "I heard you filmed *Nude on the Moon* in a nudist park—did they know you were filming there?" (In the film, thirty nude girls are running around, plus these guys in astronaut suits.) She went [sarcastically], "Oh, *no*—they didn't know a *thing* about it. We just *sneaked* around." There were all these college kids in the audience with notebooks writing things down, and

I think she had no idea why she was there in the first place. It was hilarious; she couldn't have been more rude.

♦ IR: Are you familiar with the films of June and Ron ORMOND? They made *The Exotic Ones,* in which a big (literally; he's 6'7") rockabilly star, SLEEPY LA-BEEF, plays the swamp monster.

♦ LI: He's got hair glued to his face, fangs and everything.

♦ IR: And Titania, the contortionist stripper, has a smart-mouthed acting role in it. She lives up to her name, Titania—like the *Titanic!* She's wild-looking, with serious cat-eye pseudo-Oriental makeup and built-up black hair.

♦ LI: [shows video] This Ormond film starts out with a narration like Russ Meyer's *Mondo Topless;* he calls the women "buxotics"—

♦ IR: I love new words. Here's Titania—she's so bad-ass; she's boss. This is when people had to have *talent.* Her hairdo helps her keep her balance when she's upside down.

♦ LI: And she drinks a glass of water upside down.

♦ **AJ: *Stripping like that is a lost art—***

♦ LI: Strippers today look like they're doing aerobics routines—it certainly doesn't look *sexy,* coming out and doing push-ups.

♦ IR: When we were in Vegas we saw DYANNE THORNE (star of *Ilsa, She-Wolf of the SS)* in her "Bur-lesque-a-Poppin' " act.

♦ LI: Actually, she came into the audience and sat on my lap twice!

♦ IR: Dyanne Thorne goes back to the vaudeville-burlesque days; I think she's in her '50s but she's in good shape. It was an old-fashioned burlesque show with comics mixed with strippers who had a shtick . . . half of one stripper's outfit is the devil coming on to herself—you know, *that* old thing!

♦ LI: Those Ormond movies also turned us on to harmonicas. The "Skin Diver Suite" by LEO DIA-MOND (harmonica player) is unbelievable. [plays record] He also made *The Enchanted Sea,* which has splashing sea sounds, and *Subliminal Sounds*—right in the center of the cover is a lenticular hologram of an eye which is either open or shut, depending on how you look at it. The liner notes say, "The psychological interpretation of the term holds that subliminal is: 'below the threshold of consciousness or beyond the reach of personal awareness.' "

♦ **AJ: *Can you remember some of your earliest record "finds"?***

♦ LI: There've been a million of 'em. We went into a furniture store in Cleveland and bought VERN PUL-LENS on Spade Records doing "Bop Crazy Baby" which was one of only 200 pressed—it never got distributed outside Texas. Somebody bought it, came to Ohio to work in the plants, and then got rid of the record—

♦ IR: That was almost our name (instead of the *Cramps): Bop Crazy Babies.* "Date Bait" by RONNIE

Andre Williams' *Jail Bait,* © 1984 Fortune Records.
Album cover credits: cover illustration: James Hutchinson.

SELF is another early find. He was one of the wildest vocalists ever: "Ooh, Ahh/Date Bait!" Later on he wrote some hits for Brenda Lee.

♦ LI: A picture's worth a thousand words on that guy. He sounds like a white LITTLE RICHARD. Listen to "Bop-a-lena": "I got my patent leather shoes on my hound dog feet/Me and Bop-a-lena gonna walk the beat"—great weird lyrics. One look at his face and you can tell he's no Fabian. "Jail Bait" by ANDRE WIL-LIAMS is another one of the best, where he tells the judge at the end, "I ain't gonna mess around with those young girls; I'm gonna get me a girl about 42." (He was actually caught messing around with some 15-year-old.) He sings the gamut from very fast to very slow songs; there are 16 songs on the album and every one is great. He's incredibly talented.

♦ IR: He does a song called "Pullin' Time" about being in jail—after the "Jail Bait" incident, I guess!

♦ **V: *How did you get into easy listening?***

♦ LI: I think it started from buying album covers with beautiful girls, incredibly beautiful photographs, and wild titles. They have the cream of all the artwork. Easy listening records aren't always filed under "easy listening." You have to look under the individual in-strument: "harmonica" or "organ." A lot of times they're filed under "jazz."

♦ IR: Being in a band, we also had a bigger *need* for easy listening—

♦ LI: When we come home, we don't want to hear some exciting, loud rock'n'roll—

♦ IR: —you need the opposite thing to balance. Easy listening is like an oasis. It used to be so prevalent, we took it for granted without even listening to it. I didn't realize how *surreal* it could get.

♦ LI: I met Alice Cooper back in 1970 and I was

Kay Martin's *I Know What He Wants for Christmas . . .*, © 1962 Fax Records.

Kay Martin & Her Body Guards, Roulette Records.
Album cover credits: photo: Chuck Stewart.

saying, "Have you heard Ozzie? Oh man, wait'll you hear Black Sabbath!" and he went, "I don't want to know about it. I only like easy listening music." I imagine it's the same syndrome we have when we come home after exploding for two months . . .

♦ IR: R&B vocal groups are equally soothing. We're as passionate as we ever were about them—I hate saying "doowop" because that doesn't totally describe what we mean. It began in the late '40s with CATS & A FIDDLE and STEVE GIBSON & THE RED CAPS. Even earlier are the songs on a '30s-'40s compilation album, *The Human Orchestra,* by groups who used no instruments, only their voices. In their harmonies they would simulate various instruments like clarinets. The first cut, "Mr Ghost Goes to Town," by the FIVE JONES BOYS, is really great. I think during the war metal was rationed, and musical instruments were harder to get. And those all-voice arrangements have such a beautiful effect—so eerie. "Incredibly strange" doesn't mean ugly or funny; it means attractive in an *other-worldly* way.

♦ **V: After the apocalypse, you can still make music without electricity or even any instruments—**

♦ LI: That's the way the Mills Brothers started out before they turned into a crappy pop thing. They all imitated instruments and did the weirdest things you've ever heard. It's unbelievable; you'd swear you were listening to an orchestra, but it's just these five guys with their mouths. The best recordings are *before* the '50s; don't get anything from the '50s.

♦ **V: So you started buying easy listening records for the covers—**

♦ IR: One of our Top Ten albums, which we bought for the cover, is by KAY MARTIN & HER BODY-GUARDS [title]. It's a unique act: beatnik and jazzy.

We have a lot of men's magazines, and in one we found a feature on her. On her album cover she's blonde, but in the magazine photo she had dark hair. I guess she was a pretty hot act in Las Vegas—and no wonder. What she did is not easy listening—there are certain things that defy simple classification, and I don't know what this is.

♦ LI: [describing cover] The guys with the swords in the background are two photographers who were taking a picture of her; out of this encounter they formed a group. I always like it when people become a band out of nowhere and do something unique and weird.

♦ IR: The lyrics on "Swamp Girl" are incredible: "Where the crane flies through the marshes/Where the water rat goes swimming/Where the water's black as a devil's track/That is where our swamp girl dwells." There are other great lyrics: "Her eyes are like the diamondback that stretches in the dark . . . She taunts me, dares me, then she tears me like paper dolls are torn." Another song, "The Heel," sounds like a JIM THOMPSON novel put to song: "We're in a web of love and hate, where it will end is up to fate/I'll let him have his little fling, I'll be the chewing gum that clings . . . to the heel!"

♦ **AJ: The liner notes claim she's part Cherokee.**

♦ IR: That's such a romantic line—when I was a kid, everyone I knew claimed to be part Cherokee.

♦ **AJ: Well, what you make up is just as important as "reality."**

♦ IR: Kay Martin's record also has great versions of standards like "Johnny Guitar" and "Summertime," with jive-ass beatnik variations on the lyrics. The idea of this stripper and these crazy guys singing these crazy songs—! There's two more group albums: *Kay Martin at the Lorelei, I Know What He Wants for Christ-*

Kay Martin at Las Vegas, Record Productions, Inc.
Album cover credits: photos: Jess Hotchkiss, design: De Vingo.

Kay Martin at Las Vegas, Laff Records.

mas *(but I don't know how to wrap it!),* plus a few Kay Martin solo albums: *Kay Martin at Las Vegas* (released with two different covers), and one subtitled "The wild, wicked 4:00 AM Show, Recorded Live."

♦ LI: We found another record that she yodels on. But it's under a different name—

♦ IR: Her voice is really distinct; it *has* to be her.

♦ LI: It's a 45 titled "Chime Bells" by Sherry Lee Douglas, and on the label the letters are written in rope. We like a lot of cocktail vocals, where the singer's not that good; she's usually wearing a cocktail dress and singing bluesy torch songs. You just pretend you're in some lounge and that's who's singing.

Even Hugo Montenegro made a good album: *Boogie Woogie + Bongos.* We'll buy almost anything with the word bongos on it! This one has Gershwin-like piano accompanied by bongos; it's crazy.

♦ **V: A lot of albums only have one cut that's great.**

♦ IR: And it's hard to file records like these, because if you try to do it alphabetically—well, half the time I can never remember the name of the artist. We've even tried categories like "Space" and "Hawaiian" but then they'll overlap and it's "Oh no, what'll I do?"

I suspect that anything on OMEGA might be worth buying, no matter what kind of music. They did deluxe productions; it was a hi-fi, state-of-the-art label. They put out CHAINO's records. A good one is *Jungle Echoes,* and there's another one, *Night of the Spectre,* with a bloody eyeball in the center of the label—that's the hardest to find.

♦ LI: The story is that another tribe had killed every member of Chaino's tribe except for him. Some white folks found him in the jungle under some leaves and brought him to New York, just like King Kong, and he became famous.

♦ IR: Omega also put out the soundtrack for *Destination Moon,* and PAUL TANNER's *Music for Heavenly Bodies* which features a theremin [an instrument with a hauntingly ethereal sound, used in many '50s science fiction movies]. I love theremin—I want one so bad. We saw an incredible presentation of a Russian silent science-fiction movie, *Aelita, Queen of Mars,* which was accompanied by a theremin trio. I always expect too much—I thought it meant three theremins, but . . .

♦ LI: It was unbelievable; they should have recorded that entire performance. They made explosions when a rocket took off—everything to go with the movie. Watching it, the audience was stunned. They've released *Aelita* on video, but it's silent—too bad.

♦ IR: They did sound effects as well as music. If the movie showed glass breaking, they made a sound that suggested that. And when the Martians spoke, the theremin trio did little Martian voices. It's an incredibly strange movie, with amazing sets and costumes. The Martian queen has three breasts . . . It's also a political allegory; the hero dreams a lot of the science fiction scenes, and most of the movie is the science fiction dream.

We talked to the theremin player afterwards and he said he had bought it from a tent evangelist!

♦ LI: I would have loved to have been at *that* service. They originally made 500 theremins, but threw 300 away because they couldn't sell 'em! It's just about impossible to get one of the original 200 theremins now. In the '50s, *Popular Mechanics* printed plans for a theremin. For awhile it was very difficult to get tubes (which a theremin requires), but now you can, thanks to the audiophile movement, because state-of-the-art hi-fi enthusiasts claim, "Hey, we can't get a sound like

A "New Orthophonic" High Fidelity Recording

RCA VICTOR
LPM-1165

Skin Diver Suite
and Other Selections
Leo Diamond

Leo Diamond's *Skin Diver Suite,* © RCA Victor. Album cover credits: photo: Mitchell Bliss.

camera for an entire song without blinking. Imagine all those '50s housewives with their ironing boards watching him. We got our Korla Pandit video from a friend who answered an ad in the *LA Weekly:* "Korla Pandit videos for sale." He went to an address in North Hollywood, knocked on the door, and the man who answered asked, "How do you know about Korla Pandit?" "Oh, I bought the albums." "*Really?* Well, that's great. Hold on a second," and he walked out of the room. Our friend was sitting there for three minutes before the guy returned: "And here's the man that made it all possible: Korla Pan-*dit!*" and these curtains opened and Korla Pandit himself came walking out doing his Bela Lugosi imita-

we used to." With tubes, the sounds you make get turned into fire, then the fire gets turned back into music that comes out of a speaker. But with transistors, your sounds go into a little piece of cold clay before they get turned into music again. It might have less distortion, but it lacks the excitement that a tube with fire generates. Engineers today *kill* themselves to get rid of every bit of excitement; they have no idea what it is that's exciting in music.

♦ IR: On Howlin' Wolf records he's poppin' the mike all over the place because of how he sings, and that sounds powerful. I think the vocalists got used to this popping and incorporated it into their phrasing and style.

♦ LI: Have you ever seen KORLA PANDIT's TV shows from the '50s? He's unbelievable. [plays video] I love it when they project clouds behind his face. Sometimes the Taj Mahal gets superimposed with the clouds. Thousands of housewives worshipped him.

♦ IR: It's amazing that his show was so popular. All he did was perform and not speak; his show was all instrumental. There would be a voice-over: "And now Korla plays . . ." and he'd play a song for ten minutes (live, no overdubs) and give you these exotic expressions, wearing his turban and flirting.

♦ LI: On his slow numbers, he would stare at the

tion. Our friend sat there open-mouthed—

♦ IR: He hypnotizes *me.* Our cats' favorite music is Korla Pandit; they come into the room as if drawn by a magnet. [a cat comes to doorway]

♦ *AJ: This video is just seething with sexuality and drama. In the '50s, with all that suburbanization in America, people were so hungry to explore exotic lands.*

♦ IR: All those tiki bars opened up. Almost every time we play San Francisco we go to the Tonga Room afterwards. Maybe there's a tiki revival now; the Tropicana in Las Vegas recently spent millions on wall-to-wall giant tikis for their tropical theme.

♦ LI: Have you ever seen a video of TED LYONS & HIS CUBS? It's Indian. [plays video] I used to think of India in terms of Gandhi—all rice and white robes—not these technicolor Max Fleischer sets!

♦ IR: This really inspired our *Bikini Girls* video. The film industry in India is huge—the biggest in the world. Almost all are musicals, and the composers have like one day to do the score for a movie. But it's amazingly good music, and weird; there's at least 3 CDs in a series, *Golden Voices of the Silver Screen.* Almost all of the vocals are done by a handful of men and women. It's just like in the '50s, when Connie Francis did voice-overs in rock'n'roll movies for actresses who couldn't sing, like Tuesday Weld.

When we were in England, every Wednesday night they broadcasted an Indian movie. One had a guy doing a wild dance on a giant bongo drum.

Another good one is *Dance, Raja, Dance* [available on CD]. These Indian musicals are really influenced by Busby Berkeley. They mix rock'n'roll dancing with classical Indian movements, in front of surreal sets, and are so dream-like. The men look like devils and the women do this incredible dancing, and sometimes a singer will start out in drag.

♦ *V: TED LYONS sounds like a mixture of cartoon music, Dixieland, boogie-woogie and rock'n'roll—all that, plus Indian music! It combines rockabilly guitar with Spaghetti Western trumpets.*

♦ IR: They cram in all these crazy elements, then burn the set down—literally! Ted Lyons has the sexiest act—it gets faster and faster, too ... We also tried checking out Mexican videos, and went to a lot of Mexican video stores but we kinda got discouraged—we struck out a lot. We did see an incredibly weird production with a woman doing a spider dance.

We inadvertently collected sobbing records; there's a whole genre where people break down and sob, like DONALD WOODS & THE VEL-AIRES' "Death of an Angel." Most people don't realize that the "woman" sobbing on the record is Richard Berry.

♦ *V: That has a great line: "I want to be beside her, but I'm afraid to die."*

♦ IR: Yeah—me too! A universal sentiment. [laughs]

♦ *V: Do you collect suicide recordings?*

♦ IR: Probably! Suicide, insanity, murder—all the good dark stuff. "The Rubber Room" [Porter Wagoner song] ones. End of the world themes, too. GENE MALTAIS's "Deep River Blues" is a real emotional rockabilly ballad about suicide—

♦ LI: "I got the Deep River Blues, I feel so sad and blue/I lost my love, what am I gonna do?" Even the Anita Kerr Singers (in the background) couldn't fuck this record up. Then he sings, "Now the Deep River Blues is a-callin', callin' for me to come home, where I'll never be bothered, and never have to roam."

♦ IR: The other side, "Crazy Baby," is such great rockabilly—equally unique vocals. There's a line where he says "your golden touch" but it sounds like "your golden crotch." I can't believe he does that. Then he *whistles* the instrumental solo—well, why not?

♦ LI: He forgot his theremin ... Supposedly "Death of an Angel" caused a lot of people to commit suicide. Another good crying song is "The Bells" by the DOMINOES (with vocalist CLYDE McPHATTER).

♦ *V: "Gloomy Sunday" (The Budapest Suicide Song) caused a lot of suicides in the '40s; for awhile it was banned from the radio. Billie Holiday sang it, and there was even a rock version by the Apochryphals.*

♦ LI: "Valarie" by JACKIE & THE STARLIGHTERS is a great sobbing record (this 45 just says "The Starlights" on it). What a singer!

♦ IR: Bleeding vocals. Now *that's* performing. Laughing records are weird, too. But I like good crying performances, because even if you fake it, you have to tear yourself up to perform. You have to reach in there to something *primal*. So even if you're trying to be funny, it ends up pretty real. Without trying, we definitely gravitate toward bleakness in records; I don't know why.

♦ *V: The crying throughout ALLEN SWIFT's "Are You Lonesome Tonight?" is unbelievable: "You were so mean to me; you cheated on me; you'd come home at all crazy hours, loaded. You'd insult me, and throw things at me . . . I can't do anything right!"*

♦ IR: It's almost a novelty song, but he refers to drugs and that saves it. Besides, he's giving his all—more than you want!

♦ *AJ: Imagine going on tour and having to do this every night.*

♦ LI: Have you heard "Noisy Village" by BOB McFADDEN & DOR? Another "Quiet Village" take-off is the FORBIDDEN FIVE doing "Enchanted Farm" b/w "RFD Rangoon." Instead of exotic sounds it just has barnyard animals—roosters, cows, goats, dogs, geese—even a cuckoo clock. It starts out like "Quiet Village," but the animals get louder and louder—by the end a hundred animals are screeching at the top of their lungs.

> **I think rockabilly was a quantum leap in culture—something happened in the evolution of people's minds. Like that rockabilly vocal style that's so emotional—it's hyper-emotionalism, hyper-surrealism. Maybe it was the atom bomb: "Let's do it now because we might get blown up!"**

♦ *V: The music sounds great, though; it's very listenable. I wonder if the FORBIDDEN FIVE made an album?*

♦ IR: Do you have that JULIE LONDON album with "Yummy yummy yummy/I've got love in my tummy" on it? It's real slow and breathy—almost *lewd*.

♦ *AJ: She sounds so sexy. It wouldn't even be funny if you didn't recall the original bubble-gum version—*

♦ LI: That's what's funny: the people who wrote these songs *knew* what they were doing. Little 12-year-old girls could listen to these lyrics, but because it didn't sound sexy, it was okay. There were a lot of risqué

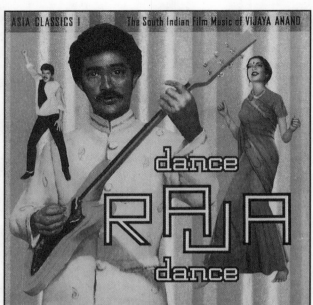

Vijaya Anand's *Dance Raja Dance*, Luaka Bop, Inc./Warner Bros. Records. Inc.
© 1992 Sire Records Company. CD cover credits: design: Alexander Isley
Design, NYC, cover illustration: Paul Bachem.

lines in '60s pop songs, but no one ever caught 'em. The Rolling Stones sang "playin' your half-assed game" in "It's All Over Now," but the sheet music said "playin' your high-class game." The STANDELLS did "Dirty Water" in which they say "lovers, fuckers and thieves" but the sheet music said, "lovers, *muggers* and thieves." It's surprising what you can get away with. There's a FLAIRS song where the lead vocalist, RICHARD BERRY, says, "I'm on that fuckin' desert, too"—clear as a bell.

There's a record called "Little Girl" where the guy goes [suggestively], "Little girl," and the girl goes, "Little boy." It's real sexy. It gets more and more exciting musically, and the girl goes [panting], "Oh, oh, oh, oh oh oh oh—ohhhhh . . . little boy!" It's like: *yikes!*—unbelievable.

This is "Don't Fuck Around With Love" by the BLENDERS: "Take a little advice from me: play around with TNT, but baby [bass voice], don't fuck around with love." It was available on "white label" records but it was never officially released.

♦ IR: A lot of groups recorded songs that would circulate clandestinely.

♦ LI: Store owners who knew their customers would bring these records out from under the counter when they came in. A lot of people think nothing like this existed before the '70s, but . . . We have a version of a song by the CLOVERS, recorded in their heyday when they had a million hit records, called "Cocksuckers' Ball"—

♦ IR: It's *a capella*—

♦ **AJ: Wasn't there a Robert Frank documentary called Cocksuckers' Ball?**

♦ IR: *Cocksuckers' Blues.* We have a Rolling Stones

bootleg: same title—

♦ LI: —in which they were singing about their manager, Andrew Oldham. Another CLOVERS song, "Crawlin'" was about being too drunk to fuck: "I'm crawlin' instead o' ballin'." There are a lot of songs that, if you really *listen* to the words—!

♦ IR: Some of the top gospel vocal groups also recorded R&B songs, like the SENSATIONAL NIGHTINGALES. They did "Standing in the Judgment" as "Standing on the Corner (she sure looks fine)"—it's got the same melody and feel. TARHEEL SLIM (real name: Alden Bunn) was in a famous gospel vocal group while simultaneously singing R&B material which a lot of people considered devil's music—you're not supposed to do both.

♦ LI: This is good "vapor" music: "Sweet Breeze" by VERNON GREEN & THE PHANTOMS—

♦ IR: And they *sound* like phantoms, like ghosts singing in the background; all minor-key harmonies. We spend hours spinning exotic vocals like these: it's another world—eerie. I love it when they mix romance with minor keys: "Oh, wind . . . wonder where my love can be/Does she ever think of me?/Bring her back to me."

♦ LI: "Flamingo" by the CHARADES is *beautiful:* "Love me, girl, like a flame in the sky/When the sun meets the sea, say farewell . . . and hasten to me"—

♦ IR: This is the music we were addicted to before rockabilly, and we still are; this is our secret passion. It's sad—these were *such* good singers and they never made money and all ended up being janitors . . . getting nothing. Yet they were *so* good.

♦ **AJ: The singer's just pouring his heart out. And it has that exotic touch—**

♦ IR: It's incredibly strange and it seems like it's from someplace else, far away and ancient—what is it? And it's made by poor people with street corner harmonies.

I never understood the power of wartime songs until I realized that the men were probably going to be *killed*—now songs like "I'll Be Seeing You" choke me up. You can think it's just romantic, but it was wartime, and people weren't thinking of my sweetie down the street, they were thinking, "Hope you come back!" I remember my mother saying she'd use an ouija board to find out what was happening with my father during World War II—which she said was not uncommon; a lot of women did that. They couldn't even communicate, because the letters were censored. It was like, "See you when the war's over—hopefully!"

♦ **AJ: Your dad made it back—**

♦ IR: Well I *am* a vampire, but—! Now I really *listen* to songs I used to regard as throwaway fluff—that my mother would sing around the house when I was a kid. You have to think about any music in the context of the time: why those lyrics were written, and who they were for. A song like "You Belong to Me" was written during wartime, about *soldiers*. And the songs become chilling when you interpret them that way: "Ugh—

that's what they meant." I don't think anyone in America—at least not young people—can imagine the world being like that.

♦ **AJ: The white culture only saw the pretty face of the vocal groups, but there must have been a whole hidden world of incredible creativity that "Cocksuckers' Ball" only hints at—**

♦ IR: It was really a subculture. But in the '50s, the subculture could always float to the top. "Earth Angel" by the PENGUINS is a hit that's an incredible poverty performance, just as hardcore as songs that didn't make it. Songs had a chance then; a "nobody" could break through. But for every hit, there was a subculture that remained anonymous.

A lot of the vocal groups evolved on street corners—it was something to do when you had nothing, and they all kinda hoped they'd make it big. There were so many of these groups; it wasn't like there were only a few people doing it. From record collecting, we always thought we'd eventually own *everything,* but there's no end to it. How could there have been so many records made, so we'll never have all of them? It just defies laws . . . the records keep coming and coming and where do they come from? Because it does seem like it's from Mars!

Sometimes groups would make 200 copies of a record just for local promotion so they could get more gigs in their area, or whatever . . . as a step to something bigger. So it's rare because there are only 200 copies, but at the same time there were a *lot* of them being recorded . . .

♦ **V: That's how something like NERVOUS NORVUS's "Transfusion" could get made—**

♦ IR: Which was a hit. That's what's so depressing about radio now. I remember when FM radio began in the late '60s, it was real exciting. There were no commercials and they'd play whole sides of albums. However, up until then you would hear a Frank Sinatra record followed by a SEEDS record, because it was just *radio,* and everybody had to listen to everything. *Anything* could creep in there, and the people who liked the awful stuff had to hear the cool stuff. Also, I don't think people had so many ideas about "this is what *I'm* into"—people could just hear a song and react to it. I don't even know if a novelty record could come out nowadays—what station would play it? Could there be a "Martian Hop" or a "Purple People Eater"?

"Now That It's Over (I still need you, need you, want you)" is by the FALCONS (not the Falcons that Wilson Pickett was in). The tenor in the background is in the stratosphere—so haunting, an experience from another dimension. When you really get into collecting records like these, you realize what's unique. The standard configuration for vocal groups is first tenor, second tenor, baritone and bass. But on this record there are *two* first tenors. The song "Earth Angel" (the PENGUINS) stands out from other vocal groups because it also has two lead tenor vocals who keep swap-ping. I think there are two versions (Mercury and Duotone) but only one has the dual tenors.

♦ LI: The records by the FLAMINGOS are like drugs. *Flamingos' Serenade* has been re-released.

♦ IR: They were a big group with hits like "I Only Have Eyes for You." That song is about as good as it gets. There wasn't much stereo production in the '50s of vocal groups, but the Flamingos did perhaps the only true stereo vocal group recording, gorgeously produced by George Goldner, a New York producer who also produced the CHANTELS. People sometimes think the best stuff is going to be the most obscure, but that's not the case here.

In the '50s everybody was *bigger than life* about everything. Their cars, their clothes, their vocal performances were all bigger than life. Sonny Burgess had red hair, wore a red suit, red shoes and played a red guitar.

♦ **V: That has exotic harmonies and it's actually strange; there's more than meets the eye—**

♦ LI: Every cut on this record is great. It slows you down, like you took a Valium. Sit and listen to this for a half hour, and you just *melt.*

♦ IR: It's heavy with the vapors.

♦ LI: LITTLE JIMMY SCOTT even more so.

♦ IR: He's in his 60s now and was in the final episode of *Twin Peaks*—the only episode I ever saw, because I knew he was in it. He was also one of Billie Holiday's pallbearers. Most people think he's a woman singing . . . he had some kind of glandular condition that caused him to not grow up. So he was Little Jimmy Scott; then at the age of 37 he grew some and became Jimmy Scott. He's been singing since the late '40s; he sang with Lionel Hampton's band. His vocal style is emotional but real clear and direct . . . it brings new meaning to the word "slow." It's very hard to accompany him, because he changes the timing in the song for the sake of the emotion.

♦ LI: Here he is live in New Orleans in the '50s, on a CD (Royal Roost label) of rare 78s on the Savoy label. If you see him today he's even better. He's really *something* to see; he looks a little like a black Frank Sinatra from twenty feet away.

♦ IR: "When you're alone, the magic moonlight dies/ There is no sunrise when your lover has gone."

♦ **V: Wow—those two phrases took about a minute.**

♦ IR: Nancy Wilson's supposed to have gotten her style completely from him, and she admits it. A lot of

people even think he's Nancy Wilson when they hear his recordings, because they sound so much alike—especially the '70s material. Nobody ever thinks it's a man.

♦ **V: Gender-crossing vocals—**

♦ IR: He's got this pure voice, unwrecked by growing up.

♦ IR: Every vocal group had their high tenor, and I'm *hooked*. We've got a lot of this material on 78, and it really sounds different—so warm, so rich. 78s have this sound that 45s don't have. They go around faster so there's more bass response on them. Rockabilly on 78 is frightening, it sounds so great. And then there's the ritual aspect of setting the atmosphere: it's night, and I'm getting out the 78 player. When you set the mood for something, you get into it even more.

♦ **AJ: In a way the technology seems to have progressively gotten worse.**

♦ LI: The RAVENS do a song, "A Simple Prayer," and at the end the singer hits a note that shatters your brain—

♦ IR: "Send me someone who cares for *meeee*." What a showoff! I'm a sucker for tenor lead vocals, maybe because the sound is richer than a woman's high voice, but it still sounds kinda like a woman.

♦ **AJ: What do they call it when they reach those incredibly high notes?**

♦ IR: Falsetto. But what makes it false, as opposed to your "true" high voice? I guess it means the note's not within your range. The lead vocalist of the TOKENS sang in falsetto, and they had a hit with "The Lion Sleeps Tonight"—people *will* respond to an exotic record if you give 'em a chance! "The Lion Sleeps Tonight" was based on "Wimoweh," an African folk song the Weavers also did. "Bwanina (the Jungle Drums)" was another incredible Tokens' production; it had their trademark euphoric sound.

Someone we know calls "Earthquake Boogie," by TERRY DUNUVAN & THE EARTHQUAKES, the "worst record ever." When the drum solo begins, it sounds like the whole band fell down a flight of stairs—but it's amazing! It ends funny, too. Drummers are all nutty; it's good they have those sticks, because that keeps 'em out of trouble. I figure that if you weren't crazy when you started, drumming probably *makes* you crazy.

♦ **AJ: Most cultures have drumming beats that help create altered states of consciousness, or shamanistic or psychedelic states.**

♦ IR: Brian Jones put out a record in the '60s featuring the Master Musicians of Joujouka. Now there's a newly recorded CD of their drumming plus pipes, and it definitely puts you in a trance . . . See, we *do* buy new weird stuff, just not by "contemporary" artists. Even if I see someone live and like them, by the time they get into a studio, it's just not happening on the record.

"There's a Fungus Among Us," by HUGH BARRETT & THE VICTORS, has cool lyrics and a real *black-leather sound* (I always visualize everything). Nobody fights as "recreation" anymore, as something *fun* to do: "There was a fungus among us, there was a rumble in the jungle/there was a static in the attic, a moanin' and a groanin'." I like the girl chorus: "Which one is the fungus?"

♦ **V: That sax solo is great and primitive—**

♦ IR: I love wicked sax. Listen to these lyrics: "I was shakin' all over, didn't know what to do/The dog and the cat they were fightin' too." They also give some great advice: "Put it to an end and *bend the trend . . .*" Yeah—I'll go along with that!

BIG JAY McNEELY still puts on a good show. He was the most *out there* raw sax player of them all. There are amazing photos of him playing on his back in the late '50s or early '60s. He's a mailman now, I think, but he still plays a glow-in-the-dark sax—the club turns off the lights and the sax'll be glowing. He was influenced by guys like T-BONE WALKER and PEEWEE CRAYTON who had really long guitar cords and would walk through the audience and go outside. Once Big Jay McNeely went out the door and didn't come back—his band was left onstage wondering why. But he'd been busted and taken away in a paddy wagon!

♦ **V: Which women rockabilly singers do you like?**

♦ IR: SPARKLE MOORE—she looked incredible with her blonde ponytail and J.D. clothes. She did rock'n'roll songs: "Skull and Crossbones" and "Tiger." "Flower of My Heart" is not typical. She looks right out of the detective mags or J.D. paperbacks of the '50s.

Not a lot of women did instrumentals back then, but CORDELL JACKSON is one. She lived in Memphis and started Moon Records. She hung around the

Dancin' & Romancin', © 1986 Charly Records Ltd. Album cover credits: sleeve design: The Raven Design Group, photos courtesy: Michael Ochs Archives.

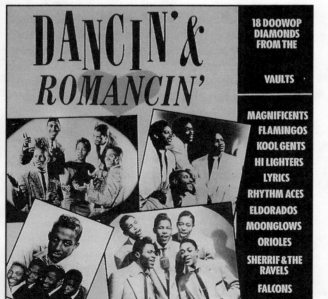

studio the entire time we recorded *Songs the Lord Taught Us,* and told us all about how she produced her records. Even though they'll say "by Allen Page" or whoever, she said she was her own session guitarist. She didn't record with bass, because bass is difficult to record . . . her solution was not to use it at all.

"Tongue-Tied" is a girl rockabilly vocal by BETTY McQUAID; WANDA JACKSON also sings a good version. It's about how she gets tongue-tied when she gets hot—she can't express herself: "I get an itchy-twitchy feelin' when he looks into my eyes/All I can say is, I'm eeny-neeny-nah, I get tongue-tied."

♦ **V: *She has such a brassy, belting, snarling delivery.***

♦ IR: Betty McQuaid is Australian; they had a lot of good rock'n'roll garage bands and white R&B bands in the '60s that sounded very American, whereas the English didn't. I don't know the true history of how the Australians were so influenced. England didn't have a '50s rock'n'roll scene; they didn't get into Gene Vincent until the early '60s. I have an EP by Betty McQuaid of six songs like "Blue Train" and it's all good stuff.

There's a song from New Zealand called "DJ Blues," which is a *cosmic* rockabilly record with lyrics like "swirling all." You know, like listening to the "swirling all" . . .

♦ **V: *Are you familiar with the punk rock that emerged in Russia in the late '80s, about ten years behind?***

♦ IR: No, but we just played Mexico City and the audience looked like 1980 American punk rock, with mohawks and everything. The band that opened for us did a cover of Sid Vicious' "My Way" and the audience went nuts. It was pretty weird.

♦ **AJ: *A time warp—***

♦ IR: Do you know "Mama Oo-Mau-Mau" by the RIVINGTONS (they also did "Papa Oo-Mau-Mau")? It's wild and aggressive: "He finally found himself a woman who could understand." [accidentally plays 45 at 33 rpm and it sounds very bassy] Do you ever do that just for kicks: play 45s slow? The CHAMPS' "Train to Nowhere" sounds really cool at a slower speed. It doesn't work with vocals; instrumentals work better. [plays 45 at correct speed] Who let him out? Put him back in the cage!

♦ **V: *That is wild—how could they move their tongues so fast?***

♦ IR: It's a group conspiracy—that's what makes it different from something like painting. These people are inspired *together* to do these things . . . express with nonsense sounds what words can't express, a vibe. When we do "Surfin' Bird" (originally by the TRASHMEN), that song has an incredible effect on people. Even with an unresponsive audience, when Lux starts that crazy "Papa Ooo-Mau-Mau" some of the audience start singing it, others are mouthing it silently and they start to look like they're in a trance.

Then they all just bust loose, and it looks like a snakepit—like this writhing thing. This happens everywhere, in any country—it happened in Mexico. Language confines your experiences so much—maybe something gets *released* by letting out these nonsense sounds. Or maybe it's a particular sound or mantra that does it. I read in the *Encyclopedia of Women* that the word "mama" is understood in any language in any culture anywhere—it has the same meaning and gets the same response.

The people originally doing rockabilly were serious *rebels* making underground music—the wildest stuff never became famous. This insane emotional expression came from within; it was a completely unfettered expression of passion.

♦ **AJ: *Certain syllables are in every language; language is actually more similar than dissimilar.***

♦ **V: *Remember Esperanto, the hope of the '50s—***

♦ IR: I remember hearing about that in school; it was supposed to be the universal language. So perhaps "Surfin' Bird" has something universal in it—

♦ LI: It does: there's nothing in it an adult or "intellectual" could stand for two seconds! And kids know that. Our version was the theme song of the Communist party radio program in Italy for several years!

♦ IR: The Red Guard held a high military officer hostage in Italy in the late '70s. When he was released, he said they treated him pretty well, except they tortured him by forcing him to listen to horrible rock music on a headset. We wondered if it could have been "Surfin' Bird"! Have you seen *Five Minutes to Live* with Johnny Cash? He plays a real bad guy—

♦ LI: —who takes a bank manager's wife hostage and tortures her by playing the same riff over and over again on the guitar—

♦ IR: [hysterical] "Do you have to play that?!"

♦ **V: *I was talking to Ken Nordine yesterday—***

♦ LI: Wow—I *love* Ken Nordine!

♦ **V: *And he, right off the cuff, started improvising some fantastic "word wanderings." I always ask artists "How do you create?" and he instantly applied his theory that "everybody should wonder-wander." He starts off consciously trying to rhyme, and one rhyme forces another rhyme that might not make sense but still takes your thoughts somewhere that logic wouldn't have taken you. [interview appears in Volume II]***

♦ LI: Ken Nordine has a great recording that no critic

can listen to and say anything back. There's a town that's really flying with this wild bop-talkin' guy, and some critic comes in and says, "Yeah, but . . ." and kills everybody's fun. Then another wild guy shows up and gets everybody all excited, and the critic does the same thing. Ken Nordine ends it with, "By the way . . . how are things in *your* town?" [the name of the song is "Fliberty Jib"]

♦ IR: We fight hard against being like robots. We think, "How did other people live? What are other ways of being?" We don't just look to the '50s, we look to any period of history, back to the dawn of man. And we're interested in physics or *anything* that could answer our questions. We have vivid imaginations for the future.

You have to beware of *language* making you into a robot; language confines your thinking. There's different thoughts in different languages, and some of them are untranslatable—so you can think more thoughts if you know more languages!

♦ **AJ: *That's where poetry gets you out of the limitations of your own language.***

♦ LI: The great thing about songs like "Surfin' Bird" is that they're beyond art—beyond good or bad. And rock'n'roll is much bigger than just records; it's a way of life—you don't even need *music* to have rock'n'roll! So criticizing it like you would criticize music seems to completely miss the point. Like judging folk music for being played really well, when it's actually someone singing about their lover being *hanged* . . . the fingerpicking or technique has nothing to do with what's happening!

Criticism of all art forms has gotten out of control: critics usually say "This stinks!" without saying *why*. It's at the point where the critic is the star and the artists are furniture. In any magazine you can see reviews of the latest albums with "A-minus" or "C-plus" . . . but music isn't about mathematics, it's about emotions. A lot of these records we've been playing: how could you give them a grade? There's something special going on—that's all there is. And the criticism should be honest and heartfelt, too.

A lot of "unsophisticated" people have something going for them (just like blind people can hear better than people who have sight). They've got an extra sense that comes from not thinking they know everything because they went to college. It's a sense of what's really real. I don't have anything against critics who actually do research, but some of them know nothing about the history of music—you can mention something so common that they *must* have heard of it—but they haven't.

♦ **V: *Where do you get your records these days— from catalogs?***

♦ IR: Sometimes, but mainly we go to the Pasadena record swap.

♦ LI: That's the best in the country; people come from *Georgia* and set up stands there. I always head straight for the Beatles collectors and look for their rockabilly box—

♦ IR: Their *junk*.

♦ LI: And you've got rockabilly collectors selling Beatles "butcher" covers and they don't know it. You gotta go to the right person; whatever they're excited about, you gotta look for something else. At the Pasadena flea market last year I was looking at a little record player and the guy says, "I got a few records here you could try it out with." I look at the records and go [forced casualness], "How much do you want for these?" and he goes, "Oh, I'll give you those for a nickel each." We ended up covering one of the songs—

♦ IR: "Shombalor," by SHERIFF & THE RAVELS. It's nonsense lyrics like "Queen of the Jungle . . . catfish knees, Frankensteino and White Albino/Somebody stole my wine-o. Of all the animals in the zoo I'd rather be a bear/climb the highest mountain just because it's there." We filthied them up—we do the *x-rated* version!

♦ LI: This group has the name mixed up, because the singer sings "Shambalar," but it's spelled "Shambalor" on the label. It's written by AKI ALEONG—he's Hawaiian and has done absolutely everything; he's had a classic surf record out, and he's the star of *Missing in Action III*. We finally figured out that "Shambalor" refers to Shambhala, this mythical place in the Himalayas: Shangri-La.

That's something people don't say much anymore: "I wish that would have continued." "Time Funnel" is a record I've put on ten times in a row. I think a lot of records were designed to make you go, "Put it on *again!*"

♦ IR: Where all animals live in harmony. Shambhala is also the name of Tippi Hedren's wildlife preserve.

♦ **V: *And the subject of the original* Lost Horizon—**

♦ LI: We went and visited where they filmed that, near Ojai . . . There's still great stuff to be found. FORTUNE Records, which had incredible records out in the '50s, is still owned by the same woman. She's just hangin' on to life by a thread, and people have been offering her like $200,000 for her catalog. But she still thinks these records will be *hits;* she told a guy who works there to go to L.A. and give some records to the disc jockeys to play. Now these records are like the wildest imaginable black R&B—there's no *possible* way they could be hits. This guy happens to be a *Cramps* fan, and he just came over to our house and gave us the records, saying, "I don't know what to do with them." Fortune Records is an old gas station, and they've got the same microphone they recorded all their records on—this thing with big tubes on it. Everything recorded there has the same sound, because it was all recorded in the gas station with this one microphone.

I'll play "Greasy Chicken" by ANDRE WILLIAMS on the Fortune label— [plays 45]

♦ **V: That starts out with a single guitar, booming drum, and this singer coming out of nowhere bursting into "Cock-a-doodle-do!"**

♦ IR: These guys are drunk: "Now this dance is back, and we gon' try to show how it go/You'll learn how to do it, in about a month or so"—I guess it was pretty complicated! We cover a song of his called "Bacon Fat" which is another dance.

♦ LI: Do you know "Zindy Lou" by the CHIMES? It's a black rock'n'roll song in the same genre. You'd never see sheet music from Tin Pan Alley that went "Ugh! Ooh-ooh-ooh-ooh!" The Chimes had quite a few great records, including a hit, "Night Owl."

♦ IR: I love songs where they say a girl's name and just sing exotic changes—

♦ LI: They don't need a lot of words to be convinced: "Zindy Lou" is enough . . . This is "Bila" b/w "Tight Skirt" by the VERSATONES—

♦ IR: It's hypnotic. It sounds really African to me, like the chants in children's games.

♦ LI: I can't figure out those lyrics. And words aren't important in the case of "Mope-ty-Mope" by the BOSS-TONES. Like: "All you people on Planet Earth/try this dance and you'll be first/To go Mope-ty-Mope Mope Mope Mope Mope."

♦ **AJ: That singer has the lowest voice I've ever heard—**

♦ **V: It's like we're hearing the extremes of what the human voice is capable of—**

♦ LI: Let's listen to "Rubber Biscuit" by the CHIPS; this song is solid nonsense words.

♦ IR: Another one in that vein is "Imagination" by the QUOTATIONS—they take this Tin Pan Alley *standard* and do a nonsense version of it. If you listen to this for the lyrics, you're missing the point!

Here's another classic, "Unchained Melody," done by VITO & THE SALUTATIONS *their* way. This is like "White Christmas," but done crazy. And to think Rodgers and Hammerstein wrote this! I think Vito changed a few words.

♦ IR: Talking about the range of human vocals made me think of CHARLIE FEATHERS, who dips low and goes high and seems to change personalities a few times within each song. Like: here's the baby, and here's Dracula!

♦ LI: He's multiple-personality rockabilly: *Sybil* Feathers! He's the guy who *invented* the rockabilly hiccup.

♦ IR: He's in his own world: the weird world of Charlie Feathers. He lives in Memphis in a trailer, I think. We covered two of his tunes: "I Can't Hardly Stand It" and "It's Just That Song." All of his songs are a little spooky.

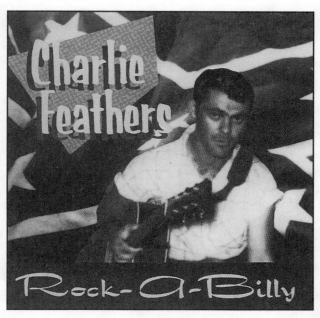

Charlie Feathers' *Rock-A-Billy,* © 1990 Zu-Zazz Records.
CD cover credits: art direction: Clive Blewchamp.

♦ LI: We also cover his version of "Tear It Up." He did a new recording of "Roll Over Beethoven" and you'd think you'd never heard it before—the way he does it is so *weird*. All his songs have this menacing quality. And it's all his family in the band—

♦ IR: His daughter and son. Charlie Feathers also claims he taught Elvis everything he knows, but he's been caught fibbing about things—

♦ LI: He taught Elvis plenty, I'll bet, because Elvis had his ear open all the time. Charlie was at Sun Records before Elvis was. He could do "A Whole Lotta Shakin' Goin' On" so you wouldn't recognize it—it's just the things he does to make a song his own.

♦ **V: Charlie Feathers must have a four-octave range, like Yma Sumac—**

♦ IR: And emotional range, too. When he sings "In the Pines" it sounds like he could have skeletons in the closet *and* under his trailer.

♦ LI: Did you ever hear "Scream" by RALPH NIELSEN & THE CHANCELLORS? [song starts with wild screaming on top of frantic beat and clanging guitar]

♦ IR: It sounds like a snuff record! They're gettin' away with murder—*musical* murder.

♦ LI: That's really my favorite kind of song: early '60s dance songs in which they go wild.

♦ IR: It sounds to me like, "Quick—let's make a record; mom and dad are gone! What's the wildest thing we could do?"

♦ **V: That has more screams per minute than anything I've ever heard—**

♦ LI: To teenagers, if their parents couldn't understand the words and were worried about it, then it was a perfect record! There was a whole teenage society that was really separate from adults, and adults knew it and worried about it, and the more they worried the

The Rivingtons' *The Liberty Years,* © 1991 EMI Records USA.
CD cover credits: art direction: Henry Marquez, design: Michael Diehl,
layout: Paul Volk, photos courtesy: Michael Ochs Archives.

better the kids liked it. "Choo-Choo" by the CABLES kinda makes fun of precise diction [vocalist sings in deliberately slurred, indecipherable moronic speech]

♦ IR: Then the chorus goes, "What'd he say? Six-seven-eight/doesn't he enunciate?"

♦ *V: It seems like we're hearing every possible permutation of an arrangement or vocal interpretation. And the song itself doesn't matter—it can be something you've heard a million times.*

♦ IR: Another thing we're really into is instrumentals—the kind that came out in the late '50s and early '60s, almost before surf. And they're not just rock'n'roll, they've become something *beyond.*

♦ *V: Like "Raunchy"?*

♦ IR: No; a famous one is LINK WRAY's "Rumble." A lot of people say that no good music came out in the early '60s, but actually that was the glory years, the peak, for these experimental instrumentals.

♦ LI: Do you remember what "War of the Worlds" by the ATLANTICS is like?

♦ IR: Ohmigod—that's an apocalyptic example! They were discovering echoplexes then. [song begins with ascending chromatic guitar chord] The drums are speeded up; maybe the whole track is. There were a few hits in this instrumental form, like the TORNADOS' "Telstar" or the MAR-KETTS' "Outer Limits." These people were pushing the limits of the technology of the time.

Another favorite instrumental is "Time Funnel" by JAN DAVIS (he was a session guy, kinda like BILLY MURE). This one starts with a scream, "Ahhhh!" Many of these early '60s instrumentals had castanets on them; isn't that strange? This one has weird chords played on the organ—it took me a half hour to figure

them out.

♦ *V: That one ends too soon; I wish that would have continued—*

♦ IR: That's something people don't say much anymore: "I wish that would have continued." "Time Funnel" is a record I've put on ten times in a row. I think a lot of these records were designed to make you go, "Put it on *again!*" It's been a long time since I've heard anything contemporary that I felt *that* way about.

♦ LI: It's usually: "Take it off!" Back in those days it seemed like people would work to find the *best* way to do the song—every note was important. At Akron's first (and probably last) psychedelic nightclub called The Birth, they once played "Land of a Thousand Dances" by CANNIBAL & THE HEADHUNTERS all night. They didn't play a single other song—they didn't need to.

♦ IR: A lot of surf instrumentals have a pseudo-Oriental, pseudo-exotic sound. "Miserlou" is a classic surf instrumental, but it's also an older Middle Eastern song. I never realized the connection until we had a neighbor in Hollywood who was an Armenian classical pianist. He played these Eastern scales, and it all sounds like the stuff you hear on surf records. I think it started with DICK DALE, who was either Lebanese or Armenian. The very fast picking might have derived from the oud or those instruments you hear in Greek restaurants. I'll bet anything Dick Dale grew up playing these instruments, and then applied it to guitar and established the style. And there were two elements in his playing that were copied by surf bands: the Eastern scales and the fast picking.

I also love DION, who is Italian and has all these crazy scales in his singing. It's all intertwined, the gypsy scales and Armenian-Spanish-Moorish influences. The sound couldn't have been just a gimmick, it must have *evolved.*

♦ *V: [looking at a pile of records] I didn't know Tuesday Weld did a record.*

♦ LI: How could Tuesday Weld be so pretty and sing so horribly? [out-of-tune, soulless vocal follows against a nice '60s organ background].

♦ *V: I know—Pretty Poison is one of my favorite movies.*

♦ LI: The liner notes say, "Orchestra conducted by H. B. Barnum"—I believe it, there's one born every minute! Actually, Ivy's related to P.T. Barnum. We started out playing at CBGBs on the Bowery, and Barnum used to own the whole block—it was one big freak show, one freak after another, down the whole street. Barnum's the one who built up the Bowery before it turned into the slum it is now.

♦ *V: You've got more than one roomful of records—*

♦ LI: We've got 'em in the basement—everywhere you look. But a lot of times, you just don't play a record if you gotta go down to the basement to get it. We're getting to the point where we think twice before bringing something home—we just can't afford the room.

We've got boxes and boxes of stuff in the basement we haven't even unpacked since we moved here years ago.

♦ **V: *What are some of your favorite places in L.A.?***

♦ IR: One of my favorite places is Forest Lawn. Forest Lawn was a concept cemetery, conceived as a cemetery for the *living,* like a park. They have music coming out of speakers in the trees, and a statue of David where you press a button and hear the story of Michelangelo. A great movie called *The Loved One* was inspired by this.

♦ LI: The trees have little buttons on 'em; you push one and a voice starts talking.

♦ IR: The world's largest painting, of the Resurrection, is there, and they present it like a movie. First they light up different parts of it, and narration comes out of each area. When they finally unveil the whole thing there's this sensurround rumbling, and you can see the whole painting of the Resurrection—

♦ LI: Which is like two blocks long—it's huge. They also have the largest stained-glass picture in the world, of the Last Supper.

♦ IR: Famous people like Jean Harlow are buried there.

♦ LI: The ad campaign for *The Loved One* went, "A movie with something to offend everyone!" And it was!

♦ IR: Liberace actually played the funeral director, and now he's buried there. We met him at a book-signing in Beverly Hills a week and a half before he died of AIDS. They had velvet ropes leading up to him; it was really controlled. And he looked so odd; we wondered if he were on drugs. Now we realize that he was near death, and that was what we were seeing. His makeup looked like the way dead people are made up, and his eyes had this weird glazed look like he wasn't seeing anything. He must have known he was near death, but he had to go out there and have the public adore him with his new book.

♦ **V: *I went to his museum in Las Vegas; I'm sure you did, too—***

♦ IR: We also went to his auction. And he did not spend money except for show. Outside of that, he had the cheapest stuff: smoked glass furniture with mylar trim, polyester plaid leisure suits, and tons of K-Mart quality stuff like Yorx stereos. And everything was worn out, too. He had a big car collection, but that too was purely for show—he'd have these Lamborghini-looking sports cars with gull-wings, but under the hood was just enough to get it to roll to a gas station—

♦ LI: A four-cylinder Toyota motor or something. He was "Mister For Show." We have something better than anything from the auction—

♦ IR: Lux gave me this Christmas present: a Liberace hot nuts dispenser! It's got an electric nut-heater—

♦ LI: You put the nuts in at the top, and as you eat 'em (so you can eat lots of 'em fast) they roll down and keep filling this up—

♦ IR: It has "I'll Be Seeing You" (his signature song)

engraved on the back.

♦ LI: That's what got him in trouble in the first place: *hot nuts!*

RANDOM NOTES:

The TRENIERS. They put out records in the late '40s, and they still perform, kinda in a Louis Jordan mode. I think they're black Egyptians; they've got that pyramid power. Their stage act is acrobatic and wild. They actually do somersaults and flips.

SAM BUTERA & The WITNESSES. They still perform in Las Vegas as the Tropicana bar house band.

MISSISSIPPI MUD MASHERS. "Moonglow" is great. It changed my consciousness; things like this keep me *away* from drugs. This sounds like it was recorded in an alley next to the trashcans.

ROY ORBISON. "Ooby Dooby" is his first record on Jewel; the label says "The Teen Kings (featuring Roy Orbison on vocals)."

JAN AND ARNIE. They wrote a song called "Jennie Lee" the night after they saw a stripper of the same name.

STAN FREBERG. In the '50s, he made a lot of money with records that made fun of rock'n'roll records. Even though he was making fun of it, they were actually good rock'n'roll records. His big hits included "John and Marsha," "St. George and the Dragonet," and a take-off on "Banana Boat (Day-O)" by Harry Belafonte.

GLEN CAMPBELL was a hot session guitarist who played on lots of records before he had a solo country and western career. Listen to "Buzz Saw" (by the GeeCees; guess that stands for Glen Campbell)—he shoulda *stayed* doin' this! EARL PALMER is on drums. A lot of famous people played uncredited on each other's records, like STEVE DOUGLAS. That's why a lot of this stuff is so good. Earl Palmer played on a million hot rod albums; he did a lot of studio work in L.A. He played on DUANE EDDY's albums, too.

DOWNEY RECORDS (where "Wipeout," "Pipeline" and a million other surf numbers were recorded) is still in Downey, California, just south of L.A. Now it's a record store, Wenzel's Records, and the guy who recorded them (and his wife) are the clerks.

Many of the recordings recommended in this interview are available from Norton Records [see intv]; Get Hip (412) 231-4766, or Down Home ($2 for catalog from 6921 Stockton Ave, El Cerrito CA 94530; tel: 510-525-1494). The *Cramps'* own recordings are available from Midnight Records, 212-675-2768.

GIL RAY

Gil Ray is a Bay Area musician (The *Rodents, Game Theory*; current band: *Shiny Wet Parts)*, songwriter and video artist in collaboration with Robert Toren and Shelley LaFreniere. Besides unusual records and videos, he collects snow globes. Gil lives in Albany, California with his wife Stacey, a musician and opera aficionado.

♦ **VALE: How did you start finding more unusual records?**

♦ GIL RAY: For the past decade I've worked for City Hall Records, which distributes independent country, bluegrass, and folk music—including the most obscure music you could ever imagine. Ironically, I grew up in the South hating country music, but got turned on to hillbilly music when I moved to California! Unfortunately the advent of the compact disc has virtually stopped the mom-and-pop record labels. There have been great reissues, but the one-record operations run out of people's living rooms have almost disappeared. But there *still* is plenty of obscure material out there—you just have to search harder.

In this day and age, just about all music seems to be more about big business than real emotion. Early hillbilly music certainly sold units, and I'm sure some shifty managers got rich—but it still sounded so *real*.

♦ **V: Why couldn't the mom-and-pop labels just switch to CDs?**

♦ GR: A lot of times it was a matter of principle. One man who puts out '30s and '40s jazz records said, "Over my dead body!" On a lot of the CD reissues you can hear the cracks and pops so much more clearly now—I don't know if that's an improvement.

♦ **V: Who continues to buy vinyl?**

♦ GR: A lot of mom-and-pop stores. The chains don't buy vinyl anymore; they're much more business-oriented now. I still find vinyl at yard sales, like this 7-LP boxed set I got for a dollar: *Young, Warm and Beautiful.*

It's like "*Reader's Digest* audio," with all the hits done elevator-music style. Something about it is very soothing. The marketing behind it intrigues me; I think it was put out for people who aren't real music fans but want to buy some records "for the house" ... who want a lot of cheap music for cocktail parties or when "company comes." Stuff our dads would buy!

Where I work we still sell a lot of vinyl overseas. People from other countries seem far more fanatical about discovering our culture than we are, with the exception of the usual "nostalgia" kicks Americans tend to go on. You know, like " '70s Greatest Hits" or *Big Chill* kind of stuff. Sometimes a record buyer from France or Japan will come in and literally pull records off the shelves by the *boxful* ... strange, loungey, cocktail jazz trio with female vocalist type stuff!

There *is* one really cool thing about CDs—if your player is able to "shuffle" 5 or 6 CDs at a time, you can throw a sound effects CD into the mix and enjoy the odd "jack hammer" or "12-gauge shotgun" blasting between songs!

♦ *V: Tell us about some of your favorite records*—

♦ GR: The *Hi-Los* were probably the *whitest* vocal group you could ever imagine: four crew-cut male singers doing "jazz" vocals that are technically quite great but ... they give me the *creeps*. Their album *Love Nest* has a picture of their heads in a nest looking like

The Hi-Lo's *Suddenly It's The Hi-Lo's*, Columbia Records.

Unfortunately the advent of the compact disc has virtually stopped the mom-and-pop record labels.

baby birds ready for the worm to be dropped in. On "Clap Yo' Hands" they're trying to sound "black," but they don't at all. They just don't sound real—they're the worst of the '50s white suburban mentality.

One of my favorite records is *The Human Orchestra: Rhythm Quartets in the '30s.* They're all vocal groups. Some are well known, like *The Mills Brothers* or *The Ink Spots,* but many are obscure. What's eerie is: the instruments you hear are being *sung,* and they're imitating bands and orchestras. The FIVE JONES BOYS doing "Mr Ghost Goes To Town" is probably the highlight of the record; "My Walking Stick" by the GOLDEN GATE QUARTET has some San Francisco interest. The FIVE JINX doing "Zasu Swing" was recorded in my home town of Charlotte, North Carolina. This is an import from Sweden. I find it interesting that countries like Sweden, Germany and Japan continue to research, collect and reissue some of the strangest music—a lot of which is obscure yet historical. Except for Rhino Records, GNP and Rykodisc, American companies tend to just go for the *obvious* money makers.

DON GIBSON is one of my favorite country writers; he wrote "I Can't Stop Lovin' You" and PATSY CLINE's big hit, "Sweet Dreams." But on *Don Gibson and Los Indios Tabajaras* he collaborated with two

Brazilian Indians and apparently they didn't get along at all—after 4 or 5 recordings everything blew up in their faces. It's a strange combination: soulful country singing with this amazing rapid-fire classical guitar behind it. I think this was CHET ATKINS' idea; he was Don's producer. The cover is worth the price of admission; it's from Bear Family who do a great job of reissuing. Their CD boxed sets come with books that tell you about every song the artist ever recorded; they're really worth it if you're a true fan of, say, JOHNNY CASH, WEBB PIERCE or ERNEST TUBB. There's a DON GIBSON boxed set, too.

One of my strangest records is a Japanese import that someone gave me: *Sound Effect of Godzilla One.* You can drop the needle anywhere and basically you'll hear Godzilla going, "Rarrr ... rarrr!" That's it. It ties in with another record I have from when I was a kid: *Famous Monsters Speak,* from the people who brought you the

The *Hi-Los* were probably the *whitest* vocal group ... they give me the *creeps*. Their album *Love Nest* has a picture of their heads in a nest looking like baby birds ready for the worm to be dropped in.

Famous Monsters of Filmland magazines—I still have boxes of them back home, although they're no longer mint; I cut pictures out and drew all over them. The Frankenstein story is told from the monster's point of view as he stalks this woman—you hear her screaming

Front cover of *Sound Effect of Godzilla 1*, Toshiba EMI.

Back cover of *Sound Effect of Godzilla 1*, Toshiba EMI.

in the background while he's panting and getting excited. My adult ears deduce a very creepy sexual interpretation, like: "I can't believe they were putting this out for kids!" In the same vein, ART LINKLETTER narrates *Where Did You Come From?*, a 1963 record (same year as *Famous Monsters Speak*). He talks about where children

One of my strangest records is a Japanese import, *Sound Effect of Godzilla One*. You can drop the needle anywhere and basically you'll hear Godzilla going, "Rarrr . . . rarrr!"

come from, but in terms of "mommy horses and daddy horses and sperms and eggs"; he says "this small tube at the bottom of the daddy horse inserts this sperm into the egg." *Small* tube? What kind of horses did you grow up around, Art?

♦ **V: It says on the back, "This album was reviewed by outstanding members of the clergy prior to its release." He wrote it—**

♦ GR: —and he did a grand job; I know everything I need to know about where I came from now. His daughter probably had to hear this over and over as a child . . .

To a lot of people bluegrass music sounds like it comes from another planet. One of my favorite albums is *Country Pickin' and Hillside Singin'* by the OSBORNE BROTHERS & RED ALLEN. The first song, "Ruby, Are You Mad?" ends with a vocal effect I've never heard before—it's amazing. They get into some high-end vocal harmonies that sound sorta like the Everly

Brothers—with a suspicious gene pool.

I've also got 4 or 5 albums with songs on them that say things like "I can't wait to see my mother up in heaven," or "Mother, when you're old and grey and wrinkled, you can always live with me." I have the DIXON BROTHERS doing "There's a Place in My Home for Mother," the LOUVIN BROTHERS doing "God Bless Her, 'Cuz She Is My Mother," RENO and SMILEY doing "Always Be Kind to Your Mother"—I guess that says it all. I don't understand these scary mountain people being so concerned—I just watched *Deliverance* and was wondering, "Do *these* guys sing songs about their mothers?" (Probably not.)

Art Linkletter's *Where Did You Come From,* © 1963 20th Century-Fox Records.
Produced by: Youth Guidance Records.
Album cover credits: design: Moskof-Morrison Inc.

THE BRISTOL SESSIONS is mostly hillbilly recordings from the '20s including the CARTER FAMILY, the JOHNSON BROTHERS, the STONEMANS who were a really popular hillbilly act, plus a bunch of little-known singers like J.P. NESTOR and ALFRED KARNES. "A Passing Policeman" and "Tell Mother I Will Meet Her"—another "mother" one—are the "hickest" recordings you'll ever hear. I wish they'd provided lyric sheets; you can hardly understand what they're saying. This is some of the most honest music I've ever heard. The reviews described this as "the definitive early American country compilation"; it's on the Country Music Foundation label.

The CARTER FAMILY is famous—they're very innovative and sold literally millions of records in the '20s and '30s—but they frighten me, probably because I grew up near hillbillies who were inbred and with no

The Louvin Brother's *Satan Is Real*, Longhorn Records. © Stetson.

The Frankenstein story is told from the monster's point of view as he stalks this woman—you hear her screaming in the background while he's panting and getting excited. My adult ears deduce a very creepy sexual interpretation . . .

teeth, spittin' tobacco. Shanachie Records put out a great video, *Chase the Devil,* which is a documentary on hillbilly music of Appalachia. There's a scene with a family playing music up a dirt road: Grandma is hunchbacked, blind and cross-eyed playing the washboard, with 3 or 4 generations of inbred-looking people just wailing. There's nothing contrived about what they're doing; it just came out of them. The Carter Family remind me of that, with songs like "Keep On the Sunny Side" and "John Hardy Was A Desperate Little Man," "Worried Man Blues," "I Never Will Marry," and "Stern Old Bachelor."

THE LOUVIN BROTHERS' *Satan Is Real* was re-released on Stetson Records, but the Stetson hat people raised a fuss. So the British record company changed their name to Longhorn Records—they're a really good reissue company; they provide all the information, including the session dates. There's a note about the making of this cover image of Satan with buck teeth: "The fiery setting pictured on the cover of this album was conceived and built by the Louvin Brothers themselves using chiefly rocks, scrap rubber and lots of imagination. The scene became a little *too* realistic, though, when Ira and Charlie were very nearly burned while directing the photography for this dramatic cover photo." All the songs are quite good, with high harmonies that sound kinda "creepy" to me. The title

song "Satan Is Real" is probably the best number. There are a lot of songs about drunks: "The Drunkard's Doom," "The Kneeling Drunkard's Plea"—I guess alcohol is the Louvin Brothers' most besetting sin. Their music is "a personal crusade against the Prince of Darkness" and I'm sure they were serious, too. But they could have built a better Satan—that one looks like *Captain Kangaroo* . . .

REX ALLEN's *The Hawaiian Cowboy* not only has a great color cover but a color picture-disc inside as well [Bear Family label]. This is mainly a YODELING album. "Texas Tornado" is a great song; "Who Shot That Hole in My Sombrero?" has a racist "Mexican" accent. "Slap Her Down Again, Pa" is "great" if you're into slapping women when they get cantankerous—we've come a long way since then, hopefully. "Chime Bells" best shows off his amazing vocal technique.

I think it was put out for people who aren't real music fans but want to buy some records "for the house" . . . who want a lot of cheap music for cocktail parties or when "company comes."

REX ALLEN narrated a lot of Disney nature specials like *Old Yeller*—almost any '60s and '70s Disney production features his voice. He did some nice western albums in the '40s, but then turned into the Wayne Newton of western singers doing a Vegas-type act. Another singer with a real "cowboy" sound was ROY ROGERS—he put out some great records with good clean vocals and a crisp backup band. I hope it's true

The Salsoul Orchestra's *Christmas Jollies,* © 1976 Salsoul Record Corporation. Album cover credits: cover photo: Joel Brodsky.

that he had his horse Trigger stuffed . . .

◆ **V: *Are there more country records dealing with abuse of women?***

◆ GR: WAYNE RANEY, a country guy from the '40s or '50s, wrote "Why Doncha Haul Off and Love Me?" which Rose Maddox covered. But you don't haul off and love somebody—you haul off and *hit* them! Another song called "My Little Yo-Yo" has lyrics like "you come bouncin' up whenever I throw you down" . . . predecessors of *Two Live Crew!* Unrelated to this topic but amazing is *The One and Only WEBB PIERCE,* which has the strangest female background vocals that almost sound like steel guitars, behind his primitive vocals.

I love/hate "The Little Drummer Boy," and to hear it disco-fied is even more special. The girl on the cover was probably naked, so they painted a Santa Claus suit over her for the Christmas market. I bet she's naked on the import versions.

This SONS OF THE PIONEERS & FRIENDS record has "Festus" from *Gunsmoke* on it. I don't think you can get much weirder than Festus singing "The Hokey Pokey" backed by The THREE SUNS, who combine skating rink music with light jazz like no other. I was impressed by that, plus the fact that there are two songs here by opera singer EZIO PINZA—my wife

The Sons of The Pioneers & Friends: Edition 6, 1950-51, © 1987 Bear Family Records. Album cover credits: photo: Fred Goodwin.

Stacey, who's an opera buff, freaked out when she saw this. You haven't lived until you hear him sing "The Little Ole State of Texas" backed by the Sons of the Pioneers.

On *All-Time Country and Western Hits,* Grandpa Jones (the old man with the mustache from *Hee Haw)* sings "Old Rattler" which is about a dog. On *Hee Haw* Roy Clark and Buck Owens would do some really great instrumental pickin'. When he was a guest, Glen Campbell sometimes would stand next to Roy Clark and one person would do the fingering on the other person's guitar while he was pickin' it—it was amazing guitar playing. Glen Campbell can be heard just rippin' on some late '50s/early '60s WESTERN SWING records. Besides being so "real," almost all of these acts mentioned can really play!

FRANKIE LAINE's *On the Trail* CD has a lot of his hits like "Rawhide," "High Noon" and "Tumbling Tumbleweeds." There's also "On the Trail" which is sung from a mule's point of view—we need to hear more songs like that (I know the mules were horribly exploited). He also does a rave-up version of "Ghost Riders in the Sky." I think most of this was recorded in the early '60s. His singing style is bombastic, but captures the essence of the Old West myth in a strange, cheesy sort of way.

Moving into the '70s, here's the SALSOUL ORCHESTRA's *Christmas Jollies* album. To hear a Christmas medley go on for 30 minutes with one disco beat is pretty special. I love/hate "The Little Drummer Boy," and to hear it disco-fied is even more special. The girl on the cover was probably naked, so they painted a Santa Claus suit over her for the Christmas market. I bet she's naked on the import versions.

I have a fascination with songs from *The Wizard of Oz,* and here is JERRY LEE LEWIS from his *Killer*

Country album singing "Over the Rainbow," with his trademark ripples-up-the-keyboard. I bought this album for that one song, just as I bought MECO performing all the hits from *The Wizard of Oz*. MECO was probably some studio band cashing in on the disco trend; it's much like the SALSOUL ORCHESTRA, one solid disco beat. I also have BILLY WARD & The DOMINOES doing "Over the Rainbow" doo-wop style— it's bizarre. It's still available on the King label which is the opposite of the Bear Family or Longhorn labels— they don't give you *any* information, and some of their reissues are not the original recordings, like *The Grass Roots' Greatest Hits* which added horn arrangements and synthesizers—they re-recorded their original hits!

I bought *Julie & Carol at Lincoln Center* (Julie Andrews and Carol Burnett) because they do a medley of '60s songs that lasts 15 minutes, featuring songs like "With a Little Help from My Friends," "The Beat Goes On," "I Dig Rock'n'Roll Music," "Gentle On My Mind," "Come Together," "Aquarius," and "Spoonful of Sugar." To hear them "get down" and sing these rock tunes with a big band behind them . . . these poor musicians are probably sight-reading their asses off; every 20 seconds a new snippet of song follows. I was impressed.

Are you familiar with BOBBY TROUP, who wrote the song for "Route 66"? He's Julie London's husband; he also starred in a '70s TV show, *Emergency*. He played the older emergency room doctor, the chief of staff. He also had a little lounge jazz trio. With his sexy, smooth voice and handsome good looks, he was quite popular with the girls. "The Three Bears" is the story of Goldilocks and the three bears done in a jazz/lounge style which is incredible: the lyrics *and* the music. "Hungry Man" is also very clever—everything gets related to food. To hear him do "Route 66" is

Julie Andrews & Carol Burnett's *Julie & Carol at Lincoln Center*, Columbia Records.

kinda special too. This is a great CD: *In a Class Beyond Compare*. It reminds me of the guitarist EDDIE HAZELL, who plays Holiday Inn-type jazz trio music; the standout on his cassette is "Gravy Waltz" written by STEVE ALLEN. Both these guys are perfect when combined with pasta, nice wine and low lights. Serious adult lovemaking music!

To a lot of people bluegrass music sounds like it comes from another planet. They get into some high-end vocal harmonies that sound sorta like the Everly Brothers— with a suspicious gene pool.

VICKY SPINOSA is a Bay Area girl who did a 45, "Dinky Little Cable Car," about ten years ago—it was a tribute to the San Francisco cable car anniversary. As you can see it's endorsed by then-mayor Dianne Feinstein. And this poor girl cannot sing a lick. Her dad was her manager and it turned out to be the joke of the warehouse; we played it constantly. Finally somebody broke the one remaining copy. But she kept at her career, and a few months ago her dad brought us a new CD. She's now known as VIKKI LIZZI, and does these sexy, vampy disco tunes: "Can't Tame the Woman in Me," and "Red Hot Riding Hood." She and her dad have been trying for a decade now—that's very charming. But I'm afraid she really is tone-deaf. They put out the sheet music, too.

There are a number of CDs of circus music from France, and here's one: *La Grande Parade du Cirque*.

Don Gibson & Los Indios Tabajaras, © 1986 Bear Family Records. Album cover credits: photo courtesy of The Tennessean.

The band plays, and when the clown does something funny you hear the crowd laughing—you feel like you're truly at the circus. For some reason I relate this to *Battle of the Organs,* a reissue from the '50s featuring LUIS RIVERA and DOC BAGBY. These guys are amazing, and there's a very romantic and sexy mood about this—it's real music, it's not sampled, and these guys are seated at four- or five-tiered keyboards with pedals just *wailing,* in real time. "Deep Purple," "Tangerine," and "Manhattan" are outstanding—standards done on a hot organ. Other good organists I like include BILL DOGGETT, a cool R&B player from the '50s; he was a huge man with a huge sound. "As You Desire Me" is a favorite track from the LP *Bill Doggett: His Organ and Orchestra.* Then there's RICHARD "GROOVE" HOLMES—some of his records are really great to dance to.

In the late 1500s the Pope, Sixtus V, banned women from appearing onstage, so the Catholic church came up with the idea of castrating young boy singers before their voices changed.

BING CROSBY's *Wartime Christmas Broadcasts* has a couple versions of "Jingle Bells" which are really jazzy and amazing. There's a brief Christmas greeting from the folks at Philco, and the Charioteers doing "A Slip of the Lip Can Sink a Ship"—war propaganda. While we're in Christmastime, here's RENO & SMI-

The Human Orchestra, Clanka Lanka (a division of Mr R&B Records). Album cover credits: sleeve design: Gene Johnson, NYC & Lasse Ermalm, Stockholm.

Don Reno & Red Smiley's *The True Meaning of Christmas,*
© 1988 Highland Music, © King Records.

LEY doing "The True Meaning of Christmas," and I don't think you've *lived* until you've heard Christmas songs done bluegrass style. Don Reno and Red Smiley—well, their vocals and musicianship are amazing, just like the Stanley Brothers and the Louvin Brothers and the Osborne Brothers.

I think a lot of the appeal of these kinds of music stems from an emotional, nostalgic aspect—they push some childhood button in me. This music seems so "sanitized," in the same way the '50s and early '60s TV shows like *Leave It to Beaver* seem. My childhood wasn't exactly like the "Beav's," but sometimes I find myself longing for those simpler days for no good reason.

I like this recording of a Wurlitzer band organ—it's calliope-like and sounds very nostalgic. This organ is really a fully mechanical band that plays itself; air actually blows into horns, sticks actually hit drums—but it's all mechanized. This one has been restored. It reminds me of carnivals, which are creepy in their own way, especially the ones with the sideshows (there's only one left now, the JIM ROSE Traveling Circus Side Show which is wild). I like *Carnival of Souls, Something Wicked This Way Comes* (the movie and the book) and *Carny* with Jodie Foster and Robbie Robertson—that's a great neglected movie, very dark. It's about life in a seedy traveling carnival; Gary Busey plays the ducking clown who yells insults at the audience, and Jodie Foster's role is even harder-core than in *Taxi Driver,* and she was still underage. It has Emmett the Alligator Man and Priscilla the Monkey Girl in it, too.

I have another calliope record, KALLY-OPE, which puts out an almighty sound. A little old lady named Barbara Taggart produces these records; she personally packs each box and writes up the invoices herself in shaky handwriting. I believe she has shown interest in possibly manufacturing CDs of this music.

Last, but not least, are a couple of CDs which my wife Stacey turned me on to. The first contains the only known recordings by the last surviving castrato singer, ALESSANDRO MORESCHI (1858-1922), recorded at the beginning of the century and kept in the Vatican archives. Even though his voice had severely declined, it still has a high vibrato which just does not sound like a female singer. In the late 1500s the Pope, Sixtus V, banned women from appearing onstage, so the Catholic church came up with the idea of castrating young boy singers before their voices changed. This practice flourished for almost 200 years until Napoleon's armies invaded Italy in 1796 and outlawed the practice as barbaric. It took awhile for it to completely die out; hence this recording.

I have a fascination with *The Wizard of Oz*, and here is Jerry Lee Lewis singing "Over the Rainbow," with his trademark ripples-up-the-keyboard and Billy Ward & The Dominoes doing "Over the Rainbow" doo-wop style—it's bizarre.

Another singer of interest is MADO ROBIN (the "Mad Robin"), the French opera singer with the highest voice in the world. She'll build up and build up and when you think she couldn't possibly hit a note any

The Collins Kids, Vol. 2, © 1983 Bear Family Records.

The Three Suns 1949 - 1957, © 1985 Circle Records.

higher, she hits it and *nails* it—there's nothing timid about this woman. It's ear-shattering; it's amazing. She's on an out-of-print CD boxed set of Delibes' *Lakme*, one CD of arias still in print, and a number of rare French LPs—I've heard that even in France it's hard to find her material. She died awhile ago. At least the town she grew up in, Yzeures-sur-Creuse-Toureine, erected a shrine to her . . .

REFERENCE:

The Human Orchestra [Clanka-Lanka CL-144,003, Mr R&B Records, Sweden] various artists; probably out of print.

The Three Suns 1949-1957 (Circle CLP-75, available from Circle Records, 3008 Wadsworth Mill Pl, Atlanta GA 30032-5899)

Holiday for Strings and Brass (Memoir Noir 503, England)

Sons of the Pioneers, Edition #6 (available from Bear Family, PO Box 1154, 2864 Vollersode, Germany. Tel 04794-1399. Fax 04794-1574)

The Collins Kids at Town Hall Party (Country Routes RFD 9002, England)

Rex Allen, The Hawaiian Cowboy (Bear Family)

The Carter Family: 20 of the Best (RCA International NL 89369, England)

Mado Robin (Accord 200022)

Alessandro Moreschi, The Last Castrati: Complete Vatican Recordings (Opal [Pearl] 9823)

Kally-Ope, $12 from Barbara Taggart, 323 Logan St., Rockford IL 61103. Tel 815-964-2789.

MIKE WILKINS

Writer and artist Mike Wilkins is coauthor of *New Roadside America*, the classic book on America's weirdest roadside attractions—like diving pigs, giant concrete insect statues, and the pickled body parts of criminals. He's been in a band, The MBAs, and coauthored the film *Birch Street Gym,* which in 1991 was nominated for an Academy Award for best live action short. In addition to records, Mike collects celebrity autobiographies/ biographies, unusual packaged foods, and promotional artifacts. He lives in San Francisco with his wife, Sheila Duignan.

♦ *VALE: Tell us about your record collection—*
♦ MIKE WILKINS: My collection is slanted toward records and music that have been used either to sell something (like Coca-Cola's *I'd Like to Teach the World to Sing)* or someone, or that otherwise promotes products, services or odd viewpoints. With most of my records, the music is secondary, and is certainly not what is being sold by the record makers.

For example, I like records by SUB-CELEBRITIES. There's a level of celebrityhood in this country that can't make easy money with that celebrity. A movie star who's famous can make money by acting or by using that fame; a newscaster can get a better contract or position. But there's a lower strata of celebrities who get famous for something, but with no obvious way to cash in! So they need a basic product that they can "name-brand." In the past there's been two principal ways to profit: books and records. Instructional videos are becoming very popular with sub-celebrities, but records, unfortunately, are on their way out.

Remember RODNEY ALLEN RIPPY, the child star of '70s Jack-in-the-Box commercials? He was this little three-year-old black kid who'd laugh and sing, "Take life a little easier! Make life a little easier!" People would say, "Oh, he's so cute!" and sing the song. But what can you *do* with that? So they released a whole album by him, and had him pose on the cover wearing a sweatshirt that says, "Take Life a Little Easier"— they tried to generate whatever income they could get from his fame. His label, Bell Records, also put out the *Partridge Family* album; certain labels specialized in this stuff.

♦ *V: He was famous just for Jack-in-the-Box commercials—that's it?*
♦ MW: Yeah! And the record's *terrible;* he wasn't a singer! Part of the charm of him singing is: he didn't quite *get* it. The theme song, "Take Life a Little Easier," was originally a commercial jingle, only 30 seconds long. It was expanded from selling hamburgers into a whole philosophy of "taking life easier." [sings] "What's to be gained by biting your nails, toting those bags, lifting those bales?"

You can't get rich off singles; singles are used by companies to push the albums. You have to have an *album* to cash in, and an album has to have ten songs. They made Rodney sing songs like "Candy Man," "The Birds and the Bees," "He's Got the Whole World in His Hands," weaving a whole persona around this bewildered little kid. This is a good example of an album put out to cash in on minor, fleeting, fickle celebrityhood.

Many of these sub-celebrities only become famous because they are very good at public relations; some people would call them blatant self-promoters. "Blatant" may be the wrong word because it connotes evil; they just know how to do it, and they have no shame about it. "Shame" is another word that connotes badness— let's say they have no *trepidation* about promoting something. On one level you can make fun of them, but on another level successful self-promoters really touch the popular imagination.

♦ *V: Can you give us an example?*

♦ MW: EVEL KNIEVEL is tops. On his record he sings, there are excerpts from press conferences; he's even written some of the songs. At one press conference Evel says "America doesn't have enough heroes . . . I don't care about death"— square-jawed things like that. He was also in a movie in which he starred as himself (called *Viva Knievel!*). The love interest is Lauren Hutton as a women's libber, so Evel says goofball things to her like, "Are you a woman or a Ms.?" There was also *Evel Knievel,* which starred George Hamilton. I visited Twin Falls, Idaho, where Evel tried to jump the Snake River Canyon in a motorized jet-cycle back in 1974. Even though he failed, that big earthen take-off ramp is still there, and so is a commemorative marker with the jet-cycle etched into it.

Photo: Robert Waldman

Another person who was really good at self-promotion is RONA BARRETT, the gossip columnist. She wrote an autobiography, she wrote a novel, and she released an album on which she sang Broadway hits. And it was straight: "Somewhere Over the Rainbow"— that kind of stuff. She was always pushing, and each item that got into the stores paved the way for another. The promo could say, "She wrote a novel, *The Lovoma-* niacs; she's a *novelist* now." It all builds on each other.

MUHAMMED ALI was a great boxer, of course, but he also had great PR instincts. He starred in an autobiographical movie called *The Greatest*. Whitney Houston's "The Greatest Love of All" is about Ali, with lyrics like, "The greatest love is learning to love yourself." He starred in his own comic book, *Muhammed Ali vs. Superman*, in which he fights Superman and wins! He even put out Muhammed Ali's Old Kentucky Cabin Barbecue Sauce ("It's the greatest.")

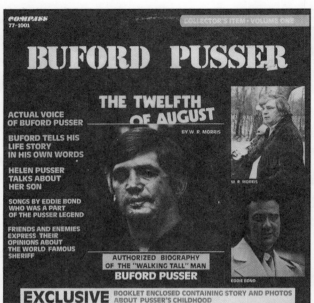

Walking Tall Sheriff Buford Pusser Talks with W.R. Morris, © Compass Records. Album cover credits: cover photos: Dewey Simpson, album design: Dan Quest & W.R. Morris.

I have an album, *Ali and His Gang Vs. Mr. Tooth Decay: A Beautiful Children's Story*. This LP includes Howard Cosell and Frank Sinatra among others, and I'm guessing that some hustler-businessman-promoter somehow wrangled his way in with this idea to see Ali. The record *features* Ali, but it's produced by Arthur Bernard Morrison whose name is everywhere; *he* is another guy who understands PR. He probably went to Frank Sinatra and said, "This is good for children, and good for the black community," and Frank probably said, "All right, I'll give you ten minutes," and then he goes to the American Dental Association with the same pitch. The back cover features this painting with all the entertainers' heads collaged in; there's Frank Sinatra, and there's Jayne Kennedy. It says "Volume One" although I doubt if there were any follow-ups. When he was pitching the story to Ali, Arthur Morrison probably said, "Then for Volume Two you're going to fight juvenile delinquency, and then heroin addiction! You're going to save the black community! But let's start small; let's start with tooth decay and build from that."

When MR. T came out with his children's album, *Mr. T's Commandment*s, in 1984, his songs could attack other problems: "Don't Talk to Strangers," and "No Dope No Drugs." Thanks to Ali, tooth decay was under control.

Here's a tribute album to Buford Pusser, who inspired the *Walking Tall* movies that came out in the mid-'70s. Buford Pusser was this six-foot-six, 250-pound sheriff in Tennessee who fought local moonshiners and organized crime, getting his wife killed in the process and his face beaten in; it took 192 stitches to put it back together. He had hero quality. But "How can we make money with Buford Pusser? Because—

look, he's *ugly;* he's had his jaw broken and his face all burnt up . . . What can we do with *him?*" Well, they made the *Walking Tall* movies about him. And he became a celebrity because "in an era spoiled by mass murders, political assassinations, child beatings and Washington scandals, decent Americans were starving for a man of courage who stood for honesty." [from LP liner notes]

There were three *Walking Tall* movies. Joe Don Baker played him in the first one, *Walking Tall*, which grossed something like 40 million dollars; Bo Svenson played him in the second (*Walking Tall, Part 2*), and in the third (*Walking Tall: The Final Chapter*) Bo Svenson plays Pusser and Joe Don Baker plays Joe Don Baker who's meeting Buford Pusser because he's going to *be* Buford Pusser in the movie! There was even a made-for-TV follow-up movie, *A Real American Hero*, and a TV series for awhile.

After the second film, Pusser died mysteriously in a car crash. His life had such a mythical dimension—he'd gotten blown up in a car but lived; he'd had his head beaten in but survived; they'd killed his wife in a pre-dawn ambush intended for him but he'd escaped. [reads LP liner notes] "Then, on August 12, 1974, the thirty-six-year-old Pusser was thrown from his new sports car and killed. Tennessee State Troopers labeled the death 'just another traffic fatality.' However, countless friends and admirers of the famous sheriff felt otherwise. They believed that Buford Pusser met death at the hands of foul play."

There's a tourist attraction, CARBO'S POLICE MUSEUM in Pigeon Forge, Tennessee that has Buford's death car; their sign has a skull-and-crossbones on it. Also, Pusser's home in Adamsville, Tennessee, is a museum: you can see his toothbrush and his credit cards. You used to be able to touch the shoes he was

Mike Wilkins (left). The MBAs' *Born To Run Things*, © 1982 Corporate Records.

Rodney Allen Rippy's *Take Life a Little Easier,* © 1974 Bell Records. Album cover credits: design & photography: Woody Woodward Grafix.

wearing when he died, but then someone swiped the wallet he was carrying when he died so everything is behind glass now.

Pusser touched a nerve. So this record, *W.R. Morris Talks With Buford Pusser,* had to come out, but there was a problem: what to put on it? Well, they include part of an interview, and then there's some songs about him and his wife ("She Ain't No Ordinary Woman"). And there's this great thing—you know about the magical numbers in Elvis's life: 2001 had special significance. Well, they've put together a horrible numerology song for Buford as well—it's so forced: born on the 12th, died on the 12th, he's 6 feet 6, 6 plus 6 is 12, and 3 times 12 is how old he was when he died. Makes you believe in a higher power, no?

Here's COLONEL SANDERS' *Tijuana Picnic.* Most people don't realize that when Colonel Sanders became famous, he no longer owned Kentucky Fried Chicken—he was used as a human mascot by the man he sold it to, John Y. Brown. Brown was a PR genius. He later married the Miss America of 1970, Phyllis George, and then became governor of Kentucky. When he bought Kentucky Fried Chicken in 1964, it was a small franchise chain. As he grew the company, John Y. Brown realized the value of having the Colonel around; you got the feeling that the Colonel looks at every bucket; he's such a decent man. So as they were pushing the chain out and expanding everywhere, the Colonel became a celebrity—yet how do you keep the fires going? Well, you release albums. So all this record is, is Tijuana Brass-type music, but it's got the Colonel's picture on the cover, and it's *selling chicken!* I'm sure no one bought this album because they thought the *music* was great. You probably got this album for two dollars when you bought a bucket . . . it was a way to sell product.

John Y. Brown finally sold Kentucky Fried Chicken to Heublein distillery in 1971 for quite a bit more than he paid for it. PepsiCo owns it today.

♦ *ANDREA JUNO: Did the Colonel get any of this?*
♦ MW: No. He had been bought out for a couple million, and he was on retainer: do the ads and show up at store openings. The same thing happened to Orville Redenbacher; he's just a shill now. Kentucky Fried Chicken is a big, multinational company, but the headquarters building in Louisville is designed like an enormous antebellum mansion. It's got columns and a big porch, and you feel like you're walking into the Colonel's house: "Well, we got ten thousand employees, but you know we still do things just like the Colonel." You walk in, and just off to the left is the Colonel's office. And when he died they preserved it as a shrine.

After Brown sold the company, they loosened the reins on the Colonel. All along he'd been a Christian, but I think that if you're someone like the Colonel— you're born in Nowheresville, Kentucky, and you suddenly become this famous guy, you think, "There *must* be a higher power, because it's not me!" So he became a *real* Christian. His autobiography was published (it's out of print now) and you could tell it was after John Y. Brown left, because it wasn't published by a major house and it wasn't used to hype Kentucky Fried Chicken; it was published by a small Christian publishing house. The first photo in the book is this great shot of Colonel Sanders being baptized in the River Jordan, and as he's coming up for air he's got this white flowing cloth on, and the preacher has his hand on his head, baptizing him. He also put out a Christian album: *The Colonel's Mandolin Band Plays Your Favorite Spirituals,* or something like that.

Rodney Allen Rippy, the child star of '70s Jack-in-the-Box commercials, is a good example of an album put out to cash in on minor, fleeting, fickle celebrityhood.

To finish up this John Y. Brown story: he used to go gambling down in Florida, where he met Jimmy the Greek. Jimmy the Greek was also a PR adept. You know how everyone's heard of Jimmy the Greek— well, *why?* What happened was: he was a small-time gambler in Steubenville, Ohio who went to Las Vegas and worked in a casino, but not as an odds-maker. Bobby Kennedy came in with his organized crime probe and said, "Jimmy, you can't work for the casinos anymore, because you're tainted." He didn't have a job, so what could he do? He started a PR firm to do PR for

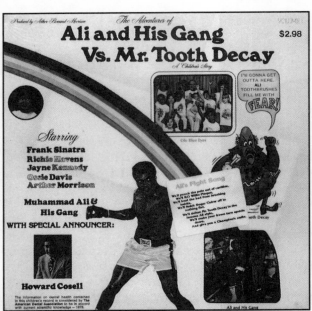

The Adventures of Muhammad Ali & His Gang Vs. Mr. Tooth Decay,
produced by Arthur Bernard Morrison.

casinos, and the way he got himself famous was, he started publishing odds on who would win the election, or what the next royal child would be—boy or girl. You'd hear on the radio, "Jimmy the Greek says the odds on . . . are . . . !" And this was a brilliant stroke, because now everyone knows Jimmy the Greek!

So Jimmy the Greek met John Y. Brown in Florida at the dog tracks or horse racing or something, and then when Jimmy the Greek became CBS's pro football odds-maker, who shows up to be the color commentator but Phyllis George! And of course, she now has a line of seasoned chicken products in supermarkets—"Chicken By George"—made by Hormel. Jimmy the Greek parlayed his nothingness into a huge money-making career—until he got fired for saying that American blacks were better athletes because as slaves they were *bred* for it. And as it turns out, Jimmy the Greek now lives in Durham, North Carolina, where I grew up. He went down for the famous rice diet.

♦ *V: What's that?*
♦ MW: When I was growing up in Durham, the only "outsiders" around were these fat New Yorkers that would come to town for Duke Medical Center's rice diet, which was mainly rice and water. It was a celebrity fat person's diet in the '60s and '70s; Buddy Hackett and Mama Cass and Totie Fields and James Coco would come down for the rice diet. Buddy Hackett, in his book of poetry, *The Naked Mind of Buddy Hackett,* has a poem of rebirth entitled "Durham." Even Colonel Sanders and his wife Claudia came down.

These celebs always mentioned it on the *Tonight Show,* and because celebrities went, a lot of other fat people came, mostly from New York. Even Al Goldstein from *Screw* magazine showed up. So you'd get all these big New Yorkers down here in this laid-back town. Part of the diet was: you had to walk. You'd see

all these really fat people in shorts and black socks walking along the road.

So when I was young this is how I imagined all New Yorkers to be: really fat. You'd see them in the grocery stores and they'd be trying to get their gum or cigarettes and get outta there, while the natives'd be looking up at them and going, "Whu-ut? You don't want to just *talk* for awhile?" Like, "So . . . you're from New York? Well, whaddaya think of Durham—it's pretty hot today, don't you think?" [angry] "YES! NOW JUST GIVE ME THE GODDAM CIGARETTES!" Another thing was, they were really hungry, so they were *really mean.* I thought, "*Wow*—New York!"
♦ *V: Continuing on with the sub-celebrity genre—*
♦ MW: Here's a good one: TED KNIGHT: *Hi Guys.* He played Ted Baxter, one of the adjunct characters, on the *Mary Tyler Moore Show.* He knew it was his big chance, so "Let's ring the cash register!" But at least Knight is doing it in his Ted Baxter voice, singing songs like "A Man Who Used to Be" and "I'm in Love with Barbara Walters."

Here's a record by Hogan's Heroes, but you'll notice Hogan [Bob Crane, the star] does not appear. Crane didn't need to do this. He went on to have a second career as a dinner theater entertainer across the country. Wherever he went he enticed all these pretty girls into orgies which he would videotape. At some point his partner, who was also his video equipment supplier, propositioned Crane. When he refused, his partner caved in Crane's head with a hammer. Anyway, when the other guys on the show were offered the opportunity to make a record, they probably thought, "This is *it* for me." They sing "The Best Songs of World War II." "A Nightingale Sang in Berkeley Square"—that's a real touching one. Carter just got a "Dear John" letter. He's really down, then Newkirk says, "Don't worry about it, Carter," and he starts singing this lovely song.

The funny thing is: most Hollywood people think they can sing. Actually, I think *most* people think they can sing! Just like everybody thinks they're a better-than-average driver, everybody thinks: "Yeah, I can carry a tune—with a little echo chamber and some strings, I could sound as good as Frank Sinatra." Why are karaoke bars so popular—because everybody thinks they've got a good voice—you just gotta *prod* 'em a little!

ROCK HUDSON's album is called *Rock Gently,* and it's an album of ROD McKUEN songs. EDDIE ALBERT (star of *Green Acres*) had an album out on which he sings some Bob Dylan songs; SEBASTIAN CABOT (Mr French in *Family Affair*) had an album out which *only* had Dylan songs. William Shatner, of course, released *The Transformed Man,* which features his mind-bending renditions of "Lucy in the Sky with Diamonds" and "Mr Tambourine Man." KURT RUSSELL made an album when he was a young Disney star. The list of TV and movie star albums is as long as your arm.

Occasionally, one of these records makes it big. John Travolta, who became a star with *Welcome Back, Kotter* had a hit single. Then he put out a couple albums, and then his brother Joey had an album out, then his sister Ellen—the Travolta collection boxed set! Then all the *other* Sweathogs started recording albums, like Lawrence Hilton Jacobs . . .

The show *Happy Days* was the same way. Donny Most (Ralphie) had an album, Potsy had an album; there's a Fonzie album, and one by Scott Baio. Joanie had an album; Laverne and Shirley, who spun off from *Happy Days,* had an album. Lennie and Squiggy had an album, and even toured. If you've got this thing that you know people are watching every week, let's lever it—*let's sell product!*

There's a record by DINO, DESI AND BILLY: *I'm a Fool,* by Dino (Dean Martin's son), Desi Arnaz Jr, and Billy Hinsche whose dad was a real estate guy. My guess is that it started out as an accounting scheme: "Look, I could give you kids two thousand dollars a year in a trust fund and not have it taxed, or I could fund your record company and have all the profits go to you, and that way I can count it as a write-off, and you can get income from it." They actually had songs that reached the charts, but I just get the feeling that this was a Hollywood tax dodge.

♦ *V: LEE HAZLEWOOD produced that album— he's pretty good.* **Nancy and Lee** *is a great album—*
♦ MW: And of course Dean Martin knows Lee Hazlewood: "Lee, write a song for my kids, okay? I'll pay you; I can write it off, and any money they get performing that song, they get. They're kids; they're in a lower tax bracket"—that's speculation.

This is a great one: BING CROSBY singing *Hey Jude.* This is right at the end of his career. In the late '60s the times they were a-changin', and these older

Muhammad Ali Fights Mr. Tooth Decay, produced by Arthur Bernard Morrison.

actors decided to get with it: "Flower power's coming; hippies are coming; this is *in.*" Did you ever see that movie by Otto Preminger, *Skidoo?* It's an acid movie, and in it all these old stars are shown: Groucho Marx

I grew up in Durham, NC where fat New Yorkers would come for Duke Medical Center's rice diet. When I was young this is how I imagined all New Yorkers to be: really fat.

smokes dope and Jackie Gleason's on acid; Carol Channing is running around in her underwear. A whole cabal of old stars suddenly decided, "Hey, we better get hip!" So, here Bing does "Hey Jude." Look at the liner notes: "Bing Crosby received a standing ovation on November 21, 1968. This on the surface would not appear to be that extraordinary. However, this particular ovation was probably the most complimentary of his career. The people who stood and gave the salute were musicians who had just backed Mr. Crosby in the recording of this album *Hey Jude/Hey Bing.* The older ones said, 'He still sings great.' The younger ones said, 'He's a *gas.'* "

♦ *V: That's sad.*
♦ MW: *George Burns Sings* is another album from the "stars go groovy" period. The cover is a Sgt. Pepper takeoff, with George giving the peace sign, Kirk Douglas in love beads, plus Frank, Dean, Joey Bishop, and Raquel Welch all hippie-style on the cover. He does one medley where "59th Street Bridge Song" segues into "Satisfaction."

Here's one by MAE WEST: *Way Out West.* It was recorded in the '60s with a nameless rock combo; she sings songs like "Day Tripper." She had a "Golden Age" revival as a spokeswoman for free love, and in 1970 she made *Myra Breckenridge* with Rex Reed and Raquel Welch. Then in '78 she made *Sextette* based on a play she had written 50 years previously.

My wife, Sheila, and I got the chance to speak with an Academy Award-winning costume designer earlier this year. He had met Mae West toward the end of her life. She was very short—only about four-and-a-half feet tall! In photo portraits she is always standing on a staircase with a long flowing gown so you can't tell which step she's standing on, or where her knees are. She always wore platform shoes, and toward the end of her career kept tripping—that's why she had muscle men on either side of her: to keep her from falling down. At the end she wore polio leg braces so she could remain on her platform shoes. This designer said that not only was she not at all feminine in look or demeanor, she actually was very masculine. I'm wondering if she wasn't a man! After all, Mae wasn't a star

'til she was 40, and always dressed like a female impersonator.

It's not just stars—*everyone* thinks they can sing. CHRISTINE JORGENSEN became famous as the man who became a woman back in the '50s. Newspaper headlines read "'Ex-GI Becomes Blonde Beauty," "MDs Rule Chris '100 % Woman', " and "Disillusioned Christine To Become Man Again!" What did she do for a living after her sex change? She had a nightclub act, she sang, and she put out an album. In 1970 a movie came out, *The Christine Jorgensen Story.* She's dead now.

BARBARA CARTLAND, the romance novelist, put out *Barbara Cartland's Album of Love Songs Especially for You* ... BARBI BENTON was forever trying to make it as a singer; she was country & western—she even had a part on *Hee Haw.* Now she's New Age. She even pitched a "How to Play New Age Piano" video on a late night TV infomercial for awhile. She's *still* trying; "I'm gonna be a star; I *know* I can do it!" Her New Age album is called *Kinetic Voyage.*

Cathy Rigby—America's first gymnastic pixie—landed the Stayfree contract. She put out an *aerobics* record selling Stayfree. Cathy can do an hour's worth of aerobics with her Stayfree and never have an "accident"!

♦ **V: Wasn't she initially famous as the young girl who married Hugh Hefner?**

♦ MW: Insiders *thought* they were going to be married, but it never happened. Hef has always been close to a girl who is then temporarily the head of the Playboy harem, and insiders would forever speculate, "This time it's *for real.*" Hef finally married Kimberly Conrad. I was at a party at the Playboy Mansion and it was great. I went down expecting to meet Jimmy Caan and Robert Blake and Jim Brown and all those people you see in the mansion photos, but ... What it was, was a party to introduce the new Playboy pinball game. And there were *no* stars present. There were eight Playmates as window dressing, but the rest of the people were the men and women of the coin-operated amusement business. Hef came out like a boxer with an entourage, smiling; Kimberly Conrad on his arm and flashbulbs going off. He comes out to the dais and says, "Welcome, thank you for coming, blah blah blah." He unveils the Playboy pinball game, plays a couple balls so people could take pictures, and then he leaves.

For the rest of the party I was walking around the mansion and the grounds, scaring the flamingos and feeding the fish. My theme for the day was posing coin-operated amusement people next to Playmates who obviously didn't want to be there—meeting people in the coin-operated amusement business was *not* going to further their careers at all! They tried to stay off by themselves huddled in a corner, but I think somebody from Playboy security said, "Okay: we want you to *mingle!"*

At one point the Playmates signed their own centerfolds for people—this turned out to be an exercise in *crowd control.* The party was in the back yard, and when they wanted it to wind up, they announced, "Now we're going to have the Playmates sign their centerfolds." They had three long tables set up with the girls signing their nude images; people would start at one end, collect their autographs, and find themselves at the front door, leaving! And since there was a big line of people coming through, they couldn't exactly turn around. It was brilliant!

♦ **V: Didn't Playboy have a record company, too?**

♦ MW: Yes, although I don't know if they had any major hits. Barbi Benton did her country & western album, *The Best Live from Japan* on it. Did you know that MARILYN CHAMBERS put out an album? She's another celebrity who, in her own way, is very good at PR. Marilyn started out doing disco, then went country & western. See, it doesn't matter what kind of music you put on a Marilyn Chambers record—that's not what sells the product.

♦ **AJ: Is she still a Christian?**

♦ MW: That's *Linda Lovelace*—I think her genius was Chuck Traynor, who then later married Marilyn Chambers. Chuck now owns an indoor shooting range called The Survival Store in Las Vegas, where he's busily promoting "Bo," the survivalists' dream girl. Both Marilyn and Linda Lovelace had all these books out in the '70s, paperbacks and intimate diaries. There was one book I wish I'd bought; it featured Marilyn Chambers and showed her topless from just above her nipples back-to-back with a topless Xaviera Hollander. That was the cover of *Xaviera and Marilyn: Intimate Conversations*—what a '70s sexuality book! Even Xaviera's husband, "Larry, the Silver Fox," wrote a book, *My Life With Xaviera,* about what it's like to *satisfy* Xaviera (or something like that).

♦ **V: Who was Xaviera?**

♦ MW: *The Happy Hooker!* Her best-selling book was followed by two or three *Happy Hooker* movies (one starring Joey Heatherton and one starring Lynn Redgrave) plus several book sequels. She even had a newspaper column for awhile; sort of a *Dear Abby* but racier. I would guess that Xaviera had an album out too, although I haven't seen it. Another porn star, ANDREA TRUE, had an album out called *The Andrea True Connection: More More More.* The cover's pink with a very soft-focus photo of her, and it was actually a big disco hit. I'm not sure that the climate is right for a porn star to do that now! Back then Mark Stevens called his autobiography *Ten-and-a-Half!*—that's like a Broadway show title. Of course, big singing star Vanessa Williams got her start posing naked. And Traci Lords, who first became famous as the jail-bait porno star (she was only 15 when she started), and then later starred in John Waters' *Cry Baby,* sings on the soundtrack of *Pet Sematary, Part II.* But if I were a current porn star trying to cash in, I'd try something like a series of "Dirty Books on Tape" for commuters, like *Ginger Lynn and Harry Reems Read Henry Miller's Tropic of Cancer.*

Overall, I think the record as sale item commemoration of people is vanishing with the rise of the CD. Like I said, instructional videos, especially fitness videos, are taking the place of albums in this regard. *Any* non-fat woman that gets famous can put out an aerobics video—or a total body makeover, new diet or ten-step fitness program. Do you remember Linda Fratianne, a skater in the '84 Olympics? *She* has a video out; she just learned how to do aerobics—that's all it took. Former jail-bait porn star Traci Lords released a workout video. Donald Trump's girlfriend Marla Maples has one out. It seems natural, but why? Why should we take *her* advice on fitness and health?

Dr JOYCE BROTHERS, who got famous participating in a rigged TV quiz show, *The $64,000 Question,* put out a record, *Thinking Thin: The Psychology of Figure Control.* There's a great album by CATHY RIGBY—she was a bronze medalist back in '72—America's first gymnastic pixie. She tried to be an actress, landed the Stayfree contract, and was their spokeswoman on TV for awhile. I think the rationale was: women choose their tampon or their Kotex when they're about 14, and once they get comfortable, well, "That's what I buy." So who did 14-year-old girls want to be like? Cathy Rigby. So Cathy Rigby put out a record—an *aerobics* record—selling Stayfree. Cathy can do an hour's worth of aerobics with her Stayfree and never have an "accident"!

♦ **AJ: So it sold a product as well as a personality—**
♦ **MW:** Right. And these albums run the gamut. Some use a personality, others don't need to. The ARCHIES were this studio band that pretended to be characters from the *Archies* comic books. Don Kirshner, who was the man behind the MONKEES, was also behind The Archies. (This was back in the days of Don Kirshner's rock concerts, which were the first TV music shows.) When you heard the voices you were supposed to go, "Oh, that must be Reggie . . . that must be Jughead . . . that's Archie . . . that's Betty and Veronica." It was targeted for ten-year-olds. There was also an animated ARCHIES cartoon series that aired on Saturday mornings. It all fed off each other; the cartoons inspired people to buy the records, and when you had a new song you could air it on Saturday morning TV (this was before MTV); it was a way to sell two million people your new song. But it was just studio musicians in the background, there never was

Stayfree's *Cathy Rigby Aerobic Exercise Album,* RCA Records/Special Products. © PPC 1982.

a "real" Archies band.

The PARTRIDGE FAMILY was similar. Again, this was pre-MTV. Every week the Partridge Family played a song at the end of the show, and even though it wasn't *them,* it was a way to advertise the record, and the record fed back on the TV series, just like the MONKEES—they'd also do a song at the end of every episode.

The BRADY BUNCH started, and they didn't plan to be singers, but the show kept going and going and probably some producer said, "Okay, you kids are older now, why don't you sing some songs?" So an episode would have the Brady kids entering a talent contest—but what can they do? "Oh, let's sing!" Then they'd sing, and two weeks later there'd be a BRADY BUNCH album in the stores. The Brady kids put out several records including a Christmas album. One record had them trying to sing "meaningful" songs like "Bye Bye, Miss American Pie"—you know, "We're not just little marshmallows; we *care.*"

Here's an album by—*the* album by—the new Monkees, called *New Monkees.* Remember them? Marty, Jared, Larry and Dino? They were put together in '87, when the old Monkees had their revival. I bought this record new for a dime, god bless 'em.

♦ **V: Who were the Sugar Bears?**
♦ **MW:** Another cartoon character rock band. Sugar Bear was the trademarked "star" of Sugar Crisps; he had a cool lounge-singer, Dean Martin-y voice. Some cereal executive probably saw some albums by the Archies or the Chipmunks and thought, "God, we can do that too." So *Introducing the Sugar Bears* came out, and you never heard of them—they never got anywhere! The trivia angle here is that Kim Carnes was one of the Sugar Bears. She probably was just hanging around the studio (a struggling singer-songwriter) and

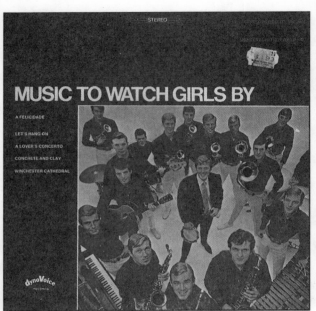

The Bob Crewe Generation's *Music to Watch Girls By,* Dynovoice Records. Album cover credits: cover photo: Ron Harris, album design: Forlenza-Venosa Assoc.

someone said, "Kim, here's $250. Sit down and write three songs about the Sugar Bears." Then, years later she has a big hit, "Bette Davis Eyes," and becomes a spokeswoman for Coca-Cola.

♦ *AJ: Is this a General Foods album?*

♦ MW: I don't know. Maybe some independent promoter thought, "What cartoon character is out there that hasn't been signed? SUGAR BEAR—I'll take it! Kids won't know any better." Several Sugar Bears songs were released as 6" 33-1/3 RPM *cardboard* records on the back of Super Sugar Crisp cereal boxes.

Here's a rather specialized album: *Music to Use the "Trim-Twist" By.* The Trim-Twist was like an executive exercise toy. You put it on your office floor and twist on top of it; it's like a lazy susan. Allegedly it helps work off those unwanted pounds. The same company also came out with an "Executive Jogger" which was just a piece of foam rubber between two pieces of wood. You could stand on it and jog in place, and it was marketed as "the perfect gift for the busy executive."

Here's a 45 to sell carpeting: "Lie Down and Make Yourself at Home" by the HORIZONTAL TREND. This was put out by a carpet mill and given away at trade shows: "Remember us when you're ordering carpet."

Every once in awhile a product-pushing song gets famous: "Music to Watch Girls By" was originally a Pepsi theme. BOB CREWE did this jingle and when it got popular he thought of a way to package an entire album around it, *Music to Watch Girls By:* "All of these are *girl-watching* songs. It's a concept album—let's ship it!" Coke had the same thing going with "I'd Like to Teach the World to Sing." I think people heard this song first because it was on the Coke ad, and liked it,

so then the Hillside Singers came out with an entire album: *I'd Like to Teach the World to Sing.* The Carpenters' hit, "We've Only Just Begun," started as an ad for a Southern California bank.

Remember the song "Little GTO" recorded by Ronnie & the Daytonas? That was done under the urging of John DeLorean, another person adept at public relations, who at the time was head of the Pontiac division of General Motors. He called up Ronnie and said, "I want you to do a song about our new Pontiac." Pontiac was the old ladies' division of GM when De-Lorean took it over and thought, "Muscle cars are going to be the next big thing. I want Pontiac to be GM's muscle car division, so I have to *reposition* its image to appeal to young people. Let's have some cool band do 'Little GTO,' and not only will this sell some records, but it'll reinforce in people's minds the Pontiac as a young person's car."

♦ *AJ: And it worked, right?*

♦ MW: Yeah, and John DeLorean went on to make the DeLorean car which he allegedly tried to fund with cocaine deals. He got acquitted, but his empire collapsed, and his TV hostess and *Slim-Fast* spokeswoman wife, Cristina Ferrare, divorced him anyway.

There are so many product records that come and go. *Pac-man* had a couple albums out; in fact there was one song that made it to the top twenty called "Pac-man Fever." It was a novelty single, and the bridge featured all these gobbling Pac-man noises. It became a hit, so of course they put out an album, and what was the theme: video games! So they had "Pac-man Fever" plus other forgotten video games such as "Centipede" and "Frogger," and the bridge on every song featured that particular video game's sound effects. And the lyrics were about the characters: "Frogger/the car's going to run you over/unless you hop real fast"—that kind of thing.

Then there was another album called *The Adventures of Pac-man,* which was a children's story album. I have the Spanish language version of that; Pac-man was really big in Mexico—in fact, you can still find Pac-man piñatas there.

Anyone that's been around for a long time, like Morris the Cat [star of a cat food commercial]—I have a ghost-written biography of Morris the Cat. Morris probably had a record out: *Songs to Pet Your Cat By,* consisting of purring noises . . . Spuds McKenzie probably has an album out; the California Raisins do have albums out.

Sheila and I once attended the annual Selma, California, Raisin Festival. (We found out about it from *Chase's Annual Events,* a directory of special celebrations throughout the world.) In the parade were all these little kids dressed up like California Raisins. They also had a Jazzercise drill team—the local Jazzercise class walking down the street doing their routines. The California Raisins appeared in person later that day. We love going to festivals in Central California—

last week was the big Woodlake Rodeo, this weekend it's the Swedish Festival in Kingsburg. You're driving down bleak Highway 99 and all of a sudden you see these windmills—it's a Swedish town! They have the Dance of the Trolls, a pancake-eating contest, Danish games, Swedish games . . .

♦ **V: You mentioned records that were put out to sell ideas—**

♦ MW: A lot of politicians used to put out albums, which sold the personality of the politician as well as the ideals that he stood for. Like this bluegrass fiddle record by U.S. SENATOR ROBERT BYRD, the famous Senate Majority Leader. This you can tell he made to give out at fund-raisers. The subtext is "Even though I'm in Washington, I still like to come back and party with my people; I still understand what it's like back home." The front cover photo shows him standing in front of a painting of Stonewall Jackson bearing the caption: "Enemy of the Union, Protector of the Confederate States of America." I'm sure that at fund-raisers he'd get up and fiddle a tune or two.

Another political "classic" is the GOVERNORS WALLACE souvenir album. That's one you buy if you're in the South, 'cause you know you're never going to see it elsewhere. George and his wife Lurleen were *both* governors of Alabama, and this LP gives the inspiring story in speeches and narration (it's not music) telling how they climbed to the top, despite the forces that would oppose good right-thinking Americans. "George was going to run for President, but who would be left in Alabama to make sure that state was looked after? Lurleen decided to accept the challenge." Lurleen became governor in '68 when George decided to run for President. He lost, but decided to run again in '72—then he got shot by Arthur Bremer. I feel

Adam Clayton Powell's *"Keep the Faith, Baby!"*, Jubilee Records. Album cover credits: cover photo: Frank Lerner, cover design: Steven-Craig Productions.

fortunate to own the biographies of both of George Wallace's wives: *Lady of Courage,* Lurleen's story (she died in 1968, after only a year as governor) and *C'nelia,* second wife Cornelia's autobiography.

Keep the Faith, Baby!, speeches by ADAM CLAYTON POWELL, is a good record. The front cover shows him on the deck of his yacht; it was recorded toward the end of his career. Powell was a Congressman from Harlem.

At that time in Congress, there were a lot of boll-weevil Democrats who controlled not only Congress but also Washington society, because they were these Southern guys who got elected for 40 years, like Strom Thurmond who's still around. And Adam Clayton Powell, being a black from New York as well as a "social justice" guy, rubbed them the wrong way. But he also was very corrupt; for one term he never showed up because he was in Bimini on a boat. He was always getting women pregnant and committing other "moral outrages." Congress voted to censure him and kick him out, but the Supreme Court said, "You can bring all this to the attention of the voters, but if the voters still want him, you've got to seat him." Of course the voters said, "That's okay with us!" and they elected him *again*, knowing that he was cruising around Bimini. I think this album was his proxy—sent back to Harlem so voters would "Keep the faith, baby!" He says "There's only two things that the white man respects from you: your vote, and your dollar"—stuff like that. "It's not *Burn Baby Burn*, it's *Learn Baby Learn* so you can *Earn Baby Earn!*" . . . Other politicians like SPIRO AGNEW had speech records out; a good cut is "Message to the Hippies." The Republican National Committee had records pressed and sent them out to people with letters, "We'd really appreciate it if you sent us ten bucks."

I also have this 45, "Come Home America" by Johnny Rivers—it was the 1972 George McGovern campaign song. Its lyrics say, "Use the power!"—you know, now that you're 18, register to vote. These campaign managers were probably sitting around thinking, "How do we *get* those young voters? Let's use Johnny Rivers—he's young; he'll get those 18-year-old votes." (By the way, this song is from the album *L.A. Reggae.*) It's a weird line you tread when you're a politician; you want the 18-year-old vote, but it's got to be sort of *clean* . . . you wouldn't want *Metallica* to do it for you, because then you might piss off their voter-parents . . . "Let's get Jackson Browne or the Beach Boys." But the flipside of the McGovern theme song is "Rockin' Pneumonia and the Boogie-Woogie Flu"!

The Army and Navy used to put out a lot of records; here's one from the Navy's 1970's fusion-jazz band, The PORT AUTHORITY. When I was a kid you could walk into the local recruiting office and get free stuff. I was 12, and at that age they're not going to take me, but I could pick up free stickers and a free album. But imagine an 18-year-old walking in and being handed a

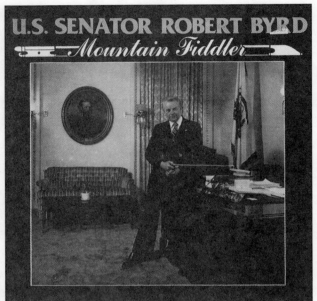

U.S. Senator Robert Byrd's *Mountain Fiddler*, County Records.
Album cover credits: Library of Congress photo: Carl Fleischhauer,
album design: Raymond Simone.

Port Authority album. Would he come back a week later and say, "I really dig this Navy music, man—sign me up!"

The military also put out records filled with 60- and 90-second promo spots. This was before the army went all-volunteer and had to hire an ad agency: "Be All You Can Be!" and all that stuff. They'd mail out all these albums and hope that "patriotic" radio stations would play them. I have an album with all kinds of different cuts; one by Gary Puckett aimed at the rock stations, Ed Ames for the country stations . . .

♦ **V: What kind of songs were these?**

♦ MW: They weren't really songs. You'd hear five seconds of an Isley Brothers song and then a male voice: "The Isley Brothers say, 'Join the Navy—it's great! You can get a lot done in there!' "

♦ **AJ: [reading] "Jerry Butler, Gary Puckett"—did these guys get paid?**

♦ MW: They probably got paid a little bit, or: "Well, Gary, we can draft you . . . or you can do this!"

♦ **V: There certainly is a wide spectrum of artists here, ranging from Peggy Lee to Gladys Knight & the Pips to the Neon Philharmonic—**

♦ MW: Military propaganda records are a genre in themselves, like this one with ARTHUR GODFREY giving one-minute highlights on the *Strategic Air Command*. Each highlight begins with the same 8-bar musical theme, "Bom bom ba-bom bom." Whenever you heard that theme you'd think, "Ah, it's another Strategic Air Command minute!" Then Arthur Godfrey would come on and say, "Operation Harvest Moon was the first time in 15 years that Strategic Air Command bombs fell on any enemy target." Then they'd have some Air Force officer come on saying, "We are more than pleased with the results—we are *delighted*.

The timing of the mission was precise; the bombing accurate. We are going into the valley to take a closer look." Then Arthur Godfrey would come in: "And that's another minute in the history of the Strategic Air Command."

♦ **V: How did you first start collecting these kinds of records?**

♦ MW: I started looking for this sort of material in high school, although I didn't think of it as "collecting" then. You know, one day you find yourself old enough to say, "God, some of these things are really idiotic!" I grew up in North Carolina and then moved to Texas—*Temple,* Texas. You know all the stuff that gets lost by the airlines? That's where it ends up for sale, in places like Temple.

I lived there in the dark time before mall-mania hit the country, so there weren't Camelot Music and Recordland chain stores everywhere. Temple didn't really have a record store. A lot of people bought their records at Gibson's, the big discount store. Or somebody would have a brother in college at Austin where they had *cool* record stores with psychedelic posters and incense. But in Temple you'd see these certain weird records and think, "I'd better get this, *now."* They were mostly 45s. That's where I got "Take a Star Trip" written and sung by Yeoman JANICE RAND, when she was trying to cash in on *Star Trek.*

♦ **AJ: She just had a minor bit part—**

♦ MW: Right—sub-sub celebrityhood! This was 1975, at the very trough of *Star Trek*—it had been off the air and the movies hadn't started yet. The songs were titled "Disco Trekin' " and "Star Child." On the back Grace Lee Whitney (Yeoman Rand) appears without her *Star Trek* uniform. I think she did a little tour of Texas department stores promoting her 45; you didn't have to be a genius to know that you probably weren't going to find that anywhere else.

This was also just before cable television. In Temple there was one TV station; you couldn't get Austin and you couldn't get Dallas. That was the impetus for cable; cable was a rural business that came *last* to the cities. The first people to get cable were rural folk who couldn't get any TV reception without it.

So if you were a kid in Temple, Texas, you had to find ways to amuse yourself. You had a lot of time, like I did, to go through all the detritus looking for things that might have special meaning. It was a way to stay interested in the world.

Some of the other 45s I got include EDWIN BIRDSONG'S "It Ain't No Fun Bein' a Welfare Recipient" (from the LP, *What It Is*). He rhymes "fun" with "recipient": "It ain't no funnn/Bein' a welfare recipi-unnn . . ." You know he's *trying* to be angry, but he's so low-key about it. He does yell one line, "Rat-infested places/that are damp—ummm, and smelly/No food for the children/No, just empty bellies."

♦ **V: Forced rhymes! . . . What else do you have?**

♦ MW: I know that you'll interview someone with a

better collection of these, but there's a whole genre of ELVIS RIP-OFF/TRIBUTE RECORDS. I like the all-spoken: "Elvis Has Left the Building" by the bass singer in his back-up group, J.D. Sumner. When Elvis would do a concert, the crowd would keep screaming for him to come back for encores until an announcer would finally say, "Ladies and gentlemen, Elvis has left the building; he's no longer here." So Sumner used this as a metaphor for his death: [low voice] "Elvis has left the building."

But there are so many more Elvis tribute records. There's a great Christmas record featuring Lisa-Marie's [Elvis's daughter] letter to Santa Claus: what she wants for Christmas. There's all this sappy music in the background, and you hear this childish voice lisping, "Santa, just tell daddy I love him. And tell him that all his fans down here on earth still love him, too. Now thank you, Santa." Somehow Santa Claus can speak to the dead. This record brings together two sure-fire money-making ideas: 1) Elvis—you put Elvis's name on a record because that'll sell it, and 2) precocious children saying deep things—that always *gets* people. Little old ladies will buy the record: "Out of the mouths of babes . . ." A couple years ago around Christmas a record came out titled, "Dear Mr Jesus." And it was the same kind of thing, featuring a sappy child. It was from Texas, naturally, and was about abused children: "Dear Mr Jesus/Please stop the hurting/of the little ones in the world." That's another genre in itself: *children saying profound things.*

Religious people are fun to have on albums, because they're so committed, like the Reverend ALBERT LONG who was a local North Caroliner. On the cover he's spinning a basketball and wearing a letterman's jacket with three or four cheerleader-type girls around him. He's "talking to teens." His message is that rock music is bad because it has the devil's lyrics and a druid, pagan beat. He's kept up with the times and released an "anti-rock music video" video . . .

I think today's best anti-rock evangelist is Bob Lar-

sen. He's on afternoon radio and is vehemently opposed to the music and the lifestyle. Troubled teens who like rock music call in and match wits with him, but he always wins, even if he has to browbeat them into submission.

Do you remember Edgar Wisenot? He was that engineer in Arkansas who had calculated all these numbers and concluded that the world was going to end in September, 1986, or thereabouts. He had a record and a book out explaining why, and it was for sale *cheap*—he didn't want to make money on it, just wanted people to be aware of it . . . But when you're interpreting from something like the Bible that was written 2000 years ago, well, the slightest little error and you're off decades! What do you expect?

ROGER HALLMARK had a 45 out during the Iranian hostage crisis. It was an anti-Khomeini novelty song: "Even our Boy Scouts/could wipe you out/We're going to come in/and we're going to blow you up!/One day soon, Khomeini/you'll burn one flag too many/Uncle Sam's got his pride/and you're about to feel his clout" (then some weird Middle Eastern noises). This was a combination of slapstick humor and "we're gonna beat you guys up!"

Here's a record for after your child is born: DR HAJIME MUROOKA'S *Lullaby from the Womb.* You play this record in the nursery and it sounds like the womb: peaceful, comfortable. This may be where Laurie Anderson got some inspiration; the very earliest New Age tendrils are emerging. Also there's this record, *Christening for Listening* by STEVE HALPERN: it's music based on the biorhythms of plants. The record's all color-coded. He took the biorhythms of different plants on different days and tried to musically emulate them. So you're not only listening to plants, you're listening to biorhythms. Both of those were real '70s things—harbingers of the New Age movement.

Another primal pre-New Age album is BERNARD GUNTHER's *Sensory Awakening: Relaxation,* which is achieved by hitting yourself in the face! You hear the record and this person says, "Now . . . lightly brush your forehead with your fingertips. Now . . . tap your forehead" (and you hear *tap tap tap* very quietly).

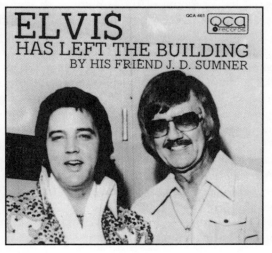

Then he tells you to do it harder and harder until you get to the face-slapping stage. I think it's related to rolfing or those other kinds of extreme massage therapy which really hurt for awhile, but then feels very relaxing . . . when they *stop*. Those face-slapping and chest-slapping cuts are inspiring.

For a time I was a country music DJ at a little radio station in Durham, WTIK (which stands for "Where Tobacco Is King"). The station manager was named Harry Welch. You may have heard of Harry—his claim to fame was: he held the world record for one-armed push-ups. And when you hold a world record, Guinness sends you a plaque and you're entitled to purchase Guinness sport shirts. Harry had five of 'em and he'd wear a different one every day—he wanted to make sure you *knew* he held the world record for one-armed pushups.

He had a daily editorial on the radio called "The Right Idea"—Harry's pun: "right" meaning correct, and also "right" meaning to the right of political center. And he would rail against the One World Government. There are people who believe in a One World Government; global events are being orchestrated by puppetmasters—socialist billionaires like the Rockefellers and the Rothschilds, so they can make more money and keep people enslaved. It's the *None Dare Call It Conspiracy* theme. Their bidding is done through puppet organizations like the Council on Foreign Relations and the Trilateral Commission.

♦ *AJ: How does this relate to being right-wing and Christian?*

♦ MW: The billionaires have made their money, and now they want socialism and a graduated income tax to keep free enterprise from really happening. They *say* they want free enterprise, but they *really* want

Ted Knight's *Hi Guys*, Ranwood Records Inc.
Album cover credits: cover design: Kissler-Brittenham Design, cover photo: Studio Five.

socialism, which as we know isn't Christian. They want our kids to be taught in the public education system because then our kids will be brainwashed (socialist billionaire myths are endemic to public schools). And that's why they will hunt down and kill people who want to educate their kids themselves— Christian creationists, for example. They want public education because it brainwashes the kids.

♦ *AJ: Are Jews part of this scenario?*

♦ MW: It depends on who you talk to. A lot of right-wing Christians believe the Jews are the "chosen people" because it says so in the Bible. But they tend to be very anti-Catholic, because they feel that Catholicism is just a new form of pagan Isis-Horus worship— Catholicism is heavy with Mary and Baby Jesus iconography, which is regarded as very demonic. They think the Jesuits run the world. But there are other right-wing Christians who think that the Rothschilds are Jewish billionaires who arm both sides whenever there's a war, and that the Jews own all the media and send brainwashing influences through it. Conspiracy theory is like a *pachinko* game—there's a huge spectrum of possibilities, and it all depends on which course you take. There are all these sub-variations of conspiracy theory.

♦ *AJ: Is Willard Cantelon against the One World Government?*

♦ MW: You bet he is! In this record album, *The New World Money System,* he explains that they control all the currencies. Then they can engineer financial panics and depressions to make more money, because *they* know what's going on and you don't. So he's saying, "Don't hang on to dollar bills; buy gold and bury it." For many years, at least since the 1960s, conspiracy theorists have been warning us about the catch-phrase "New World Order." That was supposed to be the billionaires' code word to "attack." When Bush finally used the phrase, many conspiracists got to experience that rare combination: vindication and fear.

I got this album recently (which is not available in record stores); it was offered on late-night TV: *The American Gun Album: A Celebration in Song.* It's—you guessed it—an album of pro-gun songs! If you start listening to it thinking it's a put-on, you'll find they really mean it. And with every album you order, you get a free oiled plastic rifle bag. All the classic NRA slogans are there in the song titles: "I'd Rather be Tried by Twelve (than Carried by Six)," "If Guns Are Outlawed, Only Outlaws Will Have Guns," "Never Mind the Dog—Beware of Owner," etc. The cover shows a modern family and a "patriot" family circa 1776—notice how the patriot dad looks a lot like today's husband—hmmm . . .

♦ *AJ: People think they have to look to the past for everything, yet this is a current candidate . . . How about* Selling the Sizzle?

♦ MW: It's just a short step from being a good Christian to being a good patriot to being a good salesman.

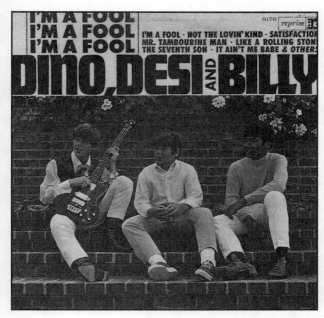

Dino, Desi & Billy's *I'm A Fool*, Reprise Records.
Album cover credits: art direction: Ed Thrasher.

That's the whole idea of the "prosperity doctrine," espoused by Oral Roberts and Reverend Ike.

In *Selling the Sizzle*, Elmer Wheeler, "The World's Greatest Salesman," tells listeners: "Go out and sell, and here's how! *You* have inner value! You can be a better salesman if when you go out and sell, you sell America too! You believe in the country; you believe in the right way. People like buying from you because you believe in America." By being motivated, you help America progress—you sell more, and then you have money to buy goods from other salesmen, and then they'll return the favor. You gotta be patriotic, and you gotta sell. I have a number of these records, many of which were put out by the Success Motivation Institute of Waco, Texas (who currently share a building with the Dr Pepper Museum, a soft drink invented in Waco). Albums like *Sell Like an Ace, Live Like a King; Personal Power Through Creative Selling; Let's Sell Success; The Man in Salesman;* and *Who Bites the Bountiful Hand.*

♦ **V: *Isn't Waco where all those WORD gospel records came from?***

♦ MW: Like I said, it's just a short step from being a good Christian to being a good salesman.

Motivational speakers like Wheeler and Dr Kenneth McFarland were popular before TV and before video; before you could order a video of a speaker (today, everyone from *Monty Python*'s John Cleese to *The Muppets* have sales and motivational videos out). These guys would go and speak to Rotary Club breakfasts and pipe-fitter conventions, and motivate them to sell, sell, sell! They are all variations on Napoleon Hill's *Think and Grow Rich,* which is still a powerful force in our country.

♦ **AJ: *Now there are TV programs that do nothing but sell things—***

♦ MW: The *infomercials.* Whatever they sell, it's a high profit margin item, like cosmetics or baldness cures—you know, 50 cents worth of stuff in a $50 bottle. One of the funniest ones is by Lyle Waggoner (who used to be on the Carol Burnett Show)—it's an impotence cure infomercial. The people that sell them, Napoleon Hill's bastard children, come and go, like Ed Beckley, who was a "No Money Down" real estate guy; he was also the world's most famous graduate of Maharishi University in Iowa. When he was big, he was the largest employer in Fairfield, Iowa, home of Maharishi University; he learned his motivational expertise from the Maharishi and then turned it into "No Money Down" real estate courses. But he went bankrupt because he offered people a money-back guarantee.

But where he falls off, somebody else comes along. Dave Del Dotto—he's around; Tony Robbins, the ex-fire walker; Tom Vu—all these people come along on their tours selling tapes. They'll set up at the local Holiday Inn and give a speech and sell books and stuff. And what they're selling is—*yes,* they may sell real estate "No Money Down," but what they're *really* selling is self-worth. The money is fine, but if you are your own boss and you have a better sense of your self and you can live the "good life" you want—it's a 21st century Christianity, in a way, *without* God.

♦ **AJ: *For most people, a "higher purpose in life" used to mean patriotism or god. And now it is money—now you can revel in money, guilt-free.***

♦ MW: AMWAY is the country's largest direct marketing operation—which means that its distributors sell the products (like soaps and cleaning fluids) door-to-door. Distributors are recruited from the ranks of everyday people, and those with the "right" combination of guts and imagination become wealthy beyond their wildest dreams—a few, anyway. The whole trick to Amway is to keep the sales force *motivated.* There's a record album out of AMWAY songs: hymns that Amway people can sing in their cars. There's also a biography of the founders (Rich DeVos and Jay Van Andel), *The Possible Dream* by Charles Paul Conn. You can visit AMWAY headquarters in Ada, Michigan and tour the facilities. The place is usually teeming with Amway distributors who've pilgrimaged to "Mecca."

♦ **V: *Do you have any more records?***

♦ MW: I have a couple examples of PRISON RECORDS; they were a big sub-fad in country & western. When I worked at the radio station they had about 20 prison album compilations, plus CB and Trucker records. Here's a great prison record by MACK VICKERY: this slicked-back hair guy playing live at the Alabama Women's Prison. The cover shows Mack on the outside of the bars, overweight but still looking like a stud with his guitar over his shoulder, and in the background are these Playboy-type models in gray prison frocks with their hands on the bars sighing, "Oh, if only I were free I would have *you,* Mack Vickery."

I'm also starting a shelf of country disaster songs.

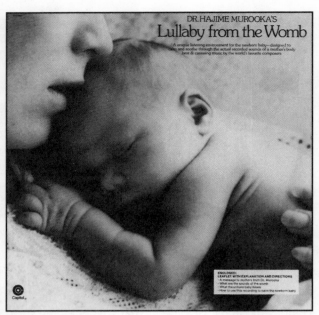

Dr. Hajime Murooka's *Lullaby from the Womb*, Capitol Records.
Album cover credits: art direction: Roy Kohara, photography: Rick Rankin.

These have a long history stretching back to the train wreck songs of the early 1900s. There's a wonderful book out about train wreck songs called *Scalded to Death by the Steam* (by Kate Letcher Lyle, Algonquin Books, 1991) which tells about the wrecks made famous in song, and quotes the song lyrics, too. Apparently these were very popular with bluegrass and country bands before WWII. Most of the wrecks immortalized, naturally, took place in bluegrass country—Kentucky, the Virginias and the Carolinas: "The Wreck of the Old '97," "The Church Hill Tunnel Disaster," and "Billy Richardson's Last Ride." "The Hamlet Wreck" was about a train that started in Durham and crashed in downtown Hamlet. Tobacco workers made up the tune.

But disasters of all sorts are endemic to country music—though TV news and shows like *I Witness video* have rendered these nearly obsolete. Bill Monroe did "The Little Girl and the Dreadful Snake," about a man finding his daughter just after she's been bitten by a poisonous snake and then watching her die. Roy Acuff's "The Wreck on the Highway" updates the train wreck theme to automobiles ("there was whiskey and blood all together/mixed with glass where they lay/they played their hand in destruction/but I didn't hear nobody pray.") My favorite is Carl Smith's "It Takes Four Feet to Make a Yard." The singer is this poor man whose son gets killed by a car and whose wife leaves him because she blames the accident on him. ("Remembering is hard/How he chased the ball I kicked out into the street/And fell beneath the speeding car"). The "four feet" obviously belong to his wife and son, and the "yard" is the one around their home, which he just doesn't feel like keeping up anymore.

Here's my album: *The MBAs: Born To Run Things,*

which came out in 1983. We made it into *People* magazine. Originally we had created a pro-business rock band as a put-on; we made fake record labels and fictitious news clippings that made it look like we were a "real" band. Of course, none of us were musicians—this was pure PR. We sent a press packet to the *Wall Street Journal,* and they called us up and said, "You're great—we want to talk to you." On a Thursday front page they printed an item about the MBAs. They mentioned a love song we wrote for Bethlehem Steel (at the time Bethlehem Steel looked like it was going under) called "Bessie." And so the Bethlehem, Pennsylvania newspaper called us up and printed a story. Then it started to snowball. A business school in Florida asked, "Could you come down and play for our graduation?" We asked each other, "Jesus—what do we do *now?* How do you cash in on this? Hey—we'll put out an album!" So we wrote the lyrics and invented a mythology (but we didn't write the music or play it; we didn't know how. We just had some studio people do it, like the *Archies.*) We had a pro-business rap song ("Do It on the Floor"), reggae ("Amortize It"), even a spiritual ("Jesus H. Chrysler"). And to this day a radio station in San Diego still plays "The Tao of the Dow."

♦ *AJ: That's probably how a lot of these "novelty" records got made: first there was a concept, then the press, and then someone said, "Let's put out a record around that."*

♦ MW: "How can we cash in?" That's what we did.

♦ *AJ: Did you sell these?*

♦ MW: We sold 10,000 of 'em. I'll tell you the mistake we made: we also had 2000 tapes made, and sold maybe a *hundred.* I guess a lot of people bought it as a gift, and somehow a little cassette just isn't as appealing as a record.

♦ *AJ: In the '60s a line of "adult" greeting cards came out on the High In-Fidelity label: you opened them up and inside of an LP jacket you got a record-shaped insert that said, "I bought this album for you as a gift. . . . Sorry, I couldn't afford the record!" It's sad to have the 12" LP going out; half the fun is reading the liner notes and having this huge photo or artwork on the cover to appreciate. . . . Did you make up any of the press releases, like this* **Wall Street Journal** *clipping?*

♦ MW: That was real. We knew that business magazines *hurt* for something that's not stultifying, so we got lots of press. We got a "Dubious Achievement" award in *Esquire* and were mentioned over and over in business magazines—all that legitimized us. We took those clippings and sent them off to *People* and CBS News and just rode the wave. Of course we got ripped off—a band called the VPs stole our idea, claiming, "*We're* the first pro-business band." And reporters believed 'em. Media sloth can work for you or against you . . . [The MBA's album, *Born to Run Things,* is still available on tape or record for $15 ppd from Tick-

Tock, 520 Larkfield Road, East Northport, NY 11731.]

♦ **V: *Anything else come to your attention recently?***

♦ MW: Well, the Japanese have just introduced a great cable radio service. Cable radio is music that comes into your home via your TV cable, and is played through your home entertainment system. It's digital, it's commercial-free, and you pay for it monthly like HBO. Cable systems in the United States offer cable radio to subscribers under names like Digital Music Express, which provides about 30 channels of music (rock, jazz, classical) 24 hours a day.

But in Japan there is a service which offers *440* different channels! 440! Try and think of different kinds of music: how many do you come up with? A hundred? Two hundred? This has 440, with plans to go to 1,000!

The program guide is amazing. In addition to all the music you'd expect (24 hour Beatles or Elvis) you can get 24 hour commercial-free Swiss yodeling tunes and Peking pop music. There's a "Scary Music" channel, one playing only "Japanese Army Songs and Music of The War Years," plus "Spiritual Music for Cultivating Innate Ability." There are specialty channels like "Rooster Calls and Bell Ringing," "Songs from TV Cartoons," "Mother's Heartbeat," or "Counting Sheep" for insomniacs. Background noise from a pachinko parlor is one of three "alibi" channels. About 20 channels carry background music designed for different businesses, like "Bank (Slow)," and "Bank (Up-tempo)," that resembles our Muzak. All this at your fingertips in the privacy of your own home!

Disasters of all sorts are endemic to country music—though TV news and shows like *I Witness video* have rendered these nearly obsolete. Bill Monroe did "The Little Girl and the Dreadful Snake," about a man finding his daughter just after she's been bitten by a poisonous snake, and then watching her die.

♦ **V: *Do you know much about Muzak?***

♦ MW: It was started by a military man, a General Squier, who was in the US Army Signal Corps. In the mid-'30s, his company started providing "wired-radio" services to grocery stores and restaurants: Muzak! Then, in the late '30s, industrial psychologists found that the proper music made people do boring work faster with less errors. Muzak started being introduced into offices and factories and when the war came along, it boomed.

I have an old magazine from 1944 called *Progress Guide: Articles of Permanent Value* which features a piece called "Rhythm for Rosie [the Riveter]." It describes the early experiments. They tried hymns ("deadening the production line"), foxtrots, polkas, even stirring marches ("except those which bring back painful memories of sweethearts overseas"). The piece closed by saying, "Music is like a shot of cocaine. A small dose invigorates, but too large a serving is fatal."

It's amazing how widespread Muzak is—something like 100 million people a day hear it. It was played on the Apollo lunar spacecraft and in the embassy when America evacuated South Vietnam. Lyndon Johnson owned a Muzak franchise in Austin, Texas, although the White House has had it since Eisenhower. I had a cousin who had a nervous breakdown and the doctor prescribed Muzak for her home. You'd go over for dinner and Muzak would calmly surround you.

♦ **AJ: *I read that you don't just buy a Muzak album, you subscribe to a complete system. During the day, the Muzak would get more upbeat till just before the coffee break, then after the coffee break it might be more relaxing. They had this scientifically calibrated biorhythmic cycle—***

♦ MW: The key to Muzak is their concept of Stimulus Progression. In their brochures, they say that to understand Muzak, think of it as a management tool rather than as entertainment. "Muzak programming is based on practical scientific principles, as valid as those used in creating good interior design, lighting and climate control."

Every song is given a rating, from one (slowest) to six (most stimulating). The songs are arranged to get more stimulating in the mid-morning and mid-afternoon, to perk up flagging workers, and to actually get less stimulating around the lunch hour to calm workers down. Of course, the same tunes not only make workers more productive, but make shoppers stay longer and spend more. And even if it didn't really work, it was something an office operations manager could understand. Scientific measurement: "This makes sense; it makes perfect sense!"

I had a weird experience: I was in an office where Muzak was playing, and I was calling someone 400 miles away who put me on hold, and the *same* Muzak was playing over the phone—both companies were getting the same satellite transmission at the same time. It was like: the greasepaint cracks, and you see Big Brother!

New Roadside America is available from Simon & Schuster/Fireside (mail order: 1-800-223-2336).

Chase's Annual Events is available from Contemporary Books, 180 N. Michigan Ave, Chicago, IL 60601.

NORTON RECORDS

NORTON RECORDS was founded by Billy Miller and Miriam Linna (early *Cramps* drummer), who met in 1977 in New York City. During the past 15 years they have produced *Kicks* magazine (obscure rock'n'roll), *Bad Seed* (J.D. paperbacks), *The Smut Peddler* (adult paperbacks), plus numerous records. Their band, *The A-Bones* (Billy, vocals; Miriam, drums; Bruce Bennett, guitar; Marcus the Carcass, bass; Lars Espensen, sax) was recently featured in the movie, *I Was a Teenage Mummy* (soundtrack available). For a great mail order catalog send $1 to PO Box 646 Cooper Station, NY NY 10003 (Fax 718-398-9215).

♦ *VALE: When did you meet the CRAMPS?*

♦ MIRIAM LINNA: In 1975 I was going to Kent State, and I had seen Lux and Ivy around but didn't know them. Then my sister and I went to New York for the summer. We were at a burger stand and Lux came over and asked, "Hey, aren't you from Ohio?" They visited me a couple weeks later and said, "Hey—ever think of being in a band?" I'd never even *thought* of that possibility: "Gee, I don't know ..." At the time I was planning to move to California with Bradley Field, who was a local "wild man," but then he was arrested for pissing on a policeman and got thrown in the clink for 30 days. There went the dream of fruit and nuts ...

Then a gal named Tracy Lacy said, "Let's all go to New York!" (I remember she'd had an abortion that afternoon) and that night all of us (including James Sliman, who went on to manage RUN DMC) piled into her Karmann-Ghia convertible. I got to New York, gave Lux and Ivy a call: "Here I am!" and moved in with them for awhile. I'd never played drums or held drum sticks before. The CRAMPS' first publicity pictures had been taken with Bryan Gregory's sister Pam on drums, but she dropped out and I replaced her. I learned just by listening to records and playing—there was no formal instruction, I was just getting this *thing* out of me! Although there was no formal statement of our

philosophy, I presume it was: you love the music, you have something to say physically ... do it!

TELEVISION in the early days were really great; we'd seen them play at this Ohio glitter rock hangout, the Piccadilly Inn, and they'd astounded everybody because they didn't look like the glitter people of the time. When we moved to New York we weren't really part of the "art rock" scene—I've got to hand it to Lux and Ivy for saying, "Even if these people you respect don't dig you, *so what*—you know what you're doing is right." They had an unshatterable confidence in what they were doing.

When Lux and Ivy first visited me, I was in my pink pajamas and we talked for awhile, then went out. I was sitting in this bar when I realized I still had these pajamas on—maybe that had some kind of impact on them! At the time I was listening to a lot of '50s and '60s rock'n'roll records, and a lot of the wannabe punk-rockers getting into the scene weren't into old records, so that was a connection between us ... finding something in those old records that was really a *basis for living.*

♦ *V: It's not just the records; the movies, books, magazines, clothes and everything are all connected—*

♦ ML: Yeah! I was raised with a strict Pentecostal upbringing; I grew up wanting to be "good." But when those hormones start going wild, you get really mixed-up—you can't have fun *and* follow the straight and narrow at the same time. My mom believed in suffering and obeying the scriptures: "It doesn't matter how rotten things are down here on earth—you're gonna have a fine life when you're *dead*." To me it just didn't seem worth the wait.

♦ *V: A lot of people buy records when they're young and then give it up, but you didn't—*

♦ ML: It's baffling to me how people could *give up* their teenage interests. Like: people being crazy rock'n'roll fans and then something happens to them and they become "adults"? Do you remember your parents saying to you, "When are you gonna grow up?" They think that whatever was happening in your teenage years you're supposed to grow out of. I've always felt that your teenage years are the greatest: when those hormones start igniting and those mixed-up emotions and feelings start being expressed. And if you're able to continue that energy—well, I've never grown out of that.

♦ BILLY MILLER: Some people accuse us

Photo: Robert Waldman

of being into nostalgia and being narrow-minded because we don't listen to the "latest" music, but it's not nostalgia—I *wish* I'd heard all these obscure records when I was a little kid.

♦ ML: Also, I don't know if we're consciously trying to "correct" people's thinking about records from the '50s and '60s, but it's really repulsive to see something like the '50s turned into just *style:* ponytails, bobby sox and full skirts . . . so that anybody who doesn't have the right "vintage" appearance couldn't possibly be "cool" in their minds or their thinking. Or: if you're

into the '50s, then you won't listen to the SONICS or other garage bands from the '60s. But we're living *now:* we've got all this music from the past to listen to—why confine yourself?

We've been on the road for a month, and everywhere we go, these kids who are record nuts come up to us with some obscure record and ask, "Have you got *this?*" Then they put it on and we go, "Holy cats— what's the story behind *that?*"

♦ BM: The nights when we're *not* playing and could get a good night's sleep, we end up listening to people's

Hasil Adkins, 1976   Photo courtesy of Norton Records.

records later than if we played a show. Because everywhere you go, people have discovered different, regionally produced and distributed records—

♦ ML: There's an endless wealth out there; there's never going to be a point where you've heard it all.

♦ BM: That's why the "Rock'n'Roll Hall of Fame" is such a con, as though rock'n'roll is only a medium for superstars. "The '50s was Elvis Presley, Carl Perkins, Bo Diddley—end of the line." Not to knock *them,* but there are so many *other* great people like HASIL ADKINS and ESQUERITA who are still relatively unknown.

♦ ML: Hasil has never changed with the times or moved with the trends. Records he cut in '67 while *Sgt. Pepper* was happening sound like they were cut in the Sun studios in '56.

♦ *V: How did you two meet?*

♦ BM: I saw Miriam play a couple times in the CRAMPS, but I actually met her at a record swap in '77, when she was running the FLAMIN' GROOVIES fan club. I sold her some records—

♦ ML: I didn't think of it then as record *collecting*—it was just: getting records that you *liked.*

♦ BM: You could still go to a flea market and walk away with an armload of records for $5.

♦ *V: For many people, you opened up the world of juvenile delinquency: books, films, records, magazine articles, everything—*

♦ ML: A lot of people identify the "J.D." phenomena with switchblades and violent teenagers: "Whaddaya

rebelling against?" "Whaddaya got?" And that *is* a glamorous aspect of it. But what *I* get out of the books and from talking to the writers (Hal Ellson, Harlan Ellison, etc) is: they were trying to write from the young people's perspective, and it wasn't "I'm the greatest! I'm gonna go out and kill!" Rather, it was about being a teenager then, and having all these *loves:* of the cars, music, clothes—all that makes teenage *teenage.* It wasn't this glamorous, violence-ridden life, it was more a lonely kind of life: being totally alienated—not really wanting to be, but *having* to be. And like anybody else, getting really defensive about it when you've got something great (the music, the way it feels going through your body when you're dancing). Yet you're being put down for it. Well, whenever you try to suppress something that's really *positive,* there's gonna be a rebellion.

Before World War II "teenagers" didn't really exist as a phenomenon. After the War women started working, all this money came in and kids had all this free time, plus the technology became available to do things like make their own records. It wasn't like Elvis was this oddball guy, a total freak of nature, who went in and recorded a record and *that* started the whole rock'n'roll craze—no, there were zillions of would-be Elvises making a racket, but they just weren't in the right place at the right time.

♦ BM: He had what it took to make people stand up and take notice. He was the catalyst—

♦ ML: You can tell from the endless number of records by obscure artists that just keep surfacing; you listen to them and go, "Holy Cow!"

♦ BM: And guys like Hasil Adkins heard someone like Elvis and thought, "I'll try it *my* way." In the same way, the early Beatles were the catalyst for a lot of garage bands that were—

♦ ML: More raw, more primitive. It's depressing to watch one-time rock stars who made a few great records but then changed their style to "go with the flow." In our book they're total losers, like: how could they *do* that? And they *never* want to talk about their early records: "P-U!" We started getting into "first" records by certain musicians, like we just got NEIL YOUNG's first surf record and it's fantastic—

♦ BM: David Gates (from BREAD) cut some wild early records—doubly wild since Leon Russell was playing on them.

♦ ML: And it's great digging up guys like RUDY GRAYZELL or ANDY STARR. When you first talk to them they're a little bit subdued—

♦ BM: —like ANDY STARR, who cut some really frantic records in the '50s. He started out saying things like, "Yeah, we had a good time. It was the era of Elvis Presley . . ."—it sounded like I was talking to *Eisenhower.* Next time I talked to him he said, "You know, Bill, I didn't tell you, but I had sex with over 5000 women! . . . Did I tell you about the time this guy was shooting at my car—his wife was hiding in the back seat while I had two blondes in the front!" He called me up and said, "Billy, I'm doing these *big* shows now—I'll send you photos." Then he sent these pictures, and he's singing in front of a potato chip rack. I don't know if he's in a grocery store, or where this "big show" took place. He sent me a poster and it said, "Andy Starr—The Ultimate Rebel." He also ran for President once.

♦ **V: *Tell me about HASIL ADKINS—***

♦ ML: Hasil, rhymes with Basil—and that's also his brother's name. He totally blew our minds when we first heard him. Then when you meet him, you realize he's the genuine article.

♦ BM: I first heard "Haze" in the '70s when I found a copy of "She Said." What's wild is: that record was produced on a Brooklyn label about a mile from where we live! Then a friend showed me "Chicken Walk" and I went, "Wow—this guy made *two* records?" Another friend, who generally only looks for R&B groups, located Hasil in West Virginia. The great thing about him is: his personality, his vision, his talent were still intact—that's rare; most of these guys who are *really* crazy fizzled out or drove off mountains. He started sending us tapes which mixed up old and new recordings—you couldn't tell which was which. One tape sounded straight outta the '50s—I thought he was yelling, "Hey, we're rockin'!" but it turned out to be "Hey there, Reagan!"—it was new. Every record he does he sends to the White House—Nixon actually sent him a "thank you" letter.

♦ ML: We went to West Virginia and brought him to New York and people went crazy over him—

♦ BM: —much like the script of *King Kong*.

♦ ML: People are hungry for that kind of emotion.

♦ BM: Hasil doesn't sleep; he drinks about 30-130

Hasil Adkins' *Peanut Butter Rock-n-Roll*, © 1990 Norton Records. Album cover credits: cover art: Pete Ciccone at Immaculate Concepts.

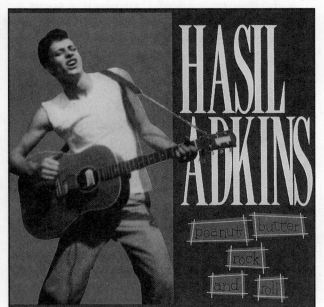

cups of coffee a day.

♦ ML: He eats more meat than any other human being we've ever met; he carries around Vienna sausages in his pocket. "What would you like for lunch?" "Meat." "Any special kind?" "Meat."

♦ BM: He'll go to a restaurant and order three separate hamburger platters, just eat the patties and say, "Hey Billy, you want these french fries?"

♦ ML: Just meat and coffee. He has an endless supply of girlfriends; girls are always chasing him, fighting over him—he's really a popular guy in that respect . . . but also a really *sensitive* guy. His personality is like: either really *up* (totally up there) or so down that you can't even get him to talk. He's among that 1% of manic-depressives who cannot sleep—

Hasil Adkins eats more meat than any other human being we've ever met; he carries around Vienna sausages in his pocket. "What would you like for lunch?" "Meat." "Any special kind?" "Meat."

♦ BM: He'll "sleep"—like all day long he'll lay down, but he'll get up periodically. Our sax player stayed with him and at 4 AM Hasil woke him up, saying, "*Come on, Lars, let's go out and play some music on the porch!*"

♦ ML: He was the youngest of 9 or 10 children and was born long after his nearest sibling. He grew up with his mom and lived with her until she died in 1985—that really destroyed him because he loved her so much. He had lived his entire life, including his adult life, in this house where he also did all his recording. His mom cooked for him and took care of him for all that time; he'd never married. When his mom died, that sent him into this intense dimension of *blueness*.

♦ BM: But he's also this outgoing wild man who takes out a couple girls and drives into telephone poles for laughs—

♦ ML: —and puts rattlesnakes in the back seat of the car just to watch girls scream!

♦ BM: He was playing in a club one night—he's a one-man band, playing drums and guitar at the same time. The ceiling fan was whirling around, making a creaky sound, and without missing a lick he reached down, pulled out a gun and shot it down—it was interfering with the song.

♦ ML: We took Hasil up to Canada when he was on parole for shooting up a guy's trailer home—that was over some woman. When we got back there were all these anxious messages from his parole officer: "Where do you have Hasil?" It turned out that Hasil's cellmate from jail had gotten out and scalped his family (he hadn't actually killed them, but had removed their

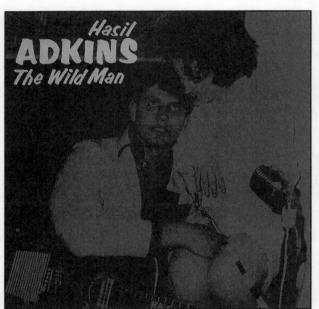

Hasil Adkins' *The Wild Man,* © 1987 Norton Records.
Album cover credits: cover art: Kicks Magazine.

behind the times—all the gals in Madison, West Virginia wear their hot pants; they're in the top of style. These New York women don't know how to dress!" He's got his own views as to what's great in the world.
♦ BM: We got him a show opening for Public Image in Toronto and after soundcheck, Haze wanted to go out to our van and put on his western shirt. When he got outside, there were all these Johnny Rotten fans in line wearing ripped-up threads. Haze just shook his head and said, "Maybe I won't change my shirt—people in this town don't seem to care *what* they look like!"

One night Hasil played in Philadelphia and we went to stay with our friend Ben Vaughn who was putting us up for the night. It was 5 AM, everybody was slumped down in their chairs, and I pulled out a record and asked, "Hasil, you want to hear some Hank Williams?" and he went, "Hank Williams, Larry 'Williams—it don't make any difference." He's funny; he's into both Slim Harpo and Lightnin' Slim but he thinks they're the same person: "Lightnin' Slim Harpo." I gave up trying to convince him that it's two different guys.

A film company that does documentaries on Appalachia was filming a documentary on Hasil, interviewing his family and friends. And in the film Hasil's walking around with this girl on his arm, a real sweet blond girl named Karen who wears a cowboy hat and coos, "Ooh, Hasil . . ." At one point the director asked her, "Hey, how long have you been Hasil's girlfriend?" and she replied, "Oh—I'm not Hasil's girlfriend; I just *play* his girlfriend in the movie!"
♦ *V: What does his house look like?*
♦ ML: A typical Appalachian 3-room shack.

Miriam ran into Andy Warhol and she said, "Stay right there!", ran into a deli, got a can of Campbell's soup and had him autograph it. We had it on a shelf in our house for years. Then Hasil stayed at our house, and I said, "Haze, I'm going out for a while; there's plenty of food in the 'fridge." I came back and asked, "Did you have lunch?" and he said, "Well, I just fixed myself a can of soup." You guessed it—

scalps along with the hair). When arrested, the cellmate had given his name as "Hasil Adkins," and that had inspired a temporary search for the real Hasil. Hasil has actually gotten some song ideas from this guy. He writes about things that really happen; he's like a news reporter talking about what he knows.
♦ BM: Many years ago Miriam ran into Andy Warhol—he was standing on a street corner, and she said, "Stay right there!", ran into a deli, got a can of Campbell's soup and had him autograph it. We had it on a shelf in our house for years. Then Hasil stayed at our house, and I said, "Haze, I'm going out for a while; there's plenty of food in the 'fridge." I came back and asked, "Did you have lunch?" and he said, "Well, I just fixed myself a can of soup." You guessed it—
♦ ML: I was going through the garbage trying to find the can—
♦ *V: You should have had Hasil autograph it.*
♦ BM: He's a wild man, but he is also a great musician. A lot of people think he's just *bashing away* because he goes way out of tune when he plays, but he actually has perfect pitch. He'll break a string in a show and replace it with a piece of fishing wire lying in the parking lot—he might come home and have some fishing line, a banjo string, some wire that was wrapped around a barrel (6 wires, none of which are guitar strings) but they're all tuned perfectly.
♦ ML: When Hasil came to New York he was extremely distressed there were no hot pants stores.
♦ BM: It was Easter Sunday, and he wanted me to take him to buy hot pants with rivets on them that say "New York" across the butt for his girl. He was bellowing, "All these stores, and no hot pants? Where do they get their hot pants?"
♦ ML: He was thinking, "Boy, New York is really

♦ BM: He's so far back in the woods that the landlord gave up driving out to collect the rent, which was $40 a month. He has ponds where he fishes and woods where he hunts. In his front yard is a broken-down New York City bus that says "HUNCHIN' BUS"— that's where he has his parties. The bus is actually bigger than the house.

♦ ML: The house has record covers and memorabilia tacked up on the walls—not only on the inside but the outside as well. He collects discarded mannequins. One time he took some local kids fishing. Previously he had attached a mannequin head to the end of a line that was dangling in the water. At some point he yelled, "Oh—I got a big one!" He reeled it in and this head popped out of the water—the kids screamed and took off running. He loves to scare people with that kind of stuff.

Hasil has that song, "I Need Your Head," which I thought was just some original concept he cooked up, but it turned out to be a true story. I found this 1957 detective magazine with an article titled, "I Need Your Head." Sure enough, it happened right in West Virginia: a guy had escaped from Moundsville Prison, kidnapped a family and sent a note to the warden saying, "I kidnapped these people and won't release them unless you send me my cellmate's head on a platter." This fugitive was hiding out in Hasil's neck of the woods. Having a head-chopping psycho in the neighborhood had to be big local news. He's just re-telling what he knows.

♦ BM: He must have thousands of songs. He has a big Buick Satellite car with polka dots on it, and we suggested he make a hot-rod song out of it, like Chuck Berry's "Maybelline." He said, "Yeah, okay"; the tapes were rollin' and he just invented it on the spot. It was pretty amazing.

♦ ML: The great thing about his singing is, not only does he sing in his "natural" voice, but he'll imitate female roles: "Oh, honey, why doncha . . ." And then somebody is knockin' on the door [deep voice]: "Whaddaya *doin'* in there?" It's like a radio show where all these characters are talking.

♦ BM: He said that when he played roadhouses in West Virginia, he'd be singing his songs like "She Said" and people would give him money to go back to singing Hank Williams-type music. He said, "Those kind of songs are great, because I get paid to do them, and get paid *not* to do them as well!" He does have a country side; on *Moon Over Madison* he does JIMMIE RODGERS-type music—

♦ ML: And they're not just romantic ballads, they're really lonely, howling songs with owl sounds on them, where you really feel the depths of his sadness . . . He was sending us a tape and I asked how much music was on it and he said, "About five pounds!"

♦ BM: One thing about Hasil's reel-to-reel tapes: they'll have cheese-whiz and crumbs and dirt on them, so you have to run them through once to transfer 'em, then put the originals away.

♦ V: *How did he support himself all these years?*

♦ BM: He is an expert mechanic and radio repairman—he does odd jobs like that.

♦ ML: Plus, he hunts and fishes for his food; he hunts deer and snake—"good eatin'!" Maybe that's why he eats meat; he has such an abundance of it there.

♦ BM: We were in New York, right by Union Square Park, and we saw a squirrel running up a tree. Hasil asked, "Billy—you do much squirrel huntin' around here?"

Hasil Adkins was playing in a club one night—he's a one-man band, playing drums and guitar at the same time. The ceiling fan was whirling around, making a creaky sound, and without missing a lick he reached down, pulled out a gun and shot it down—it was interfering with the song.

♦ ML: He lives in the middle of this beautiful wilderness—

♦ BM: —a coal-mining wilderness, though. One time when I talked to him on the phone (he doesn't have a phone anymore) he said, "I got my line in the water fishin' for my dinner, and I'm sittin' back watching Solid Gold on TV." It's like *Huckleberry Finn Goes to Mars,* or something. The thing about Hasil, he's been playing his one-man-band act since he was a kid because nobody could keep up with his sudden wacky chord changes. When he was young and listening to Hank Williams, he thought Hank was playing everything (drums, guitar, bass) at the same time, so he learned how to play like that. Now, I think that if we didn't put out Hasil's records, he'd still be at home making the same tapes.

But the Haze is no dummy; he's really on the ball. Everything he knows he taught himself. He only went to school about one day in his life, but recently he gave a lecture at a college on the topic of music—he was real proud of that.

♦ V: *What other "characters" are on your label?*

♦ BM: A friend in Texas found these acetates with titles like "My Love for You Is Petrified," "Constellation of a Fool," and "A Bald-Headed Woman and a Long-Haired Man," sung by JACK STARR, who oddly enough was born in *Norton,* Virginia. He had a total fixation with monsters and outer space and recorded tons of songs in his mom's bathroom. Throughout the late '50s-early '60s he hung out in Jack Ruby's nightclubs in Dallas when CANDY BARR was there—in fact he's got a song called "Candy Baby" about her. He was an extra in *The Giant Gila Monster* that was filmed in Dallas by Ken Curtis of *Gunsmoke.* They were looking for someone with a cool hot rod, and Jack's friend had the best car in town and managed to get his buddies into the film, too. Then, when he was 17, Jack

got invited to Hollywood by AIP to become a make-up man but his folks wouldn't let him go, so he just stayed at home making these movies and tapes.

He started making home monster movies with rock'n'roll songs in them, and he'd make home-made posters for them with titles like "Monster Rock'n'Roll," "Rumble At Flagpole Hell," "Charlie Hong Kong Meets The Spider," and "Venus Beast." He also made porno movies, and unfortunately *all* of his films got confiscated by the Dallas vice squad—I guess they're lost to the world forever. He's quite a character—he did magic shows, and is always marketing things. Right now he's marketing Jack Starr Cologne—he doused his last demo tape with it, and I had to put it out on the window sill for about four days.

We brought him to New York to play and he was the *real* thing—we couldn't even practice with him. We had a list of songs and he'd say, "Let's do 'Beat Doll' "—then go into a totally different song. We'd say, "*Jack*—we're doin' 'Beat Doll'!" Then he'd say, "Oh, I'm sorry; I got *six* songs named 'Beat Doll'!" We got nowhere rehearsing, so before the show he said, "Look. I'll just start the song on the guitar, and you just follow me—we'll keep it simple." Naturally when the first song started he hit about three chords and threw the guitar away . . He's still recording in his mom's bathroom, marketing cologne and the "how-to" magic books he's written.

♦ *V: You also had ESQUERITA on your label; who came first—him or LITTLE RICHARD?*

♦ BM: Little Richard recorded *gospel* for RCA in the early '50s, before he went to Peacock Records. Between RCA and Peacock he met Esquerita who showed him how to play piano the way Little Richard plays piano. Little Richard applied that to his rock'n'roll

Esquerita's *Vintage Voola*, © 1987 Norton Records.
Album cover credits: cover art: Kicks Magazine.

recordings for Specialty. Then Esquerita said, "Hey—*I* showed him how to do that! Now I'll outdo him." Esquerita was about six-and-a-half feet tall, he wore jewelry galore, had hair a foot high, one eyeball, and his hands were big enough to palm a Volkswagen. He was the most flamboyant gay guy—he was hosting drag shows in New Orleans, just playin' and screamin'—totally crazed. Members of Gene Vincent's *Blue Caps* got him to record on Capitol, and it's wild that those records came out on a major label.

Esquerita was about six-and-a-half feet tall, he wore jewelry galore, had hair a foot high, one eyeball, and his hands were big enough to palm a Volkswagen. He was the most flamboyant gay guy—he was hosting drag shows in New Orleans, just playin' and screamin'—totally crazed.

♦ *V: Didn't he die of AIDS?*

♦ BM: Yeah, in 1986. We booked his last shows. In fact, at the last show he did, this gay guy we know went, "Ohmigod, that's *Fabulash!*" Apparently Esq used that name when he got *way* out! Esquerita thought the world of Little Richard, but he also had this thing like "That shoulda been *me!*" However, Esquerita was too insane for that to have been him. He called up one day when I had a Little Richard hair tonic commercial on my answering machine and yelled, "Billy—how come you got Richard on your damn *arcocon?*" (that's what he called the answering machine). He was still yelling about that the next time I saw him.

The A-Bones and the Lyres once put a band together for a party in someone's basement in New York. Esquerita showed up and we said, "Why don't you do a couple numbers with us?" He said, "Well how much does it pay?" I said, "It doesn't pay anything." He went, "Billy—I'm *surprised* at you. You're a professional musician and you're doin' gigs for free." I said, "It ain't really a gig—we're playing to about 15 friends who are totally plastered." He said, "Well, I'll just sit here and enjoy myself." Then we started doing one of Little Richard's songs, "The Girl Can't Help It" and Esquerita stood up at attention, came over and tugged at my arm: "Announce me. Announce me." He couldn't stand people enjoying a Little Richard song without getting into the act and showing how it was *really* done. He got up and did a bunch of numbers; he would turn around and yell out song titles, and at one point he wanted to do LARRY WILLIAMS' "Slow Down." So he kept turning around and yelling that to Miriam [who was playing drums], and she kept slowing down more and more while he was yelling, "No, no—'Slow Down'!"

♦ **V: How did he dress?**

♦ BM: Well, in the '50s he wore wild shades, tear-away shirts—onstage he could tear off the sleeves and just rip these shirts to shreds. He said that once this white woman in Dallas fainted at the sight of him. His reputation is: he's gone the farthest out that man has ever gone. There are a lot of weird tales about him—supposedly he killed a guy in Puerto Rico. But that's not the sort of thing you ask somebody about in detail—especially when their fingers can go around your neck seven times!

One of the last times I saw Esquerita I was at his house just chatting away, and this girl came in. She said, "Esquerita—what are you getting me for Christmas?" He said, "Go in the kitchen"; then he said, "Billy, excuse me—just make yourself at home." Next I heard all this yelling and screaming and *bam! bam!* and he's yelling, "You muthafuckin' whore!" and she's yelling, "You faggot!" Then he comes back in the room as if nothing happened: "Excuse me, Billy," goes to the closet and pulls out some hollow metal vacuum cleaner tubes and goes back and I hear *bam! bam!* again. It sounded just like in the cartoons when somebody gets hit on the head. She went running out the back door and he came back and said, "Okay—now where were we?" like this was business as usual. *That's* why I never asked him if he really killed the guy in Puerto Rico . . .

He *was* great. The first time I ever sang with him I asked, "What song are we doing?" He grabbed me by the shirt, pulled me close to him, looked into my eyes and said, "Boy, this is the *greatest* moment of your life!" Then he threw me at the microphone. [laughs]

Esquerita, 1958

Photo: courtesy of Norton Records.

♦ **V: Who else are you releasing?**

♦ BM: GENE MALTAIS, one of the great rockers from New England, who went from town to town. He made a totally crazed record called "The Raging Sea" b/w "Gang War," which he now wants to present to MC Hammer to redo as a rap record "to stop all the violence in Los Angeles." As though this totally obscure record from the '50s is gonna bring violence to a crashing halt!

We're putting out recordings by the LEGENDARY STARDUST COWBOY (a well-documented maniac) and WADE CURTIS, a rocker who became a wrestling manager—we're gonna try to sell his records at his matches. We rediscovered FLORIAN MONDAY, who

Jack Starr's *Born Petrified*, © 1988 Norton Records. Album cover credits: cover art/sleeve: Kicks Magazine and Pete Ciccone at Immaculate Concepts.

made these insane records in Rhode Island in the '60s, and we've released these old tapes by King Usniewicz and His Usniewicztones—a bunch of drunken Polish auto mechanics who played a Detroit bowling alley lounge in the '70s. Their '74 "hit" was "Surfin' School."

♦ **V: *How do you decide what to collect?***

♦ ML: It's still kind of an unconscious process—if I hear something I like I go: "It's beautiful—I want it!" We have quite a collection of old radios, but it hasn't been: "We *collect* rare radios." Most of these things were created for working class people on a Woolworth's budget: radios with a gaudy plastic look. The same with '50s detective magazines with great covers, or '50s J.D. books. Some people call it "trash" culture but it's not trash—these things were created for people to buy and enjoy. I was never interested in consciously trying to "re-create the '50s" in my house, but a lot of the furniture you can get from thrift stores was made better, is more beautiful and is a lot cheaper than new furniture.

But it's always distressing when Sotheby's picks up on something like original paperback art, which ten years ago nobody wanted—it was cheap. Now it's considered "extremely collectible." Now there are these collectors of "future collectibles" who regard everything in terms of its "investment potential"—they'll go to a book fair with five thousand bucks in their pocket and buy mint-condition copies of the "Fifty Most Collectible Paperback Rarities" and won't read them; the books will sit there until the price goes up. That happens with records, too.

♦ BM: I *hate* the word "collectible."

♦ ML: It's really sad when that happens; you end up not wanting to tell people about any of your discoveries. You don't want to enthuse about something you

love, because then it'll get scarfed up by these creepy "collectors" who will turn it into some kind of "relic." The value in these things shouldn't be monetary; these things shouldn't be in the hands of people who are just saving them for their "investment potential." These things should be used and enjoyed and handled . . .

♦ **V: *And reissued again with decent cover art, too.***

♦ ML: I hate reissue record covers which are kitschy and garish and insult the artists on the record—implying or stating that these songs are "trashy." This has offended people like ARCH HALL, JR who had material released on a "Golden Turkey Awards" compilation LP. He was trying to create *good music*, and we think he succeeded. So why treat that material condescendingly—

♦ **V: *—that "so bad it's good" cliché which people use to insulate themselves from sincerely responding to something. People should feel grateful that these records even survived—***

♦ ML: One of the best rewards of publishing KICKS is being able to influence young kids who think that everything "cool" started in '77 with punk rock. You can just see it in their eyes when you play them a 35-year-old record that goes straight into their back-brain—they know this is what they *need*. And then to discover there's more and more available—! Once you realize you've got this whole realm of maybe joyful, maybe

Jack Starr   Photo: courtesy of Norton Records.

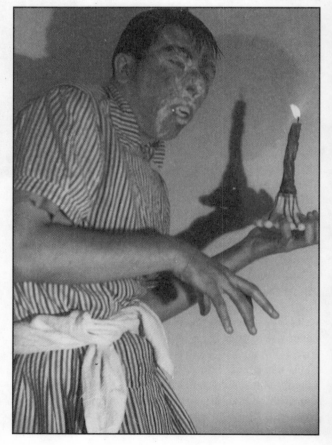

depressing, maybe horrifying or upsetting *pleasure* that is yours, and that is *endless . . .* well, you've got a whole *lifetime* to enjoy all this.

Related to these records is the realm of adult softcore fiction, which has been considered trash for so long. Sure, some of the DRAGON editions follow a somewhat standardized plot line, but it's entertaining to read them and see what appealed to men at that time. A lot of these publishers were telling stories using sexy language that is no longer used today. Nowadays, in porno books, the language used is very explicit and vulgar. It's not *offensive* to me, but I just don't care for it because I prefer language that is more "massaging" or metaphorical or witty—where *you* have to use your imagination. The writers were working within certain parameters of what was legally permissible at the time, and they went as far as they could with their language. There are great plots, and with certain pub-

Jack Starr   Photo: courtesy of Norton Records.

Jack Starr started making home monster movies with rock'n'roll songs in them. He also made porno movies, and unfortunately *all* of his films got confiscated by the Dallas vice squad—I guess they're lost to the world forever. Right now he's marketing Jack Starr Cologne—he doused his last demo tape with it, and I had to put it out on the window sill for about four days.

lishers (e.g. MERIT, NOVEL LIBRARY) you *know* you'll get exactly what you want: action-packed, sexy material!

J.D. and softcore film have been somewhat investi-

gated, but the paperbacks have largely been ignored. Often the authors wrote under pseudonyms, and the publishers went out of business or were prosecuted. That's why I'm publishing SMUT PEDDLER—to contact other people who are interested: "Let's share our information and dig into this." I've been cataloging what I have: thousands of adult books, starting in 1949 and ending around 1967. A lot of these books don't bear names or addresses, so you examine the style of the cover art and the typefaces and try to match them up. It's a big job, but when you finally figure out that "this guy" must be "so-and-so," it's exciting!

I tracked down a friend of RON HAYDOCK, Jim Harmon, and have been talking to him about Ron's career as a paperback writer (he wrote over 20 novels under the names Don Sheppard, Rita Wilde, Vin Saxon, etc), and people like him can endlessly drop names, just like RAY DENNIS STECKLER. One person leads to another, and . . . For example, FABIAN BOOKS also published under the names TROPIC and SABRE, and the owner started in the '50s. The whole scoop is in SMUT PEDDLER—at least the beginning is; I'm sure there's much more to be told.

The thing about these books and records is, once you find one, you want to know the story behind it.

61

Teen-age Riot!, Atomic Passion Records.

SON BROTHERS' "Rockin' Rickshaw" where they didn't even bother to tune their guitars. There's thousands more: "Tarzan" by The APE QUARTET, "Sapphire" by DANNY ZELLA, and "Wolf Call" by LORD DENT & THE INVADERS. I just got one today (although it's not that great): "Bowling Alley Oop" by the CAVEMEN.

I dig crazed rockers, like The PHANTOM's "Love Me"—that's just a total outburst. He went in to cut the other side (a ballad, "Whisper Your Love") and they needed something for the "B" side so he just screamed and the song took off . . . A great record came out of 'Frisco: TYRONE SCHMIDLING went into the studio thinking he would be backing somebody on guitar and the producer said, "Hey, come up with something original—we're gonna record you *now!*" He'd never written a song in his life, but he came up with "You're Gone I'm Left" with nothin' but 4 guys in the background hitting castanets on the table—he was only about 15 when he cut it. The guys don't have any sense of rhythm; it's totally demented.

Another great record is "Hep Cat" by LARRY TERRY from Missouri—we tracked him down to do an interview and sent him a KICKS magazine but when we called him he said, "Aw, I don't know—there's too many swear words in here"—he'd become religious. I kinda shot myself in the foot on that one . . . From Tennessee, BILLY SMITH had a totally nuts record called "Tell Me, Baby" on the Red Hed label. Unfortunately, he's in a nuthouse now—he followed up on the promise of his record . . . TONY AND JACKIE LAMIE did "Wore To A Frazzel"—I can play that fifty times in a row. I love one-shot records like these, where guys had one turn up at bat, got a hit and then overran the bases.

♦ **V: *What are some more strange records you've uncovered?***

♦ **BM:** There's a chain called the Waffle House—I've seen them in Arizona, Tennessee and Virginia. They all have jukeboxes, and the first 5 records were made only for Waffle House jukeboxes: "Waffle Doo-Wop," the "Waffle House Boogie," etc. Another weird record I dig is by BUD FREEMAN, "Because of LSD." It's a country record, and he sings about how his daughter got mixed up with these hippies and took LSD and *died.* That alone is great enough, but you flip it over and the other side is "Please Tell the World: A Message from the Grave"—it's the *daughter* saying, "That's right! I got messed up with hippies and took LSD and died! Don't you do it!" PHIL PHILLIPS, who had a hit with "Sea of Love," wrote that. He also put out a fantastic, bizarre record called "The Evil Dope." It starts out, "Hello. This is Phil Phillips, King of the World." When a guy starts a record out like that, he already gets four stars! It's a semi-narration about how a guy got hooked on dope, and how he goes down to Slackmouth Joe's house and scores the dope, and beats on his poor mother . . . Both of these records have

And it's up to you to find out more. If you find a record by an unknown singer you like, you want to find out all about him: where he recorded, where he grew up, who the producer is, did he do more records, etc. Sometimes people make fun of us for trying to track down something that's totally obscure, but if it has an impact on us, then it'll probably have an impact on somebody else, too. As a small publisher, we're interested in how these adult publishers survived for brief periods of time until they were shut down.

There are endless numbers of old detective magazines to uncover: over 300 different *titles* were published, starting in the '20s. And each one had a different editorial policy. Some had a "girlie" angle, while others had a garish or gory point of view. They were catering to public taste and they were selling, but not much has been written about their history. Major magazines like *Harper's Bazaar* have had big beautiful art books written about them, so that's what people think magazines are about. There is a great untold history of black publishing—not just *Ebony* or *Sepia* but also the GOODE Publications (out of Texas) who put out *Hep, Jive, Bronze Thrills,* and CHARLTON Publications, too; we'd like to get to the bottom of the barrel on this. Meanwhile, we're just tracking one guy down at a time and getting his story.

♦ **V: *Again, it's giving a voice to a neglected point of view . . . What are some of your favorite unlikely records?***

♦ **BM:** The most overlooked time for cool records was '59-'63, when everything in the charts was supposedly teen idols. But there were also tons of fantastic small label records that just got buried, like GLENN & CHRISTY doing "The Wombat Twist" or the DOT-

morals in them.

The HONDELLS do a good version of JODY REY-NOLDS' "Endless Sleep." Basically they take "Little Honda" and sing the words to "Endless Sleep." It makes dying sound like such a gas: "I looked at the sea and it seemed to say, Hey-hey-hey! You took your baby from me away—whoo!" That's pretty strange right there.

Do you remember those ads in old magazines, "Send us your poems and we'll put them to music"? The company would record them, press a couple hundred records and send them to the "poet" (for a fee). Tom Ardolino from the band NRBQ found a bunch of these records and re-released them on an LP, *The Beat of the Traps*. There's a song called "Headbands and Cadillacs," a song about Jimmy Carter, and one that just goes, "Disco, disco, disco/I'm goin' to Mt. Kisco."

◆ ML: There are some good crazy things in our Big Itch series of albums.

◆ BM: This guy T. VALENTINE does a song, "Hello, Lucille, Are you a Lesbian?" Imagine a funk band doing a bad job playing the *Sanford & Son* theme, while over the top a guy's going, "Hello, Lucille, Are you *lesbian*? Do you like to go to bed . . . with women? Whenever we go out, people say, 'It's two mens—she ain't got any tits. She's just like *him* . . . and she always wears pants—*long* pants.' " Then he goes, "What was that number: 258-9210? That's my sister's number—you got a date with my sister?! My sister is a *lesbian!*" Then the guy screams, "I hate all lesbians! I hate all lesbians! You-you-you *freak!*"

◆ ML: It's amazing *that* got recorded. He also did a record back in the '50s called "Betty Sue." There's 2 versions of it, and the earlier version is very much like TYRONE SCHMIDLING or HASIL ADKINS, where

The Big Itch Vol. Two: Memorial Album for Joe E. Ross, Mr. Manicotti Records.

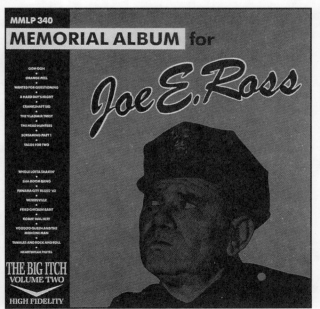

it's really off-kilter: he's just so excited and has so much to tell you; the music is going at a totally different beat—it's really good.

◆ BM: We just released a *Memorial Record to JOE E. ROSS from Car 54: Where Are You?* and copied the artwork from the *Memorial Album to Johnny Ace*. We put all these wild things like Vladimir & the Gravediggers' "Vladimir Twist" and the Rock Fellers' "Orange Peel." That one's nuts: "You loved me for a day/Then you threw me away/Like an orange peel." Between the cuts are excerpts from an amateur talent show.

We've released these old tapes by King Usniewicz and His Usniewicztones—a bunch of drunken Polish auto mechanics who played a Detroit bowling alley lounge in the '70s.

◆ **V: How has the CD affected small labels?**

◆ BM: CDs might be great for the major labels who produce these box sets and "legitimize" everything. But if you only have a few hundred bucks and you wanna record your own tape in your living room, press a few 45s and make the covers on a xerox machine—it's a shame it's getting away from that. If somebody suddenly decreed: "All fanzines must be printed and bound; there can't be any more xerox fanzines!" a lot of people would say, "Why bother?" They're just putting a pretty dress on an ugly child. A rock'n'roll fan who doesn't dig noise ain't really a rock'n'roll fan. The CD was a way whereby the record companies were able to astronomically boost the prices past the ten-dollar ceiling, plus take all these albums that were dead in the water (by groups like *Ten Years After* or *Poco*) and con all these fans into buying them again. In another ten years they'll have even *another* format, and those same people will buy them yet again. And when CDs skip, it's the weirdest thing, because you're helpless: "Ahhh!"

◆ **V: A friend of mine is meticulous in handling his CDs, yet already a half dozen of his CDs skip, and he knows he didn't scratch them. There are people who claim, "Vinyl is archival—not CDs." . . . What would you recommend people order from your catalog?**

◆ BM: Most people already own Jerry Lee Lewis or Johnny Burnette or Carl Perkins before they start ordering JACK STARR or ESQUERITA.

◆ ML: But I don't think you'll find anyone on the planet who won't enjoy a LINK WRAY instrumental record—and there are 3 volumes, with more on the

way. And the great thing about instrumental music is: it doesn't matter where you're from, you'll still be able to understand the music.

Some records like CONCUSSION or SHUTDOWN '66 are considered "uncompable" (meaning not 'good enough' to put on a compilation album). SHUTDOWN '66 is all guys who basically are in their first band, just learning how to play. They're tryin' their darndest to make a great record—maybe they're a bit inept, but they come through with so much feeling, and they're so full of emotion when they're whining or snarling about not being able to get a girl, or their parents not letting them out of the house, that . . . When a person makes a record and puts their own name on it, unless it's an out-and-out novelty or comedy record, they're trying their best—

♦ BM: Nobody put out a record to be ashamed of it.

♦ *V: I like that statement you printed in KICKS: "Most experts generally agree that when the music gets too good and too polished, it isn't considered the real thing."—The SURFARIS*

♦ ML: You see these '50s videotapes of ministers and politicians proclaiming, "Rock'n'roll has got to go!" and then they smash these piles of (now probably rare) records with a sledgehammer. Basically the same thing is happening today but in a different way; the corporate monsters are still out there dictating, and most people are still bowing down and handing them money. The people who want *real* rock'n'roll (or real *anything*) number just in the thousands.

One of the best rewards of publishing KICKS is being able to influence young kids who think that everything "cool" started in '77 with punk rock. You can just see it in their eyes when you play them a 35-year-old record that goes straight into their back-brain—they know this is what they *need*.

Of course, the big demon of the past decade has been MTV; for a lot of young kids, music *started* with MTV. Records mean nothing to them—if it hasn't been on MTV, it doesn't count. And country music radio stations have gone down the tubes: the most putrid, middle-of-the-road values are being pumped out at you by pasty-faced singers whose videos revolve around "the lovely family" and "the beautiful wife with the perfect puffy hair looking at nature." What is this crap: now the number one Country star is Garth Brooks (never heard of him) who named his kid "Taylor" after his idol James Taylor? *That's* country music?!

And these kids who watch MTV—I don't know if they can understand a record anymore. Before, if you listened to a record, that record stimulated your own images and associations—nobody told you what to imagine. But if you watch a music video, this stupid story line is beamed straight into your brain so if you hear the song on the radio, the *video's* going to come into your head, not any kind of original concept or creative imagery that's your own. What creates recording stars today is *video;* it's no longer records.

♦ *V: Do you know of any female record producers?*

♦ ML: In a man's world, CORDELL JACKSON was the first woman to have her own record label: Moon Records. She's not a one-woman band but she plays a frantic electric guitar that's completely wild, and her timing is bizarre. She was writing great songs and producing and recording other local Memphis artists back in the '50s. To look at her, she looks like a Southern Belle grandmother—she performs in long, frilly homemade dresses that her sister makes, and she wears rhinestone glasses and has a big bouffant hairdo and looks like a mild-mannered lady—but you get her onstage and she is wild! Her instrumentals are as savage as anything any heavy metal guy could pump out. And she's *still* doing it, for almost 40 years.

♦ *V: How did you start publishing Kicks?*

♦ BM: Miriam and I were writing for *New York Rocker* and other publications and thought, "Why don't we do our own magazine, and get like-minded people to write?" The first one was mainly on the Everly Brothers; the second one was better; the third was better yet . . . Now we're at the point where we can put out records by some of the people we like. We started doing our RON HAYDOCK story (*Kicks* #7) and turned up all his master tapes for an album.

♦ ML: Now we have a pretty big mail order catalog, but a lot of the records are just in small quantities—if you order, list alternates!

♦ *V: So your operation started—*

♦ ML: Really small. It basically came out of people coming over and listening to records and saying, "Gee, I wish I had that," and it would be a record that's really tough to find, like Hasil Adkins. So whaddaya do—just put them on tape endlessly for people? When we put out our first Hasil LP it was just a one-shot thing; we didn't really know we'd be doing more, but then people started saying, "Hey, you should put *this* out!" So we just kept on, and *Kicks* was basically to tell people about what we liked. The more we wrote about obscure bands or records, the more people asked, "Well, how do I get to hear this?" It all ties in: *read about it, then hear it.*

♦ *V: How can people tell what to order from your mail order catalog? Many of the artists or songs are virtually unknown—*

♦ ML: The 45s listed in the back are *all* sure-fire killers. All of 'em. You're not going to come up with a dud in the whole bunch. We went through hundreds and hundreds and picked the stuff that absolutely every *Kicks* reader would be very, very happy with. There's no duds, no sad little ballads with girl choruses in the background—they're all records that'll make you go, "Whoo!" or "Wheee!" Anything you pick out blindfolded—you'll see that they're *killers*. Several people have sent us letters like, "Send me records that are 'car' records" . . . or "Send me all your 'jungle' theme records" . . . or "Send me a selection of 'crying' records that have really frantic sobbing on them." Or somebody whose girlfriend is named Joanne will write: "Send me all your 'Joanne' 45s."

♦ BM: One guy from Japan sent us a big check with a note, "Send me a hundred R&B singles!" He'd been ordering rockabilly from us—he knew what he wanted in that area, but in R&B I guess he didn't know that much, so he decided to "try out" a hundred. I wrote him, "Whatever you don't like, send it back and if you pay for the postage I'll send you something else." It turned out he liked everything! (So, if anyone wants to send us money for a random sampling, they can send us $20 or $50 or $100 for "The Satisfaction Guaranteed Grab Bag.")

On these singles, the formula often was to put a slow song or ballad like "I Love You Dearly, Patricia" on the "A" side. And sometimes the ballad *is* the superior side. But most of the time we prefer the fast or frantic number that's on the "B" side—

♦ ML: Often, the producers didn't care about the "B" sides, so they'd permit these improvised, wild, drunken, savage songs that were totally nuts to be put on the record as "filler." But today, a lot of people prefer those "B" sides.

♦ *V: It's a lot of pressure to produce a whole album's worth of songs: a dozen tunes—*

♦ ML: Most albums just have one good song on 'em.

♦ BM: All the great rock'n'roll singers evolved through putting out singles, like Gene Vincent: "Be-Bop-A-Lula" comes out [*boom];* "Race with the Devil" comes out [*boom];* "Blue Jean Bop"—consistently great 45s, every few months. But an *album* used to be a totally different thing: they were mostly compilations of earlier 45s—the single was what you focused on. And you wouldn't even be able to *make* a fuckin' album if you didn't have good singles.

♦ *V: That seems like a much more "natural" way to evolve; plus, there's less pressure on the artist. How can you sit down and write 12 great songs in a row?*

♦ BM: In a single, you gotta deliver the goods in a couple of minutes. Whereas nowadays—I saw a guy from *Queen* on TV saying, "Well, I been working on a solo project for the past eight years, and I've got the basic tracks for about six numbers." Like: "What the hell do you do all day?!"

♦ ML: Whatever happened to the "decisive moment": going into the studio under pressure—you've got half an hour to cut a Number One record?

The Big Itch Volume Three, Mr. Manicotti Records.

♦ BM: All the great records LITTLE RICHARD made for Specialty were recorded in a year and a half—about a dozen fantastic records. Nowadays he'd put out "Tutti Frutti" and they'd have him on the road for a year and a half. Then he'd make the next record . . . and on the road for a year and a half. And these cats—when they were traveling around, a lot of 'em would stop at a *radio station* and make a record!

♦ *V: By publishing BAD SEED you've helped keep the history of the Juvenile Delinquency subculture of the '40s-'60s from disappearing—*

♦ ML: *Teenage Riot,* our juvenile delinquent album, is a compilation of J.D. 45s, and each song has a tale behind it . . . *Everything* cool has a tale behind it.

♦ *V: And everyone you meet turns you on to more records, books, magazines and films—*

♦ ML: And you never know who will turn out to be "strange." I've been having vision problems and have been going to an eye doctor in New York for quite some time—a few years back I had lost the vision in my left eye. It's come back, but it's something they have to check regularly. On my last visit I got into a conversation with my eye doctor (whom I've known for ten years) because I happened to have a copy of *Kicks* with me. I showed it to him and he went, "Oh, *wow!* I used to play in a band on Long Island called the BELL NOTES; we recorded this 45 called "I've Had It!" They were a band we'd been looking for *high and low* (the A-Bones perform "I've Had It!") and I went, "What!" He said, "Yeah, and there was one guitar player I was totally crazy about: Link Wray." I was astounded! So now, whenever I see people who are like 40-plus, I feel like asking, "Hey, did you ever make a record?"

EARTHA KITT

During a career that began in the late '40s, Eartha Kitt has played stages all over the world and chatted with Nehru, Churchill and Einstein. Orson Welles called her "the most exciting woman in the world" when she played Helen of Troy. She has released over 50 records, written 3 books (most recently, *I'm Still Here)* and appeared in more than 10 movies, making her film debut in *New Faces of 1954* and playing opposite Nat "King" Cole in *St Louis Blues*. In her dazzling stage shows, Eartha Kitt projects sensual arrogance, sophistication, easy grace and risqué wit—especially in her improvised interactions with the audience.

Eartha's fan club is run by Peter Robertson c/o 3677 North Fruit Ave., Fresno CA 93705 (send self-addressed stamped envelope). She is managed by Kitt Shapiro (888 7th Ave, 37th floor, NY, NY 10106). Eartha Kitt was interviewed backstage in Manchester, England, after her performance as the "genie" in a stage production of *Aladdin's Lamp*.

♦ *VALE: When you were invited to a White House luncheon, didn't you cause a scandal?*
♦ EARTHA KITT: In 1968, during the Vietnam War, I was invited by Lady Bird Johnson to give my opinion about the problems in the United States, specifically: "*Why* is there so much juvenile delinquency in the streets of America?" But the First Lady seemed to be more interested in decorating the windows of the ghettos with flowerboxes—she wasn't interested in hearing anything other than what she wanted to hear. I mean—it's fine to put flowers in the ghettos and "beautify America," but let's take care of the necessities first: give people *jobs,* which is what people want in order to have dignity and respect, and find a way to get us out of poverty.

This luncheon was for 50 women who were working in different communities across the United States.

I was working with an organization called Kidsville, for young people who were trying to get off the streets and develop themselves as personalities more constructive to our society. Young boys were telling me that if they were "good" and had no criminal record, their "reward" would be: having a gun put into their hands and being sent off to fight a war they were not in accord with. And when they came back from this war, they were not *retrained* to detox from their hatred against whomever they were fighting.

The parents did not want to raise children so they could be killed by foreign bullets—as toys the politicians could do whatever they wanted with. The parents had raised their children to live by the Ten Commandments, yet when they became 18 years old they were taught to go against the Ten Commandments—"Thou shalt not kill"—because the government ordered them to. The young boys who went to Vietnam came home to find out they didn't have a job. They discovered that they'd been discarded; now they were *outcasts.*

When I was a child during World War II, I remember we were taught to hate the Germans (who were blonde and blue-eyed), yet after the war when we saw Germanic-looking people we had to "check" ourselves. We were also taught to hate the Japanese—but we were never taught *not* to hate them. Of course, you should hate the person who is *instigating* these wars . . . but not the people themselves. Yet as children we were educated by newsreels to hate, hate, hate whatever group our government decided to be fighting . . .

Anyway, when it came my turn to speak, I said to the president's wife, "Vietnam is the main reason we are hav-

ing trouble with the youth of America. It is a war without explanation or reason . . . To beautify America, it seems, is to beautify her with jobs and less taxes and getting out of Vietnam." I said that the young ghetto boys thought it *better* to have a legal stigma against them—then they would be considered "undesirable" and would not be sent to the war; they could stay home. In their opinion, in this society the good guys *lost* and the bad guys won.

I didn't say this ranting and raving (like it was reported in the newspapers), but we were in a large room, we didn't have microphones, and we had to speak loudly enough to be heard. That incident, reported in such a way as to deface me in the eyes of the American people, obviously had to have been given to the newspapers by someone from the White House—probably the press secretary: "Eartha Kitt makes the First Lady cry . . ." There were *no* reporters present (all the photos and TV footage of myself and Lady Bird Johnson had been shot earlier). So this was a *manufactured furor.*

But from that incident, which was reported all over the world, the president found out he was not so much in favor in the eyes of the American people as he thought. I got letters from over 500 women saying they felt the same way I did—from places like Korea, Japan, Indonesia, Europe; this mail is still somewhere in my office in Connecticut. Mrs Johnson claimed she answered 25,000 letters in 3 weeks' time [about this] but I don't see how that was possible; I'm still (after over 20 years) trying to answer mine! And I *still* get mail about that incident; people still come up to me and say, "Thank you for helping us get out of Vietnam. Thank you for saving my son."

◆ *V: Didn't you suffer because of that?*
◆ EK: Of course—within two hours I was out of work in America. President Johnson telephoned the media and said, "I do not want to see that woman's face anywhere." They were out to get rid of me—so first of all they sent the FBI to find something "subversive" on me. And the FBI came back and said, "Her only problem is: she loves her country and she's perfectly will-

ing to fight for her country—from the *inside*"—they couldn't find anything on me. This is all in the 2000-page dossier which Jack Anderson and Seymour Hirsch of the *New York Times* got hold of.

Then Johnson sent the CIA to get something on me, and *they* couldn't find anything, either. So they began interviewing people I had worked with over the years, and if you interview a thousand people, somebody's going to say, "She's a *bitch!* She's shrewd, she's mean, she's cruel!"—usually out of jealousy or envy. And the interview that one anonymous person gave to the *Washington Post* (I know exactly who he is) stated, "She'd do *anything* to get the audience on her side." There were only two of us working on this show, *The Owl and the Pussycat,* and this man hated me—he used to kick me "accidentally" onstage and do everything he could to sabotage, because he was jealous of the audience's reaction to me.

So the government came back with all this anonymous, backyard gossip: "It is rumored that she is a sadistic sex nymphomaniac." Even if I were, what does that have to do with overthrowing the government? [laughs] Unless I were Mata Hari—maybe I should think about doing *that* if we have a war again! And this was very shocking to me, because I happen to be very enamored of my country, which is based on: "If you do not like something, you have the right to say so." Our country's supposed to be run by the people, for the people, and of the people—*forget it!* And my country also says, "We do not live in fear of our own government." But if you tell the truth, you'll be put out of work, or worse . . .

This happened in 1968, and I didn't even realize what was going on until January 1974, when Seymour Hirsch from the *New York Times* called me and said, "Eartha, we want you to give us permission to print what we have discovered on you: the CIA dossier." For all this time I had no idea why I was not being hired in America. But thank god, being an international personality, I could get contracts elsewhere—they came in from foreign countries and I was able to keep my head above water. The few American contracts that were offered me came from people who felt the same way I did and who were not afraid—such as the Plaza Hotel in New York.

My mother-in-law said, "Eartha, I understand what you said and I agree with you—but did you have to *say* it?" That was the opinion of a lot of people. But my country was split in half. The White House had invited me because they thought I'd be on "their side," but when they discovered I wasn't, they tried to make it look as though I were a bad girl, that I used foul language, that I screamed and ranted—and that wasn't true at all. But what good is it for me to say that? Finally, after 20 years, biographies are coming out that tell what kind of a person President Johnson *truly* was.

At the time people asked if I would retract myself, and I said, "Why? The woman asked me a question and I gave her my opinion. I told her what the people have told me, what the children have told me, and the way I feel myself. So there's nothing for *me* to apologize for—I think it is *she* who should apologize to me!" And I kept thinking, "Why would they pick on a little person like myself?" If Johnson had just kept his mouth shut . . . but him calling the newspapers caused this furor that went all over the world.

♦ *V: A recent* **60 Minutes** *special brought up this incident afresh for*

Eartha Kitt's *That Bad Eartha,* © 1984 RCA Records.

American viewers.

♦ EK: About three weeks after this incident, I had an engagement at an exclusive club in Texas. Some Texas property owners who came to the show invited me over for dinner and said, "We're so glad you told Mr Johnson what you felt; we feel the same way. Not only that—this man has been ripping off our property ever since he became president." Allegedly he would change zoning laws and confiscate properties whenever he wanted, and bring business in that he would get a percentage of. These people were not paying five hundred dollars to see *me,* they came to see "the girl who told Mr Johnson what should have been told him: get out of Vietnam, you're wasting our boys, you're wasting our tax money, and it's useless." These people did not want that war . . . although there's always somebody who'll go along with *anything:* "My country right or wrong." Those are the people who allow the country to go more *wrong* than right: the silent majority. If you listen to the silent majority, *nothing* will happen except what the politicians want. As long as everyone says, "We can't fight City Hall!" and don't make an effort to fight, there's no hope. So why give birth to children who will be without a future?

♦ V: *A lot of people don't think there is a future—*

♦ EK: I think that's variable—my daughter's 28, has been married 3 years, and she wants to have children. But I think *I'm* more concerned about my grandchildren than she is. My daughter and her husband see the future as, "No matter what happens, we will survive"—as though nothing will ever touch them. But that's not the way *I* feel.

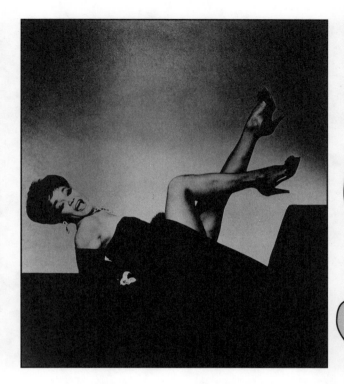

I said to the president's wife, "Vietnam is the main reason we are having trouble with the youth of America. It is a war without explanation or reason . . . To beautify America, it seems, is to beautify her with jobs and less taxes and getting out of Vietnam."

I've always grown up with nature; I've kept my fingers in the dirt. That's why I never have long fingernails and I go around looking like a bum—because that's my nature! I live on a farm—I've *always* lived on a farm. Even when I lived in the middle of Beverly Hills it was still a farm, because I had my own chickens and grew my own food. In Manhattan, my back yard was always growing fruit and vegetables.

Early on I knew that whatever the animals and the birds were eating was okay for me to eat too—up to a point. I've always told people, "Please, if you have a piece of dirt, plant your own food. And do not let the developers come in and put cement on everything, because that kills the soil—it can't breathe and will not *borne* anything. Don't chop down any trees!" I've been like this all my life; I came out of a cotton plantation. Talk about *recycling;* plastic is the worst thing to me—even god doesn't want it back!

We live in a free democratic country—as long as you toe the line! I love *England;* England has been good to me from the very beginning, when I first started to become whoever I am. It was England that first accepted me as the beautiful creature, the sensuous kitten—England made me what I am today! [laughs] Once I got a name for myself and *became* all the accolades that people were writing about me, I went back to America singing the same songs I sang in England and was a terrific flop! The club (*La Vie En Rose*) had waxed the floor and hadn't told me, so I did a dance movement and went *plop!*—fell onstage and had five stitches in my chin. That gave the club the excuse to fire me.

The William Morris Agency ran a newspaper campaign about "the beautiful sensuous creature who came in from [they said] Paris." For ten days before my opening a full page ad proclaimed, "LEARN TO SAY . . ." and in very small print at the bottom: "EARTHA KITT." And every day my name got bigger and the rest of the print got smaller; by opening night it proclaimed in big letters: "EARTHA KITT." So everyone in New York was asking, "What's an Eartha Kitt? Is it a garden tool?" because my name is so strange. I had a star-studded audience, but I was not successful. I was (like they say) thirty years ahead of my time. Nevertheless,

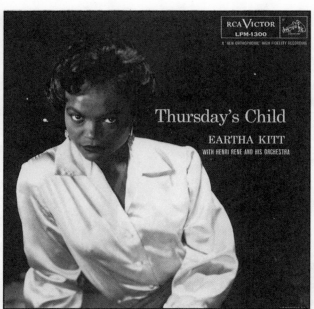

Eartha Kitt's *Thursday's Child*, © RCA Victor.

a little brown-skin girl from the cotton fields of South Carolina who was an orphan and rejected and given away by her mother still became famous—I got *even* by becoming a household name! And you have no idea what games they played on me; how the agents tried to use the "casting couch." I thought it was terribly funny—being an athlete, I could hop over the desks and chairs and run down fire escapes faster than a cheetah, you know.

Anyway, when I returned to America I had to start all over again. Max Gordon from the Village Vanguard found my address through the musicians' union and offered me a job: "I can't afford to pay you $600 a week like you were getting in Paris, but I can give you $250." I said, "Fine!" and the next day the newspapers proclaimed, "The greatest thing that's happened to New York!"—I got sensational reviews. The William Morris Agency said to me, "How can you possibly accept this job? You were making $600 a week; you cannot possibly go *down.*" I said, "Yes, but I'm hungry!" "What's that?"—as though an artist is not supposed to get hungry. You're supposed to sit there and wait and starve to death until the same-amount-of-money-kind-of-job comes along again. But naturally they took their ten percent . . .

Then they asked me to put on an audition for some potential backers, and after I started visiting the backers' homes trying to help get the funding, they got the money in a very short time. Dick and Edith Barstow—I'll never forget them—were the choreographers. The song "Monotonous" (about experiences I'd had abroad) was written in one afternoon. When we were developing the show I kept saying, "You cannot just go out and sing 'Monotonous'—by the time it's over, the audience is going to *agree.* Give me six chaise longues!" I don't

know why I asked for them, but I thought I could do these catlike movements with them. Finally one of the backers, Mr Chrysler, got me *three* chaise longues, and I worked up a skit moving from sofa to sofa, periodically singing [spits like a cat], "Monotonous!" By the time I'd worked my way across the stage, the audience was standing up laughing and applauding—we had to write two or three more verses so they wouldn't stop the show.

♦ *V: Did you ever improvise lyrics?*
♦ EK: No, I wouldn't improvise unless I really knew what I was saying. And I haven't been singing that song, because it does not work without those chaise longues.

♦ *V: A lot of your song lyrics are classic: "Nobody taught me; I figured it out for myself"; "You never get nowhere counting on somebody else" . . . I like the English translation of the song, "Paint Me Black Angels"—*
♦ EK: It's better in Spanish, though. Those are some of the songs I should be doing again today; they're very meaningful.

♦ *V: Did you get criticism for your song, "I Want To Be Evil"?*
♦ EK: Why? It's a very funny song. It's been a trademark ever since. A lot of the songs on those old records I don't even remember ever doing. Some of them were never released. I don't even have copies of some of my records.

Nevertheless, a little brown-skin girl from the cotton fields of South Carolina who was an orphan and rejected and given away by her mother still became famous—I got *even* by becoming a household name!

♦ *V: You recorded a song with PEREZ PRADO?*
♦ EK: It was terrible. He wanted everything his way and I didn't go along with what he was trying to make me do. RCA was using me to promote him; this was back in the early '50s. But he was far more interested in his own trumpet playing (or whatever instrument he was playing) than in working with *me.* Male ego, and being Latin—you know what that means! And it was a terrible record because my voice was not up to par; I was overly tired, and I told RCA not to release the record. I remember driving from New York to Atlantic City to do an engagement, and I heard it on the radio and thought, "*Uh oh*—Eartha, you were absolutely right!"

RCA and I always had a mutual agreement—if I didn't like something, they would not release it. But the people who were responsible for me (like Mannie Sacks) had died, and whoever replaced him wanted to get rid of me—Elvis Presley had appeared on the scene. Before then I was the only person who was making money for them, to the extent that when I went to the studios they literally rolled out the red carpet for me—from the door to the car, and with red roses alongside! This sounds fantastic, but it's true. And when I walked into the studio with a 34-piece orchestra (or a 64-piece orchestra), there was Dom Pérignon champagne for everyone, *and* Beluga caviar, *and* red roses everywhere. It was absolutely fantastic. They really treated me like I was a queen. I was the only person in 27 years who'd made money for them in that particular musical category, even though the man who originally got me my five-year record contract with RCA got fired on the spot. He was told, "She'll never sell any records; her voice is too *weird*. She doesn't fit in." Well—I hope I'll never "fit in"!

But when Mannie Sacks died and Elvis Presley came on the label with whoever brought him in, we were all cast aside. I remember hearing on the radio my record followed by another one, and the announcer saying, "The Beatle has a cold." I wondered, "What the hell is a Beatle? What's he talking about?" The picture came into my head of little beetles flying into America to inject something into our vegetables. Then the whole recording world gravitated toward people like Elvis Presley and the Beatles.

♦ *V: What's your critique of modern pop music?*
♦ EK: People don't write *stories* anymore. They write just one line, and the last one that I thought was hysterically funny went, "Get off your booty, get on the floor and dance." Another song featured nothing but this screaming—which can be very effective for a moment. But to kids today, everything is momentary—they don't think in terms of having a future. They want money but they don't want to work for it (maybe there's a few who do; there's always an exception to the rule).

People no longer think in terms of "my relationship to another person." Therefore there seem to be *no* relationships anymore, because it's always: "What am I going to get out of *you* if I make you my friend?" People have nothing to give, and no desire to give to begin with—they're more "takers" today. And they're getting to be more and more like that: less sharing, less caring, less concerned, because they think there *is* no future. It's "What can I get out of today?" We're not preparing our todays in order for our tomorrows to be constructed.

When I was in Paris I was reading Kierkegaard and Jean-Paul Sartre with other American kids over there, and we used to sit around the Deux Magots and the Café de Flore and exchange our thoughts, talk about what we had read—we would *discuss* things. People like James Baldwin, Brigitte Bardot and Jean Gabin would join in, too. Some of us would go to the museums . . . we didn't have any money. I was a dancer and they were students and we were all in the same boat. We'd walk 20-30-40 blocks to find a meal that only cost a dollar, but that was a seven-course meal. We would sit around places like that over maybe one glass of grog and we would philosophize, we would discuss things—we *shared* our thoughts. Well, they don't share thinking today!

Perez Prado was far more interested in his own trumpet playing (or whatever instrument he was playing) than in working with *me*. Male ego— you know what that means!

♦ *V: In America there are no sidewalk cafes or coffee houses where you can sit for hours and talk, plus—nobody reads anymore. People just go to clubs where the music's so deafening, they can't talk anyway—*
♦ EK: That has a lot to do with Madison Avenue and the business world. I'll never forget Phil Spector's statement back in the '60s: "I dictate to the kids what I want them to hear and what I want them to buy. They'll buy what I put out there." And a lot of pop music is geared toward lesser-thinking people: 13-year-old kids who can't quite make up their minds which direction to go in. They're at the stage where they have just enough money to buy a record, and enough sense to be manipulated. [laughs]

My musical director in New York who helps me with my repertoire, Maurice Levine, said, "It's Nazi music. It's all *achtung!*" You can't help but be on the beat—*boom boom boom boom*. It's all geared toward the organs of the body that stimulate sexuality. That's something I really do resent, because then you don't think about what the words are—that's *why* there aren't any words anymore! All you need is the beat plus one word or phrase or line that says, "Baby, I want you tonight!" That's all you're going to hear, that one phrase.

But to listen to a *story,* like the Nat "King" Coles and the Johnny Mathis's and people like myself are looking for . . . there's always going to be a need for storytelling songs, be they funny ones or romantic ones. All those songs I have done are a contact between me and the younger generation. They know there is an Eartha Kitt out there, and when they come and see my show, they'll never see that rock'n'roll

stuff. I'm not saying that rock'n'roll is good, bad or indifferent—but fortunately, we do grow out of it!

♦ *V: Eventually you want more subtlety, more dynamics—*

♦ EK: Nowadays it's hard to find writers who write intellectual, sophisticated wit—these days we're clubbing everybody over the head with what we want to say. We're not writing for people who want to listen, because we're not *teaching* people to listen. Therefore they don't hear anything except that downbeat with the drum and the bass which is all electronically done. As far as I'm concerned, the synthesizer is the most dangerous instrument in the world! You listen to that synthesized bass and drum—it hits you right in your intestinal organs, and you get up on the floor and you start going crazy. And after a couple drinks you don't know where the hell you are—you haven't heard a thing and you can't remember a thing. But you go home tone-deaf, because the frequencies are so loud. In America, I read about a mother who took her 13-year-old daughter to a concert. They were sitting in the center about three or four rows from the stage, and everybody *onstage* had on earplugs—but they didn't tell the audience to wear them. That mother sued the group, the system, the arena, and she won. The kids do not realize how dangerous loud sound can be—it's like being *asphyxiated.*

What rules the world is big business. And the biggest business in the world is fast food: McDonald's, Coca-Cola, Pepsi-Cola—it's all junk. (This means they'll never use me in their advertisements—well, they won't use me anyway—I'm *sophisticated.*) But junk foods create junk minds and bodies (ulcers and early heart attacks—and people die of heart attacks because everything's going so fast now). And out of that comes

junk personalities. Big business is responsible for the ruination of the ability to grow in every way—they aren't interested in humans being *intelligent,* they want them to remain stupid enough to be constantly eating their junk. Maybe I should invest in their stock. [laughs]

Modern music is—*boom boom boom boom.* It's all geared toward the organs of the body that stimulate sexuality. That's something I really do resent, because then you don't think about what the words are.

Look at what's happening to kids in Japan—they're imitating Western society, and they're getting fat from eating Kentucky Fried Chicken and McDonald's burgers. I went to Australia and in the middle of the Outback where the aborigines are there were McDonald's and Kentucky Fried Chicken. I thought, "That's the end." And in the hospital there I visited kids that were 13 years old, after they'd been raped by white Australian police who go into the reservations—well, I want to go back and do something about that. These same kids enter the hospital suffering from Vitamin C deficiency, but what do they have there—a Pepsi-Cola machine! Yet what they need is fresh orange juice. So all the doctors in the world need to get together against these fast food corporations, because McDonald's (they have *proved*) buys meat from sick, cancer-ridden cows. If the top or the bottom of the cow has cancer, they just use the other part. But they don't know how far the cancer has traveled . . . and that's what you're eating! [laughs]

The young generation have got to be *retrained;* if they'd stop drinking Coca-Cola and Pepsi-Cola they'd be able to think a little! The young people are responsible for helping the rest of us take care of the future. They can't just sit there and blame it on older people, because they're the ones who are being conned into continuing the production and consumption of junk. Even a place like the Body Shop which produces non-animal fat, no-animal-experimentation *this-and-that*—well, they charge too much. Anybody who wants to start some enterprise that would be better for our children's health, should make it less expensive so the kids would be enticed to buy it. *Then* when they get hooked—! [laughs]

Maybe I'll start something. I've got 87 acres of land in Connecticut and for a long time I've been thinking about starting a health farm. When I was a kid in New York and the boys went off to the wars, to get kids off the street they'd send girls (they called them "farmer-ettes") to help the farmers. You got room and board and ten dollars a week. So you accomplished several objectives: you helped the farmers, got off the streets, and ate healthy food too. That should be started all over again. (But then the unions would probably come in and say, "You're using kids as slave labor!")

I brought up my daughter on food out of the garden. She went through her stage of "peer-ism" eating junk food and all that, but it only lasted a moment because of the kind of training she got at home. Not my saying, "No no, nag nag nag," but by *showing*. Because I breast-fed her, gave her everything from the garden—I never thought that anything from a can could actually nourish a child. I put in her mouth what I raised myself; I mashed up the bananas and sweet peas myself. And now she's back onto that.

Eartha Kitt's *Down to Eartha*, © RCA Victor. Album cover credits: photo: David B. Hecht.

♦ **V: Do you do needlepoint, too?**
♦ EK: That's why it's sitting there. If kids don't acquire any skills from their parents—well, this goes back to: they don't think there's any future, so why learn a trade? Plus, everybody just wants to be *told* what to do; kids don't really want to work.

♦ **V: Is it true that when you were younger, for a long time you refused to talk?**
♦ EK: I was afraid. I still am; I'm afraid of attracting attention to myself. That's why for me to go around looking like (what do they say?) "the most beautiful creature in the world"—NO! I don't even want to go to parties because I have to dress up and look like what the photographs look like. I'm hiding all the time. When I was a kid, I was given away, and I never wanted to attract attention—I would hide in a corner; I never wanted to be seen. And a lot of that is still with me. I know people think that I'm "difficult" or say "she's angry" but I'm not angry at all—I'm scared to death! [laughs] I have a reputation: "She's difficult to get to know," but I'm just scared. Some people think I'm resentful, but it's not that at all—inside I'm trembling. And the moment I feel that somebody understands—"it's okay; we're not going to bite you, Eartha"—I go "Phew!"

♦ **V: You learned seven languages by an organic process—when you were abroad, you lived in people's homes—**
♦ EK: Rather than living in hotels, which I couldn't afford anyway, I lived with the people, and as a matter of interest you naturally start learning their language. For example, I lived among families in Manhattan who had fled Cuba—116th Street and Madison Avenue. There were Polish families, Italian families, Jewish families, black families—everyone who wound up in "Spic town," a derogatory term for Spanish-speaking people. Here I was living in the same block with kids who didn't speak English, so I started picking up their language. Not only that, but I'm a very good listener. Since I didn't want to attract attention to myself, I had very keen ears and a terribly good memory; I can read a script once and know approximately what it's all about.

♦ **V: In an interview, you talked about the necessity for discipline—**
♦ EK: Oh—what was my recipe? I must have been talking about playing Catwoman on the *Batman* TV series—that part was written for me, you know. People like CESAR ROMERO and I came out of the theater, where you have to memorize long scenes without a break. One day we had to be filmed doing two-and-a-

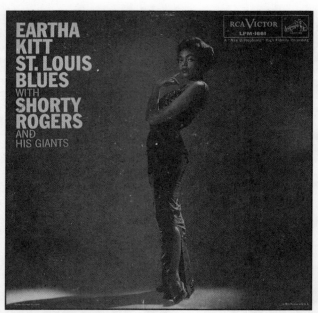

Eartha Kitt's *St. Louis Blues,* © RCA Victor.
Album cover credits: photo: Garrett-Howard.

half pages of dialogue between Catwoman and the Joker—we did it in two hours and the whole studio stood up and applauded! But when Batman and Robin came on the set with five lines each, it took forever to film; they constantly had to turn off the camera. And to Hollywood time is money—if you waste time, you're out of a job.

And one of the problems with Hollywood today is: they don't hire true stars anymore. There are a lot of entertainers with big names, but no stars, partly because "the business" (be it theater, the movies or television) wants people whom they can recycle just like *that*—one whiff of a problem and you're gone! Also, if you get too old—my friends in Hollywood tell me that if you're past 30, even if you're a *writer* . . . I have a friend who's a fantastic television writer in Hollywood, and he's 60-something years old. He writes the script, puts a young person's name on the script, and that's how he sells it . . .

This is the problem: they're not recycling intelligence; they discard rather than utilize the knowledge and intellect of an older person. That's why the business is now taken over by what we call "yuppies"— pretty sad: the young accountants, the young lawyers, the young business executives who are only interested in *quantity,* not quality. And one of these days people are going to stop and ask, "Whatever happened to quality?" I think they're beginning to. In my audience (it's amazing—so *happily* amazing) I see so many young people now. And since I am the "last legend" (they tell me), "the one and only," this may be the last tour I'm doing. I may go on for another hundred years, but . . .

◆ *V: A large percentage of the records you made thirty or forty years ago have lyrics you wouldn't be ashamed of in today's "post-feminist" era—*

◆ EK: As far as "women's lib" is concerned, I guess I've always *been* that. I didn't think about whether I'm just as important as a man—I've never belonged to any categories of any kind. But to actually think in terms of a man treating me in a different way . . . I wish the man would treat me the way the Old World was. Not in *all* respects, but—men don't send flowers anymore. They don't send chocolates, they don't stand up for women on buses, they don't respect the elderly, and they don't respect the fact that you are the feminine gender.

Now, did women's lib do that? Did it go too far in saying that women are equal to men? I don't want to be equal to men—I know I'm *ahead* of them already! If I can *borne* his children I must be ahead of him, because he can't. But why tell a man that? And I don't want to split the bill with a man who takes me out— dammit, I want him to pay for it! Because that's *also* a matter of respect—if he doesn't have enough money to take me out, he should say so. We'll go home and sit over a cup of coffee or I'll make him a bowl of corn- flakes or something. To me, a man-woman relation- ship is absolutely fantastic—I love it. But where is it?

The young kids who come walking into the dressing room and just want an autograph could at least bring me a rose, or *something* that makes me pay more atten- tion, because that person is showing, "I may not be able to buy you the world, but to show my appreciation for whatever it is you have given me and shared with me on the stage, I give you a rose." (It may be *dead*— but it's something!) I know I'm making a joke of it, but—these little things mean an awful lot. The moth- ers are not teaching their boys how to be gentlemen— that's one of the big problems. And we are not teaching our daughters to be feminine girls and ladies . . .

The man who originally got me my five-year record contract with RCA got fired on the spot. He was told, "She'll never sell any records; her voice is too *weird*. She doesn't fit in." Well—I hope I'll never "fit in"!

The ritual of woman-man relationships is a very beautiful thing, and unfortunately it's getting lost more and more with the "advances" of technology. You press a button and the dishes are washed; you press a button and the microwave cooks dinner—everything is done instantly. I asked my daughter if she uses her micro- wave and she said, "Oh mummy, I only use it once in a while." Well, to me once in a while is too much! When she and her husband come to my house for a meal, the dinner is cooked from scratch. I peel the potatoes myself, I do everything myself . . .

◆ **V: *The concept of an "interior life" has all but disappeared. People come home and instantly turn on the radio or TV—***

And the biggest business in the world is fast food: McDonald's, Coca-Cola, Pepsi-Cola—it's all junk. But junk foods create junk minds and bodies and out of that comes *junk personalities.*

◆ EK: That's exactly what we're talking about. People don't sit down and talk to each other anymore—we're screaming at each other if we have anything to say! That's one thing I can say about my son-in-law: since he's a lawyer, we have a lot to discuss. We get into tremendous debates; we are *verbally* discussing things all the time, so the three of us have fantastic, good conversations. There's no sitting around my house with people being—what do you call them?—*potato couches.*

◆ **V: *You've written three books—***

◆ EK: I'm a very disciplined, solitary person. When the publisher asked me to write *I'm Still Here*, I had to think a lot about fate, which has a lot to do with my behavior. Because I really do believe in fate—fate put me in show business and there must be a reason why I'm still here in the business. As I said, it happened by accident and I took advantage of the opportunity that presented itself.

◆ **V: *How do you write?***

◆ EK: Here in England I try to have my dressing room set up just like I would have it at home, with nothing but plants—lots of 'em. (By the way, you're not supposed to come in here without a plant in your hand, so send me one when you leave!) I can't have my kitty cats and my dogs—they're at home being taken care of. And every morning at 10:00 I come into the dressing room and sit there and write for three or four hours *longhand.* Then I give it to my secretary and she types it up. It took about ten months to write *I'm Still Here.* Also, I maintain the self-discipline of regular exercise—having the body worked out constantly; I go to a gym or at home I run four or five miles a day. I do the writing first thing in the morning. I walk around the dressing room and drink a lot of coffee and think and get the pictures and the words in my head and then I sit down and write until the brain becomes empty or the fingers get tired.

◆ **V: *What's your recipe for achievement?***

◆ EK: If you see an opportunity and you're hungry,

you grab it—you want that piece of bread. You work, no matter what it is. Any job—I don't give a damn what kind of job it is—is an honorable position to be in. And I was very lucky—as a joke somebody dared me to audition for KATHERINE DUNHAM'S dance company, when all I wanted was her autograph because I had seen her in the movies and thought, "Oh, that's a nice person and she's my color. She's a beautiful woman with a marvelous company; I'd like to meet her." So when the opportunity came, somebody dared me to try out for her class, and I said, "Oh, you *dare* me? Okay!" and I jumped in and won a full scholarship. That's how I got into show business. And I'm still looking for a job!

SOME CDs:

Live in London (2-CD set; highly recommended)
I'm Still Here
Thinking Jazz
In Person at the Plaza

Eartha Kitt's *I'm a Funny Dame,* © 1988 The Official Record Company.
Album cover credits: photo from the Frank Driggs Collection.

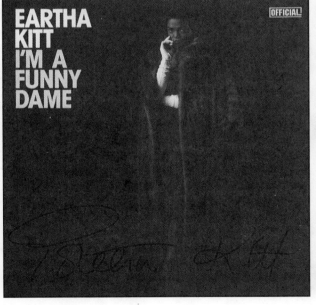

MARY RICCI

Mary Ricci is a San Francisco computer programmer with a growing collection of records and paperbacks with lurid covers. With partners Al Ennis and Prax Gore she started the first incredibly strange video outlet in San Francisco, Wild Wild Video. She has a firm belief in the sanctity of vinyl and shuns compact discs.

♦ **Vale: Why do you think there are so few female collectors?**

♦ MARY RICCI: It's a conspiracy—an evil plot by male collectors so *they* can score the best records! Actually, women are socialized to have more "responsible" pastimes, while men are expected to have hobbies. I think a lot of women defer to their partner's musical choices, so they don't spend much time in record stores. Most people don't start out actually *collecting* anything, they become collectors by normal exposure gone awry! It wouldn't surprise me if some women were put off by that "boys' club cool" so often associated with record collecting. I personally don't care if someone thinks I'm uncool for not knowing some tidbit of information about a musician or label or genre—I'm not afraid to ask questions. I find that women *and* men are often uncomfortable asking questions, but I got over it—it's such a good way to learn. I might never have become aware of two of my favorite musicians (JIMMY BRYANT and SPEEDY WEST) if I'd let the "You mean you don't *know* who Jimmy Bryant is?" crap get in my way. No one is born with a catalog of great music in their head—but some people would like you to think that! Fortunately, most people are happy to tell you about their favorites—I love going over to friends' houses and listening to their new acquisitions, and I love having people over to hear mine.

There's also an element of chance associated with record collecting, because you usually can't hear it until you get it home. That record with the $15 price tag might be unlistenable. I don't really like taking chances with my money, but—what if this record turns out to be my favorite *ever?* That's how I've acquired such a large "Records That Suck On Ice" collection!

Besides that, women still earn 59 cents on the dollar—my perception of the division of labor between the sexes is that women have simply added a 40-hour work week to their old schedule. How many housewives have the time (much less the money) to go out record scouting? Another unrelated aspect is that collecting—the actual shopping—is best done alone. I never begrudge anyone a great score, unless I'm in the store when it happens.

♦ **V: Why do you collect records?**

♦ MR: Because music is my last big mystery. Whenever I'm really fascinated by something, I try to figure it out (and usually can, to my satisfaction) but . . . how can you explain the incredible seductiveness of a certain song? It's not just a matter of "that particular chord progression causes a salivary response in females between ages 22-43"—it's an entirely personal phenomenon. For example, I love hearing people laugh while they're singing. RIC CARTY's "Mellow Down Easy" is a very sexy song to begin with, but when he throws in a cool giggle, it really *sends* me! What would Freud say about that?

Records and books are about the only things I care about possessing. If I could spend the rest of my life just collecting, listening and reading—that would be heaven.

♦ **V: What kind of records do you collect?**

♦ MR: Mostly old rock'n'roll (rockabilly, instrumental surf, boogie woogie) and anything that looks *twisted.* I

Photo: Mary Ricci

especially try to find music by women. I like old time women's blues, especially the raunchy sex songs: "If I can't sell it I'll keep sittin' on it, before I give it away/ You've got to buy it—don't care how much you want it, I mean just what I say/Just feel that nice soft bottom, built for wear and tear/I really hate to part with such a lovely chair."

I love risque themes or double entendres in popular music. A song that goes "she just wants to dance and dance and I can't keep up" is pretty obvious. Animal metaphors (cats, dogs, fish) usually refer to females— whenever I see something with an animal reference in the title I grab it, especially if it's on 78. Another recurring subject is "Little Boy Blue" and "Little Bo Peep." Maybe it's a coincidence, but every version I've heard has been a real rocker.

I look for "uptight" stuff, too. I just scored a BAR-BIE (as in Barbie doll) single that was put out in 1961. She and KEN do a duet called "Nobody Taught Me" (how to fall in love). Well, maybe they didn't think it was necessary, seeing as you two don't have sex organs! The flip side has Barbie singing "Ken," which actually contains the line "I've got a yen/for Ken"— awful rhyme. The label is really cool—it has full color cartoon drawings of Barbie and Ken.

I'm always on the lookout for songs that are really about sex, even though the lyrics state otherwise— BENNY JOY doing "Money Money" immediately comes to mind. This song is basically an instrumental,

the only lyrics are "Money Money" which he says three or four times. I know that sounds innocent enough, but I still wouldn't play it for my parents!

There are at least seven albums in the *Hot Boppin' Girls* series of '50s female rock'n'roll. They contain essential, impossible-to-find songs—long live compilation LPs! I picked Volume Five for LINDA AND THE EPICS' "Gonna Be Loved" (a single I'd mortgage my

Music is my last big mystery . . . how can you explain the incredible seductiveness of a certain song?

house for) and was really wowed by other songs. One of my faves is NONA RAE doing "Real Kool Kitty"— she actually purrs! Her voice is kinda off-key and annoying, perfect for this song: "I'm a real kool kitty, do you want to hear me purr?" (hilarious purr sounds here) "I'll scratch you like a tiger if you try to rub my fur." The bad thing about this series is the lack of liner notes—I *love* liner notes!

Volume One contains BUNNY PAUL's "Sweet Talk," which is all she really wants from her lover. The best part is at the end; she fades into echo and moans: "Ooooh, give me some sweet talk/Ooooh, Elllllvis/Talk

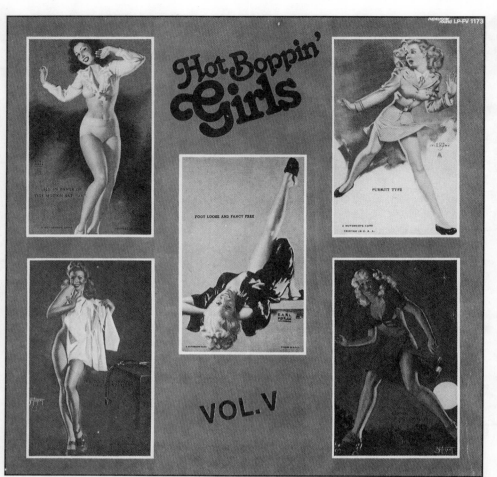

Hot Boppin' Girls Vol. V, Supersonic Sound Records.

that scratchy sound). Taped inside was her autographed business card from "Spivy's Roof," her popular nightclub for urbane New Yorkers in the '40s. Spivy would play and sing at one piano, and have another (probably more talented) pianist at another—I heard this was one of Liberace's first gigs. She was a stocky, no-nonsense lesbian with an imposing demeanor—you know how people are intimidated by strong women. Her voice was low and husky, and she didn't really sing so much as talk. She could twist a verse around better than anyone I've heard, and her lyrics were funny (some written by leading songwriters of the day). A good number is "Alley Cat."

My favorite SPIVY song is "I Love Town," which was her answer to a man who tried to persuade her to live on a farm: "I love town/[where] you see fair hair of purest peroxide/And you breathe fresh air of carbon monoxide/I hate farms, where the food is freshest and the light the crudest/Give me nightclub life though it seems the lewdest/But a gal gets paid for going nudist." Then she continues, "I can't sleep in lonely country rooms; I rush and buy a ticket/Yet I snore through the traffic smooth without a goddamn cricket/I love town." I found this in a thrift store for six bucks, and even though it's worth a lot of money, it's worth more to me on my shelf.

Collecting 78s is great—I bought my 78 player for $10 at a thrift store, and records usually cost between 25 cents and $2. It doesn't take long to figure out what's going to *rock,* and you can give your "mistakes" to older relatives as thoughtful novelty gifts. So you can't lose! 78s could be the last frontier for cheap collecting.

Another great 78 find is ROSE MURPHY—she's billed as "The Chee-Chee Girl." On "Busy Line" she sings about calling her boyfriend and getting a busy tone, which she pronounces "brrr brrr brrr brrr busy line." Her boyfriend's *busy* all right, making time with some other woman—a common theme. She's got a high voice which is not quite as suggestive as BETTY

to me." She also does "History": "Behind every great man stands a great woman," but with a funny sexual slant: "Buffalo Bill was a hero brave/But he had a woman made him her slave/Oh yeah, that sure is right/Honey love me, we'll make *history* tonight."

I like records that would never be released today because of contemporary "moral" attitudes. I picked up a reissue of HARTMAN'S HEARTBREAKERS, recorded in the late '30s, featuring BETTY LOU who sounds like a 10-year-old girl. Every song has sexually suggestive lyrics like: "Daddy, don't be so mean/Look up on the shelf and get the Vaseline." I'm sure it was meant to be funny, but there's something pretty scary about it, too.

One of the worst songs I've ever heard is VAUGHN HORTON's "Chick Inspector." It's a trucker song about a guy who spends most of his time "prowling the interstate, checking up on trucker bait"—basically, looking over the waitresses at truck stops to ensure top quality. One verse goes, "I go for curvy chicks built like a ton of bricks/What good's a brain with no foundation?" Somebody should do a female spoof of this—maybe call it "Dick Inspector."

Lately I've lucked out finding great 78s; my best score to date is a 3-record set by SPIVY, "Seven Gay Sophisticated Songs." It's mint (not that I care; I love

LOU's. On "Girls Were Made to Take Care of Boys," she gives both sides of the argument as to who's more devoted and loyal in relationships—males or females. In the end she wisely settles on the gals.

One of my favorite 78s is "Hey, Zeke! (Your Country's Calling!)" by The FOUR KING SISTERS. It's a WWII call to arms: "Hey, Zeke! Your country's callin'/ Can't you see the way the whole world's been brawlin'?" This record is a great piece of history, exhorting country boys to get off the farm and into battle: "You bet by cracky the boys in khaki will drive 'em wacky down in Nagasaki." There are some nice guitar licks on it—I always feel so lucky when I find something like that!

You can find the roots of rock'n'roll on 78s. One of my all-time favorites is LOUIS JORDAN's cover of "Caldonia." I defy anyone to come up with a more satisfying moment in rock'n'roll than the chorus "Caldonia, Caldonia, what makes your big head so hot?" Drums and vocals were never better together. Talk about uncontrollable urges—I go off my nut when I hear that. And that's a pretty easy record to find. I also recently picked up BILL HALEY & HALEY'S COMETS' "Crazy Man, Crazy" b/w "Whatcha Gonna Do." It's a 78 and I love it.

One of my favorite LPs is the ROBERT MITCHUM *Calypso Is Like So . . .* The color cover is priceless and the songs are hilarious. Now I love Robert Mitchum—*Night of the Hunter* is a favorite film, and at 25 he was the sexiest man that ever lived; perfection itself. I just don't think that calypso singing was his forte. My favorite song is "Mama Looka Boo Boo," about a guy so ugly his kids make fun of him: "I wonder why nobody don't like me/Oh is it the fact that I'm ugly?/ Their mother told them, 'Shut up your mouth; that is your daddy!'/Oh no! My daddy can't be ugly." His hot-

Robert Mitchum's *Calypso Is Like So . . .*, Capitol Records.

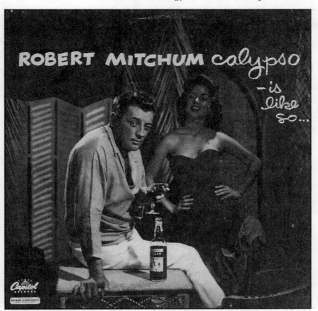

rod tune, "Thunder Road" (recorded to publicize the fabulous movie?) is truly great; it's on the *Shut Down* hot rod compilation LP which also has GARY USHER productions on it. I wish Robert Mitchum had recorded more hot rod songs. Gary Usher is responsible for the great *Go Sounds of the Slots* LP by the Revells. Anyway, I don't listen to the calypso record very often, but I do gaze longingly at the cover every day.

I just scored a BARBIE single. She and KEN do a duet called "Nobody Taught Me" (how to fall in love). Well, maybe they didn't think it was necessary, seeing as you two don't have sex organs!

I'm fascinated by religion (precipitated by 12 long years of penance in Catholic schools) and have an unnaturally large collection of singing nun and religious oddity records. I have never purchased one myself, but for some reason my friends think them crucial to my existence, and buy them for me! One of the nicer ones is *Melody* from The Immaculate Heart of Mary High School in Westchester, Illinois. Side one is by the 21-nun chorale ("Scarlet Ribbons" is the most promising title, but they're all unlistenable) and side two is by a girls' chorale—five lucky students! They get to sing hep "young person" songs like "Chim Chim Cheree," "Winter Wonderland," and the truly moving "Yum Ticky Tum."

I've also got a lovely *Soeur Sourire—The Singing Nun* record which comes with a booklet telling the heartwarming story of a young girl going off to the convent with a guitar under her arm and a song for Christ in her heart. The cover has a drawing of her playing while a group of teenage girls looks on—I swear one of them is gazing at her with intense lust. Another good religious record is *The Rugged Cross,* one of the sickest things I've ever seen. It's a full LP of religious songs as only the great WAYNE NEWTON could interpret them. The most reprehensible album of all is *God Isn't Dead* by GERTRUDE BEHANNA—it's a pre-Betty Ford look into the personal downfall of a poor little rich girl. Gertrude was advised to seek psychiatric help for her drug and alcohol problems, but instead turned to the "Great Physician" for help. The cover features a drawing of a hypodermic needle. I must admit that I would have actually bought this record myself—I might have gone as high as 50 cents. I used to keep a few of these holy gems on display, but then they started to give me the willies . . . especially this JIM & TAMMY BAKKER one—yuk!

I bought a few records for their covers and was pleasantly surprised by the music, such as this gor-

Boogie Blues, Women's Heritage Series, © 1983 Rosetta Records. Album cover credits: photos courtesy of Frank Driggs & Molly Major.

geous 78 set called "Hot Piano" by the JOHNNY GUARNIERI TRIO—it's full of swinging tunes. SLAM STEWART, famous for his "singing bass," can be heard on it. It's basically jazz standards, but they're hot indeed.

Another thing I love is getting a good booklet with a set of records. The first one that comes to mind is the SUN collection: *The Rocking Years*. It includes 12 LPs plus a 50-page booklet of bios, interviews, photos and news clippings. Another surprisingly good set was put out by the Country Music Foundation—*Get Hot or Go Home: Vintage RCA Rockabilly '56-'59*, released with a very informative 8-page booklet. Only two LPs are included but they're definitely "desert island" material, such as the three tunes by JANIS MARTIN. Two of them are live cuts that kick the crap out of the studio versions, and all three are essential listening for any gal with brains! There's also a fabulous version of "Now Stop" sung by husky-voiced MARTHA CAR-SON—boy can she swing! In a great moment of studio patter she says, "I'll try my bestest"—then she just rips into the song. There's also great tunes by guys on it, including a whole side by one of rockabilly's main men, JOE CLAY, as well as a whole side by the man who sings closest to my heart (as well as other parts of my anatomy): RIC CARTY. ROY ORBISON sings one of his best, "Almost Eighteen," and JOEY CASTLE does the hilarious "That Ain't Nothin' But Right" (words to live by!): "I like my coffee black and strong/ I like my hot rod big and long/I love my woman both day and night/Now that ain't nothin' but right." Every day I pray to the gods of fair play that a woman will record songs like this.

Another great set I picked up is the ELVIS '50s box—140 songs! It comes with a big booklet and some nice 8x10" glossies. All of my friends have said the

same thing—"More Elvis than you could ever want"— but I'm happy with it.

The ground-breaking "Women's Heritage Series" on Rosetta Records is well worth finding. The compiler, Rosetta Reitz, obviously tried to be as thorough and informative as possible. Next to familiar blues artists like BESSIE SMITH are obscure singers who really knock me out, like Bertha "Chippie" Hill and Martha Copeland. A lot of the songs deal with women being left behind in the South when their men went north to find work. The liner notes not only talk about the artists but their context as well; she even discusses musicians not included. My favorites include "Boogie Blues" and "Sorry But I Can't Take You—Women's Railroad Blues." Blues records provide an incredible history of life in the United States, and I'm glad people are working to preserve them.

Reissues of swinging female musicians seem to be getting easier to find, such as DOLLY COOPER's *Ay La Ba* (Official Records). "Ay La Ba" is her patois pronunciation of "Hey Lover." She does "My Man" with the lyrics: "Now he may be your man, but he comes to see me sometime/Well he comes so often, I'm beginning to think he's mine." Another song begins in a shouting match with her man: "Why you dirty dog you, comin' in late again/Where've you been this time?/ Baby—I just been around the corner/Around where?/ Around there"—*there* being a place he comes back from with lipstick stains. She did straight blues as well as "teen dream" material which I don't like, but it's worth the price of admission for the stuff that swings.

Every day I pray to the gods of fair play that a woman will record songs like Joey Castle's "That Ain't Nothin' But Right."

Another record that jumps is by NELLIE LUTCH-ER. The album is titled *Real Gone Gal!* so I had to get it. I think she was fairly popular in the late '40s through the '50s. She sings in a solid, unique voice and plays the piano—she's really hot. Besides writing a wild instrumental, "Lutcher's Leap," she wrote some rocking vocals including my favorite, "He's a Real Gone Guy": "I met a guy while walking down the street/He looked at me, I looked at him/He took my hand, he held my hand/He's a real gone guy and do I love him? 'Deed I do." Apparently she fell into obscurity when rock'n'roll took over. It's too bad that people don't have more diverse tastes—I think there should be room in everyone's collection for Elvis *and* Nellie Lutcher.

I have a few 78s by MARGARET WHITING, who

recorded with a lot of different bands. My favorite by her is with FREDDIE SLACK: "Ain't That Just Like A Man." It's a bluesy boogie number: "A woman always pays, yeah she's a victim/A man's got fickle ways, you can't predict 'em/There ain't no use debatin', a man's exasperatin'." It goes on to lament the common female quandary—men! I think this was recorded before Freddie Slack began working with ELLA MAE MORSE, one of the finest, most versatile singers of all time—if you see a record by *her,* don't pass it by.

I always feel like I've struck gold when I find good rocking instrumentals by women—I don't know if they're rare or if I've just had bad luck locating them. One of my favorites is "Charmaine" by JULIA LEE & HER BOYFRIENDS which I found on 78. Julia plays piano, JACK MARSHALL plays guitar, and they churn out some great rock'n'roll licks—now I comb the 78 bins searching for anything else by them. I also found a great instrumental by MARY LOU WILLIAMS. She's also on Rosetta Records with MARY LOU WILLIAMS' GIRL STARS, a female band that played great boogie woogie. DOROTHY DONEGAN is another favorite— she plays a hot piano.

Even though most of the records I collect were made more than 25 years ago, I don't think that the future is entirely bleak. There are a few bands making great records now, and it's so swell to be able to see them live. BIG SANDY & The FLYRITE BOYS write great songs, make great records and put on great shows. They've recently added a steel guitar player who has those SPEEDY WEST licks down—he's a lot of fun to watch. They even released a 78!

There's also a groovy female band around now called The TRASHWOMEN: three gals playing good instrumental surf music. One of their tunes, "Nightmare at the

Nellie Lutcher's *My New Papa's Got To Have Everything,* Juke Box Lil Records (a division of Mr. R&B Records). Album cover credits: sleeve design: Lasse Ermalm, cover photo courtesy of Orkester Journalen.

Drag," is in my top ten. They wear faux leopard fur bikinis on stage and are all really beautiful—but not like those awful MTV *anarex-aerobic* fake women. These are real gals playing real instruments having real fun!

REFERENCE:

Various—*Women's Heritage Series:* Rosetta Records compilation series of early American music made by women, from early blues to boogie. Great photos and liner notes.

Jimmy Bryant: *Country Cabin Jazz* (Stetson) and *Guitar Take-Off* (See For Miles Records, Ltd). Both feature Jimmy Bryant and Speedy West doing some of their best stuff.

Benny Joy: *Rock-A-Billy With Benny Joy* (White Label). Why Benny Joy wasn't the world's biggest rock'n'roll star is one of life's greatest mysteries.

Various—Surf: *Diggin' Out* (Mr. Manicotti). Some of the hottest instrumental surf ever recorded with the Avengers VI, Chevells, Phantoms, Goldtones and lots more—every cut is great!

Various—*Bison Bop #30.* I've heard that all of the Bison/Buffalo Bop volumes are worthwhile, and I've yet to listen to one that isn't. This is one of my favorites, with Johnny Reed, Harold Shutters & The Rocats, and Don Ellis & The Royal Dukes—the latter two shared members in common, if not the same lineup. The LP runs the gamut from raw to more polished rockabilly.

Women's Railroad Blues, Women's Heritage Series, © 1980 Rosetta Records. Album cover credits: cover photo courtesy of Duncan Schiedt.

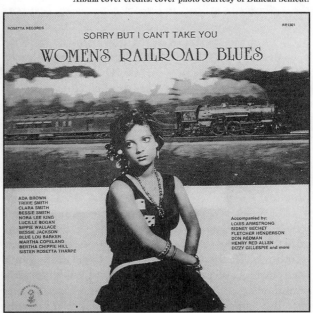

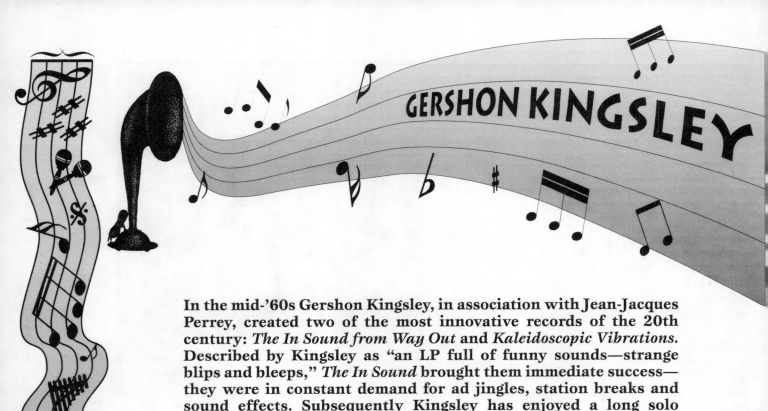

GERSHON KINGSLEY

In the mid-'60s Gershon Kingsley, in association with Jean-Jacques Perrey, created two of the most innovative records of the 20th century: *The In Sound from Way Out* and *Kaleidoscopic Vibrations*. Described by Kingsley as "an LP full of funny sounds—strange blips and bleeps," *The In Sound* brought them immediate success— they were in constant demand for ad jingles, station breaks and sound effects. Subsequently Kingsley has enjoyed a long solo career as composer, arranger and performer—his big hit being "Popcorn." Gershon Kingsley can be contacted c/o 150 West 55th St, NY NY 10019. A CD of *The In Sound from Way Out* plus *Kaleidoscopic Vibrations* is available for $20 ppd. from RE/Search Publications, 20 Romolo #B, San Francisco, CA 94133.

♦ *VALE: As an artist, do you feel you've gone against the grain?*
♦ GERSHON KINGSLEY: Once you get me going on *that* topic—yes, I'm definitely a maverick. Look: there is no easy way of doing something in the arts. People ask me, "Who did you study with?" and I reply, "Mozart and Beethoven." If you study their scores, you find that nobody can teach you how to compose—the "masters" always break their own rules. So I'm always suspicious of fancy super-teaching systems like "Learn to Play Piano in One Day," because you develop your *own* system. Through your own experience you develop how you work, how you write, how you live, how you get up in the morning: do you first go to the toilet, or make breakfast?

I was always interested in sound. In 1947 I went to a psychic who told me that one day I'd produce some "crazy music that everyone would dance to." I didn't take her seriously, but later on somebody else told me the same thing. I became involved in electronic music, and in 1972 I wrote a pop tune which doesn't fit into any particular category, yet it's been the biggest instrumental hit of the past 20 years—
♦ *V: "Popcorn."*
♦ GK: Yes. This classically-oriented electronic pop

tune has since sold millions of records, including 500 cover versions all over the world. People still come up to me and say, "*You* wrote 'Popcorn'?!"

♦ *ANDREA JUNO: So much of what is produced today sounds so derivative—it's easy to pick out the references or the primary sources of inspiration.*
♦ GK: I strongly believe in the power of the individual—creative personalities will always emerge. One of my favorite composers is JOHN ADAMS, who composed *Nixon in China* and *The Death of Klinghoffer.* He takes newspaper ideas and makes operas out of them. I regard myself as a metaphysical or spiritual person; I would love to write a work which would have the same effect on people as the Bach *B Minor Mass,* by using only electronic sounds.

♦ *V: How has your life changed over the past two decades?*
♦ GK: When you create, you try to be as honest and true to yourself as possible—which is, of course, very difficult because you're always influenced by your surroundings. In the '60s I was part of the avant-garde with JOHN CAGE and others. We would give concerts where we would rub stones together and recite poems over the "music." Or I'd give the audience ping-pong

balls to throw against the microphone and then we would modulate the sounds and give them back again. That was only 30 years back, but now it seems like *ages* ago.

In 1947 I went to a psychic who told me that one day I'd produce some "crazy music that everyone would dance to." I didn't take her seriously, but later on somebody else told me the same thing.

It's crazy; for years I have felt very happy living in my cocoon. But now my inner reality seems to be merging with the outside world. Symbolically everybody seems to be moving away from *fat:* greed, materialism, things to hang on to—what George Carlin calls "stuff." And as St. Francis said: "The moment you

own stuff, you're no longer free, because you have to protect it." But the artist usually is less concerned with stuff, because he gives up his creations to other people.

At the same time, everybody is searching for meaning. There are so many different spiritual philosophies (e.g. Buddhism, Krishnamurti) one can learn from. I think ethnic and cultural differences are important, but at the same time it's wonderful that all people can share their philosophies of life. It's almost like a kaleidoscope: if one color is missing, then we don't have a full spectrum to enjoy. Whether it's Judaism or Taoism or Buddhism in religion—

◆ *V: You believe in religion?*
◆ GK: I believe in spirituality. I want to come back in another 100 years; I lived before my time.
◆ *V: What are your thoughts on originality?*
◆ GK: Originality is not such a big thing to me—sometimes I encounter a homeless person on the street who is very original. A more difficult question is: How can you find the essence of your own inner being? Sometimes you don't even know what that is, or you may have once known but then destroyed it.

I was in psychoanalysis for years to become more

"conscious" about myself and to deal with fears; it was very fashionable in the '50s. I'd discover, "Ah, yes! Now I *know* why I do what I'm doing." Then I'd confront a situation and realize I was still making the

The Moog synthesizer fascinated me: this strange contraption that looked like an elephant switchboard and made sounds I'd never heard before.

same mistakes I made in the past; I'd realize that *it didn't work.* I think there is something wrong with our common brainpower; I think our brains are very *decadent.* There's a story about Richard Strauss, who like me loved to talk and speculate about life. When they were at parties, his wife used to say, "Do us a favor, Richard—go back home and compose."

♦ *V: But it's important for artists to be verbally articulate—*

♦ GK: One of my most important software programs is called *Articulation*; it allows you to *accent* the music you write. This is the basic ingredient that makes music *music:* instead of *bup-bup-bup-bup* you can make it *bop-bup-bop-bup.* You need this articulation—the same applies to all human behavior. I keep a journal and am writing fiction about a character I call "G"; for example, "The only thing 'G' wanted to do was write a hit tune, because everybody wants to write a hit tune." Then I describe how he achieves his aim—then undergoes all this tribulation.

♦ *V: How were you affected by the holocaust?*

♦ GK: I'm an indirect holocaust survivor. When I left Germany in 1938 I was fifteen; this was just before *Kristallnacht.* I belonged to a Zionist youth group and we were very motivated to come to pre-Israel to till the land and live in a kibbutz. My mother was Catholic (she later converted to Judaism), my father was Jewish. That's already going against the grain!

In Palestine, I worked hard in the fields as a farmer, but would come home and study music, plus read everything I could get my hands on. Then in 1941 I had to join the British army.

♦ *V: So you had some musical training as a youth?*

♦ GK: Oh yes, but I trained myself. My father was a pianist, but not professionally. He was very talented and could play by ear anything he heard; he had perfect pitch (which I don't have, by the way). I inherited my ability for improvisation from my father, and this is one of the most important parts of my musical personality. It's also the basis of composition: if you cannot improvise, how can you compose?

♦ *V: You went through some formal academic training—what did you study?*

♦ GK: Keyboards, composition, orchestration and conducting. I did all of these things quite well, and this is one of the bad things about me: if I had concentrated on *one* aspect, I probably could have been a better composer (or conductor, or whatever). Instead I turned

Gershon Kingsley's *Popcorn—First Moog Quartet,* © 1972 Audio Fidelity Enterprises, Inc. Album cover credits: cover design: Sheila Benow.

into a jack-of-all-trades. My saving grace is that eclecticism became part of my palette; my music draws from many styles.

♦ *V: How do you compose?*

♦ GK: *I think, therefore I compose!* A psychoanalyst once told me that "We're all swimming in water, but everybody can stand on his own *terra firma.*" I never attempted to imitate anybody; I tried to find my *own* earth.

The older we get, the more we think of our failures and our successes, and about death and life. We ask the impossible question: "What is after life?" All we know is that we have to work toward what Jung calls the reconciliation of our opposites. Man is made of two halves, and when we reconcile the light and the dark sides, the *animus* and the *anima,* we balance our personality. Only when we become conscious of our evil side—when we realize this is part of our own personality—can we control it.

On television, there is so much unconscious expression of hate. All the anger—whether it's in the family, the state or among nations or ethnic groups—is being expressed. And it takes tremendous strength on the part of every individual to keep from falling into that deep emotional morass. Hate is a very powerful emotion, just like its opposite: love. Hate often has more *energy* than love. And never before has hate been more expressed in music than today—just listen to heavy metal. Sometimes I feel very pessimistic . . . but I believe in the power of the individual, and I really think that beauty and love can only be felt and expressed if you know the darker side of yourself.

"Mr Moog, I'm a musician, not a scientist—how can you explain this to a musician?" He replied, "Don't you understand? This is the future!" I was down to my last $3000, and that's what the Moog cost back then—I decided to take the chance.

In the '60s, a lot of people thought that everything that came from the East was *better*—that as long as you knew your chakras you were set. But why not try understanding Hegel or Aristotle along with *haiku*? For the past 30 years I've been studying the works of C.G. Jung—although, as Jung himself used to say, "Thank god I'm not a Jungian!" When I first started reading him I wasn't as mature as I am now. The problem with wisdom is: it's wasted on the wrong age!

♦ *V: Earlier, you downplayed originality—but aren't you striving to do original work?*

♦ GK: I was *always* striving for originality. But I also made enemies because I was outspoken about every-

Gershon Kingsley's *Music to Moog By*, Audio Fidelity Records. Album cover credits: cover design: Sheila Benow.

thing. If I see something unjust, it drives me up the wall. And my music has always been honest music. If only five people around me enjoy it, then I'm happy. I cannot pretend, I don't want to impress anyone. Sometimes you come to this realization late—maybe when I was younger I wanted to impress people. If you want to really become a true individual artist, then you might have to do like Philip Glass did—for years he drove a cab. His music is very controversial and you either hate it or you love it. But still it has a personality—

♦ *V: It's instantly recognizable. Can you summarize how your musical career developed—*

♦ GK: As I said, I grew up in Germany, but because I was Jewish I had to leave and move to Israel. I was an autodidact—I taught myself to read scores and played in some bands. We would listen to the BBC (on shortwave radio) and imitate the music of Benny Goodman, Glenn Miller and Teddy Wilson. In 1946 I came to America intending to go to Juilliard, but they wouldn't accept me because I hadn't attended high school. I moved to California where my brother was living and answered an ad: a violinist was looking for an accompanist. At the same time I went to night school, finished high school, and then went to the L.A. Conservatory (now Cal Arts) where I graduated.

If you want to survive as a composer you have three choices: 1) get tenure in a university and work in academia, 2) work in the commercial world of movies, television, commercials, etc, or 3) marry a rich woman . . . *Me*—I married out of love! [laughs] But I always tell my students, "Don't follow in my footsteps." When I was young I was a *musical whore*. I did *everything* to survive: played for children's dance classes, gave lessons, etc. Then I worked in the theater; I conducted many Broadway shows and worked with one of the

most successful producers, David Merrick. I was the first music director for a show called "The Entertainer" with Laurence Olivier in 1958.

The Moog synthesizer fascinated me: this strange contraption that looked like an elephant switchboard and made sounds I'd never heard before. I began learning about things like oscillation and frequency modulation and finally decided to meet Mr Moog himself. I went to the Catskill Mountains and there he was, sitting in a basement with a few technicians working away. I have tapes of him trying to explain his theory

I did a few programs with John Cage. In one "happening" he recited something by Buckminster Fuller while Merce Cunningham danced and I improvised on the Moog. The word "avant-garde" has "derriere-garde" built into it. These performances were too intellectual for me.

to me. I remember saying, "Mr Moog, I'm a musician, not a scientist—how can you explain this to a musician?" He replied, "Don't you understand? This is the future!" I was down to my last $3000, and that's what the Moog cost back then—I decided to take the chance. In a few weeks I'd earned my money back doing my first Moog commercial. Then I met a lawyer, Herb Wasserman, and he asked, "What would happen if you put four Moogs together? What would you call it?" I said, "The First Moog Quartet." He said, "Let me talk

to Sol Hurok."

I got a call from the office of Mr Hurok: "We'd like to visit your studio." (At the time I had the only Moog-equipped studio; later on everybody copied me.) When Sol Hurok appeared, he *looked* like an impresario: white hair, silver-handled cane, big white flower in his lapel, a uniformed chauffeur. This was the man who had launched the careers of Heifetz, Horowitz, and Rubenstein. He simply said, "Play me something." Of course, I tried to impress him with all my weird new sounds, but he wanted to hear a melody: "Can you play 'My Yiddish Mama'?" I had a "whistling" sound programmed and I used it to play the tune for him. Almost immediately he asked, "Do you have a phone?" He called his secretary and asked, "What opening nights do we have at the end of '69?" Then he said to me, "You have a concert at Carnegie Hall on January 30, 1970. We'll let you know the details."

Now first of all, I didn't *have* four synthesizers, so I called up Bob Moog and asked, "Can you build me four more Moogs?" But he needed money to build them, so Herb Wasserman (a very smart man) went to Audio Fidelity Records with a proposal: "I'll offer you the recording rights to this concert at Carnegie Hall if you give us an advance of $25,000." With this money I bought the Moog synthesizers, and auditioned about 150 young musicians, mostly from Juilliard. I needed people who could play jazz as well as classical, and who could improvise with dexterity. It took a week to audition 150 people; then I was down to four.

First, I taught them the Moog. Second, I needed a repertoire—I didn't have a program yet; what would we play? So I composed the first piece, which was titled (appropriately) "In the Beginning." It started out with white noise and little random cricket noises, like the beginning of the world.

A week before the concert, nobody had bought any tickets. But Hurok said, "Don't worry." Three days before the concert, NBC and CBS talked about it . . . and it was sold out! By the way, this was an early multimedia event. We brought in a huge screen and projected movies (like rock groups do today), and we brought in dancers. Everybody came—the magazines, all the press, and it was so controversial. People in the audience went up to Hurok and said, "How can you present a piece of shit like that?!"

The next day the reviews came out. Some were horrible—the *Times* murdered me. One writer for the West Coast equivalent of *New York* magazine wrote an incendiary review saying that I was a fake; I had no right to call this music! But about a week later, I got a call from Arthur Fiedler of the Boston Pops Orchestra, saying, "I heard about your concert. Do you have a piece for four Moogs and symphony orchestra?" I said, "No, but I can write one. When do you want to do a concert?" "In four weeks." So I got together two orchestrators and in two weeks I completed a 30-minute work, the *Concerto for Moog,* which was performed on TV and became a hit.

Then under Sol Hurok we began touring and playing colleges, universities, and concert halls with major symphony orchestras. I wrote more avant-garde music. Years later in Kyoto, Japan, I performed "Popcorn" in different styles (Japanese, Hungarian, etc) with a Japanese student orchestra—they were marvelous. That one tune sent my daughter to university and paid a lot of bills.

♦ *V: You can't just sit down and write a hit, consciously—*

♦ GK: No! But record companies are greedy; they want you to do it again. After "Popcorn," I recorded "Cracker-Jacks," "Sauerkraut"—all these stupid titles about food. "Sauerkraut" was a minor hit in Germany. "Cold Duck" featured a girl singer recorded very slowly and then speeded up; it became a small hit in France. But nothing ever hit again like "Popcorn."

Then I became very busy doing work for television and movies; it seemed like I was vomiting music out from morning to night! [laughs] I've been waiting all my life to do something for the theater. Now I've written both a Broadway show and an opera about

Christopher Columbus; the opera was just performed in Germany. All my music is visual and theatrical, even my religious music—you can *stage* it . . .

♦ *AJ: Can you tell us more about your involvement with early performance art?*

♦ GK: I was only on the periphery, but I did a few programs with JOHN CAGE. In one "happening" he recited something by Buckminster Fuller while Merce Cunningham danced and I improvised on the Moog. But I think I was always aware that the word "avant-garde" has "derriere-garde" built into it. These performances were too intellectual for me—despite all my craziness, I'm pretty "down to earth."

The In Sound from Way Out was both fun and painful, because each piece took a solid week of tape splices to prepare. What we did preceded sampling; we recorded the sounds and spliced them together. Nowadays you just record the sound and digitize it.

♦ *V: Let's talk specifically about* **The In Sound from Way Out.** *How did you meet Jean-Jacques Perrey?*

♦ GK: In 1964 someone told me about "a stout Frenchman who has a very strange sound." Perrey invited me to his studio where he demonstrated his "Ondioline" for me. Years ago when you went to a piano bar, the pianist would often have a little organ-like keyboard—he would play a melody with the right hand and piano accompaniment with the left. The Ondioline was better—its inventor in France had figured out how to produce tones that sounded more like a *real* violin, a real trumpet, a real trombone, etc. I had an idea; I said, "Look. You talk with a nice French accent; why don't you work up an act playing the Ondioline?" And he began to make a living with it.

Later Perrey invited me to his studio, and showed me a reel of tape with all these splices on it. I asked, "What is it?" and he said, "Listen." On the tape I heard *boom-chuck-a oom-chuck squeal oo-chuk*—it made me laugh. Then he explained, "I took a sound, recorded it and spliced it together according to measurement—an eighth note might take exactly one inch of tape." At the time I was a staff arranger for Vanguard Records and I asked Seymour Solomon, the company president, "Would you be interested?" He said yes, so we made a demo tape and he loved it. Then we went up to his studio and recorded an album on a 3-track Ampex. We began our collaboration at a time when ad agencies were looking for new sounds to use in advertising;

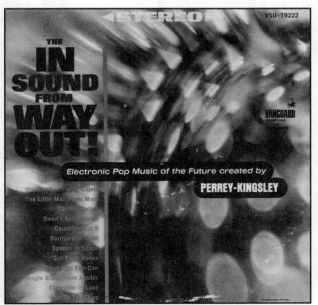

Perrey & Kingsley's *The In Sound from Way Out,* Vanguard. Album cover credits: cover design: Jules Halfant.

consequently almost every track we recorded was sold as a commercial—we made a fortune. "Baroque Hoedown" is still used as a theme at Disneyland. After recording a second album, *Kaleidoscopic Vibrations: Spotlight on the Moog*, we split up.

A lot of people wonder why horror movies are popular. Well, it's because we *like* to be afraid! Even though man has rationalized away "god" and most superstition, they re-enter through the back door in the form of horror movies . . . that emotional dimension which sometimes separates life from death.

♦ *V: What's amazing is the humor—how can humor embody itself in sound?*

♦ GK: I was always interested in the relationship between sound and humor. First of all, our greatest composers have written humoristic music. Bach wrote the "Coffee Cantata," Haydn wrote the "Surprise Symphony," Mozart wrote for the glass harmonica. You cannot be a great artist without humor being part of your personality. You have to have a certain distance from yourself, and humor can provide that.

♦ *V: You must have had fun making* **The In Sound from Way Out**—

♦ GK: It was both fun and painful, because each piece took a solid week of tape splices to prepare. What we did preceded sampling; we recorded the sounds and spliced them together. Nowadays you just record the sound and digitize it. Now I can generate sounds on my *Kurzweil* and compose with my computer.

♦ *V: Why did you call your album* **The In Sound from Way Out**? *Did you feel you were in tune with the '60s, after the horrible '50s McCarthy era*—

♦ GK: Someone else named it. And to me, every era is horrible and good at the same time. In the '60s-'70s I had a house in Woodstock and of course was aware of the whole youth movement then. I was never a hippie, but I had friends who were hippies; I never took drugs, but I had friends who took drugs.

Besides *The In Sound from Way Out,* I made another musical innovation: in 1969 I wrote the first rock service for a synagogue, "Shabbat For Today," which has been performed all over the world.

♦ *AJ: You've blended the worlds of classical and pop music*—

♦ GK: To me pop is an aspect of the whole, larger culture. On the radio you can hear pieces by Stock-

hausen next to Pink Floyd and they can sound not dissimilar. Electronic music bridges those worlds and makes the question, "Are you a serious composer or a pop composer?" harder to answer. What's the difference? In a negative sense, you could say that pop music is trying to appeal to the lower aspirations of the masses, like the fantasy of instant success. You see that in film, you see that in television soap operas. But there are a lot of different, smaller markets opening up, whether it's New Age, or Minimalistic music, or whatever you call it. All so-called mass market ideas are slowly getting dissolved; as a market becomes more global, you find regional groups starting their own variants. For example, in San Francisco there are at least 3 or 4 little companies bringing out New Age music, which is a category that didn't even exist 10 years ago.

♦ *V: How do you deal with criticism of your work?*

♦ GK: If you want to survive you have to develop *elephant skin.* You have to trust in your own ideas. When I performed with the Chicago Symphony, one of the reviewers said I should go up to a tall building and jump off! For an artist, the *act of creation* is what matters. When I'm finished with a work, it's not so important anymore—the *doing* is the best part. And I don't want to become involved with business—I *write* and that's all. I may only have another 10 or 20 years left, so I want to use my energy to just work. I'm still in good health and can work 12 to 14 hours a day.

♦ *V: How do you handle periods of discouragement?*

♦ GK: I look at each moment to experience and know that it can all change in the next moment—still I go on. When I compose, I go with a theme for hours or weeks and suddenly—bingo; it's like *Zen and the Art of Archery*—you've hit the target without even trying. The moment you become too conscious of "it"—you lose it. And I think that my most important work is not done yet.

♦ *V: That's a good way to feel.*

♦ GK: The '90s are going to be awful—terrible. Yet to me, *hope* is the essence of living—if you give a homeless person a quarter, then he has hope, if only for the moment. I'm a survivor; I pick myself up. It has something to do with self-respect; if you don't have respect for yourself, how can you respect other people? Respect your own personality (including its dark side), and know that even if man destroys the earth, the universe will keep going—the universe is more than the earth. When you go out into nature and examine how a plant or butterfly works—well, this didn't just happen by *coincidence.* And all creation involves destruction; it comes out of destruction and chaos.

♦ *V: People are brought up to not contemplate their dark side; to pretend they only have a light side*—

♦ GK: There are many times when you feel like killing someone, or you hear voices saying strange things. In order to work, you must distance yourself from this.

By projecting the dark side onto something external, like another person, people have tried to pretend this is not a part of their personality. This reminds me: recently some old prayer benches in a medieval church in Italy were undergoing restoration. When they opened them up, they discovered some very pornographic wooden sculptures inside! The past 40 years have shown that many of the pillars of our puritanical society who go to church on Sunday also have a dark side—what they do in their private life is being exposed. My wife and I have a certain understanding; when we have a fight, we say (to the dark side that flares up between us), "We accept you."

♦ V: *When you argue, do you conceptualize a "dark" entity that embodies both of you?*

♦ GK: Yes. And I feel that the most interesting things in life are caused by their opposites. New York has such great energy because there is so much evil and darkness in the city. The energy comes out of that dark chasm. Sometimes when an idea comes I think, "Oh-

The pause or silence has largely disappeared from music because silence has largely disappeared from our *lives*—and I'm trying to put it back in!

migod, I think I'm going crazy." It's interesting how close creativity is to insanity. Many modern psychiatrists let the "insane" express themselves through drawings and paintings . . . so that through intuitive means the creative imagination can be released.

Perrey & Kingsley's *Kaleidoscopic Vibrations*, Vanguard. Album cover credits: cover design: Fred Holtz, photo: Frances Laping.

I've made friends with my dark side; it doesn't haunt me anymore. In 1951 I returned to Germany thinking I'd forgotten about Hitler and about what had happened with Nazism. But I'd be waiting in line or something and find myself getting really angry—I didn't understand why. This got worse and worse. Finally I went to an analyst and we discussed this strange dream I was having.

In the dream, I was sitting in a chair surrounded by a circle of people who were all looking right through me, as though I didn't exist. I wanted to get their attention, but couldn't. Suddenly out of the air came a pointing hand that came down and went right through me and out the other side. I got goosebumps; I began to say these Hebrew words which people say when they fear that they're about to die. Then I would wake up in a cold sweat.

After months, finally I understood that this dream had to do with the fact that I'd always negated my background. Always I had said to the Germans, "I'm half-Jewish; my father was a Polish Jew but my mother was a *real* German Catholic" (before she converted to Judaism). After psychoanalysis, I could look people in the eye and say, "Look, I'm Jewish—so what? I have a Christian mother but I was raised Jewish." I had ac-

Inside cover of Gershon Kingsley's *First Moog Quartet,* Audio Fidelity Records. Album cover credits: designer: Heidi Auer, photo: Johann May.

cepted my heritage. You see: what Hitler had achieved was to make many Jews *ashamed* of being Jews.

Sometimes when I walk on the street I have this strange feeling of being in the eye of the hurricane—a place where everything's very peaceful, yet on the street there's all this insanity going on—the cars, the bicycles, the people all rushing by. And I feel, "I am my own eye of the hurricane."

♦ *V: Do you watch TV?*

♦ GK: Yes, I can watch TV without being brainwashed by it. In fact I very often find myself amused by what I see. When you become more aware of your true self, you don't have to be afraid it's going to brainwash you. I follow the ingenuity and the technology in the commercials—some are very clever and humorous. I love to watch old movies. But I don't have that much time to watch *anything*—if you're an artist, the most important thing is *doing.* I keep clippings for my kids of all the press I've received, but I don't look at them. A friend of mine (I won't mention his name) who was once an artist and who retired has now become his own audience and his own critic, but that's very bad. My rule is: Don't look back.

♦ *V: You worked in film—*

♦ GK: I did the score for *Silent Night, Bloody Night*—remember that? It was also called *Deathhouse.* Then I scored a softcore porn movie, *Sugar Cookies.* I did a film on drugs which won an award at the Venice Film Festival, plus a movie called *The Dreamer* which was Israel's entry in the Cannes Film Festival. There were a few more whose names I've forgotten. Those were the days when I was still trying to pay for my studio.

A lot of people wonder why horror movies are popular. Well, it's because we *like* to be afraid! Even though man has rationalized away "god" and most superstition, they re-enter through the back door in the form of horror movies. Man seems to enjoy renewing his sense of fear . . . that emotional dimension which sometimes separates life from death.

♦ *V: By the way—was learning computers easy?*

♦ GK: There are big problems working with computers. It took me a long time to learn computer technology, and you have to constantly upgrade. I think back to when we were making *The In Sound from Way Out*—we had to be *crazy* to sit down and make those tiny tape loops. We would take sounds and splice them together *manually,* with scissors. Then we would add a rhythm underneath and a melody on top—it would take a solid week just to do one number. Today you can do this so much more quickly with a computer (but the sounds we produced are still original just *because* no one today would have the patience to do manual splices day and night). Recently someone referred to me as "the grandaddy of electronic music"—now I've become a collector's item!

In 1975 Stuart Kranz wrote *Science, Technology and the Arts,* which profiled all these unusual artists and visionaries like John Cage, Dennis Gabor (father of holography), Stan VanDerBeek (multimedia artist), and Dr Jan LaRue (computer musicologist who did musical scores). It's a fascinating book in that it shows how much technology has changed. Now it seems back in the Neanderthal Age, yet it was only 20 years ago.

♦ *V: How did you write your biggest hit, "Popcorn"?*

♦ GK: Well, it only took me about two minutes to invent the whole song, but I could never do that again! It's a *mystery* how people write hits—especially instrumentals. Look at the song, "Winchester Cathedral"—whatever happened to that group? Nobody knows. Most people only write one or two hits during their lifetime.

Dissonance is a very philosophical concept—one man's dissonance may be another man's consonance! Today if you go to a heavy-metal or hard rock concert, you hear sounds like guns going off, sounds of violence. Guitars have become dangerous weapons!

The topic of "inspiration" reminds me of James Burke's book, *Connections.* Everything has a connection. Mozart could not have been Mozart without Bach; Beethoven leaned on Mozart, and the evolution of electronic music is based upon the evolution of instruments in general. One of the original electronic instruments is the organ; it's the predecessor of the synthesizer. And evolution is ongoing. Right now I use a Macintosh computer, eliminating the need for carrying around instrument modules; everything's getting smaller and more refined. And who knows about five years from now?

I don't like to use the word "machines" because then we'd have to call the piano a machine, the flute a machine— they're *all* machines.

What did Beethoven hear when he wrote his "Pastoral" Symphony? Hoofbeats, insects, birds, folk dances, thunderstorms. *Now* look at what composers put into movie scores or television soundtracks or commercials. Electronic sounds and noise are part of our society; artists always reflect the changes in their environment. The evolution of sound will continue—

♦ **V: In general, people's tolerance for dissonance continually increases—**

♦ GK: Dissonance is a very philosophical concept— one man's dissonance may be another man's consonance! Today if you go to a heavy-metal or hard rock concert, you hear sounds like guns going off, sounds of violence. Guitars have become dangerous weapons!

The pause or silence has largely disappeared from music because silence has largely disappeared from our *lives*—and I'm trying to put it back in! I have to react the way I feel inside. I'm not Philip Glass, I'm Gershon Kingsley, and whatever I do (whether it's in a pop vein or in a more serious vein) can only express the way *I* feel. I have 25 minutes on *Cruisers 1.0,* a "New Age" CD from the Hearts of Space label, and some people think it's boring and awful while others meditate to it and feel wonderful.

♦ **V: Do you consider yourself avant-garde?**

♦ GK: Well, I don't support the obvious or the commercial . . . I guess that makes me a bit avant-garde. The avant-garde was always about shocking the bourgeoisie. Well, one thing about getting older and living a long time: nothing can shock me anymore. Even moral infractions and injustices no longer shock me, because I *expect* them.

♦ **AJ: In your music were you trying to integrate spirituality with machines?**

♦ GK: First of all, I don't like to use the word "machines" because then we'd have to call the piano a machine, the flute a machine—they're *all* machines. The "purest" instrument probably is the voice; the moment you use strings you're creating a machine. What's important is: if you use a clarinet, you use your own personality to create a sound or tone by the way you blow into it. The problem with new synthesizers today is: even though they're touch-sensitive, a lot of the sounds sound alike.

It's so easy today to produce *notes*—anybody can become a synthesist instantly with one of these instruments that can even be programmed to compose. But composers are now sampling their *own* sounds, a truly new development in creating *new* sounds to express your own personality. The future of electronic instruments will be to use the modern technology so that the musician can play an instrument like the violin, but also create different sounds with it. PENDERECKI in Poland combines electronic sounds with live "traditional" instruments or voices. In the end it's your own personality that determines how successful you are at creating your *own* musical sound . . . and whether people like it.

When I die, maybe I'll have an electronic tombstone with a television monitor so that people visiting my grave can push a button and my face comes on the screen: "*Hello*—nice of you to come! What would you like to hear—*Popcorn?*" If it's solar-powered, maybe it could last for eternity.

DISCOGRAPHY

AS COMPOSER:
First Moog Quartet (Audio Fidelity)
Music to Moog By (Audio Fidelity)
The In Sound from Way Out (Vanguard)
Kaleidoscopic Vibrations: Spotlight on the Moog (Vanguard)
The Best of Perrey & Kingsley (Vanguard)
Popcorn Machine (CBS Records, Germany)
Popcorn (Audio Fidelity)
Anima (KS Records)
Tierra (opera, Bavarian Radio)
Cristobal Colon (musical, KS Records)
Shabbat for Today (Prime Time Records)
The 5th Cup (KS Records)
Cruisers 1.0 (Hearts of Space; 4 compositions)

AS ARRANGER & CONDUCTOR:
Three albums for Jan Peerce (Vanguard)
Two albums for Julia Migenes (Ariola)
Mozart After Hours (Vanguard)
Fleury, Greek songs (Vanguard)
Shoshana Damari, Israeli (Vanguard)
Songs of the Auvergne (Vanguard)
Ernest in Love
Fly Blackbird (Mercury)

Electronic music pioneers Jean-Jacques Perrey and Gershon Kingsley created two of the most original LPs of the '60s, *The In Sound from Way Out* and *Kaleidoscopic Vibrations: Spotlight on the Moog* (both re-released on one CD titled *The Best of Perrey and Kingsley* $20 ppd. from RE/Search Publications, 20 Romolo #B, San Francisco, CA 94133). Using only tape recorders, scissors and splicing tape they literally pieced together a humoristic vision of the future which has not dated. Since then Perrey has produced numerous solo albums, soundtracks, commercials and "therapeutic sounds for insomniacs." Jean-Jacques Perrey still composes music, and is looking for a record company. He can be contacted at B.P. 2744, 03207 Vichy CEDEX, France. (Translation by Caroline Hébert.)

WHEN I TURNED 30, MY LIFE BECAME A TRUE FAIRY TALE . . .

When I recall the *movie* of my life, I realize that when I turned 30 my life became a true fairy tale. And in this tale the name of my fairy godmother was Edith Piaf, the great lady of French singing. The magicians were Charles Trenet and Jean Cocteau; the wizard Merlin was Walt Disney, and my magic coach was the cruise liner *S.S. FRANCE* . . .

I was born January 20, 1929 in a little village in the north of France. On Christmas Eve 1933, Santa Claus brought me an accordion and I became possessed by a "little demon of music." At an early age I had a great thirst for learning and knowledge. During school and later at university I had the good fortune to have exceptional teachers who awakened in me the urge to research and the drive to create. I began reading science fiction and devoured everything I could find by Isaac Asimov, H.P. Lovecraft, Aldous Huxley, A.E. Van Vogt, and especially Arthur C. Clarke and Ray Bradbury, both of whom I later met in the United States.

In 1939 World War II broke out. When the liberation finally happened in 1944, like all French people I felt a profound gratitude toward the Americans who had freed us from the Nazi Occupation—I could not

know that 15 years later the Americans would play a key role in my professional career. After graduating from the Lycée d'Amiens (Somme), I attended medical school in Paris for four years. Even though I aspired to devote myself to scientific research, the little demon of music kept needling me.

In 1952, while attending medical school, I met a genial inventor, one of the French pioneers of electronic music, Georges Jenny. He had invented the "Ondioline," which may be considered an ancestor of the modern synthesizer. I already knew Maurice Martenot, the inventor of the Ondes Martenot, which could produce only very limited sounds. I preferred the Ondioline, which on its small keyboard allowed one to produce new and original sounds as well as sounds from existing instruments such as the violin or flute. I was fascinated by the Ondioline and felt it had a great future.

At this point I did not know a lot about music—and still don't, never having studied music seriously except for a 2-month stay at the Conservatory at Amiens where I was kicked out because of a rule forbidding students to perform in public. I was playing accordion at small local events and the director gave me an ultimatum: cease these performances, or leave the conservatory. I knew that performing in public was very important for me—already I had a taste for the stage, so . . .

The little demon convinced me to quit medical school in 1953. I decided I would become not a doctor but rather a musician and composer . . . a *creator*. Within a few months I learned (on my own, without a teacher or sheet music) to play the piano by ear. I managed to get hired by Georges Jenny, who was looking for someone to demonstrate his invention. As a sales representative for the Ondioline, I began traveling a lot—first in France, then abroad to international music fairs. In a few years I became acquainted with all the great cities of Europe.

Then my little demon whispered in my ear: "You have proved yourself to be gifted in music and to have imagination, but you must develop this talent further. You must get yourself noticed. You haven't achieved enough!"

Once more I took its advice. To supplement my salary as sales representative, I began a new type of cabaret act using the Ondioline and the piano. In Paris I had a true success with "Around the World in 80 Ways." I started out as opening attraction at theaters, but since I spoke English I went on to bigger European stages in Germany, Sweden, Switzerland, England, etc. Thus began an international career . . .

In 1956 in Paris, I had the good fortune of meeting the great singer/composer Charles Trenet, who was very impressed by the magical new sounds of the Ondioline. He suggested I accompany him onstage. I recorded some records with him, including one song which became an international hit, "The Soul of the Poets" ("L'âme des poètes"). My collaboration with him lasted a year—thanks to which I was able to meet other great artists of the singing world such as Yves Montand and Jacques Brel. I made my debut on radio and French television, not only as an accompanist of great singing stars, but also performing my own musical act.

At the same time, I was investigating the influence of sound on the human body, and the idea of music as therapy. In 1957 I recorded an "auditory prescription" for insomniacs titled *Prelude to Sleep*. The fruit of several years of research, it was the first such recording, and helped many insomniacs to regain natural rest. It was tremendously successful in Europe.

In 1958, chance (if chance exists!) brought me a meeting with an extraordinary individual who said, "You are a pioneer. You *must* continue. But like all innovators you will have difficulties, and in France you will often feel yourself misunderstood. You should try to become well-known across the ocean. You have a mission on this earth, because you were born to create. Thirty years after you're *dead* you'll be able to retire rich!" This person—this giant of the arts whom I profoundly admire—was Jean Cocteau.

The encounter with Cocteau marked me profoundly. Our brief meeting was a determining moment in my career. It must have brought me some luck, because the next year I appeared at the Olympia Theater (the greatest music hall in Paris) with Edith Piaf. Edith herself was very impressed by the immense possibili-

Jean Jacques Perrey's *The Amazing New Electronic Pop Sound*, Vanguard.
Album cover credits: cover illustration: P. Bramley.

ties of the Ondioline. From her I learned many "tricks of the trade" having to do with show business and song arrangement. She gave me money to buy studio time which allowed me to record on magnetic tape a few pieces that were a showcase for the Ondioline. She even decided *herself* which pieces I should record to obtain maximum effect. She was impeccable—very demanding of results. When she had decided that the tape was "almost perfect," she told me, "Now you must mail this to a person I'm going to give you the name and address of in New York. I will write him as well to let him know of your forthcoming correspondence. You'll see; he will answer you." It was impossible to debate with Edith; one always had to do as she decreed! Three weeks later I received an envelope from America. There was no note enclosed—only a round-trip plane ticket with an open return date, plus one word written (with a big felt-tip pen) on the envelope: "COME!" And thus began the fairy tale . . .

In March 1960 I arrived in New York with a little traveling suitcase in one hand and my faithful Ondioline in the other. My sponsor met me at the airport. I will never forget this man—also one of the magicians presiding over my career. He was the first to offer me such an opportunity to express myself; by his financing he gave me a chance to *live*. His name was Carroll Bratman and he directed Carroll Music Service, which rented musical instruments to recording studios, theaters, music halls and TV studios. He had a lot of business contacts and influence in the music world—all of which he shared with me. I feel an immense gratitude for his generosity and his heart.

New York—this was a dream come true for me, an unknown Frenchman! At the risk of failure I had to conquer this new continent, this *land of opportunity*. I had faith in myself, feeling rash (or foolhardy) because

I felt protected by the good fairies and magicians I had met in France. And when one is 30, one still has the soul of an adventurer—one needs to take chances.

I was fascinated by New York, this great metropolis through which sooner or later all the giants of music and show business pass. I spoke English, but I myself had a lot of difficulty understanding what people were trying to say to me. I admit, humbly, that I was often afraid. But the warmth and kindness of Carroll and his staff reassured me, and soon I managed to find a niche for myself. Apparently people liked the "Frenchie" with his accent and his European sense of humor. Because I was a Frenchman I had to pass a few administrative hurdles before I could legally be employed. I needed resident alien (green card) status; I also needed a Musicians' Union card (NY Local 802), and with a wave of his magic wand Carroll arranged that, too. Finally I had gotten a break—now it was up to me to prove what I could do. And this is one of the things I appreciate most about the United States: people will give a chance to an artist if he can prove what he can do—if he's original and creative. Whereas in France, the spirit is more narrow-minded, distrustful, conservative, reserved, and often envious or jealous. Thanks to my new friends and my rapid progress in learning the American language (especially the slang, which made people laugh), I was soon ready to face my challenges. Carroll has now left us, but I pledge him eternal gratitude.

My first appearance on American TV was on the Jack Parr Show. Thanks to my accent, a little humor, and the novelty of the Ondioline, I managed to surprise the audience and make them laugh—the show was a hit! Then followed radio appearances—the Arthur Godfrey Show was a big success. Later came more TV appearances, on the Gary Moore Show, "I've Got a Secret!", Captain Kangaroo, Johnny Carson, Mike Douglas, and others.

When I left France I had intended to remain only a few weeks in New York. But it took 6 months to obtain a resident alien card, so I stayed! During this time Carroll sponsored me totally, paying my living expenses at the Bristol Hotel on West 48th Street and even giving me a salary as a sales rep for the Ondioline. But he did even more. In his building, he set up an experimental recording studio completely equipped with everything I had ever dreamed of: tape recorders, various musical instruments, all the electronic keyboards existing at the time (Allen, RMI, Hammond, Martinot, etc). I felt I was living in a dream—a real fairy tale. On top of my own experimental research, I was doing demonstrations of the Ondioline for his clients as well as for the more creative ad agencies. Carroll was importing Ondiolines from France and they were selling well; Georges Jenny was ecstatic—and me too! Little by little I was becoming accustomed to the American way of life, and getting better and better at American slang.

In my research studio I worked hard—sometimes 36 hours in a row. I especially liked to work nights (the night is more propitious to research; one often finds inspiration on the doorstep of sleep). At Carroll's I met a great musician, Harry Breuer, who is now unfortunately deceased. Harry and I were linked by a true friendship which lasted well after my ten-year-stay in the United States. We composed and recorded many radio and TV jingles with the new sounds of the Ondioline, and we had enormous success. Together we created an LP for Pickwick Records, *The Happy Moog.* His loss greatly affected me because we had the knack of working together practically in symbiosis.

I also met a young composer, BILLY GOLDBERG, who composed the soundtracks for *Kojak* and *Columbo.* Thanks to Billy, I met one of my idols of science-fiction literature, Ray Bradbury, for whom we created the musical decor for the theater version of *Dandelion Wine* which played at Lincoln Center, New York. With Andy Badale (now known as Angelo Badalamenti), who did the soundtrack for David Lynch's *Blue Velvet,* Billy and I composed an instrumental called "Visa to the Stars," which later became the generic theme for an Esso TV commercial. As a team we produced many TV and radio jingles for ad agencies.

In 1961 my little demon of music imposed himself once again, saying, "You must go even further. You must create a style which is particular to yourself—very *personal*—and which will make you known beyond that which you have already achieved." Once again I followed his advice. One night, in my alchemical laboratory of sounds, I invented a new process for generating rhythms utilizing *musique concrète* sounds such as noises of machines, animal cries, insects buzzing, etc. Once the sounds were recorded I would knead them, chop them, run them through filters backward

at twice the speed (or half the speed), and in this way they would become practically unidentifiable. Little by little I created a "library" of sounds. I would isolate each of these sounds on magnetic tape, making an inventory according to various parameters (frequency, attack, envelope, tonality, etc), and then associating these sounds rhythmically according to well-determined, calculated patterns using repetitive loops and sequences. The result was astonishing. I had discovered an incredible goldmine, until then unexplored.

I would spend hours, days, and nights gluing these little bits of magic magnetic tape which were sometimes no bigger than a half-inch. Thus I was able to create a new style of rhythmic sequences. *Finally* I had found an original niche, my own style, humoristic and unusual. While we're on this subject I want to say that I never had any preconceived notions as to *selection*—that is, preferring one sound over another; I was as if possessed by recording bulimia! I was recording *everything* I possibly could, and thus accumulated more than 3000 basic sounds, heteroclite and varied, knowing that one day or another I could incorporate them within a rhythmic sequence.

In a beehive in Switzerland I recorded kilometers of magnetic tape on my Nagra recorder. When I returned to New York, I was able to produce the melody of Rimsky-Korsakov's "Flight of the Bumble Bee" using my recordings of live bees. It took a titanic amount of labor: 46 hours of cutting and gluing itsy-bitsy pieces of magnetic tape (1.03 centimeters long) together for the final result—2 minutes of music. When I recall this episode, I think I was a little crazy back then—but the result was so gratifying! At that time only 4-track tape recorders existed, so to complete this piece Carroll obtained for me a Scully 4-track machine; I recorded the melody (obtained from the bees) on one track, and the accompaniment on the remaining three. What a job!

As far as random chance goes, in my musical creation it never played a predominant role. Surely chance exists at a certain level of inspiration in artistic creation, but a true creator must know how to use it without being dominated by it. It's the job of the creator to *master* chance. An artistic creation, whatever it is, is too important to be left entirely to pure randomness. As a source of inspiration, the artist must take it into account but learn how to master it . . . and consider it as a wink of the eye from destiny.

In 1962 I had the extraordinary experience of playing one of the largest stages on the East Coast: the Radio City Music Hall of New York. I was there for six weeks, seven days a week, four times a day, in front of more than 6000 spectators at a time. This was fantastic and exhilarating. And in 1963 at a cocktail party, I had the luck to meet a man who for me was Merlin the Wizard: WALT DISNEY. We had several long conversations during which he explained his views on the search for perfection in creation. He would say things

in Montreal in 1965, when my stage number, "Around the World in 80 Ways," was produced at the Salle Bonaventure. It met with a lot of success and I appeared on several Canadian TV shows. In Montreal I encountered my friend the stage magician Michel De La Vega, whom I had first met in Paris while studying at medical school. We collaborated on numerous TV shows. I then distanced myself from stage music and jingle production to spend more time researching the influence of sound on the human body, and created my second "sleep" record.

like, "You must never let your creation get out of control. You must always *improve* it. *Work without respite.* Perfect your work without interruption, without allowing random events to direct you." He was an inspired person, a true giant of professionalism and one who could be called a "great initiate." He always encouraged me to go *further* in my research and to be a *perfectionist*—I owe him a lot and pledge him eternal respect and veneration. Unfortunately Walt left us in 1966, but for me he is still alive. Thanks again, Walt, for your teaching and your advice which I always try to follow to a "T"! Your suggestions and your advice were so precious and were always infinitely helpful to me during my entire career.

In 1964 at Carroll's I met a musician and composer of great talent, GERSHON KINGSLEY, and we became associates for awhile. Together, using my new process of rhythmic sequences of *musique concrète,* we elaborated the material necessary to the realization of an LP of 12 original pieces for the Vanguard Record Company, *The In Sound from Way Out.* This was followed by a second album, *Kaleidoscopic Vibrations,* played on the Ondioline and the Moog synthesizer. These 2 albums were reissued in 1988 on one compact disc called THE ESSENTIAL PERREY AND KINGSLEY. One of the titles of this second album, "Baroque Hoedown," is still used at Disneyland in the Main Street electric parade. Another title, "The Savers," became the basis for a TV commercial which in 1968 won the prestigious Cleo Award. Gershon and I had met ROBERT MOOG in New York, and we made a number of TV appearances and commercials using the Moog synthesizer and the Ondioline.

I also keep an unforgettable memory of my sojourn

(Note: I must say that I love and admire America a lot. It is the rare country where one finds professionalism and exemplary perfectionism in the field of show business and in the artistic world in general. Artists are considered real human beings and not "products" used to make money, as they are in France—especially at this time. I understand how one would be proud to say, "I am an American citizen.")

Anyway . . . I would return to France, sometimes twice a year. The fairy tale was continuing, because thanks to my stage number, I could travel for *free* First Class on the magnificent cruise liner, *S.S. France,* in exchange for 3 shows per cruise. So I was living the true life of a billionaire without being one. From 1962-1970 I did 18 round trips on the *S.S. France,* and met great personalities such as Alfred Hitchcock, who was a fascinating man, unusual and unpredictable. One never knew if he were joking or talking seriously. He was very impressed by the Ondioline and interested in my research; he encouraged me to continue. I met many other interesting personalities, but the list would be too long . . .

Each time I went to Europe, after only a few weeks I would return to New York, which attracted me like a magnet. I was always possessed by an intense desire to create . . . by an unquenchable thirst to accomplish *more.* I felt like I was living at a hundred miles an hour. I was literally treating each day as if it were "the first day of the rest of my life."

In 1968 I began working with Laurie Productions in New York—a great team of professionals including my friend John Mack and the composer Dave Mullaney. We did TV commercials together, and at this time I recorded my 4th album on the Vanguard label,

Moog Indigo. I was at the apogee of my American career—this was "the good life." I cherish vivid memories of the '60s, not only because it was a time of great personal success, but because it was a prolific period for music in general. There have been other "golden ages": Mozart, Johann Strauss and Offenbach have marked their eras by infusing humor into music. But in the '60s, humor sparkled in the music like champagne . . .

If we look at what has been happening during the past few years, we see humanity at a transition period. The era of Pisces is ending; little by little we are tilting into the age of Aquarius—and this does not happen without risk or inconvenience. Human beings are faced with numerous stresses: the eternal specter of world war; the dangers of increasing pollution and vandalism; political scandals; recession; unemployment; anxiety at the coming of the Year 2000—and much more. Technology has developed faster than the general consciousness; spiritual and moral values have *not* been preserved. Like Dr Frankenstein, man has been surpassed by his own creation and technology. People feel a crippling *desensitization.*

The human soul has lost its sense of magic; people have lost their sense of humor and everything is now banalized—instead of "joie de vivre" people feel "mal de vivre." So *the future is not what it was,* because humanity did not correctly manage its inheritance, Planet Earth. Now everyone is increasingly worried, anxiety-ridden, preoccupied and under pressure—and this generates sadness, intolerance, and violence. This can be felt in contemporary musical productions, which always reflect not only the present but also what lies ahead.

This is why I always deliberately introduced humor into my creations: I sincerely think that *humor* will help save humanity from the swamp into which it is sinking. Today we can't afford to be pessimistic, so let's try and keep a sense of humor bolted onto our hearts, soul and spirit! Let's shove pessimism aside for better days . . . when we will be in better shape to handle it!

For family reasons I had to return to France for good in 1970. I became the administrator and then the musical director of a French ballet company for 3 years. Because of my American experience, I was in demand to create radio and TV commercials "in the American way." I recorded other humoristic records, one for a Canadian company and 6 for a French company. I continued recording movie soundtracks in France and in Europe, plus jingles and cartoon music for French TV. I also oriented myself again toward research in therapeutic sounds, and my new "therapeutic prescription" was recently released . . . this time with the goal of inducing a state of relaxation and well-being in persons who are stressed and anxious.

I now live in the center of France in Vichy, happy with my companion who stimulates and encourages

me to continually create more humoristic music. My little demon of musical creation has not left me—he and my companion constantly remind me: "Your mission is not yet over; you must continue."

Mission . . . continue . . . create . . . these obsessive words resound like a litany in my head. Yet the times have changed. In France at present in order to create, realize and especially *produce,* one has to have significant financial backing. One must be part of the system. I know that I still have a lot of things to do . . . just recently I had one of these *luminous ideas* capable of revolutionizing the musical world, in a contemporary style, by using modern technology. If somewhere in the world there were a production company to trust me once again, I am sure they wouldn't be disappointed. EDITH, JEAN, WALT, if you hear me up there, please help me one more time! I still have one more message of humor to give, and bursts of laughter to pass on.

—*Jean-Jacques Perrey*

DISCOGRAPHY:

Mister Ondioline. Recorded in France, 1960. Pacific (double 45rpm set), Ref. 90.338 B Med.

The Happy Moog. Recorded in USA with Harry Breuer. Pickwick SPC-3160.

The In Sound from Way Out. Recorded in USA with Gershon Kingsley. Vanguard VSD-79222.

Kaleidoscopic Vibrations: Spotlight on the Moog. Recorded in USA with Gershon Kingsley. Vanguard VSD-79264. (The last 2 LPs were re-edited together on CD, $20 ppd. from RE/Search Publications, 20 Romolo #B, San Francisco, CA 94133.)

The Amazing New Electronic Pop Sound of Jean-Jacques Perrey. Recorded in USA. Vanguard VSD-79286.

Moog Indigo. Recorded in USA. Vanguard VSD-6549.

Dynamoog. Recorded in France for Canadian Company. CREA Sound Ltd #46.532.

Moog Sensations. Recorded in France. Montparnasse 2000 #MP-25.

Moog Expressions. Recorded in France. Montparnasse 2000 #MP-26.

Moog Vibrations. Recorded in France. Montparnasse 2000 #MP-27.

Moog Mig Mag Moog. Recorded in France. Montparnasse 2000 #MP-35.

Moog Is Moog. Recorded in France. Montparnasse 2000 #MP-106.

Kartoonery. Recorded in France. Montparnasse 2000 #MP-131.

MICKEY McGOWAN

Starting in the late '60s, Mickey McGowan was among the first to collect neglected music (15,000 records) *and* to play the music for thousands of visitors to his Unknown Museum, possibly the world's only archive of over 100,000 American '40s-'90s pop culture artifacts (toys, dolls, lunchboxes, promotional giveaways, etc). Far more than a trip down Memory Lane, the Unknown Museum preserves America's greatest contribution to art history—unselfconsciously produced pop culture—and is now endangered; funding, plus a permanent location for the archive (now in storage) is needed. Mickey McGowan can be contacted at PO Box 1551, Mill Valley, CA 94942. He lives with his wife, Finnlandia.

♦ *VALE: In your Unknown Museum, you've preserved so much forgotten American popular culture. When did you start collecting?*
♦ MICKEY McGOWAN: I was born in Los Angeles in 1946, and raised near buildings shaped like giant donuts and hot dogs—I assumed this was the way the world was! My first primitive collections were cigar bands, matchbooks, shells, rocks—the usual stuff that kids can get for free. I had a big sheet of plywood, and whenever I found a bottle cap I would take it home and nail it to the board—before I quit I had over 200 different ones (*Ne-Hi, Birely's,* etc) from the days of great bottle caps. I didn't care about "preservation"—I just pounded a nail right through the center! Which could be my roots as an artist, because over the years I've done a lot of nailing in the service of art . . . *artistic nailing.*

I had the classic single bed with a headboard where I kept my little Sears portable record player. After school I would go to the listening booths at Wallach's Music City near Playa del Rey and spin 45s for hours. What excited me most were records like SHEB WOOLEY's "Purple People Eater" and DAVID SEVILLE's "Witch Doctor"—they just sent you off into another land. I also remember "Delicious" by JIM BACKUS

(the voice of Mr Magoo). It's just Jim and a girl drinking champagne; occasionally someone giggles "Delicious" and laughs hysterically. This goes on for two minutes and 12 seconds, and somehow it got released and was a big AM hit. That's why the 45 was such a great medium; there's *no way* you could release an LP of that!

♦ *V: Did you plan to be an artist early in your life?*
♦ MM: I grew up near L.A. Airport so I figured I'd work for the airlines—I applied at United and fortunately did not get the job! When I first started consciously doing "art," I was inspired by assemblage artists such as Ed Kienholz. I beachcombed for rusty tin cans and pieces of metal, and started going to thrift stores and flea markets . . . then I'd take the things I'd found, paint them and nail them to wood. From the age of 14 I would ride my bike to a thrift shop in old Venice and buy a tropical shirt and get sent home from school the next day for wearing it because it was too "loud." Also, I went to the Gashouse where the beatniks hung out—I thought *this* was the way life should be.

When you mention the '60s most people just think of the hippies, but there was so much more to that decade—the first seven years seem to be completely forgotten. Yet there was outstanding music, fashion and art being produced—the greatest happenings and art statements of (perhaps) the century were made during that period. L.A. had quite an art underground; when I was fifteen I saw Warhol's *Sleep* and early BRUCE CONNER films at the Cinematheque 16. To me this was rebellion, and L.A. is the place to be rebellious in—it just cries out for alternative life.

♦ *V: How did the Unknown Museum start?*

♦ MM: I left Los Angeles in '68, went to Mexico for a month, then moved to Sausalito and hung around the Sausalito Art Center, which was a beautiful old elementary school converted into studios. A lot was going on there: the ALAN WATTS dancers,

Photo: Robert Waldman

Indian-influenced "spiritual" events, Greek folk dancing, ceramics, and crazy happenings. I continued to collect things and make assemblage art, but I gave it all away—at the time it seemed that art was not something you *kept*. (As a child I didn't keep that bottle cap collection or the model airplanes hanging from my ceiling; I collected mainly *memories.)*

From the age of 14 I would ride my bike to a thrift shop in old Venice and buy a tropical shirt and get sent home from school the next day for wearing it because it was too "loud."

A couple of years later I saw an ad for a 2000-square-foot building in downtown Mill Valley at 39 Corte Madera Ave. I called the landlord and said, "I want a big space where I can do some art," and he warned me the building was due to be torn down soon (although it lasted for 12 years). I rented it and made art in it until the Unknown Museum got going in 1974. That's when I began acquiring things in earnest.

I was rooted, had space to do something in, and I met other people who had collections, particularly DICKENS BASCOM, who made the original decorated car of all decorated cars—the archetype. It was a Ford Falcon completely encrusted with tennis shoes, typewriters, beads, toys, ceramic figurines, plastic fruit—everything you could think of. We started setting up displays, and we brought in other "gluers" (who did glue art): Larry Fuente, Lois Anderson, and David Best. On Pearl Harbor Day (December 7), 1974, the Unknown Museum officially opened to the public.

I was still working in other art mediums, but I discovered that through a *display of objects* I could communicate any statement I wished to make regarding any event or topic—whether it be an economic crisis, the birth of the Dionne Quintuplets or the Space Shuttle disaster. Remember the '70s—when the "What Is Art?" question was uppermost in people's minds? At the Unknown Museum, people would point to a pile of old teddy bears and Humpty-Dumptys and ask, "Is this art?" and I'd reply, *"Possibly!"* To me it was display art, and by not trying to arrange the objects artistically you could circumvent the "artistic" factor.

When setting up the Museum, I assumed that other people had the same memories I had. I was an average American kid and that's what gave me my *credentials.* I had free access to television, which of course goes

hand-in-hand with all this pop culture. TV has been my biggest influence; it started about the year I was born, and I'm a perfect example of what it can do to you—for better or for worse.

♦ *ANDREA JUNO: Does the Unknown Museum have a goal?*

♦ MM: I'm trying to release the past; people have started "coming to grips" with their past interests. The prevailing mind-set used to be "Don't look back," but to not look back now is *foolish.* When the Museum was open, I lived in the back as the resident curator, and I'd

The overall environment of the Unknown Museum is an artistic statement about American culture and its underlying neuroses; its fantasies, daydreams, bad dreams, wet dreams.

hear this laughter that was a different kind of laughter . . . not like you hear at comedy shows, but more like some incredible kind of therapeutic release, which was laughter but was also joy and reminiscence—a rekindling. I got addicted to that sound; that's why having the Museum be public is so important—what's important is not just the objects, but people's *interaction* with them. One of the main goals of the Unknown Museum is to stir up the knowledge you already *have,* like the memories of that old chemistry set from the '50s, or that Mister Peanut bank from your childhood.

♦ *AJ: The museum is like a recovery center for cultural amnesiacs—*

♦ MM: I like to think of it as physical therapy, except that it's the *memory* that's being exercised, not the body. Some people visit the museum and experience a delayed reaction: at the moment of seeing the ball-and-jacks or the skip rope they threw away they may feel nothing, but two weeks later it'll hit them. The synapses have been sparked and something will

work its way up to the surface to release who knows *what.*

Nothing on display is rare or arcane; the goal is to display the *common object.* Sure, it's fun to go to a museum and see the throne King Louis XIV used in 1692. But to us, the things that relate to *our* past are what really matter. Life has changed so fast and is changing even faster; it's increasingly difficult to make sense of everything and to "keep a level head." The Museum can help.

I hope people don't just say, "There's this Unknown Museum; let's go see what this guy Mickey has collected." That's not the idea; the idea is: "There's this Museum; let's go see what we've lived and experienced." Sure, somebody has put it together, but I want to stay in the background. In the '70s, when you visited the Museum there was never anyone there watching over your shoulder. I had a big panel (actually, a portion of Christo's running fence) separating the Museum from my living quarters and studio, and I could hear (if something fell over, sure, I'd run out) but it was unguarded. Those were the days when these things were not valuable. In the '70s almost nothing was stolen; back then everything was so easily available. We had our pillars of lunch pails (which have since become so collectible) out in the open.

In 1985 I moved the Museum to a two-story house at 243 East Blithedale in Mill Valley, and finally the objects were in their proper settings. In 1989 that building was demolished to make way for condos. I'm now seeking a permanent location.

♦ *AJ: These common objects have other implications, political as well as personal. They elicit some of our best (and worst) memories—*

♦ MM: Many people do have problems with their past,

Photo: Robert Waldman

so perhaps they wouldn't want to visit a museum like this; the objects *can* evoke memories of bad experiences. The crib with all the dolls in it might trigger some long-suppressed trauma—I've seen people run away from the museum crying. The overall environment of this museum is an artistic statement about American culture and its underlying neuroses; its fantasies, daydreams, bad dreams, wet dreams—every kind of dream. It's also the American Dream gone haywire. To this day I still regard the Unknown Museum as going inside America's brain: if you could imagine yourself shrinking (like the crew of *Fantastic Voyage,* with Raquel Welch) and being injected into the brain, then every little thing you see as you walk through the museum is a memory cell reflecting some facet of your past. If you don't relate to one object, I'm sure that a foot away there's something else you either *did* own, or recall.

♦ *V: What kind of objects aren't in the museum?*

♦ MM: Well, I *do* edit. Things have to be affordable as well as *properly used.* Some of my stuffed animals may have been slobbered on or have an eye missing, but to me this usage represents history and the passing of time. We don't get to see decay anymore; we're so quick to say, "Oh, that's got a chip on it—toss it in the garbage!" But it's fun to see things decomposing in your lifetime—I don't mean that in a morbid sense, but you can learn something from observing the process of aging.

♦ *V: Do you collect contemporary objects—the collectibles of the future?*

♦ MM: Anything that's really *big* you should pick up, if you're running a museum like this. I have to admit the '80s haven't been as rewarding as previous decades. I've acquired a few yuppie objects, but right now I'm focusing on '70s artifacts like the pet rock, Farrah Fawcett memorabilia, *Dukes of Hazzard* mugs, and things related to car chase programs like *Starsky & Hutch.* From the '80s I've collected Cabbage Patch Kids, Masters of the Universe memorabilia, and Garbage Pail Kids bubble gum cards. Anything from the year I was born to the present day is fair game. I try not to go beyond those years; there's no "antiques" here.

Endless vistas of memory unfold as you walk through the Museum. The kitchen alone reveals the fantasy heroes of the food empires: *Bob's Big Boy, the Kentucky Colonel, the Pillsbury Doughboy, Mister Potato Head, Davy Crockett*—all the icons that have been put on food items, lunch pails, thermos bottles and serving trays. The only contemporary items are paper cups with the straws and the lids from Round Table Pizza and other fast-food joints. In the future those will be important and revealing—as well as *any* form of hamburger packaging. The museum is a mirror held up to the last four decades of American history; it's there to reflect back your life.

The Museum is very popular with teenagers, many of whom are experts on the *Brady Bunch*—they know

Photo: Robert Waldman

more about them than most people who lived through the '60s. In this day and age when everybody moves frequently and storage costs are astronomical, not everyone has been able to drag their heritage with them . . . except in one place [points to head] where the rent is free. The memory cells will always be there, and at any moment they can be stirred up and accessed by the proper cue or artwork. And that's what I'm after: to stir up those thoughts. There's a multilayered effect caused by thousands of items hitting you within the space of an hour, and that includes the sound—a very important aspect of the experience.

I feel a *duty* to preserve these archives for future generations. I'd like to see a public agency house the collection permanently, but only if it could be done correctly. Right now everything can be touched and handled, but as things become more valuable, it won't be possible to leave them out in the open. Things *are* becoming harder to get; now *everything's* popular and "collectible." But I don't worry too much about the bathroom scales or the electric irons—if they get taken, the joke's on them!

I remember the first time something was stolen from the Unknown Museum. I was kind of *pseudo-angry* until I realized, "That old TV doesn't work

of visiting the Museum. I could create subtly surrealistic moments in sound by overdubbing a dog barking when a cat is purring, having Kennedy's motorcade approaching Dealey Plaza, WILLIAM SHATNER reciting from the *Transformed Man,* etc. I called it "the perfect moment" when something on the audiotape coincided perfectly with what you were looking at (for example, having the "Wedding March" come on just as you spotted the "Bride" display). Imagine viewing the *Star Trek* display and hearing the voice of MR SPOCK singing "Highly Illogical" (from the great *Two Sides of Leonard Nimoy* album)—that would be a perfect moment. Or if you were in the "Mom and Dads' Room" looking at a golf trophy and the voice of Arnold Palmer came on telling you how to play the 9th hole. I wanted to run out (like Groucho Marx on *You Bet Your Life)* with a prize for the people who experienced those!

In general, I selected recordings that incorporated sound effects, natural sounds and the spoken word with orchestra. Perhaps that was the direct influence of television which, if you think about it, does just that.

♦ **V: *What are the key ingredients for a great record?***

♦ MM: Well, a truly great record should satisfy two major criteria: 1) be able to be played in the background without disturbing you, and 2) be able to be played in the foreground without *boring* you. You should be able to listen to it with all ears and be totally entertained, or put it on without it disrupting any creative activity you might be engaged in. That's a perfect record! Then again, there are those that do one or the other—they're *half*-perfect. Of course, the volume is always important; you want to turn it down (or up) for the creative process.

I think that to be "incredibly strange," music has to be original. It has to challenge you in some way that you haven't been challenged before. Otherwise it won't be strange—it'll be familiar. And this has nothing to do with "good" or "bad." If you haven't heard the piano rolls of CONLON NANCARROW, then you've never heard the piano played that fast, so that's strange. All sound may be construed as music, but the people who've mixed sounds with orchestra have really hit the nail on the head—they've bridged that gap between the familiar and the unfamiliar.

♦ **V: *Why don't you go through a pile of records and comment on them by category—***

♦ MM: Okay. One of the greatest series ever produced is *Soothing Sounds for Baby,* three volumes recorded in the mid-'60s by RAYMOND SCOTT. This isn't an "in the womb" recording of heartbeats and little murmurs—these records were intended to lull your baby to sleep. My copies were used, and inside one I found a letter that said, "I bought these records because I thought they might help the tots I take care of get to sleep at nap-time. To my amazement I found the music (?) not only pleasant but much too sophisticated for

anyway, and now they'll have guilt for the rest of their life!" Even the most hardened criminal knows that a *curse* goes along with all this stuff. So watch out—if you steal from the Museum, Mister Potato Head's ghost will be after you! Of course, many of these things came from estate sales after their owners passed away, so there are spirits here in that stuffed animal or that doll, that softball glove or that erector set.

♦ **V: *Why did you choose the "Unknown Museum" as a name?***

♦ MM: In the '70s, "unknown" was a term in vogue—there was the "unknown comic" who performed with a bag over his head. Also, a lot of the objects summoned up the mystery of the unrecoverable, the unobtainable, the unknown in our past. Sometimes I think of the archive as "The Museum of the American Dream"—that's an unofficial official name. This is also the Museum of American Television Age Culture—that's the binding thread. TV has been our most influential source of information, our picture window to the world (or rather, what's *supposedly* going on in the outside world).

♦ **AJ: *How did you start getting into other worlds through sound?***

♦ MM: The sound was always vital; I mixed tapes from my recorded archives to enhance the experience

children. They'll never appreciate how clever this conglomeration of sounds really is . . ." *Right.*

Raymond Scott also recorded *The Rock'n Roll Symphony* (just like it sounds: orchestral music, but with rock drums!). He composed *Dinner Music for a Pack of Hungry Cannibals* (great cover) which was performed by Dave Harris and the Powerhouse Five. Millions of people have heard him without realizing it, because many of his melodies were orchestrated by CARL STALLING for those Warner Bros. cartoon soundtracks—now *that's* probably the most widely-heard and influential incredibly strange music!

"Come Up and See Me Sometime," an invitation made famous by Mae West, was put on a parakeet-training record.

♦ ♦ ♦ NOVELTY ♦ ♦ ♦

Mad Twists Rock'n'Roll is one of the most inspired albums of all time. You could order it (and other *Mad* albums) from *MAD* magazine in the late '50s. Who knows what stars may have been recorded here, but the credits list GENE HAYS & The DELWOODS. The album opens with "Throwing the High School Basketball Game" and continues with classics like "She Got a Nose Job," "Somebody Else's Dandruff on My Lover Baby's Shirt," "Blind Date," and "When My Pimples Turn to Dimples." These are all delivered very competently in a white doo-wop rhythm 'n' blues style—this is not just a comedy album, it's a serious musical venture. "All I Have Left Is My Johnny's Hubcap" is like the SHANGRI-LA'S "Walking in the Sand," but pre-dates it. Johnny got sent to "juvey" for stealing cars, but she still has his hubcap on her wall—it's *tragic.*

♦ ♦ ♦ BIRD RECORDINGS ♦ ♦ ♦

I love bird recordings—they're my special hobby within hobbies. In my house anything with canaries is always welcome. A favorite is *The Canaries,* with music by the ARTAL ORCHESTRA, which mixes canary songs with waltzes such as "Jeannie with the Light Brown Hair" and "Wine, Women and Song." Our feathered friends outside are the real stars of the sound world; I listen to them every morning.

An all-time great record is JIM FASSETT's *Symphony of the Birds.* In the early '60s Fassett, a sound engineer at CBS, took field recordings of birds and manipulated the tapes to create an incredible, almost electronic-sounding symphony. And he's proud of it, too; he gives a spoken-word introduction that says:

"You'll be amazed that this is nothing but birds." He made a few other records using non-musical sound sources, including *Strange to Your Ears*—that album lives up to its title! This genius must not go unnoticed—that's why this museum exists: to give people like Fassett their due.

Besides a recording of Brazilian Canaries singing "Swanee River," I also have dozens of 78s of live canaries from the turn of the century. I have all kinds of parakeet training records which say things like "Come on in, the door's open." I have Pancho the Parrot from the San Diego Zoo singing "I Left My Heart in San Francisco." There are '40s recordings of canaries performing live on the radio, such as *American Radio Warblers.* The trainers would put their caged birds up to a microphone and they would perform with organ accompaniment—magnificent.

The Audubon Society and the Cornell University Dept. of Ornithology released a number of field identification recordings (Dr. Kellogg and A.A. Allen were the masters of this). Some of them are narrated by ornithologists Jerry and Edith Stilwell—a classic older couple: "Now here we have a red robin, and it's going to tell us what a great day it is to be out in the meadow." She'll say this very gently and it's wonderful—they always know *exactly* what the birds are saying. But actually, aren't bird calls about territory or sex? At least half the time they're calling for their mates.

Bird Songs and Literature compares birds to famous writers; it tries to show how the tawny owl is like Samuel Taylor Coleridge, or how the house wren inspired William Forbish to write *Birds of Massachusetts and Other New England States.* It's all baloney, of

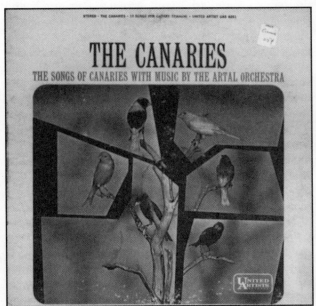

The Canaries—12 Songs for Canary Training, United Artists Records.

Eden Ahbez's *Eden's Island*, Del-Fi Records.
Album cover credits: photographs: Brad Fuller,
layout & design: Garrett/Howard, Inc.

course, but it's fun to hear them trying to prop up their theories!

"Come Up and See Me Sometime," an invitation made famous by Mae West, was put on a parakeet-training record. It's bizarre—just a high voice repeating, "Come up and see me sometime!" in different ways. Another favorite record has to be a put-on; how can you *possibly* teach a bird to say, "That's absolutely preposterous!" I've also got duck- and geese-calling records of people tempting birds to come and get *shot*.

◆ ◆ ◆ EXOTICA ◆ ◆ ◆

◆ AJ: These canary records pre-date MARTIN DENNY, with his bird calls—

◆ MM: Yes, but I would never say a word against MARTIN DENNY or LES BAXTER—they are all-time greats. *Forbidden Island, Afro-desia, Primitiva* and *Hypnotique* are among Denny's best records—actually, *all* his records on the LIBERTY label are classics. The great Les Baxter LPs include *Ritual of the Savage, Jungle Jazz,* and my favorite, *The Passions* featuring the emotionally overwrought vocals of BAS SHEVA. Les Baxter made many incredibly challenging recordings, but on *Space Escapade* where he's attempting an outer space theme—again, the results were less than stellar—it sounded like being on earth! It's strange, because when he *tries* to be weird, he's the least weird . . . whereas *Tamboo!, Ports of Pleasure, Sacred Idol,* and *Jewels of the Sea* have that special greatness. Baxter's *Barbarian* has a great cover, but is more symphonic. *Bora Bora* is up there with the hard-to-find *Que Mango!* on Alshire.

One of the truly strange masterpieces on record is EDEN AHBEZ's *Eden's Island.* He was one of the first long-hairs; supposedly he was a Big Sur guru before he moved to the tropics where he garnered the experience to make this one album of his career. *Eden's Island* sounds like: *if* Martin Denny had gotten together with Jack Kerouac, and Kerouac had gone to a desert island and not become a beatnik—! "To Live Beneath the Sun" is a classic *dropout* song that encapsulates what later became the hippie philosophy: he talks about the joy of just sitting under a coconut tree, where the open air is your cathedral. He was also a vegetarian, and practiced yogic breath control. I have a 45 by him, "Mr K." which is similar to "Tequila" except that he substitutes the word "Vodka." It's about Nikita Khrushchev drinking vodka, so obviously he has a sense of humor.

◆ AJ: On the back it says, "The story of a wanderer . . . the lone man in nature."

◆ MM: There are many stories about him, and one biography claims that he was born in Chinook, Kansas under a different name. Another claims he was born April 15, 1908 in Brooklyn. In the '40s, his very first song-writing attempt was a number one hit—Nat King Cole's "Nature Boy." He wrote this after studying yoga and Eastern philosophy; it has lines like, "The greatest thing you'll ever learn/Is just to love and be loved in return." His song titles are so evocative: "Land of Love," "Let Me Hear You Say I Love You," "Runaway Boy," "Jalopy Song," "Soft-Spoken Stranger," "Song of Mating," "Oh My Brother," "Nature's Symphony" and "End of Desire."

◆ V: Candi Strecker [who will be in Vol. II] gave me a Life magazine article about him. He tells about being stopped by a policeman (probably for his long hair) and saying, "I look crazy, but I'm not. The funny thing is: other people don't look crazy, but they are." He's quite a philosopher; he also said, "It's not so much what you want; it's keeping away from the things you don't want."

◆ MM: Some other favorite exotica records were made by ELISABETH WALDO: *Maracatu, Rites of the Pagan,* and *Realm of the Incas* (GNP Crescendo label). She was a violinist and a composer and is very serious about her work, which uses all kinds of native instruments, percussion, strange harmonies and choruses to create her special ritual music.

◆ ◆ ◆ ABSTRACT FEMALE VOCALS ◆ ◆ ◆

The abstract female vocal: female vocals without words, is a favorite genre. The undeniable master is YMA SUMAC, who recorded *Voice of the Xtabay, Legend of the Sun Virgin,* and *Fuego Del Ande. Mambo* might be considered her best, but *Legend of the Jivaro* (with its pseudo-head hunter oogum-boogum stuff) is really good. Another abstract female vocals classic is LEDA ANNEST's *Portrait of Leda* (1958). It's an Adventures In Sound production [Columbia], and it's unbelievable. More abstract tonalities can be heard on MIRIAM BURTON's *African Lament*—it's gorgeous.

Now we get to one of the truly strangest records of all time: *Cosmic Remembrance* by KALI BAHLU, released in 1967. In the liner notes Kali reveals: "In the beginning I knew I was not from this earth, but rather a visitor trapped in a horrible broken game called earth." Then she strings together the most unlikely thoughts: "Who knows if Buddha drinks *coffee?* . . . A strange thing happened; [I found myself] locked in the tunnel of changing time. In the tunnel I found a room where the magic mirror is." I played this record for somebody who said, "This girl's on acid," but I don't think so—I think she's like Yma Sumac, in a realm of her own. Maybe she got "turned on" and made this record, but whatever the cause, it's very bizarre and truly inspired. This was produced by Richard Bach who started WORLD-PACIFIC, a great label with integrity—I'm sure he believed this record was important. "Cosmic Telephone Call" and "A Game Called WHO AM I?" are standouts.

◆ *V: Here, the mind-boggling albums of LUCIA PAMELA and LINDA PERHACS also come to mind.*

◆ ◆ ◆ **SOUND EFFECTS** ◆ ◆ ◆

◆ MM: It's hard to believe that DEAN ELLIOTT's *Zounds! What Sounds!* was ever made. You hear coffee cans, costume jewelry, dogs barking, ping pong balls, mechanical teeth, raw apples and carrots—everything but the kitchen sink. In a similar vein is JACK FASCINATO's *Music from a Surplus Store*—it's the same idea, and includes the sounds of sandpaper and drills mixed with an easy listening orchestra. Old records like these reveal something long forgotten: the beauty of the One Take. *Zounds!* had guys over on one side chewing celery and guys on the other side ringing diving bells; *Music from a Surplus Store* had hoses and pipes and springs clanging away, and I'd like to think there were a bunch of people in the studio doing it all at once.

The CREED TAYLOR Orchestra made *SHOCK Music in Hi-Fi,* which bore a warning, "Don't dare listen to this music alone!" It's a masterpiece from the

Kali Bahlu's *Cosmic Remembrance,* © Liberty Records, Inc. Album cover credits: cover painting: Kali Bahlu, design: Gabor Halmos, art direction & photography: Woody Woodward.

beginning, starting with loud heartbeats. "The Crank" effectively conveys the fear which a crank phone call can inspire. "The Secret" features a man and a woman laughing conspiratorily, and raises the question: "Is a secret still a secret once it's told?"

Creed Taylor's follow-up album was *Panic: the Son of Shock.* Both of these LPs should also be credited to the film composer KENYON HOPKINS (who did *Baby Doll, The Fugitive Kind,* and *The Hustler*—all good beatnik jazz soundtracks). You hear heavy breathing, whispering, clapping, heartbeats, shudders, screams—a whole gamut of effects. After these two masterpieces, Hopkins hit paydirt in the mid-'60s with *Nightmare,* which has the sound of a plague of locusts coming in for the kill. "Chamber of Horrors," besides sounding like a horror music soundtrack, really *is* beautiful.

◆ *AJ: These records were calculated to shock?*

◆ MM: Of course! He used the sound of a telephone ringing to create incredible suspense; he used footsteps, creaking doors and glass breaking to dreadful effect. Later in his career, Creed Taylor founded ABC-Paramount and the jazz label CTI. He recorded a few more albums including *Lonelyville,* which is great private-eye jazz. Incidentally, I'm a *big* fan of the type of jazz that beatniks listened to: West Coast, cool jazz. I also like TV jazz, like *Music for a Private Eye* and *Murder, Inc* by composers like PETE RUGOLO and HENRY MANCINI.

◆ *V: What else did Kenyon Hopkins do?*

◆ MM: He recorded a series of *Verve Sound Tours,* in which he took the music of a given country (e.g., France) and mixed in the sounds of people at a sidewalk cafe in Paris. These records sound quite pleasant, not scary, and have nice fold-out covers. He also did

Jack Fascinato's *Music from a Surplus Store,* Capitol Records.

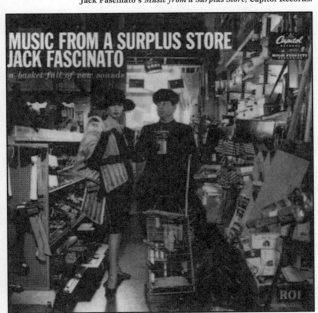

The Creed Taylor Orchestra's *Shock*, ABC-Paramount.
Album cover credits: cover photo: Tony Triolo, cover design: Matt Schutz.

Rooms on the Cadence label, which is a pre-*SHOCK* production, and *Riding the Rails*—the cover shows two fashion models who've just "hopped a freight"!

I love records like "New York Sweet," written by PHIL MOORE who was a protege of Duke Ellington. It opens with taxicab sound effects, beautiful jazzy underground subway-type music, and then a KEN NORDINE-like voice comes on telling how great it is to be at the top of the Empire State Building looking down at all the twinkling city lights. Phil Moore also composed *Fantasy for Girl and Orchestra* with sound effects that pre-date Laurie Anderson. While the violins build, a girl recites things like, "It sure is lonely in a room designed for two when there's only one around." He also did *Symphony in Green*—his musical description of the color green.

Some interesting sound effects were produced by ELSA POPPING & HER PIXIELAND BAND (actually, a pseudonym for a French composer, Andre Popp). It has backward vocals and other tape manipulations plus some pretty humorous orchestration. The pixies have high voices—it's almost like Martian polka music!

♦ ♦ ♦ PROMOTIONAL ♦ ♦ ♦

Many companies issued private pressings to promote everything from vacuum cleaners and tile to soap; U.S. Steel released *Rhapsody of Steel*, which has a beautiful symphonic score over which people promote steel products. *Music to Make Automobiles By* mixes assembly-line sounds with orchestra to inspire the workers; a promotional LP for the Volkswagen mixed assembly-line sounds with jazz. *Music to Burn Your Oil By* (a re-issue of *Music to Light Your Pilot By*) was put out by the Heil-Quaker Corporation which manufactured heating and air-conditioning units. Sometimes these records would feature entire Broadway casts

with an orchestra and chorus performing *original* compositions—the companies sunk a ton of money into these.

♦ ♦ ♦ SOUNDTRACKS ♦ ♦ ♦

♦ **V: You mentioned earlier that you like TV jazz, despite the fact that jazz aficionados consider it "watered down" or not "cutting-edge"—**

♦ MM: Some people want jazz to be dominating, so they go for the more intellectual music of Coltrane, Albert Ayler, Sun Ra and Marion Brown. And no doubt about it—it's great. But if you're just working around the house or relaxing, sometimes the less-demanding background jazz provides just what you need. TV jazz falls into the category of background music: it was intended to accent a situation, not create one. Anything Henry Mancini did is excellent—especially the jazzy numbers, like on *Experiment in Terror. Rock, Pretty Baby* (from '56) is a rock'n'roll instrumental soundtrack, while *The Versatile Henry Mancini* contains Hawaiian/tropical numbers like "Bali Hai" and "Poinciana"—again, it lives up to its title!

In the mid-'60s, a lot of soundtracks came out with a sophisticated, light jazzy sound: *Modesty Blaise, The Tenth Victim, Fathom* (with Raquel Welch), *The Party* (with Peter Sellers) and *In Like Flint*. Basically, whenever I want that mood that existed in the post-private eye/James Bond pre-psychedelic era, there's only one place to go for it: a 1965-era soundtrack with an animated cartoon cover. Very few of these albums are totally great, but each contains tunes that are magnificent. I collect soundtracks, and my rule is: if I only get two good tracks off an album, that's enough!

BIKER SOUNDTRACKS: there's *always* good stuff on these; American International Pictures (AIP) re-

Music to Burn Your Oil By, © Heil-Quaker Corporation.
Album cover credits: cover photo: Al Clayton, art and layout: Illustration Design Group, Inc.

Music to Light Your Pilot By, © 1967 Heil-Quaker Corporation. Album cover credits: cover photo: Al Clayton, art & layout: Illustration Design Group, Inc.

leased a ton on the TOWER and SIDEWALK labels. Anything with "angels" in the title is probably a biker film: *Angels Die Hard, Hells' Angels on Wheels, Hells' Belles, The Wild Angels*—anything with Bruce Dern! These soundtracks had to be "outlawish" in their sounds, so they're imaginative.

When the psychedelic era hit, soundtracks got even more interesting, because composers were *forced* to imagine drug state-suggestive sounds and incorporate them into their music! An early example is *The Trip,* starring Jack Nicholson as a hippie in San Francisco. By '69 a number of good ones featuring sitar or John Cippollina-style guitar had appeared, like *Psych-Out* and *Sign of Aquarius.* The music was trying to be psychedelic *and* orchestrated, and it was good to hear these influences pushing each other: you could actually *hear* the generation gap! By the time the '70s hit, psychedelic-influenced soundtracks were a thing of the past. They sprouted up during the brief interval after the James Bond Secret Agent period, and before disco/soul came in.

I have at least *fifty* JAMES BOND-related albums; this is a genre of its own. Some are simple orchestrated pieces with girls cooing "Thunderball" or "Goldfinger" over the top (they do it differently than in the movie), and many are on budget labels like CROWN or CORONET. Often the cover features a girl in a swimsuit holding a gun with a silencer—she'd never shoot it, but guns were *style* back then.

♦ **V: Let's talk about CELEBRITY recordings—**
♦ **MM:** On *Shakespeare, Tchaikovsky and Me,* JAYNE MANSFIELD whispers poetry by Shakespeare, Byron, and Shelley against a background of Tchaikovsky piano tinklings. This is a wonderful and legendary recording from a legendary lady—her voice is very sexy

and breathy. Listening to it can be eerie—especially if you keep in mind how she died! Most of the great actresses have made records, too: Elizabeth Taylor (Liz & Dick's *Who's Afraid of Virginia Woolf* is classic psychodrama), Jane Russell, Marilyn Monroe, Ann-Margret and Brigitte Bardot, and sometimes the *cover* is what delivers the goods.

SEBASTIAN CABOT's voice is very rich, and the orchestra behind him is thoroughly competent—nevertheless, when he does Bob Dylan's "All I Really Want to Do" or "Like a Rolling Stone" he's using a cannon to kill a mosquito! (He also made a very sexy, *classic* album with Ann-Margret.) *Sebastian Cabot, Actor; Bob Dylan, Poet* was probably conceived as a very serious project, yet it ends up in the same domain as the now-legendary *Transformed Man* by WILLIAM SHATNER.

The whole *Star Trek* crew seem to have made records; LEONARD NIMOY made six and even Lieutenant Uhura (Nichelle Nichols) made one. Nimoy's best is *Two Sides of Leonard Nimoy;* the "Spock" side opens with "Highly Illogical," about how we build freeways and yet don't have enough gas to power our cars—Nimoy has been an environmentalist for some time. The Leonard Nimoy side is more straightforward, with wistful, dated tunes like "Gentle on my Mind" and "The Ballad of Bilbo Baggins" (inspired by the J.R.R. Tolkien craze of the '60s).

Music to Make Automobiles By mixes assembly-line sounds with orchestra to inspire the workers; a promotional LP for the Volkswagen mixed assembly-line sounds with jazz.

Another Hall of Fame record is JACK WEBB's *You're My Girl,* recorded after the early *Dragnet* series. He speaks in his trademark nasal delivery, except now he's grappling with love instead of crime. In one song, he receives a letter from his wife saying she's left him—and you know a man isn't supposed to cry. So he breaks out into poetry, and with forced rhymes like "I broke your favorite *cup*/The curtains are in ribbons/I forgot to mind the *pup!*" Of course, you can't get out of your head his TV character: the laconic, no-nonsense Sergeant Joe Friday.

Kookie by EDD BYRNES is a masterpiece. This record is still taken as a joke but I don't know why—at least half of it is beyond greatness. To me, it wrote the book on pre-rap pseudo-beatnik poetry done in a sort of cha-cha setting, super-hip and cool. A lot of TV viewers remember "Kookie" from his shenanigans working at *77 Sunset Strip*—he played a parking lot

attendant who always had little words of wisdom for anybody who pulled up (they're on this record, too). "Kookie's Mad Pad" is a total classic that describes his futuristic bachelor apartment, his furniture, his wall-to-wall TV set and his stereophonic telephone. We all know "Kookie, Kookie, lend me your comb" which was a monster AM hit—on the TV show Kookie was always combing his jelly roll (hair). Those were the days when Hollywood was trying to push Elvis substitutes like Fabian and Frankie Avalon, and Kookie was right there, too.

Another masterpiece is ALFRED HITCHCOCK's *Music to be Murdered By.* Each track has an introduction by Alfred (similar to his TV show introductions), and it's pretty funny. For example, he says, "Why shouldn't I make a record? After all, my measurements are 33-45-78!" He continues in this vein, and of course his sense of humor is very bizarre. The background music sounds like Bernard Herrmann. In a related vein is *Poe for Moderns:* Edgar Allan Poe-*try* read to private-eye jazz! It's listenable and *nice*—the spoken interpretation falls within the acceptable parameters of recorded histrionics.

On *The Real McCoys,* the Latin farmhand PEPINO (who drove the tractor) would occasionally appear and give a little commentary. That was a popular TV show from the late '50s: "From West Virginia they came to stay/In sunny Califor-ni-a/Now Grandpappy's the head of the clan . . ." The family lives happily on this farm and goes into town once a week. Pepino got a chance to record *The Many Sides of Pepino,* and he could sing and play the vibes—he actually had *talent.*

♦ **AJ: So many of these second-string stars made records—**

King Guion's *Emotion, Inc.,* ABC-Paramount.

Jackie Gleason presents *"Oooo!",* Capitol Records.

♦ MM: GENE BARRY, star of *Burke's Law* and *Bat Masterson,* made an album. DOBIE GILLIS (Dwayne Hickman) did a fine record on Capitol when his show was popular. TELLY SAVALAS made a series of records, one of which is outstanding—it's the one where he recites (when he tries to *sing* he doesn't make it). Actually, when *any* celebrity tries to recite, the record is usually noteworthy. ANTHONY QUINN made a masterpiece: *In My Own Way I Love You,* with deathless lines like "Our love is like the distance to the moon." I can't talk *gruff-sensitive* like him, but this record is pure and it's moving. The backing musicians must have had fun: imagine the studio with the orchestra, and Anthony sitting on a high stool in front of the mike—with a sheet in front of him; you know he didn't memorize the lines!

Other celebrities who made records include CASSIUS CLAY (*I Am The Greatest!*—before he changed his name to Muhammad Ali), DAVID HEMMINGS ('60s-influenced album; not too bad), and BUDDY EBSON (from the *Beverly Hillbillies*)—that's a good one. While he was filming *The Fugitive,* DAVID JANSSEN made *The Hidden Island,* a romantic record about a desert island far away in the Pacific. He was searching for true love and happiness, away from the rat race—something we're all looking for.

Of course, we mustn't forget MIKE CURB, California's lieutenant governor a few years back. He was the main producer and part-owner of the '60s SIDEWALK label which released all those great biker soundtracks. One masterpiece was *Teenage Rebellion* which had such classics as "Pot Party," "Young Girl's Mistake," "Make Love Not War" and "Gay Teenager"—none of this was ever brought up during his political campaigns. Of course, if he had tried to go to the White House, I'm sure we would have heard all about it!

The Sidewalk house bands were always great: garage bands with double-neck guitars, like DAVEY ALLAN & The ARROWS. *Freakout USA* is a classic psychedelic compilation LP. "Poisons in My Body" by the International Theater Foundation is about drugs; you hear subliminal sounds and a harmonica going up and down the scale using the little chromatic button. Other good tracks include "Yellow Pill" by MOM'S BOYS; "Don't Try to Crawl Back" by the JESTERS and [personal favorite] "I Like the Way You Freak Out!" by the HANDS OF TIME.

Besides Sidewalk, there were other smaller labels like SOMERSET, which turned into ALSHIRE. Then the label became more creative and produced records like the *Animated Egg,* one of my favorite psychedelic instrumental recordings. After sales declined, the producers took the *Animated Egg* tracks, mixed in echoes and outer space effects, and re-released it as *Astro Sounds from the Year 2000* with a cover showing a girl dancing in a space suit! They were determined to get the most from their master tapes . . .

Harpo in Hi-Fi, Mercury Records.

Another masterpiece is Alfred Hitchcock's *Music to be Murdered By.* Each track has an introduction by Alfred. He says, "Why shouldn't I make a record? After all, my measurements are 33-45-78!"

Sixties records have been well-documented, so I'll just mention one more: the MIND EXPANDERS' *What's Happening.* They do "Sensory Overload," "Mandala," and my favorite, "Pictures at a Psychedelic Art Exhibition"—obviously, that's background music for a "trip"!

A SUB-CELEBRITY classic is *Folk Songs for the 21st Century* by the actor SHELDON ALLMAN—I've noticed him on *Twilight Zone* episodes. He had some songs to get out of his system, and probably knew somebody at a record company. Actually, his tunes are quite good—they're all about what it'll be like in the nuclear age: "If We Blow Up, We'll Go Out Together." "Radioactive Mama" has lines like: "We'll make gamma-gamma rays tonight . . . We're gonna rock-rock-rocket to the moon!" "The UNIVAC and the Humanoid" is about two computers that mate, and "We'll Crawl Out Through The Fallout" is self-explanatory.

A final sub-celebrity category is CELEBRITY ANIMAL recordings: there are LPs by *Mr Ed, Rin Tin Tin* ("Yo, Rinnie!"), and *Lassie.* Actually, sound effects-and-animals is an amusing topic: *The Singing Dogs of Copenhagen; Dog Training* by Barbara Woodhouse; plus albums entitled *Insects* and *Frogs.* I also like people trying to imitate animals (a favorite from my adolescence is NERVOUS NORVUS's "Ape Call") and I'm sure there are many more out there.

♦ ♦ ♦ **TV MUSIC** ♦ ♦ ♦

Sometimes it's necessary to turn down the lights when you hear a record for the first time. The cover of this LP proclaims, "From the original soundtrack of the urban eclipse silent film, *Companion to TV,*" and when I played it I discovered it was absolutely silent—there's no sound on the record! Whoever made this was *pro-television* and wanted to make sure that if you got the urge to play a record while watching TV, you couldn't possibly interrupt anything. I think this goes John Cage [author of *Silence*] one further. For sheer *listenability,* this has got to be one of the most tolerable records ever made!

♦ *V: I think TV has lowered the IQ of the world—*

♦ MM: I'm critical of television *programming,* not of television itself. I work with the TV on a lot, just like other people work with the stereo on. I like hearing the ambient sounds of *The Fugitive* or *Perry Mason—* shows of that era don't have a lot of actual violence or loud music, so at the right volume they can function as ambient sound. And even though they're staged, they're authentic documents of life at that time—you'll see what the cars and houses looked like, what people wore and how they talked.

Television commercials contain some of the strangest music ever recorded. The '50s had great ones: the deep voice of *Mr Clean;* the *Jolly Green Giant;* the *Slinky* song; the *Bosco* song; "See the USA/in your Chevrolet"; the *Chiquita Banana* tune; and the *Brylcreem* song ("a little dab'll do you"). If you forget the cartoons or visuals and just imagine the people in the

Sid Bass's *From Another World,* © RCA.
Album cover credits: photo: Wendy Hilty.

studio making these sounds—!

TV itself provides a *huge* field of quirky material, and with the advent of the VCR a new way of collecting music has been opened up. Anything that's on TV you can own, such as the great PETE RUGOLO music from *Richard Diamond* or VIC MIZZY's music for the *Addams Family.* If you have a mixing board, you can edit out the voice of Fester (or whoever) or leave in some unexpected sound effect. You can create music very much like *Shock!* or *Jungle Odyssey;* if you listen with the Dean Elliott approach you're getting the music *with* the sound effects! And there's no way to get that great *Carnival of Souls* organ music without taping it off the video.

In fact, the films listed in *Incredibly Strange Films* probably contain some of the greatest music ever recorded—it's time to examine that. That could be a book in itself: *Incredibly Strange Soundtracks.* Some of the world's most imaginative music is on film, and the reason it was never released is because it's so strange to begin with! And it never *will* be released; *The Day The Earth Stood Still* soundtrack never came out because in that industry there's so much red tape—it costs too much to get the rights. Collecting sound on videotape is the new frontier!

♦ ♦ ♦ OUTER SPACE ♦ ♦ ♦

Another major influence was science-fiction film soundtracks, especially the ones featuring theremin. I was addicted to *Forbidden Planet,* which has a soundtrack by the great electronics pioneers, LOUIS AND BEBE BARRON. I have a 1948 (the year the vinyl LP appeared) recording of them in San Francisco performing background music behind a lecture by Anaïs Nin at the SF Art Institute. I was fascinated by the tonalities the Barrons generated—the *Forbidden Plan-*

et soundtrack is still one of the most imaginative electronic music creations of all time. They did tape manipulations, generated tones of their own, and basically *wrote the book* on what outer space sounded like. *Star Trek, Star Wars* and many more movies owe a lot to that film—not just the music, either.

Other sci-fi movie favorites include *Invaders from Mars* and *Destination Moon,* plus lower-budget films like *Fiend Without a Face* and *I Was a Teenage Werewolf*—both had great theremin work. The '50s-'60s were prime years for movies, books, and records exploring the *unknown:* life on other worlds, the mystery of the infinite universe. You knew something was out there and you had to go exploring, no matter what the sacrifice. But it was an unattainable dream; the records and the movies reflected that.

WALTER SCHUMANN made one classic record: *Exploring the Unknown.* Most of his records were glee club-like and *true* easy listening, but on this one he hit pay dirt. Amidst celestial choirs you hear the deep, resonant voice of PAUL FREES narrating: "And he sat down on the face of the planet, and there were blue mountains in the distance . . ." Those words painted pictures and ideas and visions to me, as I'm sure they did to many.

When I played *Companion to TV* I discovered it was absolutely silent—there's no sound on the record! Whoever made this was *pro-television* and wanted to make sure that if you got the urge to play a record while watching TV, you couldn't possibly interrupt anything.

One of my favorite records, both as a child and as an adult, is *A Child's Introduction To Outer Space.* Almost every one of the *Child's Introduction To* series was interesting, but this one is exceptional. There are tunes such as "Meet Space Pilot Jones/He's a member of the crew/With a very high IQ"—he's a good role model! Another lyric goes, "One day there will be a little satellite in space so we can all see TV at once"—this was the '50s, and that's come true. The scientific advisor on this LP was Willy Ley (the record producers weren't fooling around) who was one of my heroes.

♦ *AJ: He actually was a rocket scientist—*

♦ MM: Yes; along with Werner von Braun he helped develop the space age. The way this record attempts to inspire kids with catchy little jingles is beautiful: "Put a penny in the scale/and you will see/How much you weigh on Jupiter." There's even a calypso tune.

Journey to Infinity was a promotional record released by Cape Canaveral: "We must back this to get out into outer space, because that's where our hope lies." This is spoken by a deep-voiced narrator expressing optimism about another life on another planet, much like that scene in *When Worlds Collide,* when the spacemen get off the rocket and just breathe (forgetting that's not quite how it is, at least on the planets we know about). This is at the top of those *space optimism* records released in the '50s and '60s.

The early attempts at imagining the sounds of what life would be like in outer space usually involve the theremin, and one of its best players was Dr SAMUEL J. HOFFMAN, who did *Perfume Set to Music, Spiral Staircase,* and *The Day the Earth Stood Still* which had *double* theremins. Another great theremin record was made by CLARA ROCKMORE. In the '60s, the theremin was revived on rock records by LOTHAR & The HAND PEOPLE and CAPTAIN BEEFHEART. Well into the '70s German artists such as CLUSTER, TANGERINE DREAM and Klaus Schulze either used the theremin or imitated it on their synthesizers, but their records aren't nearly as much fun as the earlier American LPs. However, I *am* listening to KRAFTWERK again; *Computer World, Trans-Europe Express,* and *Man Machine* are classics. They use the sounds of telephones dialing and bicycle derailleur gears spinning. More electronic sound pioneering can be found on BRUCE HAACK's *The Way Out Record for Children* and Mort Garson's *Electric Lucifer . . .*

RUSS GARCIA's *Fantastica: Music from Outer Space* with the spirograph on the cover is another great atmospheric record from the '50s. Without electronic gimmickry, he achieved that feeling of *floating* in outer space; basically the record just drifts for both sides. *Strings for a Space Age* also features some nice celestial

Ferrante and Teicher's *Blast Off!*, ABC-Paramount.

female voices ("Ooh-ooh") with violins. Another excellent '50s LP is PAUL TANNER's *Music for Heavenly Bodies;* FRANK COMSTOCK's *Music from Outer Space* is also good—inspiring!

♦ **AJ: We seem to have lost all our frontiers, and with that our hopes as well—**

♦ **MM:** That's a good point. We need hope; we need something to look forward to . . . A *darker* side of the Space Race is reflected in *If the Bomb Falls.* This was released with a booklet titled "How to Build a Fallout Shelter." In a very governmental voice it instructed you to put aside a pound of sugar per month per person, ten pounds of beans, etc . . .

♦ **AJ: But if the bomb did fall, you'd be fried to a crisp in your homemade bunker—**

♦ **MM:** Absolutely. I'd love to find a permanent headquarters for the Museum that had a '50s bomb shelter underneath, so I could display all my bomb shelter memorabilia in its "natural" setting. I have a lot of fallout pamphlets, posters, and objects like a toy atomic reactor that was sold back in the '50s when people were *optimistic* about atomic energy. I have a display of about thirty pro-nuclear books from the '50s and what they all have in common is: the chapter on nuclear waste disposal is missing!

♦ **AJ: We grew up under the specter of the bomb; we had one monolithic fear which we could balance out by the dream of exploring outer space. Today, however, the bomb is just one of many fears—**

♦ **MM:** It's time for the MELACHRINO STRINGS to issue a whole new series of recordings: *Music to Survive the Recession By . . . Music for the Greenhouse Effect.* There have been so many "Music For . . ." albums— that's a category for a whole book. Actually, I love the Melachrino Strings; they're some of the records I play most at this stage of my life. *Music for Relaxation;*

A Child's Introduction to Outer Space, Golden Records. © 1959 Bell Records, Inc. Produced by Bell Records, Inc.

Tony Schwartz's *The New York Taxi Driver*, Columbia Masterworks.
Album cover credits: photo: Alfred Gescheidt.

Music for Dining; Music to Read By—these are all from the same people, and all of them were meant to be played at a subdued volume under dim lighting.

♦ **AJ: Records like these have as their underlying premise hope for the future: that you could make your life better, or that the world was progressing. But the new generation knows that their parents had a better life than they're going to have—**

♦ MM: Increasingly I feel the same way. I don't live in the past, nor am I nostalgic, but there's no reason to *ignore* the past, as I've said before. Consequently, if you remember what it was like in the '50s—well, I remember I could go out at *any* hour and walk any street without fear. Maybe there were a few weirdos out there, but nothing like today. And this is a good reason why I think a museum of this sort is needed more than ever, because hopefully the good things that were the *keys* to that past way of life can be re-assessed, re-trieved, and possibly re-integrated into our present situation. That's how the past can function as a teacher: certain things *were* better, and let's bring them back!

This is not to deny all the technological advances in medicine and science; computers *are* great. It's just that little boys don't sit on the floor and play FRANK LUTHER's *Raggedy Ann Songs and Stories,* and little girls don't play with their kittens anymore, like that girl on the cover of *A Child's Very First Songbook.* Today, genuine wistfulness and innocence appear to be obsolete. Now it's like *Dennis the Menace* [points to LP cover with close-up of Dennis's bratty face aiming two six-guns at the viewer]. He was a forerunner of the '90s [laughs].

♦ **V: [looking at LP] Who is TONY SCHWARTZ?**

♦ MM: Tony Schwartz, one of my favorite persons, made a number of early recordings on private labels which were recorded on the streets with hand-held tape recorders. He did "concept" records like *Sounds of the Junkyard* for Folkways, but he also did his own "When I was a boy in Brooklyn" albums, and recorded nostalgic sounds of playing stickball in the street, all beautifully narrated. He rode around in New York taxicabs taping the cabbies' views on everything from baseball to weddings, and then released *New York Taxi Driver*—a "philosophy" record. He also recorded *It's a Dog's Life,* which equates our lives to that of a dog's.

♦ **AJ: [pointing to LP] Sounds for Sick People—*is that soothing sounds to help sick people get well?***

♦ MM: [laughs] The tunes are about *being* sick, like "St James Infirmary," "Fever," "Don't Get Around Much Anymore," "Dry Bones"—all arranged very nicely. This recording was made by a studio band: people who came together just for this date. Sometimes the "studio band" concept is nice because the people involved aren't concerned about touring or creating an "image" or things like that—they just want to get the project done. *Music for Crazy, Mixed-Up People:* records like these were quite successful at making fun of the reality of life.

♦ ♦ ♦ **COMEDY** ♦ ♦ ♦

♦ **V: Tell us about some favorite COMEDY records—**

♦ MM: *La Dolce Henke* by MEL HENKE has some amazing tracks, with hip, sophisticated repartee between male and female voices. This is sort of a swinger's party record; it had that wonderful, sexually-repressed battiness of the early '60s: [cool jazz comes on, then a hipster monologue:] "Man, what a body! Dig those crazy bumpers and that rear-end suspension; wow! What a power plant—just right for a drag strip . . . Like, let's see how it feels! . . . Cool . . . Built for comfort . . . I'm going to swing with it . . ."

Mel Henke's *La Dolce Henke,* © 1962 Warner Bros. Records, Inc.
Album cover credits: cover photo: Sid Avery.

[female voice:] *"Let's go! . . . Take it easy! . . . Easy! . . . Slower! . . . That's better! . . . [breathy] Yeah!"* I wish people still talked like that—life would certainly be more fun.

♦ *V: You have an album titled* **Music for Rat Fink Lovers**—*what was a rat fink?*

La Dolce Henke is sort of a swinger's party record; it had that wonderful, sexually-repressed battiness of the early '60s.

♦ MM: That's a tough question. I think it was a state of mind. The term could be good, it could be bad, it could be sneaky, it could be really great, it could be someone you love, it could be someone you hate and despise. Nobody knew for sure. On this record, the music is all easy listening tracks performed by a studio orchestra. But what makes it special is: at the end of each track, a girl's voice says, "Oh . . . you rat-fink!" And she says that in twelve different sexy ways. One track has a heavenly choir and strings interrupted by hysterical laughter, winding down to "Oh [gasp] you ra-rat fink . . . oh-h-h . . ." Then it immediately goes into another track, which ends with more coital laughter: "You *dirty* [laugh] rat fink . . ." It's a very sexy record, no doubt about it.

Another ratfink album, *Rods n' Ratfinks,* was released by MR GASSER & The WEIRDOS, who also put out *Surfink!* and *Hot Rod Hootenanny.* Mr Gasser, of course, was ED "BIG DADDY" ROTH. He, along with fellow hot rod aficionados and assorted freaks, were backed by some great studio musicians. On these Capitol recordings, GARY USHER (a surf music producer) and other professionals backed up these amateurs who were yelling things like "There's termites in my Woody!" to produce some wild, nutty records that just hint at the real fun that existed at that time. I don't think they sold all that well; they represented the "bad" side of the "Beach Blanket" films. These original characters were too *weird* to be put on the screen with Annette Funicello and Frankie Avalon and the gang.

There were a lot of monster records released, like FRANK-N-STEIN & HIS GHOULS' five great instrumental dance albums. One of my favorites on VeeJay is *It's Monster Surfing Time!*—just surf music with monster sounds. "Surfin' Time in the Creature's Lagoon" opens up with a ghoul yelling and then breaks into a great instrumental (similar to all the hot rod albums which blended car sounds with surf music). This was the rebellious music of its time—parents thought monsters were "creepy," so kids wanted them even more!

And all this spawned two great TV shows in '64: *The Addams Family* and *The Munsters*—both well-written and fun, and nobody ever got really hurt, either. Sadly, the Munsters never had an official soundtrack LP, but there was a band called the MUNSTERS which played surf music.

One of the bizarre men of our time is YOGI YORGESSON. He was an American who thought he could make a name for himself as a Scandinavian, so he adopted this name and recorded an LP of songs like "Yingle Bells," "I Yust Go Nuts at Christmas/That Yolly Holiday"—basically, every "j" sound gets pronounced with a "y." He put out a lot of singles, and I also have a compilation album by him, *The Great Comedy Hits of . . .*

KATIE LEE recorded *Songs of Couch and Consultation*—all folk songs about being psychoanalyzed on a couch, having paranoias, and not being able to cope with life when "you *can't* do this and you *can't* do that." My favorite cut is "Repressed Hostility Blues."

MICKEY KATZ made a series of absurd answers to the SPIKE JONES records. He took on this Yiddish personality and in "The Knish Doctor" he sings a parody of "Witch Doctor" (which was a big hit at the time) but substitutes "Knish." "K-nock around the Clock"—same thing. Basically what he did was parody recent song hits such as "The Poiple Ki-kish-ki-eater"; "The Yiddish Mambo," "Katz Puts on the Dog," and "Sing Along with Mikele" (instead of "Sing Along with Mitch"). And musically, these are excellent—he made a half-dozen records. He probably wrote these tunes in the Full Belly Deli on the East Side. He's the Jewish Spike Jones.

♦ ♦ ♦ **BEATNIK** ♦ ♦ ♦

A favorite beatnik record was recorded by JACK

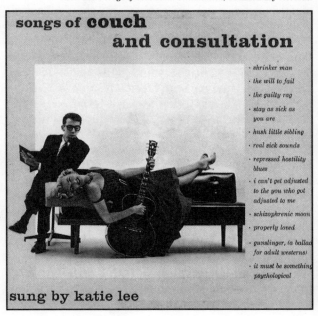

Katie Lee's *Songs of Couch and Consultation*, Commentary Records.

songs of **couch and consultation**

· shrinker man
· the will to fail
· the guilty rag
· stay as sick as you are
· hush little sibling
· real sick sounds
· repressed hostility blues
· i can't get adjusted to the you who got adjusted to me
· schizophrenic moon
· properly loved
· gunslinger, (a ballad for adult westerns)
· it must be something psychological

sung by katie lee

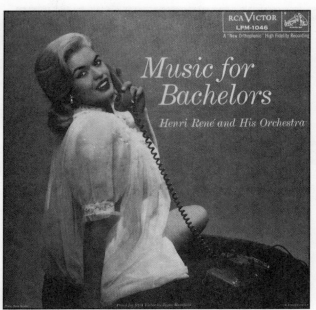

Henri René's *Music for Bachelors*, © RCA Victor.
Album cover credits: photo: Barry Kromer, posed for RCA Victor
by Jayne Mansfield.

KEROUAC with ZOOT SIMS and AL COHN: *Blues and Haikus.* He says something and they answer on the sax. On one song he talks about walking across empty baseball fields: "Branches jumping/Bluebird—*no,* blackbird!" [tenor sax]/"Branch still jumping/In the open air!" Kerouac is in top form, just before the alcoholism hit. You can tell why the legend was formed, because this is great stuff—this recording alone is enough to justify his reputation as a truly inspired improviser of hip poetry.

How to Speak Hip is a Beat era record that came with a *manual.* One of its speakers, John Brent, later joined the San Francisco *Committee Theater* which was produced by a great, forgotten scene-maker, Bill Love. The hipster-narrator tells you what you should have in your pad to be groovy, what kind of stash you should have; how to be cool and not get hung up, what you should dig, and how to not be paranoid. In the section on how to be cool, he tells you that it's uncool to claim that you used to room with "Bird"; it's uncool to claim that you *have* birds. It defines such terms as to "wig out," to "cook," to "cut out"—everything you need to know is explained . . .

♦ *V: There are also recordings of beatnik poetry readings by Lawrence Ferlinghetti, Allen Ginsberg, and Kenneth Patchen. I found a Japanese poetry-with-jazz record by KAZUKO SHIRAISHI backed by SAM RIVERS, and it sounded so strange; one number is titled "Once Again the Season of the Sacred Lecher." [?!] Her inspiration was Kenneth Rexroth—the godfather of reading poetry with jazz . . . Also, any recording by WILLIAM S. BURROUGHS will be entertaining; he has such a sarcastic, unique delivery, and often his material is* **nightmarish.**

♦ MM: FRANKLYN MacCORMACK made a lot of spoken word records; he's sort of a "straight" KEN NORDINE. His finest work is *The Torch Is Burning,* which he recites in a deep, resonant voice. I've actually seen people cry while listening to "Smoke Gets in Your Eyes."

♦ ♦ ♦ EASY LISTENING ♦ ♦ ♦

The JACKIE GLEASON easy listening series is often talked about, and there *are* some masterpieces. *Oooo!* is my favorite; the cover shows a beautiful woman pursing her lips. Usually there are female voices in the background humming celestially—a lot of easy listening records feature choruses like that. Gleason often has great covers—*Lonesome Echoes* has a Salvador Dali painting on the front and a photo of Gleason with Dali on the back. But unfortunately it doesn't *sound* very surreal.

♦ ♦ ♦ CHILDREN'S RECORDS ♦ ♦ ♦

Children's recordings are a very fertile territory. The *Bozo the Clown* records (*Bozo and His Rocket Ship, Bozo Goes to the Moon*) are amazingly influential on all of us, whether we admit it or not. They came with books; you put on the record and read: "Hello, I'm Bozo—now turn the page!" (ding!) "Now here we are in Brazil. There's a parrot on his shoulder. Next time you come bring crackers!" (ding!) "Did you turn the page? If you did, you are now in Greenland . . ." If that doesn't inspire you as a child, you may as well give up!

When adults make records for children, they think they have to come down to a different level and be playful . . . and sometimes they create these amazing things. *Sparky's Magic Piano* is one of the all-time greats, in which a piano comes alive and talks to Sparky through a "Sonobox" (a voice synthesizer you

Mickey Katz's *The Most Mishige*, Capitol Records.

put by your throat, similar to what Laurie Anderson used). Children's records are chock-full of imaginative arrangements, vocals and other innovations because they *had* to be—children *have* imaginations!

♦ **V: *What are some other great children's records?***
♦ MM: All the records in the FRANK LUTHER series were good: *A Child's First: Toys, Games, Pets, Christmas,* and *Birthday. Health Can Be Fun* is all songs about health. Adults can really gain insight from these records. There's so much tension in the world today, and there's nothing like a few minutes with Frank Luther to straighten you out!

All the *Child's Introduction To . . .* records are good, including the one on sex (although on that one they didn't quite deliver the goods as much as on the outer space ones). *Stories for Children Who Ask Questions*

asks, "What are stars? What makes rain?" It's not bad. *How to Tell Children the Facts of Life* doesn't. *A Day in the Life of a Dinosaur* is a classic, and *Songs of the South* contains Uncle Remus songs like "Zip-pi-dy doo-da." A *great* Disney record is "The Enchanted Tiki Room," with fake talking parrots.

When I was growing up, one of my big influences was *Rusty in Orchestraville,* a real imagination-enhancer. It tells about a little boy who doesn't like his piano, whereupon a voice tells him to go to Orchestraville where the instruments are *happy;* they'll talk to him and be his friends. He goes there and all of a sudden he's happy; he comes back and says, "Mom, I *want* to study the piano!" This is an *optimism record.*

Now's a good time to tip our hats to the great MEL BLANC, just for coming up with the voices for Bugs

Max K. Gilstrap Whistles, Gilstrap Records. © 1958 Zilph Gilstrap. Album cover credits: photo: Ansel Adams.

Bunny, Porky Pig, Yosemite Sam plus hundreds of others. His vocals were astonishing; in a split second he could leap from one cartoon voice to another, and these records weren't overdubbed, they were done in one take! Records like *Tweety & Sylvester* and *Woody Woodpecker's Picnic* all had Mel Blanc's voice and CARL STALLING's music, and they're all fantastic investigations of the childhood psyche. Mel Blanc has an autobiography out titled *That's Not All, Folks* (co-written with Philip Bashe)—it's funny.

♦ ♦ ♦ OCCULT ♦ ♦ ♦

Actually, there were a lot of astrology records released from the '50s through the '70s; I can't recall seeing any from the '80s. There were also a number of witchcraft records, including one made by an actual witch: LOUISE HUEBNER's *Seduction Through Witchcraft*. It has an electronic atmosphere provided by Louis and Bebe Barron, and is definitely very strange. The '60s paved the way for recordings of music to grow your plants by, plus a host of occult and satanic records like *The Occult Explosion* and those records by VINCENT PRICE. Another '60s artifact worthy of mention here is TIMOTHY LEARY's *Turn On, Tune In, Drop Out*—it's exactly like you'd expect it to be. It's pretty good, and has been re-released.

♦ ♦ SPORTS INSTRUCTION RECORDS ♦ ♦

The CARLTON HOW TO series of instructional records includes *How to Handle Your Boat; How to Skin-Dive* (by Lloyd Bridges); *How to Improve Your Bowling* by Billy Golembiewski; *How to Play Baseball* (by a Yankees manager); and a favorite: *How to Plan the Perfect Dinner Party.* These are all spoken very clearly and distinctly—they truly *are* instructional. And taken as pure poetry, they're magnificent: Billy Golembiewski (who was a famous bowler in the '50s)

tells you in his "Joisey" accent to concentrate on the *third* dot in the lane—that will help you curve the ball a certain way . . .

I listen to exercise records from the '50s and '60s, and I like the ones that have a tune for every sport. Often the voice is mixed with perky music from an orchestra with percussion, and such records can *invigorate* the tired listener. I prefer them to more recent records with modern aerobic beats; when I pass those storefronts that have been converted to "exercise centers" I feel a huge aggressive burst coming out the door at me. Whereas these older records have a smoother, more lilting tone: "Okay, *touch* the top of your head/And *touch* the bottom of your foot." You can find instructional records for almost every activity: remember the old Hatha Yoga records by Richard Hittelman or Magana Baptiste? There are also karate records, skiing records, swimming records . . . self-improvement was big back then, and it's no different now.

♦ ♦ ♦ WHISTLING RECORDS ♦ ♦ ♦

Whistling records have always been a favorite because of their purity and simplicity; as Lauren Bacall said, "It's easy—you just put your lips together and blow!" FRED LOWERY, the blind whistler who was a preacher, was a master of putting his lips together and blowing. He had some gospel-oriented recordings out, but his gems were on the Decca label: *Walking Along, Kicking the Leaves* and *Whistle a Happy Tune. Whistling for You* is an early 10", and he made some records with bird sounds, too. Just listen to him doing "The High and the Mighty"—you'll never be the same! It's great just imagining someone in a studio before a big oval microphone just blowing at it, while an orchestra plays in the background.

Another famous whistler is a ranger from Yosemite National Park, MAX K. GILSTRAP. He whistles bird calls and bird songs, and on the back of his albums it says that he also gives whistling lessons! I bought six of his records at a flea market, and they're definitely in a class of their own . . . Another great whistling record was made by ART COATES. But probably the most famous whistler of all (he was on TV) was MUZZY MARCELLINO, who has a beautiful tone and quite a range as well. His LP has a colorful parrot cover.

Of course, the key whistling records for me involve people who would like to be birds—perhaps they were birds in their past life. RALPH PLATT is one of the masters; again, he's got religious roots. "And the Birds Sing His Praise" is one song which expresses how much he'd like to be a bird—perhaps because they live up in the trees and are closer to heaven. And who's to say that's not the way we were meant to talk—perhaps somewhere along the way we got derailed by adding all these vowels and consonants. Maybe if we all *whistled* at each other, we might be able to communicate better!

♦ **AJ:** *A lot of these whistling records have a naivete and genuineness which society classifies as "corny"—*

♦ **MM:** Lost innocence . . . unfathomable to us today. No matter how hard you try, you'll never be able to really get into the mind-set which produced records like the "Music for Gracious Living" series. Of course, I always emphasize that I'm not trying to live in the past. I love all the new inventions like the VCR, but I say: use that to examine the software of the past. Now we can freeze-frame the *Monster from Piedras Blancas* and see if the make-up artist did a good job on the left eye . . . like in *Blow-Up.*

♦ **V:** *What do you prefer collecting the most?*

♦ **MM:** The museum's been my *life,* but if I have one *hobby,* it's been the acquiring of records like these. The story of America for the past 40 years could be told by a chronological layout of all these LPs. You could infer the social mores, the fads, and see how this country has changed—just by laying out all these records on a wall (if you had a wall that could stretch for 5,000 feet). Take *Music for Gracious Living*—this kitchen scene would not be the same if it were shot today. No longer does the word "gracious" enter into *anything;* you just don't hear that word anymore. Because—are things gracious anymore? I'm not cynical—I'm just asking the question!

With the political, cultural and commercial situation the way it is now, we'll never have records like these made again. Not only are albums like these being tossed out every day, but obviously the CD is trying its best to make the 12" LP obsolete. Actually, even though I don't have a CD player, I love CDs! My approach is: "Welcome to the world of sound!" which embraces

The Nutty Squirrels' *Bird Watching* (Sascha Burland and Don Elliott), Columbia Records. ® 1959—Goodford. Album cover credits: cover photo: Columbia Records Photo Studio—Henry Parker.

everything: wax cylinders, 78s, 45s, 8-track tapes (which are almost extinct); 16-2/3 rpm records (like Jimmy Swaggart's *Guided Missiles, God, and the Atomic Bomb*), and those giant 18" V-J discs released during World War II. (They contained radio shows and selections by people like Benny Goodman and aren't particularly strange, except that the hardware isn't available today.)

But it's the CD *snobs* that I don't appreciate; they say, "Oh, you *still* have records?" [laughs] I say, "Welcome to CDs!" and they say, "Unwelcome to everything else!" I know people who have sold records because they've "gone CD," yet many of the records they sold will never *be* on CD. It's so simple to have *both.* (I think my main criticism of CDs is: you need magnifying glasses to read them. Soon there'll be a generation of people who need reading glasses before they're 20!)

It's silly to close your mind to the history of recorded sound. So many 78s have been lost, so many master tapes are decaying or have been lost. All the great novelty recordings of the '20s and '30s are largely gone; even the master tapes of the great SPIKE JONES are probably lost. All those soundtracks from the great cartoons of the '30s-'50s: how would you hear them? You'd have to tape them off TV. The *films* have been preserved, but not the soundtrack masters. Now, a few people are putting out compilation LPs of nearly-lost recordings (for example, *Las Vegas Grind),* and that's great.

Actually, people *were* trading in their LPs like mad, but that's slowing down, now that the seeds of doubt have been bandied about. And even if the disc isn't there, the LP sleeve itself is a great piece of art. Some-

Peter Barclay's *Music for Gracious Living: After the Dance*, Columbia Records. Album cover credits: photo: Hedrich-Blessing.

Communist Party Songs, High In-Fidelity Records. © 1963, Kanrom. No LP enclosed.

times the only existing photo of an artist is on the back cover. I've seen LPs in frames and they look beautiful; top photographers and artists were hired to create them, and some of them are in '50s colors that are impossible to duplicate today.

♦ *V: Do you weed out your monaural duplicates?*

♦ MM: From late '57 on, *stereo* became the buzzword, and some companies knew what they were doing with it and some didn't. RCA *did* with their "Living Stereo" series, whereas some of the Warner Bros stereo records seem to leave out details that are in the mono recordings! Capitol Full Dimensional Stereo is quite good, but their regular stereo and particularly their Duophonic ("playable in mono or stereo"; the *Beach Boys* are an example) was a disaster. "Electronically rechanneled stereo" is bad—all the early rock classics like Chuck Berry or Gene Vincent or Chess blues artists like Muddy Waters are better in mono because they were *recorded* in mono. You can compare a mono to a stereo record and notice that a cymbal or a tapping of a foot or even a background vocal is missing! Phil Spector said, "Back to mono," and I don't agree with that because stereo *can* be astounding, but always check— in fact, keep both versions if you like the record, so you have the option. Especially of your favorites.

♦ *V: A lot of 45s are superior to the LP or CD versions: they're louder and have more bass and "live" presence—*

♦ MM: Very true. It makes sense that if the grooves on the 45 are larger, then more information can be picked up. With a lot of recordings, 45s are the most pure form of the release. Often a 45 would come out on a small label and then be picked up by a larger label (for example, the CHANTAYS recorded "Pipeline" on the Downey label, but once it became a hit, DOT picked it

up). So if you're a purist you want that first pressing, even though *every* record (after the initial studio source recording on 1" tape) is a repressing.

However, LPs are my main focus; I call them "the perfect square foot." The Golden Age of the LP was 1955-1965—that's when they were the most innovative in terms of sound experimentation. I love them because there's room for great cover art, extensive liner notes, plus I like the round labels in the middle of the record—sometimes *they're* art, too.

♦ *V: What makes a record strange?*

♦ MM: First of all, it has to be different—that goes without saying. It should be challenging, unfamiliar, even intimidating. It has to take you to *another* level. Often a strange recording is done by people just having fun . . . trying to reach that pinnacle of personal self-expression. Sometimes it seems like people weren't as afraid to be different back then, although now people want to be different even *more*—but it's harder because so much has been done! It was more innocent: just the fact that KALI BAHLU got released on vinyl is strange enough. Another key factor is: a lot of these records were done in one take—*live,* with no overdubs. They were just, "Let's get together and have fun!" That's why something out of tune or out of rhythm (like the SHAGGS) can be strange.

What dictates "strangeness" is also one's heritage. If you were raised in Madagascar and had never heard the Sex Pistols or Tom Jones or Barry Manilow, you might find them strange. Which would a Martian prefer: Jack Jones or LUCIA PAMELA? So it's the associations you've had in your life that set the stage for "strangeness" as perceived by the listener.

I'm a big fan of exotic and world music. Good Zulu and aboriginal music is outstanding, as is almost any-

Tony Schwartz's *A Dog's Life,* © 1958 Folkways Records and Service Corp. Album cover credits: photos: Ken Heyman.

118

thing from New Zealand or New Guinea or Africa. The liner notes might say, "This is a tribal dance to invoke the spirit of romance for a wedding," but when you listen to it you don't get that—you're just hearing strange sounds. Northern Sahara has some eerie incantations and guttural sounds, and anything from

The story of America for the past 40 years could be told by a chronological layout of all these LPs. You could infer the social mores, the fads, and see how this country has changed.

Tibet or Nepal is from another world—relaxing and frightening at the same time (something most music can't achieve). To hear those monks chant is to know that you should be doing it too—it's intimidating, in a way. Labels like Lyrichord, Folkways and Capitol went into villages the world over with tape recorders, much like John Hammond did with bluesmen like Robert Johnson.

♦ **V: What standards do you use to weed out records?**

♦ MM: Every two years or so I sweep through my records to 1) refamiliarize myself, 2) get rid of a few duplicates, and 3) get rid of what I don't like anymore. You have to keep the collection alive and moving. Any library has to be thinned out now and then. I try to keep my personal record collection around 10,000; if I kept everything I'd be like the Library of Congress. There was a time I wanted to keep everything, but then I realized, "I don't need the twelfth Bruce Springsteen album for my archives; I'll let somebody else take care of that." But I *do* need every PERREY & KINGSLEY album.

I've gotten rid of reissues in later packagings; greatest hits packages; ones that are unplayable and that *don't* have a redeeming cover. I retained records which were musically historical for the Museum—ones which everyone would recognize or have some personal relationship with (that's one of the keys for *all* the records on display). Hopefully, in the future I'll have a '70s room, and if it's the early '70s I'll display *Carpenters* records. I personally feel that *Twiggy* was responsible for Karen Carpenter's death—that pressure to be thin killed her!

♦ **V: And she had a record out, too:** **Please Get My Name Right.**

♦ MM: With regard to exceptional records; I think the element of *surprise* is also a vital ingredient. If it doesn't surprise you, it can't get to first base on being strange, because that would mean you'd heard it before.

♦ **V: Time and history renew the context. After you've read how Karen Carpenter died, you can't**

listen to her records the same way again.

♦ MM: Yes. And even with sounds that are strange to almost all of us, preferences arise. For example, I prefer the high pitch of the red-winged blackbird to the deeper tones of the Baltimore oriole.

♦ **AJ: A lot of more consciously "experimental" records don't sound as marvelous to me as the wild naivete of KALI BAHLU—**

♦ MM: Of course, it's much better to hear her now than when the record came out in '67. This is a good example of how the past can be such a great teacher. In the '60s, Indian music was supposed to be holy or sacred, but when Kali Bahlu got together with some Indian musicians, together they created something which at the *time* might have seemed in poor taste or gauche, but in retrospect may turn out to be eminently more listenable than a Ravi Shankar album—for somebody looking for *entertainment,* anyway. Back then Kali Bahlu probably just seemed like part of the psychedelic context . . .

Also, a good barometer for a really strange record is how rare it is to find. Usually it didn't sell and wasn't bought in the first place. Whether a record was ahead of its time or in tune with the times means *nothing* (whether it be records, plastic toys of the '60s, or board games)—it's what it says *now* that matters. Because the best music is timeless. I can't say for certain that Kali Bahlu will be considered "classic" in the year 2130, but I do know that some of the music we thought *would* be preserved, won't. Personal vision, of course, is a factor.

♦ **AJ: Individuals who had this** **one record** **to get out of their system—**

♦ MM: One record—exactly. That's all they wanted to do, or all they were able to do. Didn't Einstein say that

Zounds! What Sounds!, Capitol Records.
Album cover credits: cover photo: Capitol Photo Studio—George Jerman.

Henri René's *Passion in Paint: Famous Paintings Set to Music,* © RCA Victor.

most people only have one or two truly original thoughts in their lifetime?

♦ **V: A lot of writers have only written one great book—**

♦ MM: The same goes for visual artists, musicians, car designers—Harley Earl developed the tail fin. (He kept restyling it, but it was basically *one* idea.) Bucky Fuller: the geodesic dome. Whatever it might be: pick the name, pick the development. In a way, if you could make the perfect record, why do others? Well, there are a number of "reasons": 1) commercial, 2) activity: idle hands are the devil's workshop! Even if what you do next isn't as good or original as what you did before, you have to do *something.*

♦ **V: I like the fact that Duchamp stopped his painting career just as he was "making it"; he proclaimed that retinal art was dead.**

♦ MM: Sometimes the surprise factor can't be activated until you've gone into hyperspace and sleep for 20 years until you're awakened, like in *Alien.* Maybe good music goes into hyperspace for 20 years to reach the audience that needs it. The surprise never has to die; there's always new generations to hear it—any great work of art will do that. A lot of records never got their proper exposure; they weren't onstage long enough to have their originality appreciated. And if I've never heard a record before, it may as well have been released yesterday, because I'm hearing it for the first time today.

Sometimes an original record springs from a concept; someone might think of a phrase like *Songs for Sick People* and then try to record an album illustrating that—although in this particular case the music isn't really very strange; it's just a *concept* album like Mel Torme's album about the moon. I could make up

a 90-minute tape just of all the different versions of "Peter Gunn" that have been recorded: from Mancini's original to remakes by the Anita Kerr singers, Duane Eddy, bongo versions—all the way up to the Art of Noise. The same goes for "Unchained Melody."

♦ **V: Everyone should make their own pet "theme" tapes—**

♦ MM: I could compile anthologies of songs about nuclear weapons and atomic energy, different versions of the *Route 66* theme, tunes about automobiles, tunes by and for dogs—we all remember the singing dogs who did "Oh Susannah" and "Jingle Bells." Hey, you could compile a tape of all songs about coffee: "Coffeetime," "Coffee Break," "You're the Cream in My Coffee," etc.

There's so much music that never *gets* on a record, such as GRIMES, the Human Jukebox, who performed at Fisherman's Wharf. During the bicentennial celebration back in '76, Philip Garner wired together various appliances to "play" the melody to "The Star Spangled Banner." This should have been recorded.

♦ **AJ: This hearkens back to those vaudeville performers who tried to extend entertainment possibilities as far as they could. There was the cat-o-phone: a row of cats with their heads in stocks. I guess the owner would pull their tails when he wanted a certain pitch of "meow."**

♦ MM: Can you imagine him on the same stage with the singing dogs? [laughs] Of course, now he'd have the animal rights activists after him. You just can't do anything anymore—uh oh, I'm probably getting into hot water here . . .

On the topic of unrecorded music: somebody performed a *Symphony for Car Horns* out in the desert. I'm sure the Dadaists and Futurists and even the New York loft scene in the '60s came up with some sound creations that we're not remembering properly. YOKO ONO mustn't be forgotten for her contributions to strangeness; she was certainly underrated—not highly listenable, for many people, but that's not what we're after here. There are some great tracks on *Fly,* and I'm sure her early gallery pieces had interesting moments, before she ever got on record. Her *Onobox* retrospective has been released by Rykodisc.

♦ **V: What about this record subtitled Famous Paintings Set to Music?**

♦ MM: Sometimes you spot a record jacket and get excited—that happened to me when I found *Passion in Paint* by Henri René and His Orchestra. I thought, "This is going to be really amazing," because one of the paintings on the back was Duchamp's "Nude Descending a Staircase"—I mean, how would they interpret *that?* There was also a Dali "soft watch." Unfortunately, the record turned out to be very pedestrian—it's not strange at all. So, sometimes the idea is better than the product, as far as the ears are concerned.

♦ **V: Can you think of any other characteristics of**

Leda Annest's *Portrait of Leda*, Columbia Records.
Album cover credits: photo: John Engstead.

exceptional music?

♦ MM: When we grew up, we were taught that there are five senses. But there *is* a sixth one that's missing in most records: *the sense of humor!* [laughs] See-hear-smell-touch-taste are the ones we take for granted, but this is the one we need the most. And certainly, people have proven that you can get by without taste—most people do!

NOTEWORTHY:

ROSS BAGDASARIAN's first big hit was "The Chipmunk's Song." After that, every time there was a new musical fad he would pop up with "Chipmunks Go Disco" or *Chipmunk Punk.*

Other EXOTICA records include Frank Hunter's *White Goddess,* Danny Guglielmi's *Adventure in Sound* (featuring vocals by Dena), Robert Drasnin's *Percussion Exotique*—there are many more.

Other good CELEBRITY recordings are by Andy Griffith, Allen Ludden, Dennis Weaver, Laurence Harvey, George Sanders (remember, his suicide note read, "I leave you to this sweet cesspool"), and *An Evening with Hugh Downs.*

SCENTED records: *Lady Chatterley's Lover* was actually impregnated with the smell of roses. *Aphrodite* was released on scented red vinyl.

EXPERIMENTAL: In 1918 MARCEL DUCHAMP composed "Glass Music," which was designed for glass marbles passing through glass funnels and dropping onto glass plates. It was performed at one of the Dada

events. Now there's a CD of Duchamp's music available from Edition Block, Schaperstrasse 11, D-1000 Berlin 15, Germany . . . A British composer, ANNEA LOCKWOOD, recorded using glass instruments in the '60s and '70s—check it out! . . . BRUNO HOFFMAN: *Music for Glass Harmonica.* The glass harmonica is a row of champagne glasses—different amounts of water produce a different pitch, and if you rub your fingers on the edge, you can get some beautiful theremin-like sounds. A CD is available now . . . TOD DOCKSTADER made *Apocalypse* and *Drone* (on Owl Records), plus another LP on Folkways. He called his music "organized sound," and it involved tape manipulations, natural sounds and electronics, like Jean-Jacques Perrey . . . Of course, almost all of the records by Harry Partch and Moondog deserve a listen.

SOUNDTRACKS: LEITH STEPHENS composed *The Wild One, Private Hell '36,* etc—he's great. So is NINO ROTA. Another good soundtrack is *Sweden: Heaven or Hell;* side one ends with assaulting, double-edged guitars sawing away at your brain—a great tune unlike any other guitar instrumental you've heard.

OUTER SPACE: JIMMIE HASKELL's *Count Down* incorporated the outer space idea into rock'n'roll; it's "asteroid hop" music with electronic walkie-talkie voices and other sound effects . . . In the early '60s FORREST J. ACKERMAN put out *Music for Robots,* and it's a little like *Forbidden Planet*—quite good. The RICHARD MARINO Orchestra recorded *Out of This World*—that's a masterpiece. *The Twilight Zone* wasn't music from the show, it was space music, and it's a gem. *Rocketship X-M* is another theremin classic. Finally, an example of *loving* robotic music is DICK HYMAN & MARY MAYO's *Moon Gas* which sounds warm and fun—you can imagine toy robots talking in the background.

Debbie Drake's *How to Keep Your Husband Happy,* Epic Records.
Album cover credits: cover photo: Henry Parker.

LYNN PERIL

Lynn Peril is pursuing an advanced degree in Women's Studies at San Francisco State University, and invites correspondence from other record collectors toward the goal of eventually publishing a discography of outstanding recordings by women artists.

♦ *VALE: Why aren't there more women record collectors?*

♦ LYNN PERIL: Why aren't there more women artists, writers, musicians, or *women anything?* Women aren't supposed to have *interests;* they aren't supposed to *compete* with the boys. If you're a woman and you go to a used record store to trade in records, they assume you don't know what they're worth. You have to be able to say "No" when they don't give you enough. That right there will disqualify a lot of women, because we aren't socialized to be aggressive, or even trust our own judgment. This extends to areas like buying stereo equipment: if you walk into a store the assumption immediately is that a woman couldn't *possibly* figure out an audio system all by herself. Women are only supposed to know about clothes and makeup; their bodies are their only officially approved area of obsession.

Also, why *should* women care about records when they're mostly by men, about men, and from a male viewpoint? I'm attracted to records from a female point of view—but not necessarily (god forbid) "women's music." You have to piece that body of history together; it's not handed to you. Adrienne Rich says we live in a culture of "manipulated passivity"—men and women both are so used to having everything handed to them. You need *audacity* to find things out for yourself. I happen to love discarded cultural artifacts that are now in thrift stores, and surrounding myself by the things I love is one way to fight this passivity. It's the opposite of consumerism. Most consumerism is just acquiescence to aggressive mass marketing, and it's even harder for women to resist that.

♦ *V: How did you start collecting?*

♦ LP: When you're growing up you don't think about record *collecting;* if you buy records, you buy what you like and play it until it's completely scratched! It wasn't until I was a teenager (in the late '70s) that I started collecting punk records. At the same time I also started finding rockabilly records and going to thrift stores. I hate to admit it, but part of my record collecting as an adult came from living with a male collector. Now I'm in a little group of record collectors, and that helps a lot—I don't feel so "weird" anymore.

From a feminist perspective, women don't have as much disposable income as men. If you hit 35 or 40 and you've got kids, you're not going to be out buying records. Also, with some of the men who collect—well, it's the wife who has the *real* job and who is tacitly supporting *his* habit! And perhaps women aren't quite as susceptible to all-encompassing greed; the "my collection is bigger than yours" syndrome. Although I'm sure there are women completists out there who have every Elvis bootleg ever made—every recorded fart.

I have enough records to definitely classify myself as a collector. If only I could have just *one* obsession—unfortunately I have to support a *book jones* as well. I'm interested in women artists, in cover art that exploits women, in all kinds of exploitation material. I'm big on going to the Goodwill—recently I was talking to a friend about that wonderful moment in every collector's life when you score big—when you've just found, for 79 cents, a record you've wanted for years, like LES BAXTER's *Barbarian.* I also have a certain small obsession with a Japanese all-girl band, the *5-6-7-8s.* I

Photo: Mary Ricci

have their CDs but I don't own a CD player. They do songs like "Edie is a Sweet Candy" (about Edie Sedgwick) and "I Was a Teenage Cavewoman." They are completely into American trash culture. There is a certain pride in collecting obscure things—I admit it!

♦ **V: Tell me about your favorite woman rockabilly singers—**

Rose Maddox's "Wild Wild Young Men" is all about how she uses her sexuality to compel young men to fall in love with her.

♦ LP: BARBARA PITTMAN went to Sun Records at the age of *twelve* to audition and was told by the receptionist to go away and become a secretary or something! At least she didn't let *that* stop her—she went on to record some classic rockabilly songs like "I Need a Man," delivered in an incredibly sensual, guttural growl: "There's just one thing that I can see/There's a world full of men, but there's none for me/I need a man to love me . . . someone I can tell my troubles to." She also did "Sentimental Fool" which should be required listening for every woman. It's one great, *true* song, a common-sensical anthem from a feminine view-

point. Basically it's a warning against letting your feelings run away from you. I especially like these lines: "If you try to show your feelings they'll be trampled on like dirt/'cuz a sentimental fool will always wind up getting hurt"—a woman *had* to have written that. At the end she tells you how she knows what she's talking about—she was a sentimental fool herself.

But Barbara Pittman isn't as heartbreaking to me as JANIS MARTIN, who was billed as "The Female Elvis." She began her career at the age of 11, and was actually given permission to use the title "The Female Elvis Presley." She produced some great, raw songs including the standout "My Boy Elvis." But at 15 she married her childhood sweetheart and at 18 gave birth to a son—of course she gave up her career. That happened a lot to these really hot rockabilly women singers: LORRIE COLLINS (of the COLLINS KIDS) who at the age of 15 recorded "Mercy" (one of the hottest, sexiest songs on the face of the earth) got married and ended her career at 18.

Another great song is "Welcome to the Club" by JEAN CHAPEL, with lyrics like: "If you've loved before and you've tried again/And the world marks you as a woman of sin/If you've tried to do the best you can/Still they label you as the ruin of a man." Yessir! MARTHA CARSON, who's Jean Chapel's sister, also cut a wild song, "Now Stop," with lyrics which basically say: Don't tease me unless you intend to *really*

Les Baxter's *Barbarian*, American International Records.

please me! And even though it's not radical, LINDA & THE EPICS' "Gonna Be Loved" intrigued me because it's by a female rockabilly singer from Santa Cruz (of all places) on the tiny Blue Moon label of Santa Cruz, California.

Another incredible female singer was SPARKLE MOORE, who did the classic, "Skull and Crossbones." She *hiccups* the lyrics with so much feeling—and what lyrics: "You should be labeled with a skull and crossbones/You're a jinx to my soul/Well you're a menace to women/They better open up a prison/'Cuz you look like a child/You're drivin' everyone wild." She met Sammy Davis, Jr and he told her that she looked like James Dean. Then he took his glasses off, put them on her nose and said, "Now you *really* look like James Dean!" She only put out two singles, "Skull and Crossbones" b/w "Rock-A-Bop" (both written by her) and "Killer" b/w "Tiger." On "Killer" she wanted lots of echo and crazy screaming all the way through, but the record company cut out all the screams except for a little one at the end, telling her that "A *young lady* doesn't do that!" She felt they ruined the song. As usual she left the music business when she became pregnant; she felt that pressure to "raise her baby right" and "get a regular job."

ROSE MADDOX's "Wild Wild Young Men" is all about how she uses her sexuality to compel young men to fall in love with her: "Wild men whoop and holler and yell, 'Whoo-ee!'/They all wanna be mine." They drink wine and scream and show off "but they don't kill me." Then she describes how she winks an eye, heaves a sigh, wiggles her hips . . . and leaves 'em high and dry! Unfortunately, it wimps out at the end when she says: "When I tame one/that'll be the best." But it was *close*—really, really close!

In the JUVENILE DELINQUENCY category is

"Nightmare" by the WHYTE BOOTS, from the *Girls in the Garage* series, Volume Two—everyone says Volume One isn't so great. This is about a fight to the death between two girls (over a boy, of course). It's in that Shangri-Las *teen-death* vein, with a chorus in the background chanting: "She didn't want to fight/she didn't want to fight" and the lead singer concluding, "Oh my god . . . she's dead." The BLUE ORCHIDS' "Oo Chang-a-Lang" and The GIRLS' "Chico's Girl" are also pretty good. Chico is your typical misunderstood gang lout, but Chico's girl loves him because she knows the "real" side of him. She probably grows up to be Loretta Lynn singing about the pill, because she's been pregnant 9 times in the past 10 years after she marries Chico . . .

RAY CAMPI is one of my all-time favorite rockabilly artists because I think he actually cares about a problem *I* can relate to: how to please a woman. His song "Eager Beaver Boy" has the lines, "I'm just an eager beaver boy/And I'm as playful as a wind-up toy/So won't you join me in a friendly game/I guarantee you'll never be the same/When I still the water in your stream/I wanna hear your little beaver scream!" That one line gives me the idea that Ray really knows how to *satisfy.* He also does "Sack O' Lovin' " which is like a voodoo song: he has to leave town for awhile and knows that nylon hose, airplanes, and Cadillac cars won't keep her faithful, so he's gonna give her a "sack of loving" that'll set her hand on fire! He also did a *kiss-off* song, "It Ain't Me": "I've seen you out with some other cat/I can plainly see where I stand at/You think I'm jealous over your new beau/But I'm so happy 'cuz now I know/IT AIN'T ME." It goes on to talk about how she's gonna talk this other guy into marrying her, and at the last minute he'll realize it's a big mistake, because she's horrible. After a bad breakup, I put "It Ain't Me" on my answering machine—just in case that person should call.

Another novelty 45 I found is by Little Bob & His Electric Uke, featuring a great *surf ukelele* number appropriately titled "Rock That Uke."

I love making compilation tapes of my favorite material, and I've started getting a lot of great music from VIDEO SOURCES (which I hadn't thought of taping from before) like *The Wild, Wild World of Jayne Mansfield*, *She-Devils on Wheels,* and even *Top Secrets,* a late '50s promotional film for a preacher whose gimmick is spinning tops while he delivers sermons.

A sub-category of NOVELTY RECORDS is NON-

SENSE LYRICS, and one of my favorite examples is by the SAXONS: "Camel Walk." It contains word-coinages like "a-clee-dough," "dur-no-voy" and "ca-mel me-dough" which made me realize that there *is* meaning in human existence! DEJA VOODOO's "Coelacanth," done to the tune of "I'm a Man" ("I'm a Coelacanth") is a great piece of catchy absurdity which I place in the context of a classic pseudoscience book, *In the Wake of the Sea Serpents*. (Deja Voodoo are a current group with albums out on the Ga-Ga-Goodies label.) Another novelty 45 I found is by LITTLE BOB & HIS ELECTRIC UKE, featuring a great *surf ukelele* number appropriately titled "Rock That Uke." I found my copy in a thrift store in Seattle, and finds like this inspire me to keep on pawing through the singles.

Loretta Lynn's "The Pill" is about her real strength that comes from having control over her fertility, now that she's got this *weapon,* the pill. Have you ever heard anyone else sing about contraception—male or female?

Another sub-category of NOVELTY RECORDS is *Improbable* Novelty Records, and here "She's a Fat Girl" by the ROCKABOUTS is amazing—who would think of writing a song so pejorative? The lyrics go: "She's a fat girl" (chorus: "That ain't no lie")/"She's ugly" ("That ain't no lie")/"She's cross-eyed" ("That ain't no lie")/"She got big ears" ("That ain't no lie")/"She got buck teeth" ("That ain't no lie")/"Do I love her?" ("Yes, you love her"). It's got great horn charts on it. I found this "Chubby Chasers' Anthem" on a compilation reissue album, *At The Party* (Candy label). It's also on the *Fat! Fat! Fat!* compilation. Here I'll say that some people might claim I'm not a *real* collector because I don't pay $35 for a single, but I can't afford that. I'm happy to collect these reissue compilations which are hard enough to find—if you see one and don't buy it, you might never see it again! A lot of these are semi-legal bootlegs put out by collectors who just love the music and want to share it with a few others. Usually they're done in tiny limited editions, so in a few years these reissues will be almost as rare as the originals.

In the category of EXTREME MALE CHAUVINIST RECORDS is PRINCE BUSTER's "Ten Commandments of Love," which are the ten commandments of complete male dominance: "The ten commandments of love as given to woe-man [sic] through the inspiration of I, Prince Buster." It contains such gems as "Thou shalt not shout my name in the streets if I'm walking with another woman, but wait intelligently

until I come home; then we both can have it out *decently.*" And, "Thou shalt not commit adultery or the world will not hold me guilty if I commit murder"—that's a scary one. "Thou shalt not drink nor smoke nor use profane language, for those bad habits I will not stand for"—another double-standard line, I'm sure. After years of searching I found a whole *album* by PRINCE BUSTER, but it was all just ordinary ska—I traded it in for something else.

When I was making a compilation tape I had to put PRINCE BUSTER next to LORETTA LYNN's "The Pill." Her entire song is great, beginning with the idea that: "You wined me and dined me when I was your girl/You promised if I'd be your wife you'd show me the world/But all I've seen of this ole world is a bed and a doctor bill/I'm tearin' down your brooder house 'cuz now I've got the pill." Then she lists the miniskirts and hot pants she's going to wear; her maternity dress takes up far too much yardage. There's a repeated "brooder hen" theme: "this chicken's done pulled up her nest . . . this incubator's overused." She feels this real strength that comes from having control over her fertility, now that she's got this *weapon,* the pill. Have you ever heard anyone else sing about contraception—male or female? I think it's a revolutionary, radical song, even though it wimps out in the end (as usual).

Related to "The Pill" is another song I like: "Abortion Is Illegal," written in the '20s by Bertolt Brecht and Hans Eisler. It's just as true now as it was then, with lyrics like: "First you want to have the pleasure/And then do not want to do your duty/When we make something illegal/We know what we are doing/So relax and take it easy/And just leave this whole thing/To *those who know better,* ok?/You're going to make a love-

Westminster Pop Sampler, Westminster Records.

Vintage Libby Holman, Take Two Records. Album cover credits: art consultant: Garo Enjaian, photo courtesy of Joe Kearney.

ly little mother/You're going to make a hunk of cannon fodder . . ." With the recent gutting of *Roe vs. Wade*—well, we could *all* be humming this one soon!

SOPHIE TUCKER did "If Your Kisses Can't Hold the Man You Love," which is right up there with "Sentimental Fool." It starts out saying something like "Every time that I hear a woman cry/'Cuz her man has left her flat/I just feel like saying/Don't be such a fool, you fool." It has the line, "Laugh and the world laughs with you/Weep, and you sleep alone." But then she says, in effect, *So what!:* "Don't cry for him or chase him/Just go out and replace him."

LIBBY HOLMAN was a blues and jazz singer who started out on Broadway. She married Zachary Smith Reynolds, the heir to the Reynolds tobacco fortune. One day in 1932 she and a friend of his were at the family mansion and the heir wound up dead with a bullet in the head—there was a big scandal (documented in the book, *Libby Holman: Body and Soul).* Her repertoire included songs like Cole Porter's "Find Me a Primitive Man": "I don't mean the kind that belongs to a club/But the kind that has a club that belongs to him." She rode out the scandal but was never again the star she had been beforehand—she had a minor comeback in the '50s doing folk ballads in clubs. The record I have is *Vintage Libby Holman: Early Original Recordings from 1927-30* (Take Two Records).

I'm also interested in INFANTILIZATION in music. Have you heard "Rock City Boogie"? It's sung by a girl who's 8 or 9 years old—I don't know who did it because I heard it on the radio, and my tape ran out before the credits. This teeny munchkin voice is singing these incredibly suggestive lyrics like "Tell mama she's spending the night with a friend/And she's not gonna be home 'til dawn." LARRY COLLINS [one of

the COLLINS KIDS] sang "Whistle Bait" when he was only 11 years old—another incredibly suggestive song for a little kid: "Her heels are clickin' as she walks by/ The dress of pink sure fills the eye/She's a whistle bait/She's the one for me." There are videotapes of the COLLINS KIDS performing live at a Town Hall Party—Larry's trademark was playing a double-necked guitar as big as he was (and he was a whiz too); they do all the right "adult" moves. Larry went on to write "Delta Dawn" for Helen Reddy . . . THE BANTAMS are 3 brothers (ages 10, 11 and 12) from Milwaukee, Wisconsin: "The Biggest Little Band in the Land; Three Pre-Teens with the Rockin' Sound Three Times Their Size." They covered songs by the Beatles and Freddy and the Dreamers—again, singing "adult" themes. They are yet another example of *kidploitation:* "pre-voice-change rock"!

Also in the INFANTILE RECORDS category is HELEN KANE, who was the original "human" inspiration for BETTY BOOP—she actually had that face and that teeny voice. She worked in vaudeville, nightclubs, and on Broadway, and she was a film star in the late 1920s. In 1934 she sued the Fleischers for appropriating and exploiting her image, but lost. The Fleischers claimed that Betty Boop was "not intended to resemble anyone living or dead" and also that the phrase "boop-boop-a-doop" had not originated with Kane, but with a black artist named Baby Esther. On an album, *Helen Kane and other Boop-Boop-a-Doopers,* she did a great song, "I Want To Be Bad," which was basically about wanting to be sexual, but sung in a tiny, infantilized voice. This is yet another example of how hard it is for women to express a truly "adult" sexuality or eroticism in music (let alone in real life) without

Flappers, Vamps and Sweet Young Things, ASV Living Era. Produced by Kevin Daly. Album cover credits: sleeve design/illustration: Phil Duffy/Fred Robinson, P.D. Graphics Ltd.

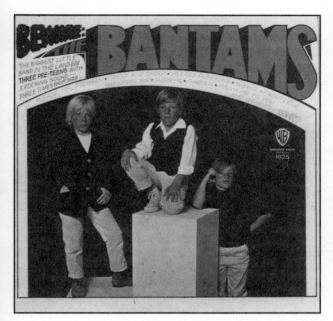

The Bantams' *Beware: The Bantams!*, Warner Bros. Records.
Album cover credits: cover photo: Tom Tucker, art direction: Ed Thrasher.

having to water it down or contain it. Infantilization and helplessness appeal to a *lot* of men. On the same album is MAY QUESTREL, who was the actual voice of BETTY BOOP in the cartoons (later she became Aunt Bluebelle in the Bounty paper towel commercial).

In the RISQUE category is GERTRUDE LAWRENCE, who sang: "Do do do/What you did did did/ Once more/Let's go again to heaven"—it's about sex, right? (The Gershwins wrote that.) That's a bit more "ladylike" than "I Want a Hotdog for My Roll" by BUTTERBEANS AND SUSIE—that's from one of those *Copulating Blues* albums, all of which are great. And MAE WEST is of course over the top, especially when she sings "Great Balls of Fire" or "Whole Lotta Shakin' Goin' On"—really scary! (Think of that Diane Arbus portrait of Mae, and the story about the pet monkey's turds being ground into the pale blue carpet, recounted by Patricia Bosworth in her biography *Diane Arbus.*) I also have the MAE WEST Christmas album where she does songs like "Put the loot in the boot, Santa."

♦ *V: How did you get into older blues and jazz records?*
♦ LP: FLAPPERS, VAMPS, AND SWEET YOUNG THINGS (ASV Living Era label, 1982) is the compilation album that got me into '20s and '30s female jazz vocals. (Almost anything on the ASV label is hot: the MILLS BROTHERS, CAB CALLOWAY, and other '20s and '30s American jazz artists.) I really like blues singer BESSIE SMITH—I love her for the same reasons that I love MARIA CALLAS or early ENRICO CARUSO: because the singing *moves* you. Bessie Smith is this incredible woman singing her heart out, with a voice that just rips your soul; how can anyone not

relate to that? It sounds like she's singing through a megaphone, but I like that sound quality (including the scratches and the pops) for the same reason that I hate CDs—to me they're artificially perfect, just like those airbrushed "women" in magazine ads.

Listening to BESSIE SMITH is like going back in time: this sense of the past is an inseparable part of the experience of listening to early jazz and blues recordings. Why would you want that beauty sucked out of it? The sound isn't *meant* to be clean—that was the state of the recording technique at the time . . . just as when you walk into a used bookstore there's that great smell of old books (which is a very *sensual* experience); why would you want that taken away from you? Why not take a Van Gogh and smooth out all the brush strokes so you can see the painting better?

Larry Collins was doing an incredibly suggestive song for a little kid. There are videotapes of The Collins Kids performing live at a Town Hall Party—Larry's trademark was playing a double-necked guitar as big as he was.

Another old jazz singer I like is ELLA MAE MORSE; *she's* a goddess! While still only a teenager she started singing with Jimmy Dorsey and then moved on to the Freddy Slack Trio. Unfortunately, she stopped recording when she was only 33. In a sultry, halting voice that was very sexy she sang R&B and pop standards

Ella Mae Morse's *Barrelhouse, Boogie, and The Blues*, Capitol Records.

The Girl From U.N.C.L.E., MGM Records. ®© Metro-Goldwyn-Mayer Inc. Album cover credits: cover design: Acy R. Lehman.

like "Daddy Daddy" and "40 Cups of Coffee."

Recently I've taken the plunge over the edge into 78s. The other day I was at a thrift store and a friend I was with—not me—scored this portable 4-speed transistorized record player from the early '60s for $12— you flip the needle over to play 78s. She spotted it before I did, and—that reminds me of a recurring anxiety dream. You're in a thrift store and find this record you've been looking for forever, and you reach out for it—then suddenly the bomb drops—it's *Armageddon*: there's that white flash and everything goes black!

If you see a book or record that's pretty rare, you

Battle of the Blues, Vol. 4, © 1987 The Official Record Company APS, Denmark.

have to buy it (no matter what state your finances are in) because you may never find it again. The worst thrift store experience is remembering those few things you didn't buy, but should have—those memories haunt you for the rest of your life. I was only in Berlin for 36 hours, but I went twice to that great flea market there (which is now gone). There was a set of five glazed art nouveau tiles that somebody must have ripped out of a wall above a fireplace, and I was exhausted and didn't buy them—but I *still* think about them.

SEXPLOITATION is another category of records— especially the cover art. And when you like the cover, you never have high expectations for the record itself. One of my favorites is *Touch* by the MYSTIC MOODS ORCHESTRA; it's easy listening with sound effects. The cover has a die-cut circle showing just the faces of a man and a woman underneath kissing. But when you pull out the cardboard inner sleeve, you see that they're both nude. Some other Mystic Moods 2-part nudity covers include *Night Tide, Love the One You're With,* and *Erogenous.*

I also collect old etiquette, self-help, beauty and sex manuals. Today I found *Practical Child Training,* by the International Academy of Discipline! "If you find a child masturbating, do *not* terrify him. *Consult the doctor.* A minor operation, *circumcision,* will stop the irritation which often induces this bad habit . . ."

There's a record on the Crown label, MUSIC FOR BIG DAME HUNTERS, with a great cover showing Irish McCalla (in her *Sheena of the Jungle* leopard skin bikini) on a tree branch. Even the 101 STRINGS put out a 12" disco single and a sexploitation album with a woman moaning orgasmically on every track. ORGAN FANTASY is one of my favorite covers from a budget label: this woman's got her arms wide open, reaching out toward all these phallic pink and purple balloons. There's another cylindrical balloon pointing toward her butt.

Another SEXPLOITATION example is GROUPIE GIRL: "Sex-hungry fan of the pop stars: they don't collect *autographs* [heh-heh] anymore." This is the soundtrack to an English film; there's a band on it called *Virgin Stigma* which anticipated punk rock by about 12 years. Lastly, here's my ED McMAHON album. He looks like a chipmunk and sings the most disgusting, sick version of "Thank Heaven for Little Girls," with a spoken intro that says something like:

every time he sees a little girl he gets a *joyous urge.* Perfect.

Another celebrity record I have is the ODD COUPLE—imagine Jack Klugman and Tony Randall doing "You're So Vain." They do a back-and-forth commentary on the lyrics that's kinda funny and kinda sick. It's hard to listen to it more than once. The question with bad celebrity albums always is: "Who put them up to this . . . and why?" A friend of mine went to India and Southeast Asia for six months, so as a farewell present I made him a tape with this song (as well as others, like William Shatner *speak-singing* "Mr Tambourine Man") and told him not to listen to it until he got really homesick for the United States. Finally he played it on a completely crowded bus in Bangkok and started laughing hysterically . . .

The flip side of a really intense and overwhelming singer like MARIA CALLAS, whom I love, is FLORENCE FOSTER JENKINS. She was a society matron with a burning ambition to sing opera, and she had enough money to rent concert halls and put on performances. On her album, *Florence Foster Jenkins: The Glory ??? of the Human Voice,* she *massacres* these arias. She became quite a cult figure, and thousands of people would go see her because she was so bad.

♦ **V: What kind of books do you collect?**

♦ LP: It's not just a matter of "want"—I collect what I *need,* to enrich my life. Art books, pulps, pseudoscience or cryptozoology (like Heuvelman's *In the Wake of the Sea Serpent* and *On the Track of Unknown Animals),* and books on women. *Le Petomane,* about a performer who could fart at will—everyone *needs* that one! And what is life without sleazy biographies? A favorite is *Jayne Mansfield* which was written by her friend, the writer May Mann—allegedly Jayne came back from the dead to tell her to write this. TINY TIM wrote an autobiography published by Playboy Press; it's replete with repressed gay sex, bizarre heterosex—it's just chock-full of guilt and repression. SPY magazine did a total comparison chart of celebrity biographies: first sex, big regrets. Mamie Van Doren wrote *Playing the Field* in which she talks about "doing it" with Rock Hudson. Florence Aadland, this Hollywood stage biddie, wrote a total exploitation, trashy book called *The Big Love* about her underage daughter's affair with Errol Flynn. She said, "There's one thing I want to make clear right off: my baby was a virgin when she met Errol Flynn."

Another kidploitation book is *My Life With Chaplin* by Lita Grey Chaplin. She was 12 when she met Charlie, 15 when she first slept with him, and 16 when she had her first child by him. I have another book, *Chaplin vs. Chaplin,* which is basically transcripts of their divorce proceedings. She was testifying as to what went wrong in the marriage and said that he made her do "unnatural things"—meaning fellatio. When questioned, he replied, "But *all* married people do that!" This caused a big scandal at the time.

Music for Big Dame Hunters, Crown Records. Album cover credits: photos: Joseph Tauber, cover design: Hobco Arts, cover model: Irish McCalla.

Pamela Des Barres's *I'm With the Band* is totally sleazy, as is *Neon Angel* which was written by the lead singer of the Runaways, Cherrie Currie. Of course, there are lots of books about Elvis written by relatives and bodyguards (like *Elvis, We Love You Tender).* The best ones are all *dirt.*

I also collect old etiquette, self-help, beauty and sex manuals. Today I found *Practical Child Training,* which is copyright 1917 by the International Academy of Discipline! The frontispiece is a photograph of a mother (who should be holding a whip) looking down on her ramrod-straight son. There's a caption: "Practice deep breathing and exercises on rising in the morning.

Organ Fantasy, Riviera Records.

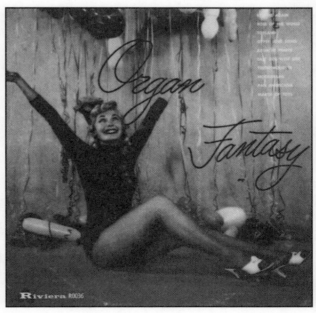

Outer sleeve of Mystic Moods' *Touch*, Soundbird Records. Album cover credits: cover concept & design: William S. Harvey, photography: Peter D'Aprix.

Inner sleeve of *Touch*.

Principles involved: suggestion, approval, cooperation and expectancy"—that's like training a fuckin' dog! And it's all about your *boy*—there's almost nothing about (god forbid) your daughter, if you were so unlucky as to have had one! And the "sexual purity" section contains such gems as: "If you find a child masturbating, do *not* terrify him. *Consult the doctor.* A minor operation, *circumcision,* will stop the irritation which often induces this bad habit . . . The habit, if persisted in, will endanger reason, give rise to abnormal ideas, and cause general ill health and irritability of temper throughout a lifetime."

More insight into the origins of our present social dysfunction can be found in *The Secret of Married Happiness* (1925), which contains advice on keeping a husband's respect: "Don't disrobe in the presence of your husband; don't joke or make light of the sacred relationship between man and wife; don't flaunt your bodily charms; don't expose yourself in a way to arouse your husband's passion." Luckily, there's a companion volume (the sequel?): *Secrets Revealed from Divorce Courts.* Obliquely related to this is *Beauty Plus* (1938), whose author seems obsessed with "proper elimination"—the cure for all ills. The book also contains a "Personality Quiz" which asks such burning questions as, "Do you, in an effort to become the life of the party, habitually drink too many cocktails and pass out on the bathroom floor, requiring several solicitous friends to take care of you?" See how your score compares with that of your girl friends!

I recommend Evan S. Connell's *The Connoisseur* to people who collect things, because I think it explains (or at least describes) the process by which collecting [anything] takes over your life. It's about the beautiful side, or the almost spiritual nature, of obsession and collecting. Collecting not only brings you things you

love, it's also a way to *grow.* You find that one thing leads to another; automatically (and relatively painlessly) you start learning more and more. There can be a social aspect as well—if you're lucky you'll have friends who bring you the things you collect, like this "Praying Hands" lamp on my bookshelf, which was a birthday present.

For me and my friends, the acquisition of material goods has turned into a form of *self-expression* . . . as well as answering the burning question: can a copy of *Jailbait* really soothe the soul? I'm here to report that, yes, it can!

For me and my friends, the acquisition of material goods has turned into a form of *self-expression* . . . as well as answering the burning question: can a copy of *Jailbait* really soothe the soul? I'm here to report that, yes, it can! When I found my copy of *Jailbait* (at a time when I was really depressed), I realized that 1) *nothing* is as bad as I thought it was, and 2) life *could* be really good. The back cover reads: "Shocking, but true. Here at last is the real story of teenage sin the headlines have never dared reveal: of twelve-year-old callgirls entertaining four men each night . . . of sexual misconduct raging like a plague in schools from Maine to California . . . of secret orgies between teenage girls and men in their forties . . . and here is the startling truth about what goes on behind the walls of our reformatories after dark." The *Cleveland Plain Dealer* says, "If anyone doubts the seriousness of America's delinquency problem, *Jailbait* will quickly dispel that notion." When I look at this book I wonder: How can anyone *not* be attracted by a pulp paperback with a sleazy cover? How can anyone not have their life made more full by a sexploitation record cover?

Besides acquiring *Flesh Peddlers* by DON SHEPARD (pseudonym of multi-talented rockabilly artist RON HAYDOCK), I also found this other sexploitation book, *All Woman,* by Matt Harding. It's a classic for all the wrong reasons: "Which would he do: beat her, or love her—or both? . . . She had the kind of body no man could pass up—not even Frank Fillmore, to whom she was a punching bag, a toy, a helpless beauty to be beaten and brutalized . . ." That's a quintessential example of male violence against women portrayed as a *norm.* It's further described as "a revealing novel of public and private sex spots, and a woman's struggle for respectability." But what does her "struggle for respectability" have to do with her being beaten up? Reading further: "She rolled on her side. She reached out and touched his face lightly . . . She wet her lips. Would she *ever* get enough? Was it *possible* to ever get enough?" So in this book, the woman is punished basically for having sexual feelings in the first place, and then wanting to fully experience them. It's her fault; it's *always* her fault!

In general I like books and records on *borderline* subjects—as in "*pushing the . . .*" People come over and are surprised: "You've got all this great stuff, all these records, all these books . . ." It's very flattering, but a part of me goes: "You mean other people don't have this stuff? I mean—*why live?*"

ing garage rockabilly. Try writing them at 2-19-26-204 Setagaya-ku, Tokyo, Japan.

Strummin' Mental is a great series of instrumental compilations. Vol. 5 includes THE LOSERS' "Snake Eyes" (sound effects of dice rattling; a singer with a very deep voice repeats "Snake Eyes" throughout) and RON THOMPSON & HIS ROWDY GUITAR's "Switchblade" (a totally hot surf instrumental featuring the sounds of screaming women and whip noises). Available from Link Records.

Hollywood Teen Fair Surf Compilation. Allegedly limited ("600 pressed") reissue of teen surf bands doing hot numbers, like THE VESTELLS covering Dick Dale's "The Wedge."

Red River Dave: "The California Hippie Murders." The only song about Charles Manson with yodeling. From *Infernal Machine* by JOE COLEMAN; one side has his band STEEL TIPS, and the other is an anthology of songs about murderers and psychos. Between the tracks, people like HENRY LEE LUCAS talk about their crimes. Beautiful production with a picture disc and a booklet of Joe Coleman's art. (Blast First Records, 262 Mott St Rm 324, NY NY 10012 or 429 Harrow Rd, London W10 4RE, U.K.)

Jackie & The Cedrics; hot Japanese surf trio. (No source.)

Chrome, Smoke & Fire, an anthology of hot rod music compiled by artist Robert Williams. Beautiful picture disc with great songs and excellent commentary. (Available from Blast First, address above.)

REFERENCE:

Flappers, Vamps and Sweet Young Things. Excellent compilation of female jazz singers from the '20s and '30s, including Sophie Tucker, Helen Kane and Libby Holman. (ASV Living Era, 115 Fulham Rd, London SW3 6RL U.K.)

Rockin' Girls' Sun Favorites. Japanese compilation LP of must-haves: Barbara Pittman, The Kirby Sisters, Jean Chapel and more.

Wild, Wild Young Women. Indispensable for Sparkle Moore, Linda & Epics, Janis Martin, Collins Kids. ($15 ppd. from Rounder Records, 186 Willow Ave, Somerville MA 02144).

5-6-7-8s: *Mondo Girls A-Go-Go; I Was a Teenage Cave Woman* **(EPs).** Wild, primitive, scream-

Groupie Girl, Eagle Films Ltd.
Album cover credits: sleeve co-ordination: E.A. Berry.

PHANTOM SURFERS
UNTAMED YOUTH

The *Phantom Surfers* and *Untamed Youth* are two California bands faithful to the spirit of '60s garage/surf music. *Phantom Surfers* include guitarists Johnny Bartlett and Mel Bergman, bassist Mike Lucas and Maz Kattuah on drums. *Untamed Youth* include Trent Ruane (guitar, keyboards), Derek Dickerson (guitar), Mace (bass) and Dave Stuckey (drums). Their recordings are available from Norton Records, PO Box 646 Cooper Station, NY NY 10003. Some members from each band were interviewed together.

◆ *VALE: What's your view of record "collecting"?*

◆ DEREK DICKERSON: I think we all pretty much hate record collectors. All of us collect records that we *listen* to, but these "collectors" buy records that they have no intention of listening to, just to make a profit—

◆ DAVE STUCKEY: We all hate it when that's the spirit behind the collecting. Yet we've all got to deal with this, because we all wind up at swap meets and these guys are there and a lot of times they've got records you really want, so whaddya do?

◆ DD: And none of this ever existed before they invented the price guide—that's been the bane of my existence. Before there was a price guide, only the people who listened to surf music (or whatever) would buy certain albums. But once a price guide comes out and says that a SUPER STOCKS album is worth $150, then there's going to be a bunch of geeks out scouring garage sales for it—

◆ JOHNNY BARTLETT: And not only that, the price guide always puts more value on the "stereo" version, which is next to useless—

◆ DD: No *true* surf collector would ever want the stereo version of the first HONDELLS album—yet it lists for $50 more.

◆ DS: When you see that precious record you've wanted for so long, and it's $300—you just go, "Grrr . . ." It

just makes it all more difficult, and you gotta dig deeper. But that's reflected in every aspect of collectible stuff—by virtue of it becoming collectible, the opportunists are going to get their hands on it.

◆ DD: Plus, now if grandma's got a bunch of rare Elvis records, she's going to go to the mall and buy a price guide and next thing you know: there's no good records getting into the Goodwills and Salvation Armies anymore.

◆ DS: Just the *existence* of a price guide makes people think that anything old—any old piece of junk—is worth money. The worst junk shit albums are priced at $5 apiece, because someone thinks, "Oh, these albums are from the *fifties.*"

◆ JB: At a garage sale I saw this guy selling a completely hammered copy of the Beatles' *Revolver;* he exclaimed, "Whoa—this is the type of thing that's worth *bucks!*" I had to tell him, "That album is so worthless it's not even funny—they pressed millions and millions." He went, "Oh—!"

◆ *V: Still, the price guide has helped preserve a lot of things. What have you found recently?*

◆ MEL BERGMAN: I found two spoken word porno records on the KONTACT label that were full of incest stories, three-way stories, anything-goes stories, etc. According to the liner notes, "You will hear the wet and lubricious moanings of oral-genital sexuality, the

132

Johnny Bartlett in his bedroom.

Photo: Robert Waldman

soft and insistent demands of two women using their fingers and mouths to excite each other's passions . . ." Volume One was "The Adventures of Barbara," and on the back it says: "Hear the searing stories of one girl's experiences with incest, lesbianism, wife-swapping and orgies. Barbara's entire life is colored by her first initiation into sex as a young adolescent—at the hands of her own father"—*how nice!* [sarcastic] Other cuts include "Sonny & Sis," "Suburban Circus," "Three's a Crowd," "Mary Loves Laurie"—great stuff. "Actual case histories on record—hear it so well that you can see it!"

I also found on the Key Record label (which resembles the Golden Key Record label), *Inside a Communist Cell* by Karl Prussion. It's a 1958 spoken word anti-communist diatribe about all the "suspicious" activity going on in San Francisco; it contains their "Fight" song. Karl Prussion was a star witness at the San Francisco hearings of HUAC (House Committee on Un-American Activities). I also scored a country-western 45 about two brothers: one brother was a hippie, and the other went to Vietnam and got killed. It's alternately patriotic march music and "twist" music—the moral of the story is: the hippie brother is alive, and the Vietnam soldier is dead.

I grew up in Athens, Georgia and I'd pay a thousand dollars to have this regional 45 I once owned as a kid: "Swamp Guinea." Studs Terkel wrote *Blue Highway* in which he refers to "Swamp Guinea," which was a

place way out in the bayou which served huge portions of catfish with half a loaf of Wonder Bread. They sold their own 45 with the lyrics: "Have you been to Swamp Guinea?/Fish lodge, Come & Eat/It's a treat/With us./ They have ham and chicken and T-bone steak/for $2.75/Man, try them frog-legs/Whooee-alive!/Swamp Guinea/Come & Eat/It's a treat/With us." The flip-side promoted the antique shop next door.

♦ **V: Do you have any more thoughts on collecting?**
♦ MB: It goes down to: are you buying the actual object, or are you buying the music? *What* are you buying? Are you buying a baseball card itself, or are you buying the memory of when you once owned it? A lot of the baby-boomers are obsessed with collecting the things they had when they were kids (I'm one too; the *Brady Bunch* defines my generation), and any time you see a "Ten Best" list, you can bet it's another baby-boomer confessing his little fixation.

I think the first price guide that ever came out was for lunch boxes, and the story I heard was: this guy had an enormous collection and wanted to unload them for big bucks, so he hit on the idea of making this "price guide" and then sold *all* of 'em—he totally cashed in. I think he "guess-timated" all the prices he printed, and that's what *all* price guides do—they fabricate artificially high prices and create markets where none existed beforehand. I really hate going to record swaps or "collector" record stores where the seller whips out a price guide—that's like: *instant depression.* Besides, there's *nothing* I absolutely have to have.

What record do you see most often in thrift stores? It's Herb Alpert's *Whipped Cream & Other Delights.* It sold 10 million copies, most of which were seldom played, and anybody who buys the CD of it should immediately be sold a deed to the Brooklyn bridge for a quarter! I thought of buying a hundred copies (that would probably cost fifty bucks), renting a table at the next Record Swap and pricing the best ones at $100, marked "Rare Stereo First Pressing." A lot of people will laugh, but some people will fall for it—then you'll start seeing high prices on *all* of Herb Alpert's records!

♦ JESSICA: One day I found an Erica phone ('60s design that stands on its end) at a thrift store—

♦ MB: They never work. *Does* it?

♦ J: It doesn't, but . . . anyway, we both (Derek & I) saw it and I went, "Dude! I've gotta buy that." He said, "Oh no, I'll buy it." I said, "No, *I'll* buy it." He went, "*Really,* I'll buy it." So I just gave up and he bought it; for a week I harbored this quiet resentment: "Why did I let him buy it? Why did he want it so badly, anyway?" Then on our first anniversary, he gave me an Erica phone that had been rewired so it works perfectly. He said, "Well, I figured—I'd already bought you this one, and if I let you buy the other one, when we broke up *I* wouldn't have one and *you'd* have two!" Such opti-mism—like, "Happy Anniversary!"

♦ **V: *What are some of your strangest 45s?***

♦ JB: I recently found a *vocal* version of "Tequila" by the Contenders on Jackpot Records. They gave it some really stupid lyrics about going to Mexico; the chorus goes "I like tequila, I like tequila." I also found a cool 45 by E. Whitney on the budget Promenade label (six songs for the price of two!) about a water skier and his trusty boat driver, Daddy-O. It's pretty sick.

Speaking of weird records, I have a 45 called "Rubber Dolly" about a guy whose mom is gonna buy him an inflatable doll since he doesn't have a girlfriend! It's from the late '50s; the flip side is "All American Boy" which is the Elvis Presley "poor boy gets guitar, gets famous, gets drafted" story. At the same garage sale I got a '50s lifestyle record called "Frozen Dinners" by RONNIE & JOEY. The song is all about eating TV dinners (which were new at the time) and losing weight. The first line goes, "Frozen dinners gonna get me thin-thin-thinner."

One of my most bizarre 45s is "The Ballad of Troy Hess" by (of course) Troy Hess. He was 3 years old when he recorded this "song" about himself in 1968, and the label has a photo of him with his guitar, wearing a cowboy hat. Underneath it says "Troy Hess—Age 3, A Souvenir For America." Of course he can't sing. Actually, Troy's dad was BENNY "Wild Hog

From the collection of Johnny Bartlett. *Silly Surfers,* © 1964, Hawk Model Co., Hairy Records. *Hot Rod City,* © 1963 Atlantic Recording Corp. *The Superstocks: Thunder Road,* Capitol Records. *The Hondells,* Mercury Records. *Surf Route 101,* Capitol Records, album cover credits: cover photo: Capitol Photo, studio: George Jerman. *Little Deuce Coupe 409,* Dot Records, album cover credits: photos: Kay Trapp.

From the collection of Johnny Bartlett. David Rose's *The Stripper*, MGM Records. *Music of the Stripper*, © Metro-Goldwyn-Mayer, Inc., album cover credits: cover photography: Murray Laden. *Adam Stag Party Special featuring Terri "Cupcake" O'Mason*, © 1960 Fax Records Co. "Bald" Bill Hagan & his Trocaderons' *Music to Strip By*, Somerset Records, album cover credits: cover art: G.L. Phillips. Ann Corio's *How to Strip For Your Husband*, Roulette Records, album cover credits: design: Moskof-Morrison, Inc., illustration by: Howard Nostrand. Bob Freedman & Orchestra: *The After Hours Show: Music to Strip By*, Surprise 101.

Hop" HESS, a '50s rockabilly/country crooner. It's amazing what you can still find.

♦ DS: Well, there's still a lot of stuff out there that, for whatever reasons, is not collectible. Most 78s are still real cheap—

♦ TRENT RUANE: When you see a 78 for five bucks, that's a real high price—

♦ MB: Especially when it's by Eddy Duchin. [laughs]

♦ DS: I think we can all agree that he haunts all of us; there are Eddy Duchin 78s everywhere you go. Fortunately, Capitol records are still not worth a whole lot; neither are Decca or Reprise . . .

♦ JB: I think we all have this unwritten law, even though we break it frequently: don't pay more than a dollar a song.

♦ DS: Before the advent of the Price Guide, you paid whatever it was worth to you.

♦ DD: Plus, for years and years rockabilly was going for big bucks, but you could find really great surf music for nothing. Just within the last five years it's become this new collector's "thing." So you see the worst surf albums going for $25—

♦ JB: —by studio bands that were nothing but saxophones, like the Wedge and the Spinners' "Party My Pad After Surfin' "—you couldn't listen to that if someone paid you, but it's got a picture of a surfer on the cover. And some dealer goes, "Uh—these old surf records go for a lot of money." Well, some of them do

and some of them don't, and this is one that doesn't.

♦ DS: They don't do their homework. Yet they don't want to take any chances.

♦ DD: Surf music is the biggest genre of all the "budget" capitalism releases. Surf was a big fad around

The Phantom Surfers, © 1991 Norton Records. Album cover credits: cover design: Pete Ciccone/Immaculate Concepts, photo: Sven-Erik Geddes.

From the collection of Johnny Bartlett. *Spook Along With Zacherley,* Elektra Records, album cover credits: cover design: W.S. Harvey, photo: Lions-Heicklen, photo: Abramson. *Monster Mash,* Peter Pan Records. *The Munsters,* Decca Records. John Zacherle's *Monster Mash,* Parkway Records, album cover credits; cover design: Al Cahn & Elkman Advertising Co., Inc. *Famous Monsters Speak,* © A.A. Records, Inc., Golden Records. The Ghouls' *Dracula's Deuce,* Capitol Records.

1962. There weren't that many surf bands, but suddenly there were all these surf albums out. It turned out that many weren't even surf music—just really bad instrumental music.

♦ JB: The CROWN budget label actually took records that had been released in '59, like Billy Boyd (and his twangy guitar), and repackaged it as DON DAILEY—

♦ TR: And later they repackaged that again as a hot rod album; they just added some sound effects . . .

♦ JB: One of the most interesting producers from that era has got to be GARY USHER, because of his involvement with every major studio in Hollywood in the early '60s. He used a pool of musicians and recorded under several different names (he would actually sing and play guitar on some tracks, besides doing the production). Some of his recordings include: *Hits of the Street and Strip: The Competitors Play Little Deuce Coupe 409* (Dot), The Hondells: *Go Little Honda* (Mercury), The Knights: *Hot Rod High* (Capitol), The Kickstands: *Black Boots and Bikes* (Capitol), The Road Runners: *The New Mustang and Other Hot Rod Hits* (London), The Weird-ohs: *New! The Sound of the Weird-ohs* (Mercury), The Silly Surfers: *The Sound of the Silly Surfers* (Mercury), The Revells: *The Go Sound of the Slots* (Reprise), The Ghouls: *Dracula's Deuce* (Capitol), and The Super Stocks: *Surf Route 101, Thunder Road,* and *School Is A Drag* (Capitol). He had his finger on the

pulse of teen culture and was a most prolific writer of hot rod and related genre songs, ranging from monsters to model-making, and slot cars to surf music.

♦ TR: We should talk about MARK 56, the budget label that put out the weirdest records, such as *I-HOP Presents Kaptain Kangaroo Eating at I-Hop, Taco Bell Produces the Tijuana Taxi, Alpha Beta Presents The Tijuana Brass, Tijuana Brass at the Pizza Connection*—

♦ DS: MARK 56 were one of the earliest labels to put old radio shows out on vinyl, like "Inner Sanctum." Basically, they put out promotional records. It seemed like they didn't put up the money for any of their records; they got somebody else to. They were just an office front. But they did release *Good Humor Ice Cream Presents Real Cool Hits* by the AVENGERS SIX—the best surf album, ever. Not only that, they recorded that a year or two after the whole surf thing had died, around '66. I mean—let's just hear it for budget labels altogether, because—for example, the best IKE TURNER album *ever* is the one on CROWN; it's full of terrific guitar instrumentals. Almost any country or R&B artist can be found on the CROWN label. Most of the time it's different takes or weird, really primitive material recorded by artists who later became more slick. CROWN apparently would buy out-takes and "junk" from everybody—

♦ JB: All the MARK 56 albums say "A George Garabedian Production" on the back. I just scored a Mark 56 45 that was by The George Garabedian Players and—he must have been a frustrated old man like the Beach Boys' dad, Murry (not Murray) Wilson, who after he was canned as the Beach Boys' producer/manager put out a horrible album, *The Many Moods of Murry Wilson*. This record is equally unlistenable.

♦ MB: All those CROWN "Twist" records are the best—every one: *Twist with B.B. King, Etta James,* etc.

♦ DS: They all had wonderful covers painted by the same artist, FAZZIO, and a generic back cover. Apparently they didn't license anything—that's what got them busted, a hundred albums later. [laughs]

♦ JB: I think SUTTON was the West Coast subsidiary of CROWN; they had the same cover artist. Other budget labels include KENT and FOUR STAR.

♦ MB: The genius label of all is TOPS—everyone thinks, "Oh, these are just reissues by crummy guys"—but then you find a SCATMAN CAROTHERS album that just *rips* . . .

♦ TR: Mike Lucas found a DICK DALE album at a swap meet (but it was by the Lawrence Welk accordionist) and asked the seller, "Do you know who this is?" "Yeah—it's that surf guitar guy!" "Uh—no, it's *not.*" There was even a photo of the guy with an accordion on the record, but the dealer wouldn't believe it!

♦ DS: But that's the whole upshot of this "collecting" thing: guys desperately trying to get any kind of dough they can out of these records; they hear all the wrong stories. But this has been going on for decades. I heard some old air checks from the early '60s with ads by Times Square Records (a record store in the Times Square subway); they'd play some old doo-wop song and announce, "You can come down and buy that at Times Square Records for $150." Doo-wops were the very first collectibles.

♦ DD: That was a whole New York thing. Then in the late '60s all the Europeans came over and totally took all the rockabilly out of America—they combed the South. At one point there were all these juke box operators who had old juke box records piled up to the ceiling—a penny each. And the Europeans just came over and took 'em all back home.

♦ DS: There was a distributor in Memphis that was around in the '50s, the SUN warehouse, which had every Sun record there ever was—

♦ DD: And Jerry Osborne, who did the first record price guide, bought a warehouse full of thousands of Elvis Sun 45s, then cleaned up.

♦ DS: Anyway, well into the '70s, Europeans were still making the pilgrimage to the South and cleaning them out—they were still a dime (or whatever) apiece.

From the collection of Johnny Bartlett. Dick Dale's *Mr. Eliminator*, Capitol Records, album cover credits: cover photo: Capitol Photo Studio—Ken Veeder. *Surfin' Hootenanny,* Stacy Records, album cover credits: art & cover illustration: Stacy Art Dept, Brodie Herndon, Director. The New Dimensions' *Deuces and Eights,* Sutton Records. The Tornadoes' *Bustin' Surfboards,* Josie Records: a product of Jay Gee Record Co., Inc. Rhythm Rockers' *Soul Surfin',* © 1963 Challenge Records, album cover credits: photo: Bruce Brown, cover design: Gardell/Boulton. *Surfers' Pajama Party,* Del-Fi Records, album cover credits: photo: Gene Ford.

◆ DD: There's still records in people's attics, but the easy-to-find stuff is long gone.

◆ DS: Although, there are still stories—someone we know went to a little garage sale and found "Rockin' Daddy" by SONNY FISHER on 78. Who would still have that to sell?! But people die, and stuff hangs around forever . . . then somebody decides to sell it. It's so great that you can *still* come across something . . .

◆ MB: The whole insanity of this record collecting is brought to life by the ADRIAN & THE SUNSETS record I found for a buck, and some guy over the phone offered me (sight unseen) seventy-five bucks for it. And it's just not that good an album; it's been re-issued a lot and it's a lousy record besides.

◆ DS: But I would like to vote in favor of reissues, at this point. Because the greatest thing about nowadays is: you can get, for example, so much more '50s stuff (which I personally like the best) than you could when it was coming out! Because it was so regional then. And now, you can get it all. I can listen to the *Sun Rockin' Years* boxed set and never get tired of it.

◆ DD: Before the '70s (when all the reissues started coming out) whatever you could find at garage sales was *it*—if you wanted Sun 45s, you had to find the Sun 45s. Then when the reissues began, it seemed that literally thousands of great unreleased songs, many

from the vaults, were made available for the first time. Now it seems endless; stuff just *keeps* coming out. And you can't afford to buy it all—

◆ DS: There's no way you can buy all the great reissues that come out. And unlike some people I know, I will take it wherever I can get it—any format, including CD. Have to!

◆ JB: But there's already so much on *record* that you can't possibly collect; why change format?

◆ DS: But if there's a great RCA R&B compilation like BILLY VERA's *Rock'n'Roll Party*—if I could get it on vinyl, I would. But I can't.

◆ DD: A case in point is the ASTRONAUTS' *Rarities,* which only came out on CD for the first time. It was a matter of minutes before I tracked somebody down who could *tape* it for me!

◆ MB: The insanity of CDs is shown by this example: my best friend got rid of all his albums and re-bought them on CD. Johnny's comment is the best: there's just too much music to have to buy the same stuff again.

◆ TR: What sucks is: the industry that put out the CDs is not giving anyone a choice. It's: "You *have* to buy this now, because we're not going to produce records anymore. They cost more, and you're going to buy them because we say so." If there were a choice, then I might consider owning one. But I hate their

From the collection of Johnny Bartlett. *Finley's Heroes,* narrated by Monte Moore, Fleetwood Records, album cover credits: graphics: Peg Hawk, cover art: Dick Hamilton. Arnold Palmer's *Music for Swingin' Golfers,* Mark 56. Kermit Schafer presents *Golf Par-Tee Fun!,* © GPI, King Records, album cover credits: photography: David Haylock. *The Giants Win the Pennant,* narrated by Russ Hodges & Lon Simmons, Fantasy Records. *How to Bowl,* © 1960 American Sight & Sound Corp. Don Carter presents *Music for Happy Bowlers,* Mark 56.

From the collection of Johnny Bartlett. *The Beetle Beat*, Coronet Records. The Bearcuts' *Swing in Beatlemania*, Somerset Records, album cover credits: cover art: Chic Laganella. *Beat-A-Mania!*, © 1962 Pickwick International, Design Records. *Beats!!!! The Merseyside Sound!*, © 1962 Pickwick International, Design Records. The Manchesters' *Beatlerama*, Diplomat Records, a product of Synthetic Plastics Co. Brock & the Sultans' *Do the Beetle*, Crown Records.

mentality.

◆ JB: Also, with CDs you can't perform DJ scratching techniques.

◆ MB: And what's going to happen when they market CDs you can record on—they'll probably be an inch bigger, and you won't be able to play the old CDs on the new players.

◆ JB: Remember the switch from 4-track to 8-track format in the '60s?

◆ MB: My dad's best friend got duped into 4-track—that was around for about 3 weeks, right? [laughs] At least he didn't get suckered into "quadrophonic" (four channel sound).

◆ **V: Now, besides DAT and 12" laserdisk there's even a newer cassette tape format that Phillips has introduced.**

◆ DD: All I can say is: if record collector geeks ask me if I'm into CDs, I say, "Dude—I've been gettin' into 'quad,' and it's the most *amazing* thing. I've gotten through the '50s and the '60s and now I'm up to 1972—at this rate it'll probably be another 10 years before I get into CDs."

◆ MB: With "quad," the drums are all on one speaker!

◆ DS: The motives behind these format changes are absolutely despicable. But if I can't have JIMMY MURPHY any other way, I have to get the CD.

◆ DD: One thing: if I stopped buying records tomorrow, I'd be completely set for the rest of my life. [All agree] If you have 2000 records and play one a day, by the time you go through them you've forgotten what the first one sounded like.

◆ MB: And how many records in the collection have you never even stuck a needle on?

◆ TR: You know, the other thing about record collecting is the *fun in finding something.* You're at some garage sale in the boonies and you find a box and get that "feeling"—there's nothing like it!

◆ DD: When you come across something that's completely monumental and it's a *dime*—that is the best feeling in the entire world.

◆ **V: What LPs do you think are least likely to be reissued on CD?**

◆ DD: The sick ones. Novelty ones. Homemade ones.

◆ JB: Derek has an album that sticks in my mind: BILLY BARTY's *The Little Mouse That Roared.* That's one of several Billy Barty albums. I don't think any of those fake Beatle albums will be re-released on CD—the ones like The BUGGS' *The Beetle Beat,* The BEATS' *The Mersey Side Sound,* The MANCHESTERS' *Beatlerama* (which shouldn't be confused with The BEARCUTS' *Beatlemania*), or B. BROCK & THE SULTANS' *Do The Beetle.*

◆ **V: Fake Beatle albums?**

◆ JB: There was a buttload of Beatle look-alike albums put out in 1964 with the sole purpose of deceiving people into buying them. The covers either had a

139

From the collection of Johnny Bartlett. The Hillbilly Bears: *Hillbilly Shindie*, Hanna-Barbera Records. Huckleberry Hound: *The Great Kellogg's TV Show*, © Hanna-Barbera Productions. The Flintstones' *Flip Fables: Goldi Rocks & the three Bearosauruses*, © 1965 Hanna-Barbera Records, album cover credits: cover design: Willie Ito, artist: Ron Dias. *Yogi Bear & the 3 Stooges Meet the Mad, Mad, Dr. No-No*, Hanna-Barbera Records, album cover credits: cover art: Homer Jonas/Art Lozzi, hand lettering: Robert Schaefer, art direction: H.C. Pennington. *Secret Squirrel & Morocco Mole in Super Spy*, © 1965 Hanna-Barbera Productions, Inc. Hanna-Barbera Records, album cover credits: F. Montealegre, hand lettering: Robert Schaefer. *Golden Cartoons in Song Vol. One*, Cartoon Series, Hanna-Barbera Records, album cover credits: cover: H.C. Pennington, Typography: Headliners, Inc.

picture of four guys who looked like the Beatles, or featured the word "Beetle" very prominently. What's cool is that most of these records *are* truly great—and they were all pretty much on budget labels like Crown or Diplomat. There was even a *female* Beatles take-off.

♦ MB: I can bet that the LANCELOT LINK soundtrack album will never be re-released. And that's a great album, too.

♦ DS: I wonder if all those great HANNA-BARBERA albums will be reissued. All the '60s ones were reissued in the '70s—not for any collectibility, but just for the new generation of kids: the GOLDEN RECORDS. Actually, I don't think you can say there's anything that won't be reissued, because it's *all* grist for the mill. Those RUDY RAY MOORE albums are coming out on CD now. Anything that's really expensive might be reissued. But I don't think that *Go Sounds of the Slots* will be reissued—

♦ TR: —or *A Garbage Collector in Beverly Hills.*

♦ DS: The GHOULS' (sadly underexploited sub-genre of monster surf rock) album was reissued, but on *French* Capitol. And the SUPER STOCKS album was reissued on Capitol—but *Australian* Capitol. But now that they've reissued *Country Comedy Time* by LONZO & OSCAR—that proves you can't predict anything. It

is all out there, and you can get it all! And there are still gems everywhere.

♦ DD: As the collectors push the prices higher and higher up on the obvious stuff, you just have to dig deeper into the weirder stuff. At a combination sewing-machine and vacuum cleaner repair/collectible records shop, this guy had all these records priced, and they were reasonable; I got two out of his "priced" section. Then he had about 50 boxes of "junk" records that were a dollar each. I found the best surf 45 in there, plus ten or eleven other great records that were so obscure they weren't in any price guide.

♦ TR: That's always nice when they're not in a guide.

♦ JB: I guess I have three *least*-favorite collectors: the Star Wars action figure collectors, Hot Wheel Collectors, and (the all-time worst): the McDonalds Toy Collectors.

♦ TR: They'll have *bins* of these "Happy Meal" toys, all in the original plastic bags they came in; *thousands* of 'em—

♦ DS: "This came in the 1989 Happy Meal between February and March 30th."

♦ DD: And you talk to them and they say, "Yeah, I got 'em sealed—I'll *never* open 'em." Well—*they* must be fun to play with!

◆ MB: That reminds me of all those old RICK GRIFFIN posters from the '60s—they're serial-numbered, and they've got collectors' guides to them. I talked to a guy who said there's a warehouse stacked to the rafters with posters—

◆ DS: Give me a match!

◆ TR: The weirdest things anyone collects are those glass insulators on top of power poles—

◆ DD: "Well, this is the one they made between 1895 and 1910. It was only used in Pennsylvania near the Norfolk-Western railroad line."

◆ MB: Those guys probably share convention space with the barbed-wire collectors. They have an "insider" name for barbed wire; they call it "stinging rope"—

◆ TR: I can see collecting Old West badges and stirrups, but power pole insulators and barbed wire?! *Get a life!*

◆ MB: Basically, it's no fun to go to a collectors' record store and pay twenty-five bucks for something, 'cause you feel ripped off. And you know you can find it eventually. I do have a rule: Never go to a garage sale with someone you know! Derek goes out every Saturday to 20 or 30 garage sales and scores tons of cool junk—

◆ DD: Yeah, but you weren't there at the 25 garage sales I had to drive to that were just Tupperware, crappy clothes, and diapers—

◆ JB: A couple weeks ago I was at a garage sale and asked, "Got any records?" Someone said, "Well, the woman that's selling the records—she went to get the food for us. She'll be back in about an hour. If you could come back tomorrow—" and I go, "*Tomorrow?* Can't I just come back in an hour?" "Uh—yeah, I guess." I left and came back and the woman brought down *six hundred* albums she'd been collecting. I bought 15 of 'em for 20 cents each: an original *JOHNNY ACE Memorial* album, WANDA JACKSON's 4th LP, The BIG BOPPER album, and SAM COOKE on Keen Records . . . also an ADAM READER porno album from the early '60s, with a totally nude girl on the cover.

◆ MB: The whole thing, the bottom line, is: there's still a brand-new *AVENGERS SIX* record out there that's never been opened, somewhere. And someone's gonna find it. The whole thing is the *hunt*.

NOTE: Both Maz and Johnny Bartlett have record labels. Send self-addressed stamped envelope for catalog to: Four Letter Words, 1784 Dolores St. #2, San Francisco, CA 94114, and Hillside Records, 30 Westline Dr, Daly City, CA 94015.

From the collection of Johnny Bartlett. Bob Thompson: His Chorus & Orchestra, *Mmm, Nice!*, © 1960 Radio Corp. of America. Erotica: the Rhythmns of Love, Fax Records. Officer Gunther Toody of *Car 54, Where Are You?*, © 1963 Eupolis Productions, Inc., Golden Records. *Kiddie Au Go-Go: Nursery Rhymes with the Teen Dance Beat of Today!*, Happy Time Records, album cover credits: the Go-Go dress designed by Robert Love for Joseph Love. Dwayne Hickman's *Dobie!*, arranged & conducted by Jimmie Haskell, Capitol Records. *The J.C. Penney Company presents Michael Brown in Penney Proud*, J.C. Penney Co., 1962.

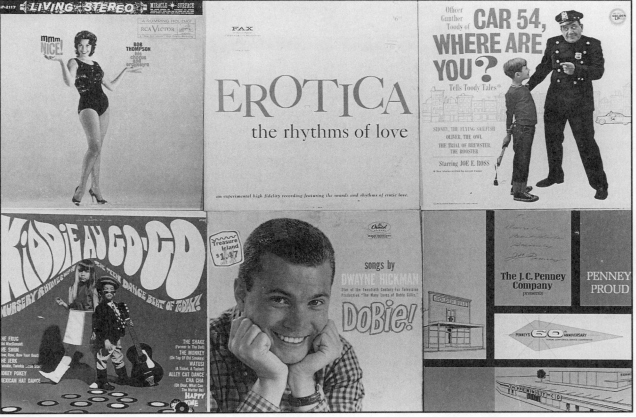

MARTIN DENNY

In 1957 composer-pianist Martin Denny had a number one record with "Quiet Village," a 45 taken from his debut album *Exotica* which featured bird calls, jungle sounds and little-known percussion instruments behind piano, vibes, bass and drums. Subsequently, a host of imitators released records with "exotic" in the title, and Denny's sidemen Arthur Lyman, Augie Colon and Julius Wechter went on to careers of their own.

Before he retired, Denny released 37 albums which sold over four million copies worldwide. Lately, he's had a resurgence of popularity: Toshiba-EMI in Japan has released several compilation CDs (plus a brand-new recording), and Rhino Records issued a "Best of" CD compiled by Stuart Sweezy and Brian King of AMOK. Recently he played five concerts in Japan! Now in his eighties, Martin Denny lives in Hawaii in a condo with a spectacular view of the mountains and the sea, from Coco Head to Black Point.

♦ **VALE: Your music conjures up visions of a tropical paradise—**

♦ MARTIN DENNY: Well, you're getting *close*. My music is a combination of the South Pacific and the Orient . . . what a lot of people *imagined* the islands to be like. It's pure fantasy, though. A lot of tourists have listened to my records, and when they come to Hawaii they expect some kind of romantic setting like James A. Michener conjured up in *South Pacific*.

The biggest hit single I ever had was "Quiet Village," which came out in 1957. It was taken from my debut album, *Exotica,* which had been released the year before. We were appearing at Don the Beachcomber's, on the beach at Waikiki, and a lot of servicemen who were stationed in Hawaii would come in, listen to us and buy our records. And when they were shipped out, they brought the records with them and played them for others. So through word of mouth our name got around: the "exotic sounds" of Martin Denny.

The *S.S. Nautilus* was the first American submarine to go underneath the North Pole. They had "Quiet Village" on their jukebox, and when they came back into dry dock after a year at sea, they mailed me my record, autographed by the commanding officer, with a letter telling me it was the favorite of the crew. So my records have literally been played from the North Pole down to the South Pole!

♦ **V: What's your musical background?**

♦ MD: Well, I have a classical background. At age ten in New York City, I studied piano under Lester Spitz and Isadore Gorn—I was kind of a child prodigy. When I was quite young I went to South America with a six-piece band and spent over four years traveling down there. As a result you can detect a lot of Latin rhythmic signatures in my music. If you take Hawaiian music alone, it lulls you to sleep—whereas Latin has exciting rhythms; it has a *beat!*

When I started my group I didn't limit myself to Hawaiian songs; I used popular tunes as well as ones I'd composed. My group included piano (I'm the pianist), vibes, bass, drums, and Latin percussion. Every-

The Martin Denny Group. Martin Denny (left).

body doubled on their instruments; the vibes person played marimba and bells (or whatever), and I leaned heavily on this interplay of percussion. Together we achieved the "Martin Denny sound," which was a blend of all these instruments. And the *hook* was these exotic bird calls.

♦ **V: Who thought of that?**

♦ MD: Well, I did—I put 'em in there! But it began quite accidentally. I opened at the Shell Bar in Henry J. Kaiser's Hawaiian Village in 1956. By this time we had four people including Arthur Lyman on vibes (later replaced by Julius Wechter, who went on to form the Baja Marimba Band) and Augie Colon (who did the bird calls) on bongos and congas. The Hawaiian Village was a beautiful open-air tropical setting. There was a pond with some very large bullfrogs right next to the bandstand. One night we were playing a certain song and I could hear the frogs going [deep voice], "*Rivet! Rivet! Rivet!*" When we stopped playing, the frogs stopped croaking. I thought, "Hmm—is that a coincidence?" So a little while later I said, "Let's repeat that tune," and sure enough the frogs started croaking again. And as a gag, some of the guys spontaneously started doing these bird calls. Afterwards we all had a good laugh: "Hey, that was fun!" But the following day one of the guests came up and said, "Mr Denny, you know that song you did with the birds and the frogs? Can you do that again?" I said, "What are you talking

about?"—then it dawned on me he'd thought that was part of the arrangement.

At the next rehearsal I said, "Okay, fellas, how about if each one of you does a different bird call? I'll do the frog . . ." (I had this grooved cylindrical gourd called a güiro, and by holding it up to the microphone and rubbing a pencil in the grooves, it sounded like a frog). We played it the next night, and all evening people kept coming up and saying, "We want to hear the one with the frogs and the birds again!" We must have played that tune *thirty* times. It turned out to be "Quiet Village."

As a result of playing in that tropical setting, I began to incorporate instruments from the South Pacific and the Orient into our act. We'd build a different arrangement around each instrument, experimenting to give each tune a different feel. Gradually the sound evolved. After a year I was ready to do *Exotica,* and I got a silver record for that—it sold about 400,000 LPs.

♦ **ANDREA JUNO: Can you talk about the origins of tiki culture? What did that mean to you?**

♦ MD: I don't know about any tiki culture. What I did was of a musical nature, and you can *associate* the sound with whatever you want. But I didn't do any research into tikis, or anything like that.

♦ **AJ: But didn't your music emerge at the same time that people began wearing '50s Hawaiian shirts and hosting tiki parties in their back yards?**

◆ MD: Part of the reason my records caught on was that *stereo* had just appeared on the market, with its amazing separation into right and left channels. People were interested in sound *per se*—and that included my so-called "exotic" sound. I guess I just happened to be there at the right time.

◆ **V: You've certainly managed to convey the feel of that balmy Hawaiian climate in your music—**

◆ MD: That climate rubs off on you, when you live here. Plus, the people I worked with represented different ethnic groups. My bass player, Harvey Ragsdale, was Chinese-English-Hawaiian. My bongo player, Augie Colon, was Puerto-Rican. My first vibes man was Arthur Lyman who was part Hawaiian. My drummer was Chinese; sometimes I had people who were Korean. Visually this was a distinctive-looking group and they were all talented musicians. It's like: if you were baking a pie and wanted to be imaginative, you might make something that still tastes like apple pie, but with a hint of mango in it . . .

Actually, a lot of what I'm doing is just window-dressing familiar tunes. I can take a tune like "Flamingo" and give it a tropical feel, in my style. In my arrangement of a Japanese farewell song, "Sayonara," I included a Japanese three-stringed instrument, the *shamisen*. We distinguished each song by a different ethnic instrument, usually on top of a semi-jazz or Latin beat. Even though it remained familiar, each song would take on a strange, exotic character.

◆ **V: It's great that instead of rejecting the bird calls outright, you immediately incorporated them—**

◆ MD: Essentially I was lucky to have a big *laboratory* where I could experiment: I was playing in a very exotic setting with a captive audience! People would come in off the street to have a *mai-tai,* and what we played seemed to blend in with the tropical drinks. I tried a lot of sound experiments; if it was good I kept it; if it wasn't, I dropped it. And the musicians I had would go along with whatever I suggested. After a while it all started to sound perfectly logical. I thought, "Let's keep it this way!" Whereas most musicians just want to play straight jazz—

◆ **V: Or imitate whatever is currently "hip"—**

◆ MD: Or they want to play for their own amazement. [laughs] Anyway, I didn't accomplish this all by myself; everyone I worked with contributed their own personality and know-how. I never took credit for their talent, but I do take credit for *directing* their talent . . . for working within their limitations, organizing and putting the sounds in the right place.

◆ **V: Most people have such rigid preconceptions that even if they accidentally come up with something original, they don't realize it. They go, "Oops—I made a mistake."**

◆ MD: Well, if I'd been on the mainland and had said to a bunch of musicians, "Hey, I want *you* to do a bird call here, and *you* to do a bird call there," they would've laughed me out of the place: "You gotta be kidding!" Since then, I can't tell you how many people have tried to copy my exotic sound, but I don't hold it against them. Imitation is the sincerest form of flattery, they say.

◆ **V: "Quiet Village" was written by Les Baxter—**

◆ MD: Long before my record came out, he'd released an album with that tune on it, a suite called *Le Sacre du Sauvage.* I took at least five or six selections from it; they're imaginative and they fit in with what I did. But he had a big orchestra at his command, whereas I only had five guys, so I had to give "Quiet Village" a different interpretation entirely. As a result, *my* version turned out to be the big record. Les Baxter gets composer's rights, so he's made a fortune off my recordings.

◆ **V: So you knew him personally?**

◆ MD: Oh yes! He did the liner notes to one of my albums. As a matter of fact, he's very grateful that I recorded "Quiet Village"—why not? It was a great piece of material for me. But I've also recorded about 35 of my own tunes which are along the lines of exotic sounds. Awhile back I recorded an album called *A Taste of India* (1969), never dreaming that someday I'd be going there to play. You know that I've traveled a lot; I've played Europe, South America, Japan and even Western Samoa.

At the next rehearsal I said, "Okay, fellas, how about if each one of you does a different bird call? I'll do the frog . . ."

◆ **V: Can you talk about the artwork for your albums, which perfectly complements the music inside—**

◆ MD: I had nothing to do with the artwork, although I got to meet the cover girl, Sandy Warner. She was a stunning model, extremely photogenic. She posed for at least the first dozen albums I did. They always changed her looks to fit the mood of the package. For instance, we called one album with an African sound *Afro-desia,* and for some reason Sandy dyed her hair blonde for the photo session; she's seen against a background of colorful African masks. When we did *Hypnotique,* which is surrealistic, she had dark hair. For *Primitiva* she was photographed standing waist-deep in water. The story I heard was that she was very uncomfortable because there were fish darting between her legs and tickling her feet. Also it was really cold—the photo was taken up at Lake Arrowhead.

◆ **V: You mean they weren't shot in Hawaii—**

◆ MD: Oh no! [laughs] None of the photos for the

album covers were ever shot in Hawaii; they were all done in Hollywood. Interestingly enough, Sandy Warner built a career as the "Exotica Girl." She even made a record, and they asked me to do the liner notes for her. But nothing ever came of it—it was just a flash in the pan.

♦ **V: So she made one record?**

♦ MD: Yes. I haven't the slightest idea what happened to it. It didn't make any impact at all.

♦ **V: Did you actually write the liner notes?**

♦ MD: Yeah. But I can't remember what I wrote—I don't even have a copy of it.

♦ **AJ: When did you last record for the Liberty label?**

♦ MD: The last one was *Exotic Moog,* in 1969. The Moog synthesizer had just come out; by recording this, the record company thought I'd be "keeping up with the times." We took hits like "Quiet Village" and "Taste of Honey," and reinterpreted them on these synthesizers. The entire group was electrified—even the drums. The introduction to "Quiet Village" was played on a synthesizer that gave it a real fat bass sound—a whole other dimension.The company aimed this at what was then called the "underground" market; this was when the hippie thing had started happening in San Francisco.

♦ **V: How did you like playing the Moog?**

♦ MD: We used two keyboards, because originally you could not play any harmonies on the Moog. If you wanted to record a chord, you had to record each interval separately. Wendy Carlos had released *Switched-On Bach,* with liner notes explaining how it had been recorded: *very painfully.* The process involved recording one note at a time, then overdubbing and adding another until it was finished—hundreds of hours later. I remember the Musicians' Union warning that the synthesizer would replace live musicians. In a way, it has: a four-piece band using synthesizers can now sound like a full orchestra and chorus.

Anyway, for *Exotic Moog* we did things like have a drummer hit gongs that were partially submerged under water. We used a new kind of electronic organ, plus other electronic effects that had just come out. The engineer played a bigger role than previously, putting all these sounds together. The album has a black cover; it's our only record with a sleeve like that. But the record never sold, so that was the end of *that.*

♦ **V: It probably didn't get distributed.**

♦ MD: I think a lot of people just weren't interested in it. Maybe they thought, "Hey—*this* doesn't sound like Martin Denny! It's a whole new bag."

♦ **V: Where did you find exotic percussion instruments like a 200-pound New Guinea talking drum? I can't believe someone would haul that back from New Guinea for you—**

♦ MD: No, they didn't. I was browsing at one of those

LST 7122
Liberty
STEREO

QUIET VILLAGE

The Exotic Sounds of

MARTIN DENNY

Martin Denny's *Quiet Village*, Liberty Records, Inc.
Album cover credits: cover design: Pate/Francis & Assoc., color photography:
Ivan Nagy, cover posed by: Sandy Warner "the Exotica Girl."

decorator's galleries in Los Angeles—interior decorators are always looking for something a little novel—and there it was. Immediately I thought of fitting it into the next album, which we were going to title *Primitiva*—primitive, in other words. When I told the fellow who owned the shop what I wanted to do, he got very enthusiastic—he didn't even charge me for using it. All he wanted was a credit, which I gave him on the album.

♦ **V: Yes, it says, "We acknowledge the assistance of Franklin Galleries, Los Angeles, Calif: loan of garamut, primitive New Guinean log drum."**

♦ MD: They had to lug that thing up to the studio. It had once been used for primitive rituals; the way you struck it had a sexual connotation. That was the one and only time I ever used that particular drum. For better or worse, I used all these really weird instruments just for effect—to make an impact.

I'll tell you something with a real romantic story behind it. The liner notes on *Quiet Village* were written by John Sturges, a well-known film director who made *The Old Man and the Sea, Gunfight at the OK Corral, Bad Day at Black Rock* and *Last Train from Gun Hill.* Knowing that I was interested in strange musical instruments, he told me he was going to Burma to shoot the background for a film with Frank Sinatra titled *Never So Few.* I told him, "John, if you come across anything interesting, would you get it for me? Whatever it costs, I'll reimburse you." And he said, "Don't worry about *that;* I'll just keep my eyes open."

At the time—I think this was 1958—I had just finished a tour and flown back from New York City to Los Angeles. In New York I had received a cable from him that said, "I have sent you some *goodies*—I hope

you like them." When I checked in at the recording studio, there were two very large packing cases addressed to me. Well, the cases were so big that I couldn't open them there, so I had them shipped back to my home in Honolulu. They turned out to be *crammed* with different types of Burmese gongs, drums, little brass instruments—everything under the sun.

It turned out that Sturges had climbed this sacred mountain to shoot background scenes at the top, and there was a Buddhist temple surrounded by little shops selling all kinds of musical instruments. He couldn't speak Burmese and they couldn't speak English, but he was able to buy up these instruments like he was in a candy store: "Gimme six of these; I'll take a dozen of those . . ." In order to get them down the mountainside, he hired a procession of monks in saffron robes—can you visualize that? When they arrived at the bottom, there was a VIP being shown around; it was Marshal Tito of Yugoslavia.

Sturges got permission to take the instruments out of the country—they're classified as primitive art—and that's how I ended up with a matching collection of eight beautiful gongs that vary in diameter from 10-14 inches. I used to have them strung together in order of ascending size, and I would play them like a scale. They gave out these wonderful sounds. There was another set of seven solid brass gongs—the largest weighed 70 pounds—and yet another set of even smaller ones. There was also a marvelous collection of Burmese drums.

Unfortunately, somebody burglarized our house and stole part of that collection. I don't think they knew what they were doing—they were probably some *delinquents*. I still have most of the collection; eventually I'll give it to the University of Hawaii. It's too valuable—in fact it's irreplaceable; it's an extraordinary collection. And Sturges charged me only for the freight, which came to about $300. Today, each one of these instruments is worth more than $300!

I used all sorts of percussive instruments—that became the signature of the group. And there's no musical notation system for these exotic drums and gongs. We used what is called a "head arrangement," just trial and error. So if a musician came up with a certain effect I liked, I'd say, "Okay, let's use that; remember how you did it." And you'd hope that the musician could duplicate it next time. So . . . there's no orchestra in the world that can sit down and duplicate that sound, because they don't have the instruments—they don't even know how the sound was made. That's what makes my recordings unique. I never thought about it at the time, but now I look back and realize, "Hey, that *is* one-of-a-kind. Where are you going to find somebody who has a collection of those same Burmese gongs?"

♦ **V: On the back cover photo of The Best of Martin Denny, *what are you playing?***

♦ MD: That's a Tahitian drum. And I'm not really

playing it—I'm *posing* for that photo—it had to look exotic, you know. *I* play the piano. [laughs] You don't believe everything you see in pictures, do you?

♦ **V: Did you get that drum in Tahiti?**

♦ MD: Heck no! That photo was taken at Don the Beachcomber's. Don had a terrific Polynesian art collection, and I had access to anything I wanted.

♦ **V: Oh—there really was a Don the Beachcomber?**

♦ MD: Oh yes. I appeared at his place for about seven years; it later became known as Duke Kahanamoku's in Honolulu. They had a fantastic stage setting with a huge overhead fan that moved sideways. People would ask, "What makes that thing move?" and the waiters would kid, "A little man up there turns the handle." There was a huge piece of tapa cloth that moved from side to side, creating an almost hypnotic effect. Wherever I played, I consciously tried to enhance the setting. For instance, to hide the metal tubes of the vibraphone, I built a bamboo frame around it and stretched tapa cloth across, so that if a photo is taken, you don't see a modern-looking vibraphone. That's showmanship—in *any* presentation, the costuming and the background are very important.

The original Don the Beachcomber restaurant was in Hollywood, then he started one in Chicago and eventually the one in Honolulu. After he lost control and it became syndicated, competitors like Trader Vic's sprang up all over the place. Don the Beachcomber was the inventor of the *mai-tai,* among many other drinks. He was a real character, and a true Polynesian buff.

♦ **V: He's one of the principal disseminators of tiki culture—**

♦ MD: He created the illusion; he was a great showman. He had brought back literally thousands of arti-

facts from his travels, and when you walked into his restaurant it was like entering a different world—Polynesia, with all these tiki figures, palm fronds, sea shells and everything you associate with Polynesian thatched huts. And people loved it. The food he served added to the illusion: more or less Cantonese dinners plus a few Polynesian dishes, which to most Americans then were quite exotic. Many of the drinks were unique, rum-based concoctions he'd invented himself. Don himself was very colorful—he always wore a bush jacket, khaki shorts and long stockings like he'd just come off a safari. He wore a hat, always had a cheroot in his mouth, and had a little moustache—he looked like a British colonel. During his lifetime he entertained kings, astronauts, con artists and stars—he's mentioned in a book called *Rascals in Paradise.* I was inspired just by being surrounded by all his artifacts, which my music *adapted* to!

Part of the reason my records caught on was that *stereo* had just appeared on the market, with its amazing separation into right and left channels. People were interested in sound *per se*—and that included my so-called "exotic" sound.

♦ **AJ: When did you last see Les Baxter?**

♦ MD: In 1976 I gave a concert in the Waikiki Shell for the Bicentennial. I used approximately a hundred people—two of my original groups, a symphony orchestra, a jazz group and a choral group—and presented a whole program of my selections. I invited Les Baxter, and he was guest conductor on "Quiet Village" and other numbers he had composed. Like I said, his material was just perfect for *me,* and I in turn helped *him,* because a lot of people discovered Les Baxter as a result of my recordings.

♦ **V: You first met him in May, 1958, at the Interlude in Hollywood?**

♦ MD: That's correct, and he gave me some other compositions he wanted me to record. Later, somebody claimed that he had put me down because I'd used bird calls on my recordings—

♦ **V: The very thing that "made" you—**

♦ MD: Exactly. Ironically, years later I got a letter from him asking if I would send him a tape of my bird calls—he was recording something and wanted to use them!

♦ **V: Perhaps he didn't recognize the innovation when it first appeared—**

♦ MD: It's hard for people to recognize innovation. But most people were just plain *intrigued* when they

Martin Denny in his home.   Photo: Ed Hardy

Ravel's *Bolero.* On top of that are layers of exotic percussion, plus the sounds of the vibes, the piano, and (of course) the bird calls. It all adds up to a modern sound that evokes some very *primitive* feelings.

Popular music has changed; now it's all "rock." But in 1958 Dick Clark, who had the hottest TV show in the country for teenagers, had me on his show. I rode the charts of *Billboard, Cashbox,* and *Variety;* "Quiet Village" was Number One for 13 consecutive weeks. I had as many as three or four albums on the charts simultaneously. I also had national hits with "A Taste of Honey," "The Enchanted Sea," and "Ebb Tide."

◆ *V: Didn't you work with Ethel Azama?*

◆ MD: Yes. She was a marvelous jazz singer who passed away several years ago. She worked both in Hawaii and on the mainland, and had several records out. She was not Japanese, but of Okinawan descent.

◆ *V: Did she use exotic sounds in her arrangements?*

◆ MD: No. I helped produce one of her records; she did another one with a big band. There was another singer I worked with who sang "Bali Hai"—an Indonesian girl named SONDI SODSAI who was going to college at UCLA. Liberty Records recorded her LP *Sondi,* using exotic sounds—she sang in Indonesian, and the musical background was written by Hal Johnson, an arranger who collaborated with me and knew my sounds. He used a large orchestra behind her, trying to get an Indonesian feel. It wasn't the greatest record, but it's strange to hear because she performs in that weird Balinese singing style.

◆ *V: Did you meet her?*

◆ MD: Oh, yeah. She came from a royal family, and had been trained in the art of exotic Balinese dancing. After cutting one album and getting her degree at the university, she went back to Indonesia.

◆ *V: You've recorded many songs with evocative titles, like "Stone God," "Love Dance," "Lotus Land," "Return to Paradise," "Island of Dreams," "When First I Love"—*

◆ MD: That last title was suggested by Omar Khayyam, and that song reminds me of the atmosphere of his Persian poetry. "Return to Paradise" was the theme song of the movie of the same title; Dimitri Tiomkin wrote it. Once I was playing it on the piano at the Royal Hawaiian Hotel and Tiomkin came up to me and said, "That's my song." He introduced himself and thanked me for playing it. Later on I recorded it with my group; it seemed to fit right in. Three years ago when I went to Western Samoa and played for the King of Samoa, his officials gave me a tour of the island and showed me a white sand beach dotted with coconut palms, where the movie had been filmed. I sat in the shade of a little thatched-roof bar sipping a drink and thought, "What a perfect setting," while the theme from "Return to Paradise" drifted through my mind.

◆ *V: Describe your house—*

◆ MD: I live right above the ocean with a magnificent

heard these wild jungle sounds coming out of us. I had a running gag I would use: when people asked if we used live birds on our records, my reply would be, "No—we come up with sounds for which there are no birds." Augie Colon was the acknowledged master of the bird sounds—he was terrific.

◆ *AJ: How would he do them? Obviously, with his mouth—*

◆ MD: Yes—with his mouth. When he was a youngster he used to go hunting in the jungle; he'd hear all these birds and was able to imitate them. You know, a lot of people say, "How come Martin Denny doesn't do any bird calls?" I personally don't do any—I can give a poor imitation of a *parrot,* but that wasn't my "thing." But to this day, wherever I go people ask me to play "Quiet Village." I can play the damn thing on the piano, but I can't do the bird calls . . . so I say, "C'mon everybody; *join in!* Be my guest—*you* be the bird!" Sometimes the record company would pressure me to include even more sounds—overkill, you know. I began to resent it; my feeling was: "I'm not selling bird calls—I'm selling music!"

◆ *V: When you first hear it, "Quiet Village" certainly has an impact—*

◆ MD: If you just hear it on record, it sounds like a whole jungle—you don't know how or where any of those sounds originated. But if you hear it "live," then you can see how it's all done, with the percussion instruments. "Quiet Village" has a compulsive jungle rhythm to it; the bass has a hypnotic effect almost like

view of Coco Head. It's a very romantic setting. I'm sitting in my den which has some of my mementoes and pictures displayed. On one wall hangs a blue marlin that I won first prize for in medium tackle—it's seven feet long. Behind me on the wall are some of my gold and silver records, plus a group of Japanese porcelain masks. The room is modern but exotic—it's got a little bit of everything. In the corner I have a few gongs and prayer bowls, plus my hi-fi equipment. To my right is an African mask with a horn sprouting out. In front of me is a Burmese drum, plus some brilliant red-and-yellow Hawaiian feathered gourds which the women shake when they're dancing. There's even some Eskimo primitive art from Alaska that someone gave me. I also have a figurine displayed, commemorating my first hole-in-one in golf. So my claim to fame is: I had a hole in one, I won first prize in medium tackle, and I got a gold record. That's not bad!

♦ **V: A multi-faceted individual.**

♦ MD: You've got to realize, I'm over 80 years old. I was born on April 10, 1911. You can see I've had a very full life.

♦ **V: One final question: when you were recording, did your producers allow you as much freedom as you wanted?**

♦ MD: I was the one who dictated what I wanted to do. I had the final say. If I didn't like it, I'd tell them. Si Waronker was the president at one time; then there was Al Bennett, who later became president, and the engineer, Ted Keep. You've heard of the CHIPMUNKS, haven't you?

♦ **V: Yes; they did "The Chipmunk Song" and "Alvin's Harmonica."**

♦ MD: David Seville came up with the idea of the Chipmunks, whose records were based on speeded-up vocal sounds. The characters were named Simon (after Si Waronker), Alvin (after Al Bennett), and Theodore (after Ted Keep). When the "Chipmunk Song" came out, Liberty was on the verge of bankruptcy—that record made over a million dollars and saved the company. The company's next big hit was "Quiet Village," followed by Julie London's recording of "Cry Me a River." Those three records saved Liberty Records. I could go on for hours, but that's all history now.

I'm semi-retired, and the only thing I can say in defense of old age is: what counts most is your *attitude.* I talked to my brother in Atlanta, Georgia on his 84th birthday and asked: "How you feeling?" He said, "I don't feel like 84; I feel like 48. A week ago I went out and bought 6 pairs of shoes." I said, "My god, you're an optimist. To wear out 6 pairs of shoes you've got to do a lot of shuffling!"

But I've had a good long career, and I've enjoyed what I do. My records got made because I happen to have imagination—that's all. Along the way, a lot of people helped me pick up on ideas. Imagination plus *organization . . .* how to take something and put it in its proper perspective. It's like making a cake: you put all

Martin Denny's *Latin Village*, Liberty Records, Inc.
Album cover credits: cover design & photography: Studio Five.

the ingredients together and sometimes you come up with a new little flavor that makes it unique. So I just added a lot of musical flavors, mixed them through trial and error, and came up with the sounds.

♦ **AJ: And it worked—good cake!**

♦ MD: Most people live their lives content with a banana split: strawberry, chocolate and vanilla ice cream topped by some nuts and a banana. And they think that's just fine. I don't know if you've ever done this, but try putting a scoop of passion fruit sherbet on half a papaya. Nobody even *thinks* of doing that, but it's been there all along. You'll end up with an unusual, exotic taste that will take you to another world!

HENRY J. KAISER AND ME
by Martin Denny

In October 1956, I was appearing at the Shell Bar at Henry J. Kaiser's Hawaiian Village when I was introduced to Arnie Mills, of the management firm of Gabbe, Lutz and Heller, one of the giants in show business. Some of their accounts were Liberace, Lawrence Welk, Margaret Whiting, and Mel Torme. Mills had heard my group and was impressed—he wanted to sign us up, and painted a glowing future for me. I felt this was the opportunity I had been waiting for: to finally get a crack at "the big time."

I talked to Alfred Apaka, who was the featured attraction at the Tapa Room next to the Shell Bar. Alfred was enormously popular and the darling of the Kaisers. He was also the entertainment director who

Martin Denny's *Exotica,* © Liberty Records, Inc.
Album cover credits: cover photography: Garrett-Howard.

had originally signed me up to play at the Village. He wished me luck, and said he would break the news to Henry J. Kaiser: that I planned on leaving the Village when my contract expired on December 31, 1956. Shortly thereafter Alfred told me that I had the blessing of Henry J. and that he hoped we could work out return engagements.

Of course I was elated. I had a contract made up offering Arthur Lyman (vibes) and John Kramer (bass) each 25% interest in any profits we made over basic union wages. I later included Augie Colon (percussion, bird calls) who was the newest member of the group, and gave him a 10% interest. The agreement was to hold good as long as they remained in the group.

However, all this changed when Henry J. wanted to record the group without my permission (my management firm had planned to sign me to Liberty Records). I refused, and the following day was read the "riot act" in his office in the presence of my group. Henry J. accused me of disloyalty, and showered me with a barrage of intimidation. He demanded I cancel the contract with my new management, telling my boys that he had great plans for the group and that I was ruining their future—that I was an *ingrate.* He carried on this tirade for a half-hour, browbeating and humiliating me. I could not get a word in edgewise.

I was stunned at his outburst. The truth of the matter was that he didn't want us to leave, as he had a good thing going for him: the Shell Bar was sold out every evening. I finally asked if I could have a word with my boys privately. They told me they were with me all the way, and whatever I decided, they would go along with my decision.

I told Henry J. my decision was still the same. At this point he told me he was going to follow my career very closely, which I interpreted as a threat. Henry J. was a billionaire tycoon used to having his way, and later I was told that I'd received the full Henry J. *treatment* (when he wanted something). He could be ruthless when he wanted things his way.

That same month I was married to my present wife, June. For over two months until the end of my contract I was cold-shouldered by all the employees (including Alfred Apaka) by orders of Kaiser. No one spoke to me, and any requests I made were ignored or treated with rudeness. It was hard on us, and I did have misgivings and self-doubt about my future, as well as my boys'. This was one of the most important decisions I ever made—but I never regretted it, even though the next few years were tough and it was all I could do to keep the group together.

My first tour was on the West Coast of California. We played for the Pebble Beach Crosby Open Golf party, and this marked our first appearance on the mainland. We were sponsored by the legendary Francis II Brown and Winona Love who kept residence there, as well as in Honolulu. His family had once owned what is now Pearl Harbor, and he was a great sportsman and golfer; we were introduced to the elite of the golfing world.

We were a big hit and from there we opened at the new Royal Nevada Hotel in Las Vegas. Word had gotten around of our "exotic sound" and many of the entertainers on the strip came to hear us, including Xavier Cugat. The Sands Hotel used "Quiet Village" as the theme for a stage presentation. While there we were rear-ended by a hit-and-run driver, and June, who was pregnant, almost aborted our baby—this was very traumatic for both of us. Our group played several resorts and finally returned to Las Vegas to play at the Flamingo Hotel. We played behind the bar on a slowly revolving stage, and by the time we'd made a complete cycle the audience would be all new faces. What was funny was the gambling bosses sending us messages to "Knock off the bird calls!" as they distracted the gamblers.

Then we had no further bookings. In desperation, I cabled Don the Beachcomber and told him we were free and could he use us? To my relief, he wired back that he wanted us to open as soon as possible. I had to leave June behind as she couldn't travel and was expecting the baby any moment. When I got back to Honolulu I was fortunate in finding an older house on 1/8 of an acre that had just about every kind of plant indigenous to Hawaii: a mango tree loaded with fruit, papaya, avocados, figs, bananas, limes, and coconuts. It also had tropical flowers, ginger, red and yellow plumeria trees, vanda orchids, wood roses and a large breadfruit tree, plus a huge lawn. The property took up the corner of the block it was located on, and was surrounded by shrubs that were 12 feet high.

Our baby was born in Los Angeles on August 6, 1957. I wasn't able to see her until three weeks later, when June was well enough to travel. We named her Christina Gwen and called her Tina. After appearing at Don the Beachcomber's for several months, I was made aware that Henry J. Kaiser had been surreptitiously sending his staff to court Arthur Lyman, my vibes man. Arthur gave notice, and informed me he was leaving in November. He took my bass man (John Kramer) and formed his own group. Later, I found out that he had been rehearsing with his group even *before* giving me notice. So Henry J. finally got his way—he wanted Arthur to play the Shell Bar with a presentation identical to mine. That way he thought he could get back at me, and break up my group.

Well, he didn't break my spirit. Augie Colon remained loyal to me and stayed on with me for over eight years. I made a quick trip back to Los Angeles to audition vibe players; Julius Wechter was highly recommended and turned out to be the best choice I could ever have made. He was only 22 at the time, and brought his wife Cissie and their infant David to Hawaii with him. Julius was extremely talented, both as performer and arranger, and played a large part in the group's development. I also added (on bass) Harvey Ragsdale, who came from Hilo on the big island.

Arthur Lyman made a reputation and career and followed my style, thanks to Henry J. This created a rivalry between us as to "who came first: the chicken or the hen?" Arthur's wife, Marie, who acted as his manager, caused a great deal of unpleasantness. Eventually they were divorced and Arthur was discouraged enough to drop out of performing.

None of the photos for the album covers were ever shot in Hawaii; they were all done in Hollywood.

Meanwhile, I kept evolving my style and when "Quiet Village" hit the singles charts, I had as many as three or four LPs riding the album charts on *Billboard, Cashbox* and *Variety*. In 1959 I won the *Billboard* award for "most promising group of the year" (voted on by DJs nationally). I was also nominated for "pianist of the year," along with George Shearing and Ahmad Jamal. Our group was featured on the *Dinah Shore* and *Johnny Carson* shows as well as the *Tennessee Ernie Ford, Bob Crosby* and *Bob Newhart* shows. That year I became incorporated when my earnings on royalties and personal appearances came to $250,000—a considerable amount at that time, before inflation. So much for Henry J. Kaiser—had I stayed with him I would *never* have known the success I enjoyed! When I left Kaiser I was earning $8,400 a year.

We all finally made our peace. John Kramer is a stockbroker and handles my account with him. In 1987 I helped coax Arthur out of retirement to come back to Hawaii, where he is still very active as a soloist. We did several projects together and he recorded with me on my last CD, *Exotica '90*, for Toshiba-EMI. Augie Colon still keeps in touch and I call him whenever I have a project going. Harvey Ragsdale died in 1990. Alfred Apaka died in 1960 and Henry J. died at the age of 85.

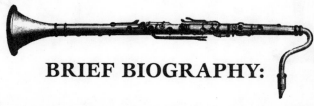

BRIEF BIOGRAPHY:

Martin Denny was born in New York City on April 5, 1911 and raised in Los Angeles, California. He toured South America with the Don Dean Orchestra for four-and-a-half years, and has performed with the bands of Gigi Royce, Jimmy Grier, and Carol Lofner. He has also accompanied Betty Hutton and Hildegarde on tours.

During WWII he served in the U.S. Air Force for 43 months and did a tour of Germany and France. After his discharge on December 13, 1945, he returned to school and enrolled at the Los Angeles Conservatory of Music, studying piano and composition under Dr Wesley La Violette, and orchestration under Arthur Lange. He also studied at the University of Southern California.

Martin Denny first came to Honolulu in January 1954 under contract to Don the Beachcomber's (which later became Duke Kahanamoku's) where he appeared for ten years. In 1955 he formed his group and signed a contract with Liberty Records. He made his mainland debut in 1957 at the Bing Crosby Golf Tournament at Pebble Beach sponsored by Francis II Brown.

Denny has performed for the Royal Hawaiian Hotel, The Hawaiian Village, The Kahala Hilton, The Kuilima, The Hawaiian Regent, Canlis' The Blue Dolphin, the Mauna Kea Hotel, The Mauna Loa, and the Wailea Beach Hotel in Maui. He has appeared on college concert tours throughout the U.S. as well as in major hotels and clubs and on TV. His publishing company, Exotic Music, has a catalog of over 36 of his own compositions.

Now active in the Honolulu Rotary Club, Denny is a member of ASCAP, the Hawaiian Professional Song Writers Society, the Aloha Shrine and is a life member of the Hawaiian Association of Music, Local 677. In 1990 he was awarded the *Hoku* award for "A Lifetime of Achievement" (Hawaiian Recording Society).

Martin Denny is married to his wife June, a native of Washington. Their daughter, Tina, attended Hawaii School for Girls and graduated from Oregon State University at Corvallis. His hobbies are golf and collecting exotic musical instruments from Indonesia and the Orient.

LYPSINKA

The Fabulous Lypsinka was born John Epperson in Hazlehurst, Mississippi, in 1955. In 1978 he moved to New York. After a visit to Paris in 1981 where he saw lip-synching drag queens performing as an art form, he "wondered if it couldn't all be put together in one character." In 1982 he began solo theater productions such as *The Many Moods of Lypsinka,* utilizing not only classic films like *Imitation of Life* but outrageous songs from musicals, lounge acts and cabaret.

Lypsinka is also a playwright and writer—his coloring book is available for $7 postpaid from Big Fat Movie Star Productions, 8 Little West 12th St, New York, NY 10014. Lypsinka is represented by Mark Sendroff, (212) 922-1880.

◆ *VALE: Your show incorporates some startling music and dialogue, taken not only from records but films as well—*
◆ LYPSINKA: I'm obsessed with films—that's really my great passion, even though I've never made any—I just like to look at them. A film I saw at a drive-in when I was a kid affected me a lot: *I Want What I Want,* starring ANNE HEYWOOD as a man who enjoys being a transvestite and wants to have a sex-change operation. I grew up in Mississippi, where they showed more films like that than anywhere else, and it possibly changed my life! It undoubtedly sparked a certain train of thought. I also saw RUSS MEYER movies, not knowing what they were or what impact they would have later. I remember seeing *Vixen;* now I know the star, ERICA GAVIN—she's the top salesgirl at Fred Segal in L.A. She looks quite different than she did then.

My absolute favorite movie is *Imitation of Life* by DOUGLAS SIRK with LANA TURNER. It functions on so many different levels. It's an out-and-out melodrama, it's a backstage story, it's a women's picture, it's a satire on American life at that time. It's a "black" comedy—in more ways than one—although you have

to see it a hundred times to realize that Douglas Sirk is making a joke out of everything. It's really glamorous—the clothes and the colors. And just the fact that Lana Turner is in it, being as phony as she can be . . .

Also, it's a ROSS HUNTER production. Ross Hunter saw only one aspect, which was entertainment and gloss; he didn't see the irony that Douglas Sirk put into his films. So in the movie there's this dichotomy: Sirk has the upper hand, but it has Ross Hunter written all over it as well. And I watch it over and over; I never tire of it. But that's true of a lot of my favorite films— every time I watch *Marnie* or *Sunset Boulevard* or *Valley of the Dolls* I find something new and exciting.

I adore *Hush Hush . . . Sweet Charlotte.* Most people prefer *Whatever Happened to Baby Jane?,* but I always prefer the more obscure things in life! It's a little more desperate. I also like the setting in the South in Louisiana, and the script is not quite as good—which makes it nutty, too. Plus, it's kind of a sequel—not the same characters but the same *style* of film.

Another film I like is *Madame X* (1966). CONSTANCE BENNETT plays to the hilt the supercilious, rich, upper-class Texas mother who despises the "trashy" bride her son brings home. As she's throwing

Photo: Albert Watson

Lana Turner out of the family mansion, she hisses, "You're still a shop-girl from San Francisco and you should have *stayed* on the other side of the counter!" The camerawork is by RUSSELL METTY (who photographed all the Douglas Sirk films) so it has the "look" but none of the irony of Sirk. Nevertheless, it's fascinating in its bathos.

NATALIE WOOD's *Gypsy* was also an early influence—I think it was advertised as "all color, all stripping!" and when I saw it at the age of eight I was entranced. It's aged rather well—just like *Hello, Dolly*. At the time, people were going, "We've *had* it with

153

Photo: Albert Watson

tion—preferably both in one. Metzger's films were little more than softcore low-budgets, but they were arty because he did them with style. *The Lickerish Quartet* has this bizarre scene with people rolling around naked on huge pages blown up from a dictionary. And *Camille 2000* had great '60s mod clothes. He also made *The Opening of Misty Beethoven.* So basically, if somebody does something with style, I want to see it!

♦ **V: How did you become "Lypsinka"? Obviously, you weren't encouraged in school—**

♦ L: I grew up in a small town in Mississippi, in a family that really didn't encourage the arts. My father is an athlete and wanted me to be an athlete, too. I tried sports, but I just couldn't get interested; I was always more interested in music and reading. I studied piano—my teacher discouraged me from playing or even listening to anything other than "classical." She got very upset when she caught me picking out "Georgy Girl" on the keys—

♦ **V: She was "high culture" oriented—**

♦ L: Right. Playing the piano became a form of escape for me. In the back of my mind I always knew that I wanted to be an actor or performer, but I was afraid to say it. Everyone in my town took piano lessons—that was accepted—but to actually make a *career* out of that was another thing. Everyone wanted me to get my teacher's credentials because they didn't think I could "make it" playing piano—I proved 'em wrong! [laughs] I ended up playing rehearsals for the American Ballet Theater for years. I also played saxophone in the high school band, and studied pipe organ as well.

My favorite organist is ETHEL SMITH. She plays the role of a music teacher in *Bathing Beauty* (1944) with Red Skelton and Esther Williams. It's set at an all-girls' school, and there's a scene where the girls come in and say, "Oh, don't play any Bach today—why

these overblown musicals!" but in retrospect Barbra Streisand was fantastic in *Hello, Dolly!* The production values made it into what is, by today's standards, a lavish, beautiful film.

I recently read *Directed By Vincente Minnelli* (written by Stephen Harvey) which changed the way I look at everything. The author dissected the themes running through Minnelli's films, tied them all together and made you realize he was almost subliminally the consummate artist. He explains why *Brigadoon* was such a big mess. Part of the problem was: should it be Cinemascope or not? So they filmed it both ways, on a sound stage instead of on location, and it just looked phony—which for Minnelli should have worked, but didn't. [laughs]

♦ **V: Why do you like RADLEY METZGER—**

♦ L: I've only seen *Camille 2000* and *The Lickerish Quartet.* But what I'm interested in most, whether it's art or music or films or theater, is *style* and *styliza-*

don't you play 'Tico Tico.' " So she starts playing it—she has a big '40s pompadour, and she just *goes to town* on the organ. That was her big recording hit; it sold over a million copies. I think she's in *Saludos Amigos* (1942), and *The Three Caballeros* where she's "live" but everything else is animated, and she's flying around the sky playing the organ. It's really wonderful. I also saw her in a hillbilly movie when I was a kid—never forgot her. CHARLES PIERCE used to take her on the road as his opening act.

♦ *V: How did you take the step of moving to New York?*

♦ L: Sheer nerve, and saving up money. When you're 23 you think, "I'm *just* going to do this!" I had played piano for a ballet class in Mississippi, so I moved to New York with a letter of recommendation and immediately got a job playing for the American Ballet. I was as "green" as they come, even at 23—nowadays, young people know so much more. But for a 23-year-old from Mississippi in 1978 who was insecure and shy (with all the baggage that comes from growing up in the South), moving to New York seemed like a major achievement.

In Mississippi I had been an *outsider;* I was taunted for being a musician and for being effeminate. The irony is: now I use that effeminacy to make my living and my "name." It's definitely been a form of revenge to say to those people who made fun of me, "Well, look at me—I'm on TV with Sandra Bernhard; I'm in *People* magazine with Madonna; and I hang out with Karl Lagerfeld. I've met my idols. I've been hugged by Carol Burnett, I've chatted with Bette Midler"—how many people have done *that*?

♦ *V: You mentioned that your father wanted you to become an athlete—were you ever a runner?*

Ethel Smith's *Tico Tico,* Coral Records. © 1973, MCA Records Inc. Album cover credits: sleeve printed by Robert Stace.

♦ L: No. I have jogged in my lifetime and got high on endorphins and freaked out and never did it again! But now I *am* an athlete—of a different kind. I train; I do a long warm-up for every performance and a cool-down afterwards. And I've been macrobiotic for ten years; it's too late to turn back now. I did go to dance classes, but I started much too late to become a great ballet dancer (or any kind of dancer, for that matter).

When I was a kid, one film that affected me a lot was *I Want What I Want,* starring ANNE HEYWOOD as a man who enjoys being a transvestite and wants to have a sex-change operation. I grew up in Mississippi, where they showed more films like that than anywhere else, and it possibly changed my life!

♦ *V: If you're not a dancer, you do a good job of faking it—*

♦ L: [laughs] Mainly what I do involves body language with my upper body, and I learned that from just watching people for years; although I move my lower body as well—and I'm in heels the whole time. I throw in moments of impersonation of famous performers like JUDY GARLAND, or famous corny LIZA MINNELLI moves. I became a dancer because I *had* to. You can't do a lip-synching performance for an hour and just stand there; you gotta give the audience something interesting to look at. I never stop moving the whole time I'm onstage.

When I was growing up I just thought of myself as this skinny, gawky kid. But when I moved to New York I realized, "Well, I *am* skinny and gawky . . . but wasn't *Veruschka?* And she made it work for her. If I ever do anything in drag, I'll do it as if I'm this tall, thin, glamorous fashion model." And that's when the idea for this character, Lypsinka, started developing.

I studied photographs of fashion models like DOVIMA—she was in two or three scenes in *Funny Face* (1957) with Audrey Hepburn and Fred Astaire. She's unmistakable: a very tall, skinny, glamorous model with a white face and black hair; I'm sure you've seen Richard Avedon's famous photo of her with the elephants. So there's DOVIMA with those eyebrows and white face and incredible long body—the longest line ever. I thought, "My body's like that, too—maybe I can use that." She became the touchstone for the "look" of LYPSINKA.

Some of LYPSINKA's "energy" is taken from another actress in *Funny Face,* KAY THOMPSON. She's an

Rudy Ray Moore presents *The Lady Reed Album: Queen Bee Talks*, Kent Records. Album cover credits: cover coordination: T. Toney.

incredible musician; she was Judy Garland's vocal coach at MGM and wrote lots of special material for her. She also wrote choral arrangements for many MGM films including *The Harvey Girls*. In *Ziegfield Follies* Judy Garland performs completely in Kay Thompson's style: high parody, very chic and soignée. She's Liza Minnelli's godmother; Liza worships her. And even though she's really the ultimate musician-performer, she's almost forgotten now.

Kay Thompson was never a movie star. She was in a Broadway show but was fired and never quite got over it. In the '40s she created her own nightclub act with the WILLIAMS BROTHERS (Andy Williams and his three brothers; the others didn't go on to fame and fortune the way Andy did). For her act, Kay Thompson created the character of *Eloise,* a little girl who lives at the Plaza Hotel and terrorizes everyone. People suggested that she write a book about Eloise, so she did, and an artist, Hilary Knight, illustrated it. A famous pastel drawing of Eloise still hangs in the lobby of the Plaza Hotel.

The actor John Houseman described Kay Thompson's act as "so mechanical, yet fascinating"—she's like that in *Funny Face* as well. There's nothing spontaneous, and yet somehow it fascinates you. So I take my "energy style" from *Funny Face* . . . from Kay Thompson and DOLORES GRAY.

♦ *V: Who's Dolores Gray?*

♦ L: DOLORES GRAY only made four films for MGM, although she did lots of Broadway shows and now has a cult following. In fact she and Kay Thompson live a block apart—I've threatened to move across the street so I can watch them with a telescope. [laughs] Dolores was in *Kismet* (1955), *Designing Woman* (1957), *The Opposite Sex* (1956), and *It's Always Fair Weather*

(1955, with Cyd Charisse and Gene Kelly). I like her energy and her presentational style. I think she had the best Broadway voice I ever heard; even better than Ethel Merman's—with the same strength and enunciation, but more beautiful. With her blond hair and large features, she was just the apotheosis of '50s glamour.

DOLORES GRAY was a singer, but she could also dance and strike poses like you've never seen. She possessed an incredible vocal instrument and understanding of high comedy. But for a number of reasons she missed out becoming a star. For example, when Judy Garland got sick, Dolores was asked to do *Annie Get Your Gun* (1950). But she was performing in the stage version in London, and couldn't get out of her contract. Then MGM was going to cast her in *The French Quarter,* a big musical co-starring Fred Astaire, but that fell through. She ended up getting the second female lead in *It's Always Fair Weather*—she's not even in the movie until the second half. She said the character was sexless and ageless and a caricature, and I said, "Look, Dolores—that's the impact. That's what I like so much: that it *is* a caricature." And she said, "Yes, but imagine a 26-year-old with a film contract at MGM having to do *that* as her first film!" She really had wanted to be a romantic lead.

♦ *V: When you were first hired by the American Ballet, weren't you excited?*

♦ L: For the first few years it was exciting watching people rehearse—GELSEY KIRKLAND was there and she was my idol. I'd seen pictures of her and seen her dance the *Nutcracker* on television, then I'd seen her dance at Lincoln Center. She was just fascinating: the incredible body, the energy, the attitude, and the beautiful face. I was *mad* for her, and used to follow her around New York like a groupie. Now she's like a friend of mine—it blows me away that I have a relationship with her. It's not a *big* relationship, but she says, "How are things going?" and "Congratulations!" and all that.

I saw the book she wrote about her downfall, *Dancing On My Grave.* At one point she tells the story of this really bad fight that she and Misha Baryshnikov had (and they had a *lot*). She mentions that a pianist was present—that was me; and she says, "The pianist said nothing"—well, Baryshnikov was my boss—I wasn't about to say anything to *him.* [laughs] Her point was: at the American Ballet Theater no one ever said anything, for fear of rocking the boat . . . which is just like growing up in the South where no one says anything. Now I've discovered that no one ever says anything *anywhere!* [laughs] Did you see *Prince of Tides?* For all its hyperbole and overblown Hollywood-ness, it does say truths about families who don't talk and end up being dysfunctional.

♦ *V: You started the "Lypsinka" character back in 1982—*

♦ L: It takes awhile for a man who dresses as a woman

to gain any recognition outside a certain community, because it's still perceived as "kinky" or "perverse." I think I'm making some headway against that, although there still are misogynistic drag performers who make fun of women, and who project really absurd caricatures with big breasts. I find that distasteful. I don't hate women—why would I even *bother* doing all this research if I didn't like women?

What really motivated me to get my career going was the AIDS crisis. I was spending a lot of energy looking for a sex life; then I read about AIDS in the *New York Times Magazine* and thought: "You don't want to die. You want a career, but you haven't really put yourself *out there* to get one. Why don't you put your energy into having a career instead?" It wasn't easy, because when I went on the road with the American Ballet, I would have to drop out of the scene; when I came back it would be like starting all over again. But in 1985 I really started pushing myself. I wrote a show called *Ballet of the Dolls,* which is a parody of *Valley of the Dolls* plus the ballet world. It was a parody not only of the movie but also the book *and* Jacqueline Susann's lifestyle *and* all the people the book was allegedly based on. I wrote all the music and lyrics and produced, directed and financed it myself, plus I played Jacqueline Susann. And I pulled it together in a month; we did 6 performances at the Pyramid Club and it was sold out every night. That's when I realized: *you can do something.*

What really motivated me to get my career going was the AIDS crisis. I was spending a lot of energy looking for a sex life and I thought: "You don't want to die. You want a career, but you haven't really put yourself *out there* to get one. Why don't you put your energy into having a career instead?"

I continued doing my character LYPSINKA at the Pyramid. Nine months later the management said, "*Ballet of the Dolls* was such a big hit—why don't you do another show? You can do it every Monday night for several weeks." So I wrote *Dial "M" for Model*—inspired by the *Millie the Model* comic books. I filled the script with references to '60s pop culture and the modeling world: David Bailey, Suzy Parker, Penelope Tree and Holly Golightly (rhymes with Truman Capote). My big number was called "He's Got Designs On Me." The sixth character in the play was "Dalian, the fashion designer"—that was taken from *Back Street*

(1961), which featured an obviously gay fashion designer named Dalian (played by Reginald Gardiner) and his lovely assistant, Rae (played by Susan Hayward). I produced, financed, wrote and starred in it, but I didn't direct it—at least I didn't have *that* responsibility. And that became a cult hit in New York; it moved to La Mama.

Then at La Mama I did *Ballet of the Dolls*—rewritten with myself as Jacqueline Susann *narrating* it. Finally, in May of '88 I co-produced the first LYPSINKA theatrical production—previously it had only been done in nightclubs. CHARLES BUSCH, who wrote *Vampire Lesbians of Sodom* (which played for 5 years off-Broadway) and *Psycho Beach Party* came to see it. Two nights later his roommate, the producer Kenneth Elliott, came and said, "We want to do this as a late-night show after *Vampire Lesbians.*" We changed the title from *The Many Moods of Lypsinka* to *I Could Go On Lip-Synching*—the title is a parody of Judy Garland's last film, *I Could Go On Singing.*

In terms of recognition, my career development happened gradually. By the time *I Could Go On Lip-Synching* opened in a full-fledged off-Broadway theater, I was already a "minor cult star." I had gotten experience and my confidence had been built up, but it still remained somewhat difficult. If stardom had come any earlier, I probably wouldn't have been able to deal with it; it would have gone to my head and I would have been insufferable.

Everyone's always surprised to find out that I'm this calm, "zen" person. LYPSINKA was intended to be as animated as a cartoon, so that's what I have to do onstage. I *can't* be wild offstage and have the control I need while performing—although now that my career is on automatic pilot, I *am* ready to sow some wild oats! [laughs] For years I did nothing but persevere and concentrate on *work, work, work*—now I'm ready to "have a life"! But that wild lifestyle that seems so intriguing and glamorous—the Warhol-Candy Darling-Jackie Curtis scene, staying out all night, taking drugs and being *mad as a hatter, darling!*—it might look tempting, but I think even Holly Woodlawn would tell you now, "It wasn't as great as it seemed," and "It's better to be alive than to be Jackie Curtis and dead." I imagine that Holly herself came pretty close to being dead in the gutter somewhere. When people read about me, they probably think that I go night-clubbing every night and carry on till all hours and lead a really wild lifestyle—just because I'm a man who dresses as a woman onstage—but it's not the case.

♦ **V: Your show contains so many obscure and outlandish references; you must be a dedicated student of film and music—**

♦ L: [laughs] That's true. My friend Mason Wiley called me "a self-taught film scholar." (By the way, Mason wrote *Inside Oscar,* which is full of anecdotes about every Academy Awards presentation.) My parents liked movies, too, so that helped. But what started

my whole film obsession was seeing *Bye Bye Birdie* with ANN-MARGRET. I was floored by her energy, her sexiness, her healthiness (sexy and wholesome at the same time) and the visual style of the film: that image of ANN-MARGRET in front of a solid blue background, with the wind blowing her hair. And then the big dance number, "A Lot of Livin' To Do," where she, Jessie Pearson, Bobby Rydell and all those chorus dancers do that "chicken" movement! [demonstrates] I also liked that telephone gossip scene where the screen gets divided into four conversations—especially when they all melt at the end.

Liza Minnelli said that when she saw the play version of *Bye Bye Birdie,* she thought, "*Now* I want to be in show business!" She was already the daughter of the "greats," but *that* was what did it for her. And the movie caused Neal Peters to devote his whole life to Ann-Margret; he wrote a book about her and got "Ann-Margret" tattooed on his arm. Now he's one of her best friends.

I'm fascinated by how, when I was a kid, I could sit in a movie theater and have my life changed by a film, while the kid sitting next to me remained unfazed. The next day I'd be at school showing everyone this dance step at recess—and most of them could have cared less. What is the *cause* of this difference? Is it because I'm gay? Is it because of a difference in people's imagination—some have it and some don't?

What started my whole film obsession was seeing *Bye Bye Birdie* with ANN-MARGRET. I was floored by her energy, her sexiness, her healthiness . . . that image of her in front of a solid blue background, with the wind blowing her hair.

♦ **V: I don't see how anyone could *not* be moved by that film—**

♦ L: And yet they weren't. Anyway, that film was the first visceral experience I'd ever had, and I'm *still* looking for visceral experiences . . . and the older I get, the less frequently they come along!

♦ **V: *What other films come to mind?***

♦ L: Brian De Palma's THE FURY is another favorite film; it stars Kirk Douglas, Amy Irving, and Carrie Snodgress. Again, it's back to the question of *style,* because the script itself is ridiculous (it's *Carrie* taken to the extreme). The film is an exercise in *violence as style:* you see people blowing up, amusement park rides going wild and people flying off them, and Carrie Snodgress being hit by a car in slow motion and crashing through the windshield! Brian De Palma may have

Ann-Margret's *Bachelors' Paradise,* © 1963, RCA Victor.

lost it now, but in the '70s he sure had it. His *Sisters* was a great film, too—an insane, over-the-top black comedy with great BERNARD HERRMANN music pounding out at you. The idea of Margot Kidder with a French-Canadian accent being one of a pair of Siamese twins who get cut apart at the hip—! He uses all these cheap camera tricks, yet it all comes together. I *love* that film. It's so violent I've seen people run out of the theater puking.

BERNARD HERRMANN is fascinating in himself; he did the musical scores for so many film classics, from *Citizen Kane* to *Psycho.* He was a nonconformist with an explosive temper who would not suffer fools gladly—someone described working with him as "sitting on top of a volcano." Some of his music is influenced by Prokofiev and Sibelius, and sometimes there's a Wagnerian influence as well. I'm pretty sure he borrowed from a Debussy piece called *Sirènes.* Yet he manages to take these influences and create something all his own—no doubt Prokofiev was ripping off somebody else, anyway.

Movies were much more of an influence on me than theater, because there *was* no theater where I grew up. I thought of moving to Los Angeles when I left Mississippi, but I didn't want to drive a car! So I moved to New York and got started in theater—it's easier. To make a film you *have* to have a camera, but to do theater you don't need anything; you can even do it in the street.

♦ **V: *What are some more favorite films?***

♦ L: I love *all* the great Douglas Sirk films, but if I named them that wouldn't leave as much room for others on my "Top 25." I like *All That Heaven Allows* (1955), another Douglas Sirk film with Rock Hudson, Jane Wyman and Agnes Moorhead. *Gigi* (1958) is one of my favorites and one of Minnelli's best—it's just so charming and so perfect. *The Wizard of Oz* (1939) is a favorite, of course, and *Cabaret* (1972)—I love that movie. *Female Trouble* (1974) is the *Gone with the Wind* of cult films. That has the classic "Who wants to die for art?" scene in it, but my favorite moment is when Divine says [hysterically], "I still *am* the Number One model—look at my legs, just *look* at 'em!"

◆ **V: Tell us about the strangest music you know—**

◆ L: I like *Ethel Merman Live in Las Vegas;* right away it poses the classic dilemma facing any would-be performer: "Who am I? What am I doing here?" That segues into "I Got Rhythm." She sings that long note ("Who could ask for anything *mooooore?"*) and for fun I took it, sampled it on the computer and repeated it until it became ridiculously long. On the computer you can equalize, you can make it sound better or worse (obviously, I try to make it sound better). You're working with the sound wave itself and you can telescope in to the tiniest moment *in* the recording and do whatever you want. If there's a record "pop" it'll show as a jagged peak, and you can just "erase" it.

SYLVIA DE SAYLES—who knows who *she* is? I found her record in Boston, and after hearing "Wild Is Love/Like a Fire Burning Beyond Control" where her voice ascends to impossibly high notes, I knew "I've got to have this!" I like KAY STEVENS' opening number from her album *Kay Stevens in Person, Live at the Copa.* At the peak of the song she sings "I've got a smile on my face/for the whole human race/'cause I love everybody I see!" Of course she isn't smiling—who could possibly love the cop who gives you a ticket, or the IRS? At the end she's screaming, "Everybody loves me! Everybody loves me!" and as Bruce Vilanch (who writes special material for Bette Midler and others) says, "She does four opening numbers at the top of her act!" In other words, she doesn't know when to stop.

Roberta Sherwood's *Clap Your Hands,* Decca Records.

Co-Star: The Record Acting Game with Tallulah Bankhead, Co-Star Records, Inc.
A subsidiary of Roulette Records, Inc.

Everybody knows who CONNIE FRANCIS is, but CATERINA VALENTE is almost forgotten. She was on *The Entertainers,* a TV show which also featured CAROL BURNETT. Caterina did an album, *Songs I Sang on the Perry Como Show,* and I like "To Be a Performer," which is from *Little Me.* The song tells it like it is: "To be a performer you must be a two-face; get ready to suffer." I also like the LP of DOLORES GRAY's nightclub act, *Let Me Entertain You,* which was recorded in London at the Talk of the Town club. (I found that record for $10 but usually it goes for $100.) Here let me say that Dolores has a picture of CATERINA VALENTE on the table next to her couch; she's one of her best friends!

FAY McKAY is a favorite. She was a protege of Liberace, and mostly she performed in small clubs in Las Vegas. On her album she sings "Mame," "Step to the Rear," "Hey Jude," and "Almost Like Being in Love," and she also does a parody impersonation of ROBERTA SHERWOOD singing "Up the Lazy River."

◆ **V: Who's Roberta Sherwood?**

◆ L: I remember seeing her on "The Lucy Show," where Lucy's in the kitchen and Roberta Sherwood is in the living room rehearsing "Up the Lazy River" over and over again. Lucy starts chopping to the rhythm of the song, and vegetables start flying everywhere—it's so funny. Later someone comes into the kitchen and Lucy says, "If I go 'Up that Lazy River' one more time, I'll—!" Anyway, back to FAY McKAY—her song, "The Twelve Days of Christmas," in which the singer becomes progressively more inebriated, is a classic. Her version is an absolutely relentless, nonstop degeneration into slurred speech and nonsense syllables—there's no doubt that by the end of the song, the singer is thoroughly soused and on the verge of passing out!

Alfred Hitchcock's *Music To Be Murdered By*, Imperial Records.
Album cover credits: cover photo courtesy of TV GUIDE.

We haven't talked much about LUCILLE BALL, but she was a big influence on me—as a kid I was just mad for her; I even made "Lucy" toys. CAROL BURNETT was also a big influence—just her personality and madcap humor and voice. So for Carol Burnett to sit in the audience and watch me perform, and for me to hear her laughing the whole time—well, that was the ultimate! The only thing left is for FAYE DUNAWAY to have dinner with me . . .

♦ *V: What are some more favorite lines or scenes by actresses?*

♦ L: ANN BLYTH played the role of the ungrateful daughter in *Mildred Pierce.* I remember my parents discussing the scene where Joan Crawford slaps her; they wondered, "Did she really slap her, or was that a stage slap?" Ann Blyth played mostly cutesy-poo parts, as opposed to TIPPI HEDREN who is so great in *Marnie*: "I know that women are stupid and feeble and men are filthy pigs!" LOUISE LATHAM who played Marnie's mother also had a good line: "You get out of my house! I don't need any filthy men comin' in my house no more, do you hear me?" And JUDY GARLAND says in *I Could Go On Singing*: "I've hung on to every bit of rubbish there is to hang on to, and I've thrown all the good bits away!" . . . SUSAN KOHNER's big claim to fame was: she played the "high yaller" daughter who was trying to pass for white in *Imitation of Life*. I loved it when she screamed hysterically, "I'm white, white, *white!*"

Another favorite record is JOAN COLLINS's *Beauty and Exercise* record; my last show, *Lypsinka! A Day in the Life* was inspired by that. I like her tone of voice, which is so supercilious. Yet what she says—in that mid-Atlantic accent of hers—is so ordinary and everyday that any fool could figure it out! But I guess a lot of people have to be *told* . . . She talks about everything

from how to eat breakfast to what kind of perfume you should wear. There's a long section about *vitamins* (as she calls them) and whether or not soap and water is really good for your face—she calls it [British accent] the soap and water con*trah*versy. At the end she says, "*Sleep* is nature's oldest and most trusted beauty treatment."

♦ *V: Are there any female impersonators you like?*

♦ L: I like *An Evening with Arthur Blake*—he was a great female impersonator who did Bette Davis (I think he's dead now). He was one of the first in a line of performers to imitate famous people—that's the tradition that CHARLES PIERCE and JIMMY JAMES are still carrying on. Arthur Blake frequently performed with JAYNE MANSFIELD; in her nightclub act he would portray Bette Davis and Louella Parsons and Charles Laughton and Noel Coward, and Jayne would interact with him. He was on the recording of her live Las Vegas act.

T.C. JONES was another fantastic, very talented female impersonator. He sings on an unreleased recording of *New Faces of 1956*. He was in the Monkees' movie *Head,* where he plays a Bette Davis-type waitress, and was also in *Three Nuts in Search of a Bolt* with Mamie Van Doren. He plays "Babette the Bald Hairdresser" in *Promises, Promises,* with Marie "The Body" MacDonald and Jayne Mansfield—that's my favorite. Jayne thinks she's pregnant, and T.C. Jones throws a baby shower for her. His maternity gift is a bag of wigs, and at the shower (all women, except for him) he puts on these wigs and does impersonations of movie stars to entertain them. Then he puts on a blonde wig and says, "Now I'm going to do Jayne Mansfield" (she's sitting right there). Then Jayne says, "Oh, I can do her *too!*" and she does herself.

♦ *V: Tell me about* **Valley of the Dolls**—

♦ L: Does *Valley of the Dolls* need any kind of introduction? It's really the great gay cult film, although I suppose it's been superseded by *The Rocky Horror Picture Show* to the world at large. I've seen it so many times and it's such a constant reference point that . . . I really am a *Valley of the Dolls* scholar. I've read scripts that were not used; I've studied stills; and to me it's beyond description—fascinating in its awfulness. Patty Duke plays Neely O'Hara, a young singer who becomes a malicious, vicious, wicked-tongued drug addict. The film is really just a mean version of *How to Marry a Millionaire.* 20th-Century Fox did lots of films about three girls, especially when Cinemascope came along, and *Valley of the Dolls* was just a sexed-up, drugged-up version of that kind of thing: about three girls trying to make it in show business, and they each end up on pills for one reason or another. Some other films in this "genre" include *Three Coins in the Fountain, The Best of Everything,* and *The Pleasure Seekers* (basically, a remake of *Three Coins in the Fountain*).

BARBARA PARKINS became famous when she was in the TV version of *Peyton Place,* and *Valley of the*

Dolls was really her greatest moment in feature films. I like her lines about that rush of loneliness that overcomes you just before the "pills" you've taken come on. The music in the background is eerie and disturbing. She was in *The Mephisto Waltz* (1971; a Satanic cult story) and a film with Faye Dunaway and Frank Langella, *La Maison sous les Arbres/The Deadly Trap* (1971).

Speaking of pills, DODY GOODMAN sings that great comedy number "Tranquilizers" on her album *Dody Goodman Sings?* She played Mary Hartman's mother on *Mary Hartman, Mary Hartman.* Some people think that song perfectly summed up the frustrated housewife of the '50s—that decade when tranquilizers were gulped down as freely as aspirin, and were just as freely available.

I like SPIVY—that great portly lesbian cabaret-owner and singer-pianist; she's profiled in James Gavin's *Intimate Nights:* "My first song is *very* sad; you must be *very* quiet." KAYE BALLARD can remember actually hanging out at her club, Spivy's Roof. And Spivy herself has a small role in *Requiem for a Heavyweight* (1962) with Anthony Quinn, under the name "Madame Spivy." She's also in an *Alfred Hitchcock Presents* episode that I saw.

◆ V: Who's Kaye Ballard?

◆ L: She was a Broadway and cabaret star, and was in *The Girl Most Likely* with Jane Powell and Cliff Robertson. She played a madam in *A House Is Not A Home,* and also does TV commercials for some Italian tomato sauce. She's a really talented person who never had her day in the sun—kind of like Dolores Gray: if she'd been ten years earlier, she would have had a bigger career. I heard she sang the theme song from "Shaft" on the *Tonight* show, which must have been hilarious

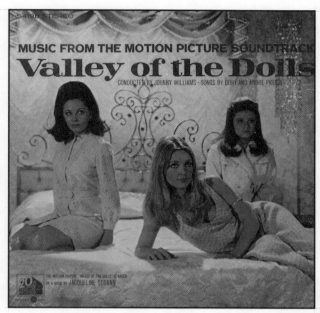

Valley of the Dolls, © 1967 20th Century-Fox Record Corporation.

because of those *lyrics.* She's a very funny lady.

◆ V: Is cabaret reviving?

◆ L: I don't know; it's always been there in New York. Maybe it's just nostalgia on our part, but when SPIVY was in her heyday, cabaret seemed more interesting because it was "underground" and forbidden. Today naughty subject matter is no big deal, unless it's like Madonna, a huge mega-pop star, coming out with a book of nude pictures of herself. If somebody sings a risqué song in a cabaret in New York—how decadent is *that,* nowadays? But back in the fifties it was like: "Ooh, we're really *seeing* something now!"

◆ V: But there's definitely been a trend toward more censorship, although it's usually sparked by just a handful of letter-writing Bible Belt nuts trying to control the whole country—

◆ L: Well, if America's going conservative, I say: "Just keep going in that direction!" because it makes naughty subject matter more enticing. And it makes performers like me more interesting. People want to see drag now—all of a sudden they *just* want to see it. And I feel like I'm riding the crest of this wave. I've seen it coming for a long time, and the movie *Paris Is Burning* just put it over the edge. My newest show, *Lypsinka: A Day in the Life,* has a lot of sexual references in it; it's already caused a small stir. So if America's going conservative, it's just going to make people like myself and KAREN FINLEY famous. This trend toward censorship isn't stopping anyone—it's just making people even more "out there."

◆ V: What other music do you like?

◆ L: I like *I Had A Ball* which was a famous Broadway flop starring Buddy Hackett and KAREN MORROW, a Broadway singer with a big belting voice who was never able to find her niche in a hit show. She sings "I Have Everything I Want"—but of course she doesn't.

Terri "Cup Cake" O'Mason, *Adam Stag Party Special #2,* © 1960, Fax Record Company.

Jayne Mansfield: *Shakespeare, Tchaikovsky & Me*, MGM Records.
Album cover credits: cover photo: Bob Vose.

The show was set on Coney Island with Buddy Hackett pretending to be a fortune teller, so he has a crystal ball—hence the play on words. And Richard Kiley who was most famous for playing in the original *Man of La Mancha* was also in this. It's amusing, but it bombed.

RUTH DRAPER was a famous monologist who has a number of great lines. I don't know much about her, but Lily Tomlin was really influenced by her. "The Italian Lesson" is especially hilarious—a very long monologue about a high-society woman whose Italian lesson keeps getting interrupted—it's just *her* but she still manages to evoke all these other people in the room. Another favorite is TERRY "Cupcake" O'MASON—a Belle Barth-Pearl Williams-Rusty Warren comedienne who sang naughty songs. She was sort of like SPIVY, but a little sexier; I found her LP (on the Adam Party Records label) in Vancouver. Besides this recording, she boasts another claim to fame: she was once the girlfriend of CHARLES BUKOWSKI! [laughs]

JORIE REMUS was a cabaret singer I like. She was born in New York and her career began in a tiny cafe called the Candlelight Room. Then she went on to play at the Hungry I and the Purple Onion in San Francisco. She's profiled in *Intimate Nights*. FAYE DE WITT was in a famous Broadway musical flop called *Flahooley*, with BARBARA COOK and YMA SUMAC—I think it was written by Sammy Fain and Paul Francis Webster. It was Yma Sumac's great Broadway moment. (The book by Ken Mandelbaum, *Not Since Carrie*, describes all the flop shows between 1940 and 1985—it's very entertaining.) Faye De Witt was also in a show called *Nightclub Confidential,* and in a series called "The Shoestring Revues"; Dody Goodman appeared in one, and Beatrice Arthur got her start there.

FAYE DE WITT's record, *Through Sick or Sin*, consists of these weird comedy routines. She gave me this recording with her blessing and said, "Use it!" The song is called "The Insecure Tango" and I use the line, "I wear contact lenses/My fingernails are false/I have a spastic colon . . ."

DOROTHY SQUIRES was a fifth-rate Judy Garland or Shirley Bassey-type. She became a big star in London but she's not well-known outside England. She recorded "I Gotta Be Me," which I love—it's hard to find recordings of women singing it. It's kinda like "This Is My Life" (which, by the way, I've performed holding a box of *Life* cereal). I think Dorothy Squires was either married to or lovers with Roger Moore in the '50s, and took him along on a trip to Hollywood. Hollywood took one look at *him* and signed him up, and he left her to pursue a career of his own.

KATHARINE HEPBURN was in a Broadway cast recording of *Coco,* about the life of Coco Chanel. This recording is blatantly "bad" and unmistakably Katharine Hepburn—you can almost hear her head shake as she's talking. She can't really sing, so a lot of it is her rapping in rhythm—really *weird*. Oh—I love *The Sensuous Black Woman* by LADY REED. She was an associate of RUDY RAY MOORE, who made that series of *Dolomite* films which are amazing, like Z-grade *Shaft* films. They made these recordings of *The Sensuous Black Man* and *The Sensuous Black Woman*, and they're just *filthy*. I love that part where she's screaming, "Fuck me! Fuck me! Fuck me!" Her recordings are unbelievable; she says things like, "Certain bitches are checkin' out them mighty black poles/they're lickin' 'em down like a five-cent popsicle in a heat wave! You better get on your job, girl: Be a *bitch* in the living room, a *lady* in the kitchen, and a stomp-down natural-born hog-fuckin' *'ho'* in the bed!"

JANE MORGAN was a popular singer in the '50s—I like *Live at the Coconut Grove*, where she talks about having sung a song at the Academy Awards. She's one of the Bushes' best friends . . . One of the most incredible recordings ever committed to vinyl is LIBBY MORRIS singing "Tea for Two" from the LP, *Ad-Libby*. When she introduces this song, she says, "We're now going to do the frantic version." She manages to go through so many styles, including a cha-cha and a Sarah Vaughan impersonation; she works in *The Three Musketeers*, sings in French at one point, and does it as a rock'n'roll song and as a cutesy-poo ballad—it's an amazing tour-de-force.

♦ *V: Right—that is so imaginative and witty, with all those personality changes. Never has the American ideal of the "perfect family" been lampooned so deftly. Her interpretation brings out all the schizophrenia and hypocrisy latent in the "family values" cliché now being mouthed by every slimy politician across the country.*

♦ L: Finally, it's impossible to resist paying homage to Bette Davis. I like a line in *The Star* where Bette Davis plays this *has-been* Oscar-winning star who is trying to make a comeback. At the beginning of the movie she has a horrible fight with her sister, and kicks her sister and her husband out of the house. Then she picks up her Oscar and says, "Come on Oscar—let's you and me get *drunk."*

♦ **V: You must have a large collection of videos and records—**

♦ **L:** Well, my collection of videotapes is pretty big, but as for my collection of records—I've seen people with bigger ones. People all over tell me about things and give me things—they know I'm looking for unusual material. When I met CURTIS HARRINGTON, who directed *Games, Queen of Blood,* and *What's the Matter with Helen?,* he mentioned Yvette Vickers (who has a small role in *What's the Matter with Helen?*). I said, "Oh, you mean Yvette Vickers who was also in *Hud* and in *Attack of the 50-Foot Woman?"* He said, "Wow—you really *are* a film scholar!" [laughs]

In *What's the Matter with Helen?,* Debbie Reynolds plays a tap dance teacher in '30s Hollywood for would-be Shirley Temple types. Shelley Winters is her best friend who plays the piano at her school, and they have a couple kids who kill someone and—it's like *Whatever Happened to Baby Jane?* Harrington's *Games* is a '60s pop version of *Diabolique*—it even stars Simone Signoret, who was in the original French version by Clouzot. James Caan, Katharine Ross and Estelle Winwood are in it, too.

Have you seen *The Big Cube?* It's the 1969 "acid" version of *Imitation of Life.* Lana Turner plays an actress-mother, Karen Mossberg plays her daughter and George Chakiris plays the daughter's gigolo-boyfriend who feeds Lana Turner some LSD. I saw that for the first time at the Library of Congress in Washington, D.C., where you can view almost every film ever made (if you have a valid reason). They take you to a little booth; you put gloves on and handle the film stock yourself. That's where I saw *Spree,* that JAYNE MANSFIELD Las Vegas documentary. I also saw *Girls' Town* (1959), where MAMIE VAN DOREN plays a bad girl wrongfully accused of a crime and railroaded into prison, where she finds the real culprit. They had *Untamed Youth* (1957) which again features Mamie Van Doren, plus Eddie Cochran, stuck on a prison work farm. Both of them get to sing, of course. I also saw *Succubus,* a Radley Metzger-type x-rated late-'60s softcore porn film about a female vampire.

I also got to see once again *The Battle of the Villa Fiorita* (1965) with Rosanno Brazzi and Maureen O'Hara, which had a big impact on me when I was a kid. DELMER DAVES, the poor man's Douglas Sirk, directed that. He directed *Rome Adventure* (1962), *A Summer Place* (1959), *The Hanging Tree* (1959), *Spencer's Mountain* (1963), *Parrish* (1961, with Claudette Colbert, Troy Donahue, Connie Stevens and even Sylvia Miles) and *Susan Slade* (1961) with Troy Donahue and Connie Stevens—she has a little baby boy and it

catches on fire! He also made *Youngblood Hawke* (1964) with Suzanne Pleshette and Eva Gabor, about a naive Southern boy who writes a novel and then becomes the toast of New York literary society. *A Summer Place* is probably his most famous movie. I *love* Delmer Daves; if there's ever a Delmer Daves cult revival I don't know what I'll do!

♦ **V: Now, you can be pretty happy doing exactly what you want to do—**

♦ **L:** Al Pacino said somewhere, "There's no such thing as happiness—there's only concentration." And I don't believe in happiness either; I believe there are fleeting *moments* of happiness that mostly come from contentment and satisfaction, just as there are fleeting moments of having fun. In that Vincente Minnelli biography I read that "the only really important thing is work." That's what it all boils down to. And I think I'm lucky to be able to work at something I really enjoy. When I see people doing boring jobs, I wonder to myself: "How do they *do* it? Could *I* do that?" Maybe some people just don't *realize . . .* "Ignorance is bliss" and "No brain, no pain"—right?

There are moments when I wish I didn't have the knowledge that I have, or the ambition. Because then I would be perfectly happy to sit in Mississippi and not know any better. Sometimes I find myself in painful situations that arise out of the nature of the business. People get jealous of me; I find *myself* jealous of people sometimes. But the important thing is to *recognize* jealousy if you feel it; otherwise it just festers. In the end, the moments of joy make up for the crap you have to take. And my personal motto is: *I'm very serious about not being serious.*

Mamie Van Doren's *The Girl Who Invented Rock 'N' Roll,*
© 1986 Rhino Records Inc. Album cover credits: package design & development: James Austin/Real Gone Graphics, photos: courtesy of Sabin Gray Collection.

AMOK BOOKS

AMOK BOOKS (Bookstore & Publishing) was founded by Stuart Swezey and Brian King in Los Angeles. Besides their avant-garde publishing (Bataille's *Trial of Gilles de Rais,* etc), they have hosted radio programs, clubs and concerts promoting music consistently acknowledged as "cutting edge." The *Amok Catalog,* a classic reference guide to essential books, has redefined "culture" in all fields ($17 ppd from 1764 North Vermont Ave, Los Angeles, CA 90027). Recently Brian and Stuart compiled *The Best of Martin Denny* (CD available from Rhino Records). For Amok mail orders write PO Box 777, Oakland CA 94504, and when in Los Angeles, visit the Amok store (far more than a "bookstore"), managed by longtime associate Mike Glass, at 1764 North Vermont Ave (213-665-0956).

♦ *VALE: How did you start acquiring unusual records?*

♦ BRIAN KING: Well, for me it wasn't so much buying records as rediscovering my parents' albums. They already had the THREE SUNS, PEREZ PRADO, and STAN GETZ, as well as records like Doris Day, Herb Alpert and *South Pacific.* My mother was always loaning her records to friends, so she put those name-and-address labels on them. I still have all of 'em.

♦ STUART SWEZEY: I always knew there was this other kind of strange music, because you'd hear it in movies or TV—like the organ in *Phantom of the Opera.* Gradually I started buying anything that might have that strange feeling to it.

♦ *V: When were you born?*

♦ BK: 1962. I grew up in Westchester, which is next to the Los Angeles Airport. It was one of the first suburbs. I remember people decorating their backyards with big tikis, or having a rumpus room with bamboo-lined walls and a shrine—this had to do with Hawaii becoming a state. The records I first heard were played at parties or barbecues, so they have a certain demented nostalgia for me. My dad would string up a volley-

ball net in the backyard and light up tiki torches. When I was about five, I got really drunk on a grasshopper (a disgustingly sweet mint-julep drink) and my parents found me passed out under a tree.

Our next-door neighbor had an incredible tiki backyard, where I used to play. Their son was in the Turtles before he got into the Tony and Susan Alamo church and had to be deprogrammed by Ted Patrick—that's a typical suburb story.

♦ *V: Who was Tony Alamo?*

♦ BK: A very anti-Catholic crusader who put out tracts saying, "The pope is evil!" In the '60s the Alamos were picking up people on Sunset Boulevard who were strung out and taking 'em in and reprogramming them. Tony got into trouble because when the parents left his group, he would try to keep the kids—he got accused of spanking them, etc. Members of "The Tony and Susan Alamo Foundation" (it says that on their vans) still drop off flyers at our store.

Susan Alamo died about 10 years ago, but Tony claims she still lives! Tony put out a really hellish country & western album (which Porter Wagoner produced) on which he sang duets with his "dead" wife. Naturally, all the songs were about reincarnation and love.

◆ *V: So how did your musical appetites evolve?*

◆ BK: My taste for unusual music was a slow evolution—I didn't go bonkers for the THREE SUNS immediately. Basically, I went from something like a SEEDS record to a VENTURES record, then getting *Ventures in Space* (which is very surreal) and going from that to the THREE SUNS. I had heard MARTIN DENNY on the radio, but never really paid attention to his name. Then at college my roommate was Mike Glass. One day he played MARTIN DENNY for me and I went, "This is *it!*" Then I went home and found the albums stowed away in my mom's attic . . .

◆ SS: I remember when Brian first brought over all these records from his parents' collection. It was like discovering a treasure trove. We've never been the same since—his parents' record collection definitely influenced *me.*

◆ *ANDREA JUNO: Did the tiki subculture of your childhood backyards only exist on the West Coast?*

◆ BK: It happened in Florida and Arizona, too. Even in New York there's Trader Vic's and the Hawaii-Kai restaurant. Servicemen stationed in the South Pacific brought back parts of that culture with them, including Filipino or Japanese wives—

◆ SS: Some of the older tiki restaurants have entrances that resemble the corrugated steel quonset huts which were built near the landing strips on Pacific islands, where military men would have their big beer busts. The guy who started KELBO'S on West Pico Blvd came back from WWII and started hosting barbecue parties for his friends. They loved his ribs so much that by '48 he'd opened Kelbo's to re-create an environment reminiscent of the days before they "settled

Brian King (left) and Stuart Swezey.   Photo: Nancy Barton

down." In their sedate postwar lives they could look back and recall all the fun they'd had while serving their country . . . when life had *meaning.*

◆ *AJ: Describe Kelbo's—*

◆ SS: My parents used to take me to the one on West Pico Blvd (they tore down the one on Fairfax). It's a big, sprawling place filled with aquariums, massive tikis, black lights, palm fronds, and seashells—

◆ BK: Plus a dance room called the Coco Bowl, where the ceiling is shaped like the inside of a coconut shell. There's also a mirrored ball hanging down and a big band-era stagefront. When I went there recently, it was deserted except for a young Marine dancing with a 55-year-old woman, and an old DJ with a raspy,

horrible voice—I think he had throat cancer. I was requesting songs by the THREE SUNS or PETULA CLARK and he was looking down quizzically at me: "You don't want to hear Michael Jackson?"

♦ SS: They get couples driving in from Las Vegas just to relive old memories. Actually, Kelbo's probably owes something to the original Don the Beachcomber's—a hot spot in the '30s where stars like Clark Gable hung out. The tiki idea became "mass" after the war; I've met people from *Saskatchewan* who've said, "Yes, there once was a little tiki bar in our town." The idea was to create an imaginary paradise, with soothing Hawaiian music and exotic-flavored drinks.

For me, the Hawaiian music influence came from my dad, who was stationed in Pearl Harbor during the Korean War. I remember him learning ukelele and singing Hawaiian songs and playing 78s of old Hawaiian war chants. My mom studied hula; my older brother Richard was born in Hawaii. My parents became totally saturated with Hawaiian culture—they actually saw MARTIN DENNY play there.

Also, in Southern California there was the swingin' singles apartment fad (which I remember reading about in old *Life* magazines). Basically, all these engineers (who moved to Southern California to work at the big aircraft plants) and single secretaries would live in these apartment complexes built around a pool. The decorative motif was tikis, and they would have luaus and hula hoop parties. In the '70s the landlords got rid of the tikis and put up redwood siding to "keep up with the times," but a lot of these apartments still have names like "The Samoa."

♦ BK: Cultural imperialism is the main theme of tiki-type music. It's LES BAXTER saying, "I went to New Guinea and learned this dance rhythm," then bringing it home to arrange it.

♦ SS: With a lot of those exotic records, the operative word is pagan, as in "Pagan Love Song." It was like an acceptable way to be anti-Christian, even though people might not have consciously realized that. These pagan tikis are phallic, they're sexual, they're non-Christian—yet you find them in the middle of Orange County. Now to us pagan might mean people chanting during a full moon, or doing some ritual. But in the '50s there was so much sexual repression that pagan meant Dionysian party-time—pagan meant *sex*. The same went for the mambo craze—anything "Latin" connoted sex, too.

At the swap meets and thrift shops, the covers provided the initial attraction to exotic records, like ARTHUR LYMAN's *Taboo, Vol. 2* (featuring a shrunken head) or *Pele*. Before I even knew who Arthur Lyman was, I saw this blond woman with big breasts coming up out of a volcano—this was the most bizarre record cover I'd seen. The lettering and the colors were wild; talk about psychedelic! Of course, the chief animator for *Fantasia* was a German artist who had been the subject of mescaline research in the '20s. And Walt

Hawaii Instrumentally Yours, Waikiki Records Company.

Disney was friends with Gordon Wasson, who researched naturally-occurring psychedelic drugs and wrote a favorable article on them for *Life*.

But in terms of my early exotic *imprinting*, the Jungle Cruise and the Enchanted Tiki Room at Disneyland have never left me. You go back and the detail is still incredible; so wild. Other influences were MARIA MONTEZ films, *mondo* films, and old *National Geographics* with the hand-tinted photos of strange, exotic people and places.

♦ BK: Tiki bars today are hellish, because even if they still have great tiki decor with lava lamps and blowfish and the whole works, they'll be playing old Shaun Cassidy records that are not conducive to the environment.

♦ *V: Why do you like the THREE SUNS?*

♦ BK: The first time I played them for Stuart he thought I'd lost my mind. In a way they're like cocktail trio music. But they aren't kitsch, they're talented musicians playing an accordion, a Les Paul-style electric guitar and an organ or piano. Each album is different: they can go from soft strings to circusy "Jalousie" organ—

♦ SS: When you play the THREE SUNS for people, everyone thinks of roller rink music. The first LP Brian played for me was one of the lush ones; I went, "That's a great cover, but are you *really* listening to this?" Then we started getting into the more bouncy, eerie, freakish recordings. I've always found something unsettling about organ music, so when we discovered GEORGE WRIGHT and KORLA PANDIT, it was like: "God—there it is, and there's so much of it!"

♦ BK: The THREE SUNS are especially odd because they have this snappy guitar and accordion (really happy music) mixed with this completely *Dark Shadows* soap opera organ. So there's a real mood split there that's hard to resolve—it's "surreal." Also, they were Mamie Eisenhower's favorite group—that's a good reason to listen to them!

♦ **AJ: Why do you like organ music in general?**

♦ BK: It's a very powerful instrument, especially "live"—it's so loud. In terms of pre-electronic music, the organ is the loudest instrument, *period* (besides timpani or drums). I love listening to BACH organ works; they can be so mathematically precise and so emotional at the same time. Even schlocky organ music like GEORGE WRIGHT is great. He plays versions of "South Pacific" and "Bali Hai" that are really schmaltzy and overwrought. His version of the *Mannix* theme is so overdone; it's bombastic as hell. There's one album where he visits Japan and it'll be real quiet and then he'll go overboard—you have to turn the stereo down all the time. He'll take a song meant for acoustic guitar and transcribe it for organ—that's always a laff riot.

On one album is a photo of him as a young man tinkering with an organ. Korla Pandit told us, "Yeah, I used to play the Rialto, but then George Wright got hold of that organ and took it apart and never put it together again." Whenever George plays somewhere, he's such a perfectionist that he takes the organ apart . . . but sometimes he gets pissed off at the owner (he's temperamental) and then he leaves the organ in shambles.

♦ SS: Everyone respects his playing ability. His mother was a theater organ player so he grew up under the keyboard, so to speak. He's considered "the best, but hard to work with." He's always hot-rodding the organ wherever he goes. He still plays once a year at the Paramount Theater in Oakland, and we got a notice from the LA Theater Organ Society that he has a CD out.

♦ BK: He has at least 40 albums out; I've got about 20. They're always scratchy; I've never found one in good condition. But they really put a chill up your spine when you listen to them.

♦ SS: He does a great "Hernando's Hideaway." There are certain songs that seem to be standards across the board, from the THREE SUNS to GEORGE WRIGHT—

♦ BK: "Caravan's" a big one; it's very Arab-Indian influenced, and was one of the first exotic songs. Plus "Quiet Village," "Tenderly," and "Hawaiian War Chant."

♦ SS: On a radio show we played ten versions of "Caravan" back-to-back and people were calling up: "Stop!"

♦ BK: But they were all so different, you could barely recognize them as the same song. Duke Ellington wrote it, and his version is really good.

♦ SS: Black people in Harlem in the '20s and '30s were into being "so sophisticated." When all the white people started coming to their clubs, they reacted by becoming more African—it was like this mocking of the white people. At the same time they got into an Arab

feeling with songs like "Caravan," or an Indian feeling with "Indian Love Call."

♦ **V: Even earlier, in the late 1800s, Western composers like Debussy and Ravel began incorporating exotic foreign influences into their music—**

♦ SS: Along with Rimbaud, Debussy was trying to conjure up "the mystery of the East." If you hear something like a Debussy flute piece played on a pipe organ—that's incredible.

♦ BK: Before he became famous, ROD McKUEN produced a BILL IRWIN album, *Organ Mystique*, which has an incredible Debussy "Clair de Lune." Ravel's "Bolero" is like that, too—

♦ SS: I like really schlock versions of "Bolero" more than regular symphonic ones.

♦ **V: In order for you to desire more unusual records, your esthetics had to expand—**

♦ SS: A guy from Germany stayed with me and looked through my records. He said, "Your records are very interesting, but *this* one is terrible." He was holding *Hafenmelodie* by HEINO. I asked, "What's so bad about Heino?" and he said, "This is so conservative." I guess Heino is identified with the *vaterland* feeling of German *oom-pah*—he offends the hell out of the younger Germans. But he's a major sex symbol to middle-aged German women. Basically, he does lively beer-drinking songs which are the MOR (middle-of-the-road) music of Germany, but he throws in a little marimba or steel guitar. And he has an imposing voice which doesn't quite go with the light tunes he selects.

♦ BK: He looks like such a swinger—black turtlenecks, shades, Wally George haircut.

♦ SS: I found out about HEINO when I was in Germany. I saw an album cover showing a guy who looked like Andy Warhol with sunglasses and white hair. I

Korla Pandit's *Music of the Exotic East*, Fantasy Records.

KORLA PANDIT

plays MUSIC of the EXOTIC EAST

Fantasy 3272 HIGH FIDELITY

thought, "This is wild—who is this?" Apparently he really *was* a Warhol fan and that's where he got his image.

With a lot of those exotic records, the operative word is *pagan*, as in "Pagan Love Song." It was like an acceptable way to be anti-Christian, even though people might not have consciously realized that. These pagan tikis are phallic.

Once you start opening up to these possibilities, you lose your embarrassment about buying some "square, dorky" record because you know you *want* it.

♦ BK: A lot of this is just instinctual. If I like a Michael Jackson song, I like it—even if it *is* Michael Jackson. And he's becoming more perverse: the Howard Hughes of the music industry.

♦ SS: I started out immersed in rock'n'roll. First it was punk rock, then SUN rockabilly records, like WARREN SMITH. Brian and I saw the BLASTERS countless times. Then I realized that rock'n'roll isn't getting people off the whole societal control thing—the rebellion that it's *supposed* to be is such a packaged con.

♦ BK: And so much of it now is a remake—why listen to Tom Waits when you can listen to Louis Armstrong? Unless the remake is *perverse.*

♦ SS: Plus, music today is self-conscious. The first time I heard the THREE SUNS or the HARMONICATS doing "Peg o' My Heart" it sounded so eerie—yet that was a number one single in the '50s.

♦ BK: While Elvis was going on, MARTIN DENNY and PEREZ PRADO had huge hits.

♦ *AJ: What do you think about listening to music from other lands?*

♦ SS: It bothers me to see "hip" musicians taking something out of a culture that took thousands of years to create, sampling it and *diddling* with it.

♦ *V: And this world beat fad: I don't like the Gypsy Kings, Dissidenten or westernized Middle Eastern singers, either.*

♦ BK: A lot of today's music is meant to make people dance, help them drive their cars, or put them to sleep—there's no intelligence to it, or emotion.

♦ SS: I hate the fake sensitivity that's come back in a big way, by people like Edie Brickell, or the Cowboy Junkies who folkized "Sweet Jane." I also think that somewhere along the way I got completely tired of words—

♦ BK: A "message."

♦ SS: Which is usually so banal. I can still listen to a song in a foreign language—I don't know what HEI-

NO's saying and it doesn't bother me. But to have somebody putting these words into your head—I got so I couldn't *think* anymore.

♦ BK: Like U2's live concert album—before they do "Helter Skelter" the singer says, "We're taking this song back from Charles Manson and giving it back to the Beatles!" When I heard that I thought, "This is definitely a low point . . ."

♦ *AJ: Word viruses encapsulated in a song can be like the "Tingler"—they go into your backbrain and stay. Ad jingles do that, too.*

♦ BK: And I reacted against these songs that are supposed to mirror social currents—U2's "Streets on Fire" is supposed to be a call for revolution?!

♦ SS: The whole idea of these people making incredible fortunes on their supposed social commentary which is eight words long, like "Martin Luther King was great" or "Mother Theresa blah-blah-blah . . ."

♦ *AJ: I love words, but I want them to throw my mind somewhere completely unexpected. I don't want to hear songs wishing for a "little cottage with a white picket fence."*

♦ BK: Something ultimately conformist.

♦ *AJ: Buying a ticket and going to a concert is now equated with political or social activism.*

♦ SS: So much more imagination went into these old records than goes into rock music today. When we talked to LES BAXTER he said, "I studied gamelan music. I'd go to the library and get 78s of Chinese music." He also had a background as an arranger for Nat King Cole. Yet despite all the great music he put out, he ended up doing soundtracks for *Switchblade Sisters* . . .

♦ BK: People give awards to Henry Mancini or John Williams every day, but for some reason Les Baxter is considered a hack even by soundtrack aficionados.

Yma Sumac's *Miracles,* London Records Inc.
Album cover credits: cover design: Marcellino.

◆ SS: Here's a record by YMA SUMAC produced by LES BAXTER in the late '60s: *Miracles.* I don't believe that story that she's "Amy Camus from Brooklyn"—I think she really *is* Peruvian. As to whether she's an Incan princess, I have no idea. Les Baxter had produced her classic records in the '50s, like *Voice of the Xtabay,* and he claimed to have invented the "exotic sound" with this one minor note. I can't remember what note it was, but according to him that was what made those records exotic. He had incredible respect for her four-octave range; it really suited the exotic style he'd been developing, but he hated her manager/husband, Moises Vivanco. He ended up having to give Vivanco songwriter credit on all these songs which he claims the guy never had anything to do with writing. Yma went on to do some really great records like *Jivaro,* where she goes into the Amazon with her husband and lives with these head-hunting Indians and does war chants. Songs like "Blood Festival" and "Whip Dance" are really great.

◆ *AJ: She was in a classic movie,* **Secret of the Incas** *(starring Charlton Heston) that was directly ripped off by* **Raiders of the Lost Ark.** *She was also in* **Omar Khayyam** *(1957), playing an Indian princess.*

◆ SS: I went to the Museum of Broadcasting in New York and they had a film of her on the Gig Young Show, from the early '60s. In the late '60s Les Baxter had been doing these biker soundtracks, and I guess Yma wanted to make a comeback and do a rock album. The liner notes to *Miracles* describe her as "the most extraordinary voice of three generations" and that's true—

◆ BK: *Miracles* sounds like The Stooges meet Yma Sumac: great acid wah-wah guitar mixed with her four octaves. It reminds me of Nina Hagen with these intense, guttural rants—

◆ SS: It's one of the most psychedelic records ever made. But she hated the cover, and after the first pressing the record went out of print. It has a really insane version of "El Condor Pasa" on it, which is Simon & Garfunkel's Peruvian song. On some songs she makes these nonsensical sounds and is very experimental without any self-conscious *trying* to be experimental. "Remember" is good. Les Baxter wrote all the songs except for the Simon & Garfunkel one.

◆ *AJ: Why did she hate the cover?*

◆ SS: It didn't make her look beautiful, whereas all the others showed this airbrushed vision of an Incan princess coming out of the Andes with volcanoes in the background. This one looks like a Monty Python collage: there's a huge guitar next to her, a Venetian canal scene, and Grecian edifices. We asked Les Baxter about this record being pulled and all he said was, "She's a very difficult woman."

◆ *V: Show us more LES BAXTER records—*

◆ SS: Here's *Space Escapade.* I really like the cheap futuristic feel of this cover: these two guys in astronaut

Xavier Cugat's *Mambo!*, Mercury Records.

suits drinking exotic purple and green drinks. The women are tinted yellow—

◆ BK: That photo has a real Ed Wood feel to it.

◆ SS: And this is supposed to be serious futuristic music. I like "Winds of Sirius," "Mr Robot" ("On our first visit to a planet, we arrive in the midst of the festivities of the *Martian Gras*"), and "The Commuter" ("Jet-mobiles roar through early Solar City traffic"). Les Baxter always returns to the idea of the busy metropolis. *Ports of Pleasure* has "Busy Port" with frantic music—

◆ BK: —that reminds you of being in a rickshaw in Hong Kong in the middle of a traffic jam. I think Les Baxter was trying to evoke the feeling of a soldier on leave who literally has 24 hours to "make the town."

◆ SS: It's *bustling.* Also, to me it conjures up being in junior high school and having a substitute teacher wheel in a projector and show you travelogues ... Unfortunately, *Space Escapade* is one of his least innovative records. The next record *is* great: *The Passions,* featuring BAS SHEVA—I think he'd lost Yma Sumac by this point. There are titles like "Despair, Ecstasy, Hate, Terror, Jealousy, Joy, Lust," and for each mood, the liner notes quote the Bible or Shakespeare. Bas Sheva does incredible nonverbal vocalizing. "Terror" starts out calmly and then "London Bridge Is Falling Down" comes in ... the singer becomes more and more frightened. A whole story is told, and it's really jarring. Whereas "Despair" is basically just passionate roaring.

◆ BK: I love records like these which are really into demonstrating the idea of high-fidelity—the full 20-20,000 cycles experience.

◆ SS: Some of these highly original records were made possible by the fact that people had these high-fidelity

stereos for the first time, and they wanted odd panning and weird tones just to test out the new technology.

Here's Les Baxter's *Music of the Devil God Cult,* which is actually the soundtrack from *The Dunwich Horror.* This was done in the mid-'60s. He put in a little *Phantom of the Opera* organ, but basically he recycled his samba-type material and Brazilian rhythms into songs like "Sacrifice of the Virgin," "Necronomicon," "Devil Cult," and "Black Mass." Suddenly it sounded like a Gothic horror tale.

◆ BK: Recently he did the soundtrack to *Born Again: The Chuck Colson Story,* with Dean Jones in the title role which is really scary.

◆ *V: How did you discover KORLA PANDIT?*

◆ SS: Again, the cover grabbed me: this man in a turban with jewels and eyeliner on. Korla says he's a Brahmin; his mother was European-born. He always wears his turban—supposedly Brahmins can't cut their hair, so maybe it's all up in that turban. The record itself lived up to the cover, to say the least.

◆ BK: Korla's music is very Indian-influenced, but there's also a Maria Montez *Cobra Woman* influence, too.

◆ SS: He had the first all-music program on TV starting in 1948, Sunday afternoons for about five minutes. He would come in, bow, and then play this enchanting organ music. His music was a strange cross-blend where he would take a real perky number like "Cactus Samba" and make it minor and mysterious. Women fell in love with him like crazy. TV was just starting out; it was a new medium and anything went, so he ended up getting a one-hour show. According to him, he was the first to play percussion on the organ.

◆ BK: In his films he demonstrates incredible technique. He'll use the flat of his hand and half of his forearm getting the samba rhythm going—it's amazing to see. Later in his career he put out albums like *Music for Meditation*—pre-New Age music.

◆ SS: Actually, that's an interesting genre: Rosicrucian albums, meditation albums, yoga albums. I have one by KRIYANANDA where he says, "I am the bubble,

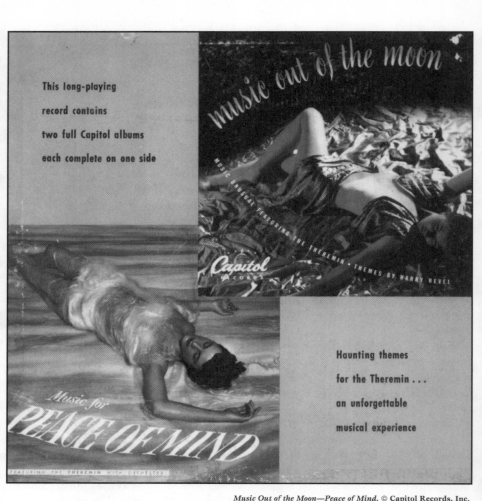

Music Out of the Moon—Peace of Mind, © Capitol Records, Inc.
Album cover credits: cover posed by Virginia Clark, photo: Paul Garrison.

make me the sea . . ." People with their little gurus were doing this before New Age became a huge movement.

◆ BK: Maybe in ten years we'll start getting into old New Age albums! [laughs]

I saw KORLA PANDIT play an old-time music hall with a theater organ where all the instrumentation is exposed—the drums, cymbals, etc—and everything's painted in fluorescent colors. There was a black light shining on it. I wasn't on LSD but I should have been. We were the only people under 65 in the audience.

◆ SS: In the late '80s we did a club, *Mecca,* with this black-light tiki environment. We didn't play conventional dance music; we played mambo and Martin Denny. Then we put on a show with Korla Pandit at the Park Plaza Hotel, which had a Masonic lodge feel plus an old pipe organ from the '20s. Korla gave a "power of positive thinking" rap between each song. Then he played the synthesizer. "Sutra Samba" was pretty good, but he also did the theme from "Cats" which was maybe too *out there* for us—I guess we wanted the Korla from forty years ago, but he had his *own* idea of what he wanted to play. Maybe he thought, "Oh—there's going to be young people there; I'll go get a synthesizer."

◆ BK: He recently played a soundtrack to the silent

film, *Phantom of the Opera,* on the theater organ at the Orpheum Theater, and it was great. *That* was the Korla we really enjoyed.

♦ *AJ: Have his albums been re-released?*

♦ SS: He has his own record company, India Records. He wants to re-release all his old *Fantasy* albums, but I think he can't get the masters . . . even though he says he owns them. One of his albums has quotes from Milton, Shelley, Pound, Whitman, Byron and Baudelaire to go with the songs, and he calls his music "a golden union of East and West." He advocated the idea of the "universal language of music."

♦ BK: He matches up "Tale of the Underwater Worshippers" with lines written by Lord Byron.

♦ SS: More cross-breeding: he was Indian, but I think he was influenced by French composers like Debussy who were also trying to create a more exotic feeling. And the results are sometimes more than the sum of the parts.

♦ BK: Let me read Korla's own words: "Music may not save your soul, but it will cause your soul to be worth saving."

♦ *V: Perfect . . . Talk about your favorite electronic pop music—*

♦ SS: Dr Samuel J. Hoffman playing the theremin is the featured artist on LES BAXTER's *Music Out of the Moon,* as well as *Music for Peace of Mind* (which features a woman wrapped in saran wrap on the cover). The liner notes describe the theremin as "a rare instrument that is closely akin to the human voice and heart. It is played by the motions of the hands in the air over an electronic field; the right hand gives pitch, the left volume, yet neither hand comes in direct contact with the instrument. The tone produced has a vibrant sweetness, with a tender, pulsing vibrato."

♦ BK: Hitchcock's *Spellbound* has great theremin—

Mike Melvoin's *The Plastic Cow Goes Moooooog,* Dot Records.
Album cover credits: art direction and cover illustration: Honeya Thompson.

whenever there's a dream sequence you hear "ooo-ooo-oooo."

♦ SS: *Lost Weekend* has great theremin, too, especially during the DT scenes! Theremins, echoplexes, and other interesting electronic devices aren't being made anymore, and they have a different sound than you can get with a Macintosh. I also like moog records: *The Plastic Cow Goes Moooooog; Moog Party Time; Moog Power* (Hugo Montenegro)—

♦ BK: *The Plastic Cow Goes Moooooog* is scary, especially "The Ballad of John and Yoko."

♦ SS: The first really big moog record was a classical one: *Switched-On Bach.* But I prefer the records that make no pretensions toward anything deeper. I love when they take '60s anthems like "Born to be Wild" and "Spinning Wheel"—tunes that were supposed to be mind-expanding or psychedelic—and pulverize them. They manage to *destroy* these "classic rock" songs that people cherish—

♦ *AJ: You mean* reinvent *them!*

♦ SS: On *Moog Power,* Hugo Montenegro does songs like Frank Sinatra's "My Way." The moog makes songs that mean so much to people—anthems—sound as if they were recorded on a different planet.

♦ BK: They'll take something like "The Magnificent Seven" theme and completely blow it out of the water with amazing, dorky sounds that make no sense in the middle of a western soundtrack.

♦ *V: The liner notes to* Moog Power *claim that "the Moog does nearly everything but rob banks!"*

♦ BK: *The Plastic Cow Goes Moooooog* says on the back, "This is the first pop electronic album with a soul." Jesus—I wish I had a soul like that!

♦ SS: *Moog Party* was done by PETE BELLOTE—he later collaborated with GIORGIO MORODER, who produced the Donna Summer sound of the "Munich

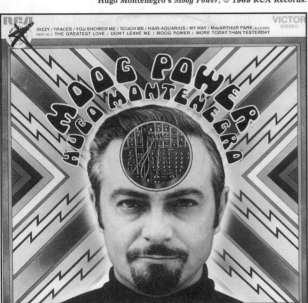

Hugo Montenegro's *Moog Power,* © 1969 RCA Records.

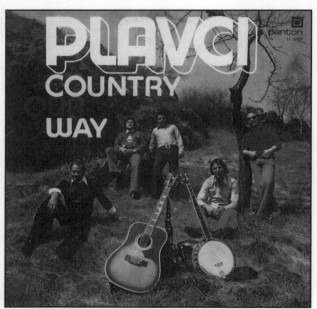

Plavci's *Country Our Way*, Panton Records.

Machine," with its impersonal, corporate aesthetics. The version of "Popcorn" here is devastating—it goes into maximum overdrive.

♦ BK: "Popcorn" was a huge hit when Stuart and I were kids. We grew up with '70s music—the most banal, horrible music in the world. "Popcorn"[makes popping sounds] sounds a bit like Moroder and has a real drive behind it. The original version was very cutesy and very repetitive, like "Chopsticks." When we played "Popcorn" at Mecca, people would immediately get up and dance to it: "Gawd, I remember this song from ages ago—I can't believe they're playing this instead of James Brown!" There was instant nostalgic identification—and you *can* dance to it.

♦ SS: Because the synthesizer is so omnipresent in music now, I like working back to the source of it all. Then you find out how much more raw and strange it was back then. They really couldn't simulate the sounds of actual instruments, so you get a much more alienated sound. They actually play up the robotism of it. A PERREY & KINGSLEY album liner note talks about "robots with soul" and claims they managed to make the synthesizer sound warm and musical, but . . . I guess it's the sheer impersonality of moog music that makes it so great. When I think about these moog records, the word that keeps coming up is "relentless." It's automated music, total artifice, with no pretensions to having a human voice.

♦ BK: We also tried to get into MECO, but—

♦ SS: I just got too bored with the MECO version of the *Star Wars* theme: awful synthesizer music with robots doing "The Bump" (remember that dance?) on a planet. It's Moroderish soundtrack music, but cheaper.

♦ BK: If anyone made a film of PHILIP K. DICK's *A Scanner Darkly* (about drug-dealing in Anaheim in the

'70s, but set in the future with surveillance devices), they'd have to use an old moog soundtrack.

♦ SS: That's an incredibly paranoid book about people who had their '60s idealism and their acid, but who just became *lost* after that era. One guy's always trying to wash the aphids off his body because he's been up for days on speed; he's always going into the shower. That's an actual syndrome of people who have done speed too long.

Eastern bloc records are promising. I found this record in East Berlin: *Country Our Way*. It's a Czechoslovakian country & western record with a version of "Blue Moon of Kentucky" that's incredible—they can't really pronounce English. We all know the Elvis Presley or Bill Monroe version, but when you hear PLAVCI doing it, the warp factor's incredible. They do "Sloop John B" too.

♦ BK: Phonetic albums are a genre in themselves—

♦ SS: I also like yodeling records. In the '30s there was a U.S. tour of Swiss yodelers and all these country singers like Jimmy Rodgers went to see them. So yodeling, which we think of as so traditional American cowboy, came from Europe—

♦ BK: And why are accordions featured in Mexican music? Because there were German colonies in Mexico at the turn of the century. Cross-breeding produces interesting music.

♦ SS: In the area of SOUNDTRACKS, the *Latin Sound of Henry Mancini* is just one of many that I like. I think Mancini is one of the most incredible composers of the 20th century.

♦ BK: For *Touch of Evil*, allegedly Mancini went to the Universal Studios music library and just lifted things like music from *Creature from the Black Lagoon* and mixed it all together. That was his first soundtrack.

Eastern bloc records are promising. I found this record in East Berlin: *Country Our Way*. It's a Czechoslovakian country & western record with a version of "Blue Moon of Kentucky"—they can't really pronounce English. We all know the Elvis Presley or Bill Monroe version, but when you hear PLAVCI doing it, the warp factor's incredible.

♦ SS: You associate him with schmaltz now, but something like "Peter Gunn" is a *basic* rock'n'roll riff. On *Latin Sound* he does "Señor Peter Gunn"—a Latin version! His "Moon River" from *Breakfast at Tiffany's* sounds timeless. Are Henry Mancini or Martin Denny or Yma Sumac "authentic"? No! Martin Denny is not Hawaiian music; "Moon River" is not a real folk song;

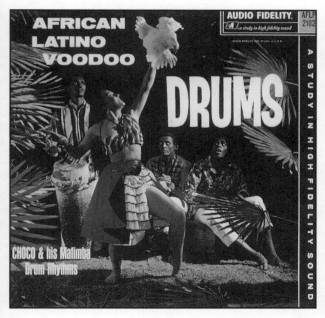

Choco's *African Latino Voodoo Drums*, © 1963 Audio Fidelity, Inc.

Herb Alpert is a Jewish guy pretending he's Mexican [allegedly]—and to me that's great! This rock critic's idea of "street credibility" where everything is "real"—well, it never is; it's always a pose. Bob Dylan started out *dressing up* like Woody Guthrie.

Once you start enjoying music like this, you realize that it doesn't matter *where* the sources come from. A rap group like NWA is "straight outta Compton"—therefore they're real "street." But they're influenced by everything that's going on—they watch TV, too. People think that by going out and buying NWA's record, they're grasping onto something that's "real." The records I buy are like grasping on to something fake that makes me *feel* more real!

◆ BK: Speaking of crossover, there was a *Flintstones* episode where a rock group comes to Bedrock and performs a song called "Way Out." These two black girls redid the song and it became a hit.

◆ SS: Totally artificial groups like the Partridge Family, the Archies, or Josie & the Pussycats can be great.

◆ BK: Who *cares* whether the Monkees can actually play their instruments?

◆ *AJ: And what is "real"? To sell us on any illusion of "street credibility" is a con—there is no fixed "reality," anyway. It's a shifting world; there are no authentic "tribes" anywhere.*

◆ BK: That's why someone like ENNIO MORRICONE is interesting: an Italian guy doing Mexican westerns. This is a clash of cultures. But he's been influenced by Duane Eddy or Dick Dale; he mixes in that heavy guitar sound with symphonic arrangements. *Once Upon a Time in the West* is like a film opera. I get a chill every time I see that crane shot over the train station, with the Morricone music—it's just brilliant. Charles Bronson played the man with the harmonica, and whenever he made an entrance it was like in si-

lent films: you play a certain chord on the organ when the good guy shows up.

◆ SS: His soundtracks are bombastic, epic and stirring—he's not embarrassed about being completely overblown. He also did the great *Exorcist II* [JOHN BOORMAN's *The Heretic*] soundtrack: an incredible hard-rock/Satanic ritual mix.

◆ *AJ: It's odd, having another culture (the Italians) deifying this mainstay of our culture, the western.*

◆ SS: I heard that got started because the Italians stopped making gladiator sword-and-sandal epics when they became unprofitable. (Morricone had done soundtracks for them, too.) So because they had these desert sets there, they decided to use them for something else.

◆ BK: Clint Eastwood started using them, too—then he became a big star.

◆ *V: What's the opposite of exotica records: ultranormal ones?*

◆ SS: I suppose, and here we have *Music to Live By*, a Mercury Living Presence compilation showing a perfect '50s family in a model interior. This exemplifies the whole idea of functional music: you would put this on to create these moods inside your perfect home. But what's this family doing—they're all sitting on the couch; they aren't exactly *living it up!* The album contains a couple popular selections, a couple jazz, a couple classical—this is the only record you'll ever need!

◆ BK: In the '50s, travelogues were big—and the music of Martin Denny or Korla Pandit is like a musical travelogue. Mood music was created to evoke a mood—

◆ SS: Can we quote you on that? Mood music was real escapism for people who didn't have much variety in their lives, and who wanted *anything* that could take them away from the ordinary and the routine. A lot of housewives bought *101 Strings Visit Cairo*—they

Naif Agby's *El Debke*, © 1962 Audio Fidelity, Inc.

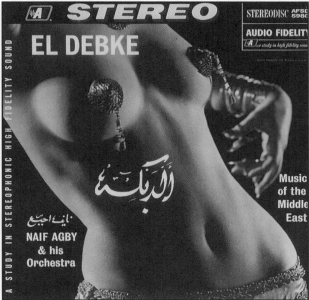

Kuwaiti Television Artistic Group Vol. 2, Bou Zaid Phone.

couldn't really tolerate the authentic music which was too dissonant or jarring, but they could take this weird mutation.

♦ **V: *Let's talk more about ethnic crossover records—***

♦ SS: This is *El Debke: Music of the Middle-East,* a belly dance record by Naif Agby & His Orchestra. Through belly dance records, Arab music which was fairly authentic became totally integrated into American life. Women would buy records to learn how to belly dance for their husbands.

♦ BK: Records like these are a hit-or-miss proposition, but the cover nudity's always nice. Belly dancing was supposed to liven up your marriage and tone your stomach besides. (I also love those *How to Strip Tease for Your Husband* type of records.)

♦ SS: And the women on the covers always have bright red hair and tons of makeup—frightening masks of mascara. They sound so foreign and wild; the music is usually pretty frantic and upbeat, conjuring up images of exotic sexual slave girls—and boys. *Music of the African Arab* by MOHAMMED EL-BAKKAR & His Oriental Ensemble has naked breasts on the cover; they got away with it because the woman was black. That and *African Latino Voodoo Drums* by CHOCHO & His Mafimba Drum Rhythms are both on the Audio Fidelity label, which has great covers and good sound quality, too.

♦ BK: We used to go to Ali Baba's restaurant in Hollywood; their belly dancer would get so close that you could practically see the hair on her breasts—

♦ SS: Because it was presented as "belly dancing music," that made it okay—it wasn't some weird Arab record. This was another way to bring sexuality into a totally repressed era: "I'm just taking belly dancing lessons, and I'll put this record on." We also got into Egyptian pop music like OM KALSOUM and FAIZA AHMED—

♦ BK: They sound so sensual and beautiful, you can fall in love with their voices. They evoke such imagery—Faiza Ahmed, especially.

♦ SS: ABDEL WAHAB is the composer-arranger for all these sweeping orchestral records, and records featuring women with soaring voices—he's like the god of this genre and is incredibly prolific. Here's one called *Colours from Abdel Wahab Melodies.* I also have him on a belly dance record—again, that was a way to make his music acceptable. In *The Sheltering Sky* Paul Bowles writes about listening to Wahab on the radio—that was Arab pop music back then, and again, it's not traditional or authentic.

♦ BK: But it's incredibly moving. There's a series titled *The Voice of Lebanon;* here's one by NAGAT (on another album, her name is spelled NAJAT). Her voice is great, and so is the album cover. She has a Barbra Streisand haircut and her face is framed between four golden candles.

Sometimes you hear synthesizer mixed in with traditional Middle Eastern instruments. We have a tape that Faiza Ahmed did with Abdel Wahab which is amazing—it has grandiose orchestral movements and squeaky synthesizer sounds that are just jolting, but it all really works well, like Chinese pop music.

This record is *Bulgarian Folk Dances—*

♦ **V: *Bulgarian vocals have been so "hip" since the '60s.***

♦ BK: Nevertheless, their instrumental music is very odd—it goes off into Banshee cries when they use reed instruments. They use bagpipes and other pipes, too. Look at those beautiful headdresses! There were literally thousands of female Bulgarian folk groups, and most of them are still unrecorded.

This next record shows TONY CAMARGO posed with two pumpkins. It's great mambo music.

♦ **AJ: *What's the difference between mambo and salsa?***

♦ SS: Salsa comes from Puerto Rico and it's really big in New York. Mambo was invented in Cuba; it's big band with really percussive horns that are occasionally dissonant and clash against the music itself. It can be really frantic. Mambo meant "cha cha cha." There's a certain dance step that goes with that, just like there's certain dance steps for rhumba. Cuban music has two basic influences: Spanish and African. PEREZ PRADO does mambo; he was one of the first to use organ in pop music as a predominant instrument (his big hits were "Patricia" and "Cherry Pink and Apple Blossom White"). "Marilyn Monroe Mambo" is good.

♦ BK: We saw him play and he looked about 90, completely shriveled up. But he was batoning along and got a great sound; he was still really incredible. Occasionally a man from the audience would jump onstage and put his arm around him while his wife took a photograph. A lot of his albums are great. *Havana 3 A.M.* was recorded in '56 during the Batista era, the most decadent Cuba ever.

♦ SS: On *Voodoo Suite* he got a little arty. It's a "tone poem" that starts out as African slave music and progresses to *Havana 3 A.M.* It's really conceptual and brilliant. Perez Prado had great album covers, too.

♦ BK: Here's *Mambo!* by XAVIER CUGAT, who wrote "Brazil" and was married to Charo, the *coochie-coochie* girl. On his tours he always carried two chihuahuas around—an L.A. restaurant called Cugie's has a painting of his face done as a dog's. He did a song called "Gypsy Mambo" that's really amazing, and a version of "Babalu" that's good, too. There are films where Cugat's performing his vibrant, maracas-shaking music.

♦ SS: Cugat was the prototype for Ricky Ricardo. But Prado was the king of mambo, definitely—I think Cugat took a lesson from him, because previously he was more restrained, more cocktailish. Prado always did these grunts, "*Di*-lo! *Ugh!*" that would tell the band to stop, or get ready for the next big charge.

♦ BK: Moving to the Middle East: *An Evening in Beirut* has good songs on it from various singers, and a beautiful photo of Beirut by the bay looking completely calm, all lit up at night. It's like Perez Prado's *Havana 3 A.M.*—a lost American empire. Beirut used to be the "Paris of the East," the big party town for the Arab sheiks who couldn't drink and get wild and whore in Saudi Arabia or Kuwait, so they'd go there. Capitol Records was a big purveyor of exotica—they put out Yma Sumac and a whole series of foreign albums.

♦ ***V: Beirut, a city that was a living work of art, was obliterated. It had an incredibly intricate irrigation system that had been there for thousands of years, plus amazing Islamic "Thousand and One Nights" architecture. All that's gone forever.***

♦ BK: This is a favorite group, the *Kuwaiti Television*

Jose Juan's *The Latin Hippy*, Wolf Records.

Elaine Minor & Earl Boveé's *The Musical Magic of Elaine & Earl*, Beem Records.

Artistic Group, Volume 2. Their music is incredibly traditional and very beautiful; it's all men, singing words I can't understand backed only by percussion. It's the male equivalent of Bulgarian music, poetic and dramatic and evocative. Some numbers are rhythmic and slow, others are very danceable and percussive.

♦ SS: Here's an ethnic crossover record I bought for its graphic value—*Jose Juan: The Latin Hippie ... Introducing The Guajison* (whatever *that* is). It shows a guy with a guitar and a Renaissance Faire cape, flowered pants, and a woman out of focus behind him. They spell "hippie" two different ways, with a "y" and an "'ie." Awful record.

♦ BK: Those Mexican album covers always have a woman out of focus in the background; it's odd.

♦ ***AJ: Look at those lambchop sideburns, and that reverential look—***

♦ BK: A real Grover Cleveland or Chester Arthur effect. That necklace is great, too, and check out that beer can opener ring ... Another crossover album is *The Organ that Talks* by ERNESTO HILL OLVARA, one of the scariest albums ever. "Pancho López" is the Mexican version of the "Ballad of Davy Crockett," and he somehow gets the organ to "talk" the words, with a vocorder-like effect. It was recorded in Mexico.

Here's a recording of a Mexican torch singer—chanteuse-type music by OFELIA DAVILA. This looks like an independently-produced album. She looks demonic and the music is demonic, too. The orchestra sounds like it's playing in another building—very muted. This guy Cimy looks especially Satanic—I guess he's Davila's husband, and he also wrote six of the songs. The best cut is "Enigma." It was recorded in the "City of the Angels," and it sounds like an Argentinean bar late at night.

♦ SS: *Dingaka* is your basic jungle African witch

Pomping Vila's *Moments of Enchantment*, Gift Records

doctor movie soundtrack, with songs like "Baby Elephant Walk."

♦ BK: Plus "Python Dance," "Thunder Orgy," "Placating the Gods," and "Cheeni Cheeni." There's narration, too. Cheap jungle movies are a lost genre. Sometimes the music on these records approaches the *Dating Game* theme—incredibly perky and weird. Joseph E. Levine produced this, and he's one of the sleaziest producers around, up there with Arkoff. He does these really bloated productions with a soap opera sensibility.

♦ V: *Don't you collect records with sitar on them?*

♦ SS: Yes; here's one by BILL PLUMMER and His Cosmic Brotherhood. He's standing by his sitar barefoot, but in a black business suit with a paisley tie—

♦ BK: His feet are so huge, too. What a nerd!

♦ AJ: *And he has short hair—*

♦ SS: It's 1967. The photo looks like it was taken in front of the Self-Realization Fellowship on Sunset Boulevard. Basically, he's a '60s jazzbo going raga, trying to cash in: instead of raga rock, it's raga *jazz*. The title is *Journey to the East*. He actually narrates "Journey to the East"—not the Hermann Hesse novel but a poem written by fellow sitarist Hersh Hamel. He tries really hard to get that Hindu feeling, and credits as significant his studies with Hari Har Rao and Ravi Shankar.

Jazz guys were always a little bit late picking up on the raga rock fad. GABOR SZABO recorded some jazz-raga records, including *Jazz Raga*. There's a JOHN McLAUGHLIN album, *Devotion,* which is all acid-guitar instrumental, no vocals, and it sounds like the introduction to an early P-FUNK record. I always hated fusion (especially when I was a kid) but this was made before it became so "technical" and Scientological. Larry Young is really amazing, too, in terms of total space-out keyboards.

Lotus Palace is a kinda *mushy* easy-listening-with-raga record by the ALAN LORBER Orchestra (Verve). They do "Mas Que Nada," "Within You Without You," and "Up Up and Away." The liner notes say, "This record is not the debut of a new musical group; it is rather an indoctrination into a way of thought and a way of life. Whatever machine you play this record on will—for the first time—earn its keep. The highs are almost limitless, the lows border on pain."

I like almost any rock records with sitar on them. HARI HAR RAO & the Folkswingers recorded an album where they covered songs like Paul Revere & the Raiders' "Kicks." When I got back from a trip to India, I took tabla lessons from Hari Har Rao for awhile. I also have ANANDA SHANKAR's album on which he does amazing versions of "Jumpin' Jack Flash" and "Light My Fire"—raw rockin' raga! When he does "Jumpin' Jack Flash" on the sitar, he takes the song out of its revered spot. Being into this music is a way to reject the rock mythos—the "Jim Morrison died for you" attitude. Just like when SERGIO MENDES does "Fool on the Hill," he kinda deconstructs it: all of a sudden you realize how stupid the lyrics are and how utterly banal and facile the song is.

♦ BK: Every Indian has probably heard a Rolling Stones or Beatles song, so why not take one and fuck around with it?

♦ AJ: *Removing the song from its original context helps neutralize songs which have become part of society's control process—*

♦ SS: Especially for people who still think they're "liberating" themselves by buying a particular record or CD.

♦ V: *Consumption is equated with self-expression.*

♦ SS: Here's an example of '60s wild hi-fi that's kinda Latin: ESQUIVEL from Mexico City. Besides original

Hyman Gold's *Hot Bagel!*, Hyman Gold Records. Album cover credits: photographs courtesy of: Har-Omar Restaurant, Hollywood.

compositions, his group did easy listening versions of stuff like the *Third Man* theme and *Spellbound,* but he put in all these odd touches. He worked with tape manipulations, too. If you put *Exploring New Sounds in Hi-Fi* on your stereo, sounds bounce around the room. Besides using cow bells, glockenspiel, accordion, temple blocks and *buzzimba,* he also inserts amazing vocal bits into the mix to break up the song. I like "Boulevard of Broken Dreams," which ends with "Boulevard of broken dreams, cha cha cha!" Into a completely ominous mood he throws in a little "cha cha cha!" as if to say, "It's *okay*—don't worry about it!" He uses a theremin on this, too.

Here's CHARLES CAMILLERI's *Spectacular Accordions.* He does the most manic version of "Jungle Fantasy." It's exotica done on accordion—he just blazes through it. As the subtitle proclaims, "Dramatic effects—thrilling realism—unforgettable listening!" Accordion records go from being really conventional (Italian restaurant music) to utterly flipped-out, and this one is frantic. The cover shows three giant accordions with a blissed-out girl in a yellow leotard sitting on top of one.

♦ *V: Tell us about homemade lounge records—*

♦ SS: Here's POMPING VILA's *Moments of Enchantment.* It's representative of all those records which were recorded at some lounge and pressed in tiny quantities—they were probably just sold at the club. This particular organist played first at the Gloucester Hotel in Hong Kong and then was brought to the U.S. He does "Sister of Satan," "Tabu"—

♦ BK: Listening to this, you really get the feeling of being in a weird Filipino whorehouse.

♦ SS: I love the obscurity of these people. The liner notes always tell you about all the clubs they played at, and who appreciated their music, and how the British officers would be sitting around this club in Hong Kong . . . a strange slice of life you'd only encounter by finding this record in some thrift shop.

Here's another lounge record: *Hot Bagel!* featuring HYMAN GOLD 'N' CELLO. The cover shows a guy with a cello kissing a none-too-attractive Jewish woman's hand, with a flaming shishkebab of bagels in the background. The record doesn't live up to the cover—it's pretty bland cello versions of tunes like "La Vie en Rose" and "Autumn Leaves." It's a little too sedate for me.

♦ BK: *I* think she's pretty attractive.

♦ SS: Here's another homemade record, *Who Will Buy?* by the SPECIALISTS on "Jazzette" Records, which was the name of the artists' Siamese cat who "says we never sang about the important things such as mice and catnip." The Specialists are Kit and Ken Kennedy, who both wear incredible sunglasses and demonic grins. It's all '60s songs like "Age of Aquarius" and "Feelin' Groovy" warped into lounge music. The cover drawing shows them on a bicycle built for two, wearing their shades and shorts. Who *did* they think would

Back cover of The Specialists' *Who Will Buy?*, Jazzette Records. Album cover credits: cover: Vivian Stein.

buy this record?

♦ *AJ: This was their little burst of creativity.*

♦ BK: Here's *The Musical Magic of Elaine and Earl*—they also write books on metaphysics, meditation, astrology and other spiritual subjects, and they want to open up an institute. I paid 50 cents for it, and at that price you can throw it away if you don't like it. It's actually quite horrible—Elaine really can't sing, and she's backed by a drum machine plus a piano/organ combination. "Girl from Ipanema" is really scary. They do the most incredible cocktail version of "Hava Negila"—at the end she goes, "Oy vey!"

♦ SS: I like some harmonica records, and the most famous group was the HARMONICATS—Jerry, Don and Al. My favorite song, where they challenge themselves to the limit, is Aram Khachaturian's "Saber Dance" on three harmonicas. It's wild—very frantic. Jerry Murad has a book out, *Jerry Murad's Harmonica Technique for the Superchronomic*—a must for all students.

♦ *V: A husband-and-wife duo, the MULCAYS, put out some great amplified harmonica records.* **Dream of Love** *features great "poetry" spoken by a deep-voiced poet, Robin Morrow, and on* **A Kiss In the Dark** *every song has "kiss" in the title.*

♦ BK: In the '50s there was a famous harmonica player, LARRY ADLER, who played all these concerts. Then he got blacklisted because he was allegedly in the Communist party, so Murad took his place on the charts.

♦ SS: According to *His Way,* by Kitty Kelley, Frank Sinatra really hated the Harmonicats because they dislodged him from Number One with "Peg o' My Heart," which sold three million copies. His record company wanted to assign him the Harmonicats' producer, and he said, "No fucking way!" Then someone

Sound Effects U.S. Air Force Firepower, © Audio Fidelity, Inc.

threw a party for him on a boat and unknowingly booked the Harmonicats to play—Frank hit the roof. I see the HARMONICATS and the THREE SUNS connected in terms of the songs they both do, like "Twilight Time."

♦ BK: They both have that roller rink feel. And the harmonica isn't bluesy, it almost sounds like an organ or a bunch of accordions.

♦ SS: The Harmonicats also do "Galloping Comedians"—Ed Sullivan-type music, when the guys are juggling dishes or the dog show comes out and everyone's frantically running around.

♦ BK: In the *National Enquirer* you always see K-Tel type ads for the *Greatest Hits of the Harmonicats.*

♦ *V: You've got a number of "twisted authority figure" records—*

♦ SS: Here's *Power of Source* by the APOLLO STARS, and here's L. Ron Hubbard on the cover with headphones on. For quite a while Hubbard lived on a boat, the *Apollo,* controlling the whole Scientology empire while cruising around the Mediterranean. Their motto was "Make Earth a Scientology planet." Allegedly he attempted to take over Morocco at one point—he was funding different factions under the king. He stayed on the boat because of tax problems, plus he claimed he'd lived all these earlier lives and had been a Phoenician captain looking for sunken treasure. Whenever they would land, the Apollo Stars would wear their uniforms and provide their own welcoming fanfare calculated to win over the "Wogs" (meaning anybody who wasn't a Scientologist). And all these fusion-jazz guys ended up in Scientology: Chick Corea, Stanley Clark, Herbie Hancock and even Van Morrison. The liner notes claim that "in 1973 L. Ron Hubbard developed an incredible new sound in music," but it's certainly not on *this* record, which is incredibly bland fusion-jazz. Nevertheless, because of its origin,

it stands out.

♦ BK: The cover's out-of-focus and everyone looks so unhappy—L. Ron Hubbard most of all. The clothes are so '70s, too—Wilson's House of Suede-type jackets. Hubbard even co-wrote one of the songs, "My Dear Portugal (Meu Querido Portugal)"—it's instantly forgettable.

♦ *AJ: This record isn't really meant to be played; it's a historical artifact—*

♦ BK: Like the JIM JONES' *Peoples Choir* album. That's really scary, because you hear children singing a lot on it.

♦ *V: I like records where these idols reveal feet of clay—*

♦ BK: Here's the *Howard Hughes Press Conference* he gave in 1972 to prove that he did exist and that Clifford Irving did not write his biography with his consent. It's just Howard Hughes going on about everything from the length of his fingernails ("Oh no, I clip them every day!") to . . . one of the reporters asks about his predilection for tennis shoes and he replies, "Oh yes, they're easy to wear and they make my feet feel good." *Citizen Hughes* talks about what he actually looked like at the time, and he looked like hell—he weighed 90 pounds; he had fingernails out to here. He was shooting himself up with some kind of speedball, like morphine and speed.

♦ SS: His voice sounds "back from the dead," because they recorded it off a speakerphone. He didn't do the press conference *in person,* he did it by phone from a hotel in the Bahamas. You wonder: How could this guy be running a multi-billion dollar empire and influencing who was President and everything else? On every question he veers off onto strange tangents. When he's asked about tennis shoes, he talks about World War II when canvas was the only shoe fabric you could wear

Sidney O. Fields' *The Communazis Exposed*, General Records.

Chad Everett's *All Strung Out*, Marina Records.
Album cover credits: front cover photography: Gabor (Gabi) Rona.

because all the leather was going for boots in the war . . . he goes on and on in a monotone.

♦ BK: George Garabedian, who made these albums, mostly produced radio show nostalgia records, like Orson Welles's outtakes, which are hilarious.

♦ SS: On one track, this poor director is trying to tell Orson Welles how to do a frozen peas commercial. Welles totally intimidates him: "YOU don't know how to be a director! *I* know how to read the lines!"

Our military has released some pretty "psycho" records, like *Sound Effects: U.S. Air Force Firepower*, with tracks like "Mass napalm attack by F-100s," and "Psychological warfare, public address from C-47," where they announce [with helicopter sound in background] "Clear the village—we are about to strafe and bomb it!" The sonic boom from a F-104 Starfighter sounds so "ambient," but then you'll have a Gatling gun immediately afterward. Another eerie cut is "Nuclear bomb explosion, Yucca Flat, Nevada."

♦ BK: And even at its most *horrible*, beautiful sounds come out.

♦ SS: And here's *The Communazis Exposed by Their Own Words: Revolution Today in the USA*. Coming into this massive collage of '60s demonstrations, swastikas, stars, and Black Panther salutes is the Fourth Reich with a peace sign in the middle of the "o" in "Fourth." The back cover shows Hitler, Lenin, Castro, Ho Chi Minh and Mao. The recording intercuts Hitler's speeches with speeches by Bobby Seale and other lesser-known '60s radicals like Bob Avakian from the RCP. They're trying to prove that the radicals from the '60s are the same as the Nazis.

♦ *AJ: Who put this out?*

♦ BK: United Sales American; Sidney Fields put it together. He produced documentary films like *Communist Accent on Youth, Communism & Co-Existence,*

and *Communist Imperialism*. He also did *The Truth About Communism*—Ronald Reagan hosted that turkey.

♦ SS: It looks like they got a tape of the Black Panther Party's National Revolutionary Conference for a United Front Against "Fascism," Oakland Auditorium, July 18-20, 1969—then they re-spliced it to reflect their own point of view. Charles Garry, one of the People's Temple lawyers, is also on it. The record begins with the narrator saying, "Adolf Hitler (infamous dead Nazi leader) said: 'Within four months we have eliminated 1.2 million.' " Then the narration resumes: "Those were the words of the Socialists of the 1930s. Now listen to the Socialists of today!" and Bobby Seale comes on. We also have a record titled *Survival of the White Race* on which the narrator warns against Jews, blacks and the "mud races."

In the genre of Educational Children's Records, here's one titled *Listen with Your Ears: Everyday Skills* by WILLIAM JANIAK. This is a record for retarded children, and the speaker is a "registered music therapist." Some titles include "We wash our face," "I have a cold," "My name is ___," "I have swimsuits," "Sit down," and "I'm getting big now."

♦ BK: You could make a porn album for paedophiles with this . . .

♦ SS: It's incredibly simplistic and the narrator sounds so deadpan, with no intonation. He says, "I have a cold" and then he'll cough and sneeze.

♦ BK: And he's backed by a really dorky synthesizer doing wah-wah-wah *Sesame Street*-type music. We did a radio show and played "I have a cold. I can't smell. My head hurts," then segued into a Kennedy assassination LP where a secret service agent describes first seeing Kennedy's head with all the brains exposed. We cut from "My head hurts" to "I saw the President's

William Janiak's *Listen With Your Ears*, Kimbo Educational Records.

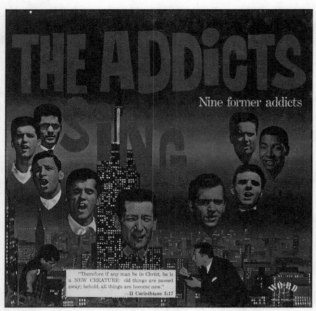

Front cover of *The Addicts Sing*, Word Records.

Back cover of *The Addicts Sing*, Word Records.

head and it was just a mass of *gore . . .*"

Another JFK record is *Can't Keep From Crying*. It's all typical blues songs about "Oh, he died for us," but it's great because they're all about JFK dying. Big Joe Williams and Otis Spann are on it . . .

Here's a record by CHAD EVERETT, who starred as Joe Gannon in *Medical Center*. He was a stud of his time; look at the width of that belt. That little choker's kinda nice too. He does "Ain't No Sunshine" which is really hellish; he can't sing. This is like WILLIAM SHATNER's album, and what a title: *All Strung Out*. I saw him in a film recently and he's gotten really barrel-chested and fat—scary looking. His skin got really weathered, too. Awful album, but it's good for the pain value.

♦ SS: I have a love-hate relationship with a lot of records. Some I instinctively love, but others you have to be in the "right mood" to listen to—ROD McKUEN immediately springs to mind. I have a masochistic relationship with some records—they're painful.

♦ BK: My ex-girlfriend wouldn't allow me to play CLAUDINE LONGET in the house—it's too irritating, especially "A Man and a Woman" or "Day Tripper."

♦ *V: Do you have any drug-influenced records?*

♦ SS: Here's *The Addicts Sing: Nine Former Addicts*. It shows shooting up on the back cover, too—a real Jack Chick-inspired touch. It's on the WORD label, "the finest name in sacred music," and was recorded in a rehabilitation camp founded by Pop and Mom Rosado, pastors of the Damascus Christian Church in the Bronx, New York. Basically it's all gospel songs. "The Addicts March" is the best cut: "We are the former drug addicts that have now been saved by the Lord," sung to the tune of "Battle Hymn of the Republic." The harmonizing's pretty incredible. Their voices are so rough—it

seems like they really *have* been through hell.

♦ BK: The album cover's great: Puerto Rican ex-junkie heads floating over the skyline of New York City, and a little Bible quote in the bottom corner. There's a tattoo on one guy. Apparently they toured the country acting out "ad-libbed real-life dramas portraying all the horrors of drug addiction"—*that* must have been fun to watch!

I like Christian J.D. concepts like *The Cross and the Switchblade* (the book, the movie, and the soundtrack). Here's a Christian J.D. album, *The Restless Ones*, a soundtrack by JOHNNY CRAWFORD produced by Billy Graham. The best thing about this album is the theme song, "The Restless Ones," on which Johnny Crawford sounds exactly like Jim Morrison from the Doors.

♦ SS: That theme song is epic: "Oh restless ones, when will you see the truth?" In *The Rifleman* Johnny Crawford played "Mark," the son of Chuck Connors.

♦ BK: Besides being in the Mouseketeers, he was also in *The Naked Ape* (based on the Desmond Morris book). He and Victoria Principal (from *Dallas*) are nude during half the film. He also did some teen star albums where his voice is so high, he sounds like a girl: "Rumors" and "Your Nose Is Gonna Grow" were his teenage hit singles.

♦ SS: Another possibly drug-influenced record is *L'sGA* (title reminds me of LSD) with the mummies of Guanajuato shown on the top part of the inside fold, plus the most bizarre liner notes I've ever seen, with really wild spelling and capitalization and grammar: "A speech is a . . . peach is an . . . ache is a Che. Acknowledging who is right or wrong is YET MOOT (Lying Dutchman). There has to be time for sobering mysteries (with a little help from one's friends)." Like—*what?*

♦ BK: It's definitely the most experimental album

ever—beyond anything else.

♦ SS: L'sGA stands for "Gassed-Masked Politico, Helium Bomb, and Two Channel Tape Ballad/Octet." The composer is SALVATORE MARTIRANO. This came out in '67 on a major label, Polydor—maybe they were trying to market it like a regular psychedelic record. I don't know what inspired him to do *this*—it sounds nothing like his other records which are boring 20th-century "avant-garde." But this sounds like a precursor to *Throbbing Gristle*—

♦ BK: And the *Eraserhead* soundtrack, too.

♦ SS: It goes from low moaning and roaring to a high-speed tape-manipulated "Pledge of Allegiance," and Lincoln's "Gettysburg Address" spliced and played at distorted speeds.

♦ BK: There's a little minuet violin thing, but most of it's just "slaughter" music—like Butthole Surfers without the heavy-metal edge. We play it at the store sometimes and people just leave. It's incredibly rare, too.

♦ SS: Here's IRMA GLEN's *Music, Ecology, and You!* This woman plays the organ and talks about ecology: "Suddenly our lives as individuals are of secondary importance. Now we want our world to be saved . . . If you're not part of the solution, you're part of the pollution!" How did this record ever come about? I guess she's into meditation music (some of her other records include *Music, A Bridge to Higher Consciousness* and *Music-Prayer Therapy & the Promises of Jesus*). She was inspired by the ecology movement of 1969—

♦ V: **The year** The Population Bomb **was published**—

♦ SS: "Every Day Is Earth Day" is my favorite by her—it's a rallying cry. The liner notes warn that "the greatest obstacles are human apathy toward the future, and human reluctance to spend money or exert effort for the benefit and welfare of succeeding generations."

♦ BK: She's an original Earth-Firster.

♦ SS: Now we're on to SCOTT WALKER, one of the Walker Brothers. They weren't brothers, their real name wasn't Walker, and they were American, but they were called the Walker Brothers and pitched as part of the British Invasion of the '60s. Scott grew up in Riverside, California and played Gazzari's nightclub on Sunset Strip. After the Walker Brothers became famous he kinda flipped out, hated his pop star image, hated all the media attention, and created this mystique where all he would do was read Camus in his London flat and listen to Sibelius or Mozart. Then he recorded some solo albums which we describe as "Tony Bennett on acid." He has an incredible voice—an amazing crooner sound. He's a weird bridge between actual crooners like Tony Bennett and Frank Sinatra, and pseudo-crooners like Bryan Ferry and David Bowie (who were heavily influenced by Scott Walker, as was Mark Almond).

When Scott quit the Walker Brothers, he took a year off and lived in monasteries in Scotland; he went to Russia. He considered himself to be a Communist in the '60s, and the inside cover of *Scott Walker Four* is this collage of Stalin and marching Russians. *Melody Maker* asked him, "What's your favorite pastime, Scott?" and he answered, "Brooding." "Well—what do you do when you're not on the road?" "I think about World War Three."

He was into acid, but afterwards he said he was against acid because he was supposed to be into reality. He was trying to counter all the psychedelic stuff that was going on. And instead of evolving from a pop group into Cream or something, he developed this introspective, incredibly morbid material—

♦ BK: Like "Rosemary," which is about a woman who plays bridge with her mother's friends and looks into the mirror and sees herself getting older.

♦ SS: Another song, "Big Louise," is about an aging drag queen in Soho. He put out four solo albums in a row [*Aloner, Scott 2, 3, 4*] plus *Scott Sings Songs from His TV Series.* Then he released *Till the Band Comes In;* a soundtrack anthology, *The Moviegoer;* a country LP, *Stretch;* and a jazzy album, *Climate of Hunter.* He also did three Walker Brothers reunion records, *No Regrets, Nite Flights,* and *Lines*—the title song is the only good track on that one. On *Scott Walker Four* there's a song, "The Seventh Seal," based on the Ingmar Bergman film: about how *he's* the plague. And it sounds like an Ennio Morricone thing with that sound of hoofbeats, and he's going from town to town spreading death.

♦ *AJ: Who wrote the songs?*

♦ SS: He wrote some great ones, and some others were written by Jacques Brel. When you *read* the lyrics (contrasted with the way Scott Walker presents them: as if they're Las Vegas show tunes) they're really staggering. There's one called "Next!" about a soldier in the French army who loses his virginity in a mobile whorehouse—

Irma Glen's *Music, Ecology, and You!*, © 1970 Numinis Recordings.

Music, Ecology, and YOU!

Original music composed and played by Irma Glen

"Suddenly our lives as individuals are of secondary importance. Now we want our world to be saved."

Claudine Longet's *Claudine*, A&M Records.
Album cover credits: album design: Peter Whorf Graphics.

♦ BK: With a gay lieutenant slapping his ass—

♦ SS: —as if they were all fags. Every time he makes love he thinks of all the gonorrhea that he's had.

♦ BK: The original Jacques Brel song is French accordion fluff—if you heard it, you'd go, "Take this shit off!"

♦ SS: There's another song called "Jackie" (which must be from Jacques Brel calling himself "Jackie"). This singer starts out in a coffee bar with an acoustic guitar, and goes on to greater and greater success. He ends up playing for old women who are decked out like Christmas trees, and everything's fake, and he's only happy when he's locked up in his opium den surrounded by Chinamen . . . He goes on about "authentic queers and phony virgins," and how he's this giant pimp to the whole world. It's just the most cynical song.

♦ BK: He talks about how he can have any girl, and how everyone in the world loves him. It's sort of this Nietzschean *Ecce Homo* thing: "Why I am so brilliant." And it's sung in such a manic way; he literally rushes the words through the entire song.

♦ *AJ: What's the music like?*

♦ BK: It's arranged-for-orchestra stuff that sounds like John Barry. Our favorite song is "Montague Terrace (In Blue)." Scott wrote it, and it's amazing—very referential to Tom Jones.

♦ SS: He talks about this little dank apartment in London and the woman across the hall: her thighs are full of tales to tell about all the men she's known, and the fat man upstairs is going to crash through the ceiling soon. Scott was really successful with this stuff in England—he actually had a TV show for a season. For awhile he was like a massive sex symbol; he was handsome, but did these perverse songs that you would never think of as being a possible pop thing. Like

"Funeral Tango," where he basically says: when I die, you guys will come to the funeral, but just go out and get drunk because I know you don't give a shit about me anyway.

♦ BK: He also does "The Big Hurt," which SANDY POSEY did, but a fully blown, completely overwrought orchestral version. And he does a ROD McKUEN song, "If You Go Away," which Rod co-wrote with Jacques Brel—were they lovers at the time? So Scott is like this incredibly cynical romantic . . .

♦ SS: An interviewer asked him, "What kind of contemporary music do you like?" and he said, "I don't like anything that's going on now. I think the only real *men* in music are Tony Bennett and Frank Sinatra." And this was when those guys were totally "out"! Scott had a nice voice to begin with, but then he really developed this crooner's deep, smooth, suave delivery. When David Bowie got into his "Thin White Duke" phase he was definitely copying the Scott Walker pose.

♦ BK: Now we have three albums by CLAUDINE LONGET, who was once married to Andy Williams. Herb Alpert signed her to A&M, and the record company tried to push her as an ingenue, a beautiful innocent flower. She did songs Astrud Gilberto would do, but she doesn't have a voice at all. She whispers the songs and has a little-girl grossness.

♦ SS: Also, it's so cheaply European—especially her version of "A Man and a Woman." Whereas the original, by Francis Lai, is lilting and dramatic.

♦ BK: She's in *The Party,* an incredible film by Blake Edwards where Peter Sellers plays an Indian actor who fucks up the production of a movie. Claudine is the love interest, and she's especially foul—she does a saccharine little guitar number. Later, she became part of the cocaine set in Aspen, Colorado and was going out with this skier, Spider Sabich. Supposedly she "accidentally" shot him to death in the stomach while he was teaching her how to shoot. The trial got worldwide media attention and she was found guilty of manslaughter—she served a month or so in jail. Andy was by her side, even though they'd divorced ages ago. I don't know where she is now . . . beneath that innocence, a killer lurked!

One of my favorite soundtracks is *Lolita* by NELSON RIDDLE (he also did the theme music for *Route 66*). The theme itself is schmaltzy; I prefer "Lolita Ya-Ya" which is sung during a scene where James Mason sees Sue Lyon for the first time in her bikini out in the backyard. The song just goes [high pitched] "Ya Ya Ya Ya Ya Ya." It's the composer's interpretation of what he thought teen music was about; paedophilia is *very* apparent in the song.

This is SONNY's solo album, *Inner Views.* The cover drawing shows him sitting in a chair looking very stately with striped bell-bottoms and Cher is like a ghost fading away . . . it's very weird. Two incredible songs stand out. On "I Just Sit There," he steals "I heard the news today, oh boy"—it's 12 minutes long and has a lot of sitar on it . . . it's excruciating. "Pammie's On A Bummer" is about this "chick" who wanted to do something but she put her body up for sale and then started smoking pot to keep herself from flipping out and now she's on a bummer. Like Rod McKuen, he has the worst voice in the world—plus he's real reactionary.

As far as I know HONEY, LTD only did one album, produced by Lee Hazlewood. The songs are in the Josie & the Pussycats vein; the girls sing in harmony, and I have the feeling Lee Hazlewood wrote them even though they're credited to someone else. "The Warrior" is about a man going off to fight in battle, and you think it's a pro-fascist song but then it tries to get a little anti-war kick in there, because "you're going to come back dead." "I've got your man" essentially says, "Fuck you; I've got him and there's nothing you can do." They also do the most excruciating "Louie Louie"—it's slow, vague, and really drawn out.

♦ SS: They're a real saccharine girl group, nothing like the RONETTES.

♦ BK: They were literally cheerleaders that Hazlewood signed up. In the late '50s, Hazlewood produced and wrote songs for Duane Eddy ("Rebel Rouser") and he also produced a country star, Leapy Lee. His roots were in pop-country. Then he made a couple of albums that were poetry *a la* Rod McKuen. On *Hazlewoodism* the liner notes were brilliant, sort of like redneck Bob Dylan.

♦ SS: He tried to be avant-garde with the layout of his liner notes. He was trying to be "the man in black" like Johnny Cash, but he comes off phony—he sings that he's waiting at a bus stop in Texas, while allegedly he was living with Nancy Sinatra in Beverly Hills.

♦ *V: Were they lovers?*

Music to Read James Bond By, United Artists Records. Album cover credits: cover illustration: Frank Gauna.

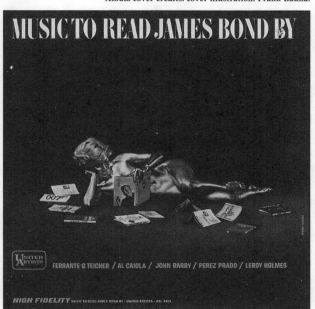

♦ BK: I assume so, but it's never been documented. Lee Hazlewood hasn't said anything about it. After he did these poor man's Johnny Cash records he hooked up with Nancy Sinatra and wrote "These Boots Are Made for Walking" and created a hit. Originally he wrote the song for himself, but Nancy liked it so much she said, "*I want to sing that!*" Lee said, "I don't think you should—I wrote this for a *guy*." But she got her way . . .

And why are accordions featured in Mexican music? Because there were German colonies in Mexico at the turn of the century. Cross-breeding produces interesting music.

Lee and Nancy worked well together. Their hits include "Summer Wine" and "Some Velvet Morning," which sort of mystifies her as a Greek goddess. She's a bit Claudine Longet-ish in that she can be such a little girl, but she can also be a biker/hooker type (like in "Boots") where she'll stomp your ass.

When she and Lee do duets together, sometimes she takes the quiet road (as in "Summer Wine" where she plays innocent), but in "Jackson" she's real balls-kicking. On a lot of their songs they do dialogues. "Let's Get Together Again" on *Nancy and Lee Again* is an impromptu session where he's playing acoustic guitar. She sounds like she's completely drunk, and he says, "Move over, Buck Owens; Hazlewood's pickin' now." It's a one-take number with a little chorus and some improvised dialogue. He says, "What do you want to do, Nancy?" and she says, "I wanna have babies." "'Whaddaya thinking?" "I was thinkin'—I won't say it." "What?" "We're the oldest teenyboppers around." He makes her sing "Howdy Doody" in the middle of the song, and then says, "Okay, I'm off to Sweden! Bye." You hear him walk out of the studio and that's how the song ends. As far as I know, Lee still lives in Sweden.

He did a couple solo albums where song after song is about an unnamed woman that he just can't stand—that he *hates*. I don't think it's Nancy Sinatra, 'cause I think he worked with her later, but it's all "You did me wrong" kind of songs. One's called *Requiem for an Almost Lady*. His *Forty* has the most depressing liner notes, written when he turned forty. He also did a horrible C&W album with Ann-Margret.

Here's somebody who worked with Lee and Nancy: BILLY STRANGE. He was an orchestra arranger and guitarist who recorded theme songs from James Bond movies, the *Munsters, Peter Gunn* as well as "Hava Nagilah." There's one album where he goes to Tijuana. A lot of his stuff is mediocre and reminds me of the

Baja Marimba Band—really boring. But he's the third element in the triad of Nancy Sinatra, Lee Hazlewood and Billy Strange.

JAMES BOND music is always great, especially when it's by the brilliant JOHN BARRY. I don't like the music from the later Roger Moore films as much. "Thunderball" is Tom Jones talking about balls—I know a number of gays who love that song. SHIRLEY BASSEY's "Diamonds Are Forever" is wonderful. NANCY SINATRA's "You Only Live Twice" is really beautiful. The *Goldfinger* soundtrack has a great surf instrumental version of "Goldfinger" with a definite DICK DALE influence. John Barry also did a classic score for *Beat Girl,* available on CD.

Melody Maker asked Scott Walker, "What's your favorite pastime, Scott?" and he answered, "Brooding." "Well—what do you do when you're not on the road?" "I think about World War Three."

Here's a James Bond-ploitation album, one of many: *Music to Read James Bond By.* I love the cover with the gold-painted girl reading the books—it's up there with the Nelson Riddle cover, *Witchcraft,* which shows a Satanic woman with black hair lying on aluminum foil—skull, books, and candle nearby. The best cuts here are FERRANTE AND TEICHER's "James Bond Theme," and "Goldfinger" by Perez Prado.

♦ V: *Do you really like easy listening music like Percy Faith?*

♦ BK: Percy Faith is a lot more saccharine, with gross piano-with-strings arrangements: complete Muzak which I can't take much of without getting vomitous.

♦ SS: It's funny—in the easy listening section you'll find Percy Faith but you'll also find ESQUIVEL, which is much more wild and wacky. But if you get stuck with the real easy listening, it's boring—there's no way around it. Like the Baja Marimba Band—I heard one album and that was enough for me!

♦ BK: Now here's *The Exciting World of Buddy Merrill & His Guitars.* He's one step below Billy Strange, and Billy Strange is a poor man's Dick Dale. The cover shows BUDDY MERRILL standing in front of the world globe at Leisure World, Laguna Hills, California—a planned retirement community where all the old people ride around on tricycles. This is a really good album; it contains the *Third Man* theme and the *Green Hornet* theme (that was my favorite show when I was a kid). This is like Chet Atkins meets surf guitar, but it sounds tinny, not deep. I'm collecting all of Buddy Merrill's albums now.

RUSTY WARREN's most famous album is *Knock-*ers Up. I also found *Rusty Warren Bounces Back,* a two-LP set with such numbers as "When a Woman Waits for the Signal to be Wanted." Another good album is *Sin-sational* (where she looks like John Wayne in drag). She's like a wacky, gravel-voiced, sea hag comedian: "Girls, let me tell you something!" It's always good to put this on the answering machine if you don't want anyone to call you. I like her a lot.

Here's SANDY POSEY: *Looking at You.* She has a wonderful beehive hairdo . . . a definite Myra Hindley look. Her genre is somewhere between '60s country, and girl group. She does songs that are so sad—she's a real heartbroken, always-getting-fucked-over kind of woman. Her albums are great, except for her final release, *Why Don't We Go Somewhere and Love,* recorded after she "found god."

♦ V: *"Born A Woman," "Shades of Gray," "Sunglasses," "Standing in the Rain," and "The Big Hurt" are so poignant. All the songs on The Best of Sandy Posey are classics.*

♦ AJ: *This reminds me of OLIVIA NEWTON-JOHN, who did some incredible songs: "Magic," "Heart Attack," "You're The One I Want" and "Xanadu."*

♦ SS: We haven't talked much about the '70s, but the BILLY JACK soundtracks have incredible songs on them. There's one by this girl with an acoustic guitar singing, "Why is there war? Why is there killing?"

♦ BK: His movies are so violent. The hero *tries* to be a just, peaceful man, but against his will he's constantly forced to knock off men left and right. The star, Tom Laughlin, is supposedly a Jungian authority now—he's written three books on Jung. My favorite scene in *Billy Jack* is when he goes to visit the shaman—was that influenced by *The Teachings of Don Juan?* I'd like to see *Billy Jack Goes to Washington.*

Rusty Warren's *Sin-Sational,* © 1974 GNP Crescendo Records, Inc. Album cover credits: cover design: Stephen Hass Studio.

♦ SS: As you come into the early '70s, the pain threshold increases dramatically. Music really took a turn for the worse—

♦ BK: Your basic "Tie a Yellow Ribbon 'Round the Old Oak Tree" type of song (that was by Tony Orlando and Dawn).

♦ *V: Didn't Tony Orlando die?*

♦ BK: No, that was Freddie Prinze—same era. They were friends and they looked alike, too.

Stuart crossed the pain threshold when he got into the Doobie Brothers and America.

♦ SS: "Black Water" starts out really slow and then goes into this weird *a capella* "I wanna hear some funky Dixieland/pretty mama come take me by the hand."

"Ventura Highway" by America defines our generation's music. It wasn't Elvis or Jefferson Airplane, it was songs like "Horse With No Name" or "Grand Illusion" by Styx. Seals & Croft, Cat Stevens, Josie & the Pussycats, Brady Bunch, Flintstones, Kiss, Linda Blair—that shit is *our* generation. Enough time has gone by that we can go back and examine this music and wonder, "How could this have been popular? What was going on?"

♦ BK: We haven't crossed the Eagles' line yet—"Hotel California" is our limit.

♦ BK: There *is* stuff we just can't handle, like Black Oak Arkansas. I've been getting into Christopher Cross, who did "Sailing" and "Ride with the Wind."

♦ SS: The CARPENTERS are great. Have you seen that Karen Carpenter film made with Barbie dolls? It's really well done and very funny. The filmmakers got sued and I don't know what happened to it. Against the '70s, the CARPENTERS stand out so strongly.

♦ BK: They represent the essence of the suburbs. Herb Alpert discovered them, and their sound is so overproduced and layered with vocals, they sound like angels singing in heaven.

♦ SS: "Rainy Days and Mondays" really conjures up a suburban house where the housewife is at home, morbidly depressed and on tranquilizers. And I like "We've Only Just Begun"—that was a cover of a bank commercial written by Paul Williams. Richard Carpenter spotted it on TV and they made a number one smash hit out of it.

♦ *AJ: You obviously enjoy the Carpenters, but they also cause you pain—*

♦ BK: There's many levels of listening to music. I never listened to Led Zeppelin as a kid, so when I listen to them now they sound completely ridiculous and bombastic—Robert Plant trying to be a white bluesman?! (They're still great!) But something like Perez Prado really *is* wonderful to listen to—it's great music and he has wonderful musicians.

♦ SS: We don't think of our childhoods as necessarily the most fun time—there is this pain value in listening to songs that we heard growing up.

♦ *AJ: You can look back on and rediscover a past*

The Exciting World of Buddy Merrill & His Guitars, Accent Records.

that you never experienced, like the Three Suns and Ferrante and Teicher—

♦ BK: I'm more alienated from the Rolling Stones than I am from America and Christopher Cross. Actually, Stuart and I are also heavily into metal music, like Sabbath (*Paranoid*'s one of the best albums), Motorhead (especially *Ace of Spades* and *Orgasmatron*), Judas Priest, early Metallica, and Deep Purple ("Space Truckin,'" "Highway Star" and "Smoke on the Water"). Venom is an incredible group; they're either Italian or they record in Italy and they're the *worst*. They go for the Satanic angle just to make some bucks, and do backward masking but it's completely technically incompetent. In that sense, they're really raw and kitsch. But you can listen to them and enjoy them on some very primal level.

There's no kitsch value for us attached to Motorhead. If there's any hero worship we involve ourselves in, Lemmy's definitely one of the heroes of our lives. But the question is: can you listen to *both* Martin Denny and Motorhead?

♦ *V: What do you think of jazz?*

♦ BK: We don't listen to Keith Jarrett or anything that's completely pretentious; we listen to what real jazzbos *hate*, like Stan Getz or Cal Tjader or JIMMY SMITH (the greatest organist, up there with George Wright; *The Champ* is an incredible album). Stan Getz's soundtrack to the Arthur Penn film *Mickey One* is really amazing.

♦ BK: The whole BOSSA NOVA scene I will definitely get into.

♦ SS: Walter Wanderly organ music can be amazing, too—almost Jetsonoid. There's a record of Walter Wanderly and Astrud Gilberto together that's fantastic. Walter had a huge hit with "Summer Samba," and it immediately reminds you of summers back in the '60s.

When I heard ABBA's "Dancing Queen" after a long time, it conjured up *so much*. They're also sonic artifacts of that time.

◆ BK: And we're definitely into alternate history. Why uphold Elvis when there was Martin Denny; why uphold the Rolling Stones when there was Sandy Posey? We are into the lesser-known, more obscure and also more absurd sides of life.

◆ SS: There *are* things people would like to forget, like BARRY WHITE.

◆ BK: He's so big and mean and dresses like a pimp—what's romantic about a 500-lb man on top of you?

◆ SS: But all these white middle-aged housewives regarded him as their record to jack off to. I once saw him "live"—he did his greatest hits; I couldn't have asked for a better show. He brought up a young black couple from the audience and asked them their names, and then said [bass voice], "Well, when Sean here makes love to you, does he make you tingle from head to toe?" and she goes [high voice], "Ooh, yes!" Then he asks, "Does he undress you, or do you undress yourself?" She said, "Well, uh—I usually undress myself." Then he said, "Junior—we're gonna have a *talk* after the show!" This poor kid's just standing there with a shit-eating grin . . . it must have been the most embarrassing moment in his life.

◆ BK: The record covers always show him sweating like an animal. All the songs are about foreplay—no insertion, just foreplay. He really likes to make it last—

◆ SS: —and make it beautiful. I remember seeing the three girls from *Love Unlimited* on the Merv Griffin show, and Merv asked them, "What's it like to go on the road with a man like Barry White?" They replied, "Oh . . . we call him the *Warden.*" When we first started listening to him, it *was* this kitsch thing, but he *is* great and we eventually got to love his records. "Love Theme" was one of the top five hits of the '70s—it's an orchestra and wah-wah guitar combination with no lyrics. "I'm Gonna Love You Just a Little Bit More" has a great groove for dancing, and the lyrics are so sleazy. When you listen to him say [bass voice], "Take off that brassiere/my dear" or "Take off your baby blue panties," you can't help but respond.

◆ BK: I'd rather hear Barry White than Whitney Houston; I don't want to listen to white black music. I like black music when it exuded Afro-Sheen instead of Jheri Curls. Barry White and Isaac Hayes personify blaxploitation films and soundtracks to me.

◆ **V: *Have you gotten into blaxploitation soundtracks?***

◆ SS: *Gordon's War* is pretty good, with the guy from *Sounder*, Paul Winfield—especially "Supershine Number Nine." *Superfly* is incredible, and so is *Shaft. The Together Brothers* is a real scary one. *Foxy Brown*—the cover looks great but it's kinda bland.

◆ BK: WILD CHERRY did "Play That Funky Music, White Boy." KC & THE SUNSHINE BAND is one of my favorite bands ever—yet I hated them when I was a

Nelson Riddle's, *Witchcraft!*, Pickwick/33 Records.

kid. The ISLEY BROTHERS' "Fight the Power" is a great song.

◆ SS: Unlike '70s black music like OHIO PLAYERS' "Love Rollercoaster" (which is great), the soundtracks aren't even real songs. They're usually sleazy atmospheric porno soundtracks that set the mood. I don't think any post-'70s music can conjure up that sense of degradedness conveyed by a certain wah-wah guitar, plus strings.

◆ BK: You think of red hot pants and long white boots.

◆ SS: You can find incredible disco songs that are so sleazy they also sound like a porn soundtrack. If you listen to them now, they're great—so refreshing. There's no rhythm machines or synthesizers on them. "Jungle Fever" by the CHAKACHAS is just this Latin woman going "Aiii! Aiii! Que Fievre! Aiiiiii!" This was before Donna Summer. At the end you hear them go [exhausted] "Uhhh," and they start snoring.

The soundtrack to *Patty,* a movie about Patty Hearst, has a song "Gotta Get a Gun" which is sung like a deep-throated gospel disco song—like the TRAMMPS' "Burn Baby Burn/Disco Inferno": "Gotta get a gun/ gotta shoot the police" and "You can't fight the police with a flower." One incredibly strange black group is the LAST POETS. They were the earliest rappers; they did graphic songs about people on heroin, like "Run Nigger Run." Allegedly Gil Scott-Heron stole his song "The Revolution Will Not Be Televised" from them—that was a song on their first album. They did great black power stuff critiquing black apathy at the time. Very simple music went with it: bongos, drums. Ten years later they were still doing rap songs—

◆ BK: And they were heavily into conspiracy theories, *Illuminati*-type raps.

◆ SS: They got into the symbolism of the dollar bill; to them "E Pluribus Unum" meant "one oppressor for the many." "Jones Coming Down" is one of the great heroin songs—not in a glamorizing *Velvet Underground* way, but the opposite, where the kid's nose is running and the wife's out hooking on the corner and the guy's dick is dripping . . .

♦ BK: It shouldn't even be talked about, it's so obvious now, but all the early George Clinton/Funkadelic/Parliament records are classics.

♦ SS: And remember, "Maggot Brain" has liner notes by the Process Church.

♦ *V: Can you think of more records featuring women that you like?*

♦ BK: A compilation album, *Va Va Voom*, has screen goddesses singing songs, and Sophia Loren has the worst voice in the world.

♦ *AJ: Whereas anything by Jayne Mansfield is sexy and fun . . . What are your criteria for judging records?*

♦ SS: A certain twistedness, where the intent was one thing but the result is something else. It could work on a lot of different levels. But what you get is something bigger than the sum of the parts.

♦ BK: The same thing with incredibly strange films: Ed Wood did not intend his films to come out the way they did. But if somebody today tries to make an Ed Wood film, it's horrible and *camp-lite*. For all their kitschiness—

♦ *V: —which is sometimes in the eye of the beholder rather than in the record itself—*

♦ BK: —these records must have *some* aesthetic and principle.

♦ SS: I think there's an unconsciousness on the part of the people doing it that makes a difference. If you get George Wright on a huge pipe organ (which you associate with cathedrals) playing the theme from *Mannix*—that's weird.

♦ BK: And *Mannix* was a show we saw when we were kids—so our appreciation involves cultural identification. Our generation didn't have the "Golden Age of Television"—we had all the *dross*.

♦ SS: A lot of these songs or pieces of music are really haunting. They come out of some strange space . . . an underside of Americana, a normality that's scary. Who was this music intended for—somebody's grandmother? What was *she* doing listening to this? It addresses normal people's desire for something mysterious, exotic, and bigger than their own lives.

♦ BK: I'd much rather experience music and film than static art (sculpture, painting, photography) because it's a lot more visceral—less elitist. I'd rather buy 50 albums for 50 cents each than buy one Warhol or Rauschenberg for $10,000. And it's nice to be able to read a book or listen to an album by yourself in the privacy of your own home.

♦ *AJ: These albums addressed people's needs.*

♦ SS: Yet a record doesn't have to have massive sales to be compelling; it could be Irma Glen's *Music, Ecology, and You*. One person's strange vision can

be very appealing.

♦ BK: And Irma Glen can be just as odd as Rod McKuen—god knows why Rod McKuen was so popular while Irma Glen just put out one album that ten people bought. And we haven't talked about John Cage—I usually hate that shit. In general I can't listen to avant-garde music. We went to a Derek Bailey concert and reacted completely on this *National Enquirer* level: "My kid could do that!" It's a reactionary stance, perhaps, but we couldn't get into it. But we *could* get into seeing George Wright play organ.

♦ *AJ: Most "New Music" events make you want to retch; they're performed by people with an academic mindset referencing what they do to other references.*

♦ BK: Stuart tried to introduce Martin Denny to these New Music Festival people, but they weren't interested. They couldn't accept the idea that Martin Denny was an American composer.

♦ SS: When academics try to create something strange, they're so cerebral. They think they're elaborating something new, but these other people come at this problem from an "anything goes" spirit, so the result of them *not* trying to address some tradition can make for music that's much more original.

For me, there's something archeological about hunting for these records. A thrift store displays all this debris, all these pieces of history that aren't in the history books yet illuminate the time. Just as a pottery shard tells you about an ancient civilization, so "Quiet Village" can tell you a lot more about 1958 than a sociology book. Records are the last cheap archeological collectibles . . .

Music to Live By, Mercury Records.

♪♪♪♪♪

The "Pig-o-Phone," devised for the court of King Louis XI, was a keyboard with wires attached to a row of 20 or more pigs. When the French Abbe de Baigne began to play, out of the strange bedlam came the notes of an old French air, squealed harmoniously by the line of singing swine. Sharp spikes at the ends of each wire effectively produced the proper squeal at the proper time when he struck the corresponding keys. —**John Hix, "Strange Music Makers"**

♪♪♪♪♪

The Bohemian general Zizka, who fought to give the Hussites religious freedom, ordered that when death should overtake him, his skin should be stripped from his body and made into a drumhead. His own skin reverberated to the beat of drumsticks at the head of the army he had once led in person.—**John Hix, "Strange Music Makers"**

♪♪♪♪♪

Without the help of poetry which fixes its ideas, music would always remain vague and indeterminate. This is why these two sciences were never separated in Antiquity. They even added to them that of the dance . . . A perfect music can never exist without the union of three things: the word that determines the idea, the melody that communicates to it the sentiment, and the rhythmic movement that characterizes its expression. Music separated from poetry and become purely instrumental is a kind of soul deprived of a body that falls into vaguenesses and lacks the means to make its beauties felt. Do not separate, if you can avoid it, the three sisters who love each other ardently and who embellish one another.—**Fabre d'Olivet, *Music Explained as Science and Art***

♪♪♪♪♪

There exists an unheard music all around us, even permeating our own bodies. All matter is perpetually in a state of vibration. The fact that a certain range of vibrations affects our sense of hearing as sound, deafens us (for better or worse) to the immensely wider range of vibrations which we cannot hear.—**Joscelyn Godwin, *Harmonies of Heaven and Earth***

♪♪♪♪♪

In a western chase scene, you have the sound of the horses' hooves blending with the background music, until it's not clear which is music and which is the sound of the horses. I think that's good.—**Louis Barron, interviewed by Ted Greenwald**

♪♪♪♪♪

Under laboratory conditions, the Swiss scientist Hans Jenny has photographed the effects that *tone* has on smoke, fluid, and the finest granular substances such as lycopodium powder: it forms them into beautiful and orderly shapes. Jenny calls his new science "Cymatics," dedicated to the study of creative vibration on every level from the molecule to the galaxy. —**Joscelyn Godwin, *Ibid***

♪♪♪♪♪

Giovanni Battista Porta wrote in 1558 that diseases could be cured by music if played on instruments made from the stalks or wood of plants having the appropriate curative properties.—**Joscelyn Godwin, *Ibid***

♪♪♪♪♪

Martianus Capella mentions the charming of stags by shepherds' pipes, the clattering sounds that cause fish to stop swimming, the strains of the cithara that attract the Hyperborean swans, and the Indian elephants and cobras that can be restrained by music, the latter bursting asunder from the effect.—**Joscelyn Godwin, *Ibid***

♪♪♪♪♪

(Athanasius Kircher witnessed, on a journey to Sicily in May 1638): The fishermen attracted their prey by sounding bells and singing a certain song—*no other would do*—whereupon the swordfish came close enough to be harpooned.—**J. Godwin, *Ibid***

♪♪♪♪♪

Music evokes emotions, heightens the sensations of coitus, and offers a different environment from the "real" one surrounding the lovers.—**Gil Lamont & Douglas Wise, *Sex in Music***

Muzzy Marcellino's *Birds of A Feather*, Liberty Records.

🎶🎶🎶🎶🎶

The musicians who were summoned asked the patient the color and size of her tarantula so they could adapt their music accordingly, but the patient replied she did not know if she had been bitten by a tarantula or by a scorpion. They began trying out their themes: at the fourth, the tarantulee immediately began to sigh, and at last, no longer able to resist the call of the dance, she leapt half naked from her bed, without a thought for conventions, and for three days kept up a sprightly dance, after which she was cured.—**G. Baglivi, quoted in Ernesto De Martino's** *La terra del rimorso*

🎶🎶🎶🎶🎶

The rhythms of heard music can guide the couple in the thrust and withdrawal of coitus, making sure that they are working in unison . . . No bedroom is complete without some method of introducing music to the environment.—**Lamont & Wise,** *op cit*

🎶🎶🎶🎶🎶

Not only does recorded music offer a topic of conversation, it also fills those awkward gaps when one can't think of the right thing to say. Silences are often embarrassing. One tends to feel self-conscious and insecure in those painful silences, and nothing can destroy a mood faster than that. This is a real problem, as every enlisted man in the Navy well knows.—**Lamont & Wise,** *Sex in Music*

🎶🎶🎶🎶🎶

Music is invaluable in crime prevention; nothing is more powerful than music in acting as an *emotional stabilizer.* A surprisingly small number of inmates have had former musical training, especially in their young years. Teach your boy to blow a horn, and he will not blow a safe!—*San Quentin Sports News*

🎶🎶🎶🎶🎶

That old legend of the Orient: the rules of music were formed in order to tame the wild animals, and to bring harmony into the world.—**Sacheverell Sitwell, "Orpheus and His Lyre"**

🎶🎶🎶🎶🎶

The "Armonica" was a strange instrument invented and played by Benjamin Franklin. Glass discs [arranged in ascending size] vibrated pleasantly when Franklin applied wet fingertips to them as they were rotated by a foot treadle.—**John Hix, "Strange Music Makers"**

🎶🎶🎶🎶🎶

A tiny pipe organ only one foot high, yet complete in every detail, was built for Titania's Palace, the famous fairy castle of visionary Sir Neville Wilkinson. The keys were so small they had to be played with a matchstick . . . J.F. Pearson, an unemployed English musician, built an organ from old tin cans, scrap lumber and string. It plays well, and critics claim that its tone is comparable to that of expensive theater organs.—**John Hix, "Strange Music Makers"**

🎶🎶🎶🎶🎶

At the World Peace Jubilee in Boston, 1872, Patrick Gilmore, the Barnum of the music world, assembled the greatest array of musicians ever to play together. In all, there were *22,860* musicians under his direction! As a climax to his mammoth musicale, Gilmore astounded his audience with a rendition of Verdi's "Anvil Chorus" from *Il Trovatore.* Ten Boston firemen beat lustily on 50 anvils, and a battery of cannon outside the great hall let go a tremendous salvo when Gilmore triumphantly touched an electric button.—**John Hix, "Strange Music Makers"**

🎶🎶🎶🎶🎶

Violins have been made from glass, metal, sugar, a

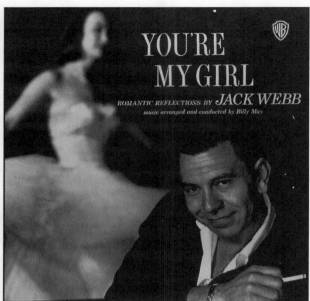

Jack Webb's *You're My Girl*, © 1958 Warner Bros. Records, Inc. Album cover credits: cover photo: Bert Six.

steer's horn, and even the jawbone of a mule. A man in New Jersey built a violin that stood 14 feet high. A St. Louis artisan made one only 2-1/2 inches long, and it really played.—**John Hix, "Strange Music Makers"**

♪♪♪♪♪

In 1875 a German invented the pyrophone, which produced *real* "hot music." It consisted of various glass tubes of different lengths which gave forth musical tones as a hydrogen gas flame played up and down within them.—**John Hix, "Strange Music Makers"**

♪♪♪♪♪

The man who invented bagpipes got his idea from stepping on a cat.—**Lord Dewar**

♪♪♪♪♪

The new style of music quietly insinuates itself into manners and customs, and from these it issues a greater force, and goes on to attack laws and constitutions, displaying the utmost impudence, until it ends by overturning everything, both in public and in private.—**Plato**

♪♪♪♪♪

Music modifies the respiratory and cardiac rhythm which is slowed down or speeded up . . . At a concert, when the musical motor shuts off, not only is there a liberating violence of ovations and handclapping but also a thunderstorm of sneezing, coughing, scraping of feet—as if everyone suddenly reacquired possession of his own body.—**Paul Virilio, *The Aesthetics of Disappearance***

♪♪♪♪♪

What we need most of all is an explanation for the probable connection between the latest changes in music and the increase in noise. The progress of music is based on and conditioned by the necessity of constantly overcoming fatigue. And the fatigue of the ear has been hastened or aggravated by the alarming increase in noise to which modern life is subjecting us. Probably our whole nervous system is affected by it, and not to its profit. Where two hundred years ago melodious street-calls announced the approach of itinerant vendors and the song of an ungreased axle merely emphasized the ordinary stillness, we have now the involved and strident counterpoint of traffic over an ostinato of policemen's whistles and automobile horns . . . Truly the art of music is hard put to devise new stimuli wherewith to counteract the growing aural disturbance.—**Carl Engel, "Harking Back and Looking Forward," 1928**

♪♪♪♪♪

Noise tenses muscles, causes stress and a sudden rise in blood pressure, and changes the diameter of the blood vessels.—**Robert Baron, *The Tyranny of Noise***

♪♪♪♪♪

When Buddy Bolden heard Jelly Roll Morton playing, he said, "That ain't no music. The notes is written out, tellin' you what's gonna come next. That's like wakin' up an' knowin' you gonna be alive at the end of the day."—**from *Jelly's Last Jam,* Broadway musical staring Gregory Hines**

♪♪♪♪♪

[describing how she created each new operatic role] You take the music and you learn it as though you were in the conservatory. In other words, exactly as it's written, nothing more and nothing less, which is what I call *strait-jacketing.* Having broken this down completely, *then* you can take wings!—**Maria Callas, quoted in Arianna Stassinopoulos' biography**

♪♪♪♪♪

The greatest difficulties lie where we are not looking for them.—**Goethe**

♪♪♪♪♪

I love the convenience of CDs, but it's too bad you can't buy the older records, too. It's almost like feeling that you can't buy *books.*—**Yo Yo Ma**

♪♪♪♪♪

When power wants to make people forget, music is ritual sacrifice, the scapegoat; when it wants them to believe, music is enactment, representation; when it wants to silence them it is reproduced, normalized, repetition . . . Listening to music is listening to all noise, realizing that its appropriation and control is a reflection of power, that it is essentially *political*.—**Jacques Attali**, *Noise*

♪♪♪♪♪

Intuition is intelligence that is speeding.—**Bernstein**

♪♪♪♪♪

In 1906 Thaddeus Cahill exhibited in Holyoke, Massachusetts, his "dynamophone" or "telharmonium," the first instrument to make music by electrical means. It apparently weighed two hundred tons and generated sounds from dynamos, transmitting them over telephone wires. Nothing now remains of this dinosaur of electronic music, apart from a couple of faded photographs.—**Paul Griffiths**, *A Guide to Electronic Music*

♪♪♪♪♪

When music was first recorded a century ago, it started on a path of abstraction that separated it from the flesh-and-blood live performer.—**Jon Pareles**, *New York Times*

♪♪♪♪♪

"Gamelan" is a general word for an instrumental ensemble ranging in size from a few small instruments to an impressive set of over fifty. The music played usually involves repeating patterns of punctuation and time-marking, mirroring in musical sound local conceptions of *cyclic time*.—**R. Anderson Sutton**, *Music of Indonesia*

♪♪♪♪♪

Originally with church and tribal music, the making of the sound itself brought you into the state of trance

Beat Tropicale, © 1956 Concert-Disc/Concertapes, Inc.

and meditation, adoration or ecstasy. Now music is used as an acoustical tapestry or, at best, something to identify with: a particular emotion that's dominating at the moment.—**Stockhausen, quoted in Paul Griffiths**, *Ibid*

♪♪♪♪♪

They tell me that I was the first gal singer to hit the big time with one record: "Cow-Cow Blues" sold way over a million, I hear. I wasn't getting royalties—man, I made thirty-five bucks on it. Isn't that the end?—**Ella Mae Morse, quoted in Nick Tosches'** *Unsung Heroes of Rock'n'Roll*

♪♪♪♪♪

People hate those who make them feel their own inferiority.—**4th Earl of Chesterfield**

♪♪♪♪♪

Nowadays the illiterate can read and write.—**Alberto Moravia**

♪♪♪♪♪

The first sampler was Frederick Sammis' 1936 photoelectric *Singing Keyboard*. Built in Hollywood for commercial purposes, it used loops of optical sound film.—**Douglas Kahn, "Audio Art in the Deaf Century,"** *Sound By Artists*

♪♪♪♪♪

Other predecessors of Sammis' instrument included the Noisegraph, the Dramagraph, the Kinematophone, the Soundograph or the Excelsior Sound Effect Cabinet . . . from whose keyboards and associated equipment came galloping horses, railroad whistles and bells, rooster crows, mockingbird calls, tugboat whistles, anvil strikes, marching feet, frog croaks, water splashes, and the blowing of noses.—**Raymond Fielding, "The Technological Antecedents of the Coming of Sound: An Introduction," quoted in** *Sound By Artists*

♪♪♪♪♪

Whistling is an off-the-wall kind of talent on which to base a life. No college of music offers a major in whistling. It is, however, a sort of magical gift, and there is always a place in the world for magic . . . People don't whistle much anymore. I guess it's a sign of the times. Whistling is a carefree, happy thing, and these aren't carefree, happy times. Everybody's uptight about something.—**Fred Lowery (the blind whistler) quoted in Richard Lamparski's** *Whatever Became Of . . . ? #11*

♪♪♪♪♪

It has often been said that music is the language of the emotions. Emotion is coextensive with consciousness;

Mohammed El Bakkar's *Exotic Music of The Belly Dancer*, © 1966 Audio Fidelity Records Inc. Album cover credits: art director: Charles Blodgett.

human consciousness itself is nothing but an uninterrupted concatenation of emotions. It would require volumes to analyze properly the emotional history of a single hour. Every thought which flits through the mind has its own accompanying emotion, or train of emotions . . . indeed, emotion is the very breath and lifeblood of thought.—**The Rev. H.R. Haweis,** *Music and Morals*

♪♪♪♪♪

We remember one strange man who bore the appearance of a North American Indian armed to the teeth, stuck all over generally with some two dozen or more instruments, and boasted that he could play most of them simultaneously. A drum, worked with a wire by one foot, rattled above his head; his mouth blew into such things as Pan-pipes, flutes, clarinets, horns and other tubes slung to his neck like an ox's cradle; one hand moved an accordion tied to his thigh, while a triangle jingled from his wrist; the other hand played the bones, while the elbow clapped a tambourine fixed to his side; on the inside of his knees were cymbals, which he kept knocking together. There was only one foot and ankle left, and on that ankle he had bells which rang with every moment. We describe from memory, and doubt whether we have detailed half the instruments.—**The Rev. H.R. Haweis,** *Ibid*

♪♪♪♪♪

Every one does not have the luck to be an orphan.—**Jules Renard**

♪♪♪♪♪

The function of the creative artist consists in making

laws, not in following laws already made.—**Ferruccio Busoni,** *Ibid*

♪♪♪♪♪

In 1928 the Soviets announced that the importing or playing of American jazz was punishable by a fine of one hundred rubles and six months in jail. The Ayatollah Khomeini imposes similar strictures.—**Evan Eisenberg,** *The Recording Angel*

♪♪♪♪♪

Clarence [who has a quarter of a million records] tells of a fellow collector in Brooklyn: "He's old now. Sweetest guy that ever lived. Oh, he has a collection that I'd love to get—he started in the twenties." The thing about this collector in Brooklyn: he's *deaf.*—**Evan Eisenberg,** *Ibid*

♪♪♪♪♪

Karlheinz Stockhausen has actually suggested using "acoustical garbage machines" or "sound swallowers" in public places which are computer-programmed to counter every noise with the contrary vibrations, thus cancelling it out and producing silence.—**Joscelyn Godwin,** *Music, Mysticism and Magic*

♪♪♪♪♪

Birds sing far more than is biologically necessary for the various forms of communication . . . the bird-song has partially escaped from practical usage to become an activity which is engaged in for its own sake: an expression of avian *joie de vivre.*—**Anthony Storr,** *Music and the Mind*

Sounds Nice: *Love at First Sight*, Rare Earth®. © 1970 Motown Record Corporation. Album cover credits: art director: Curtis McNair, graphic supervision: Tom Schlesinger, cover photography: Hendin.

NORTON RECORDS. $1 for great catalog from PO Box 646 Cooper Station, NYC 10003. 718-789-4438.

DOWN HOME Records. Call 510-525-2129 for catalog.

BEAR FAMILY Records. Send $5 US cash for catalog to PO Box 1154, 2864 Vollersode, Germany. Tel 04794-1399, Fax 04794-1574.

MIDNIGHT Records. Call 212-675-2768 for catalog.

SUBTERRANEAN Records. $1.50 for catalog from PO BOX 2530, Berkeley, CA 94702.

CIRCLE Records, 3008 Wadsworth Mill Place, Atlanta GA 30032-5899. *Three Suns 1949-1957* LP $13 ppd.

RHINO RECORDS. Send $3 for catalog to 2225 Colorado Ave, Santa Monica CA 90404-3598.

PERFORMANCE RECORDS. PO Box 156, New Brunswick NJ 08901. *Plan 9 From Outer Space; Tim Leary* LP $15 ea ppd.

SYMPOSIUM RECORDS. 110 Derwent Ave, East Barnet, Hertfordshire EN4 8LZ. Tel 081-368-8667. FAX 081-368-8667. *Emile Berliner's Gramophone* CD 13 pounds (about $27) postpaid by air. *Caruso* CD 10 pounds ($21) ppd air.

CYBERETHNIC US RENDITIONS. 1123 Dominguez St, Unit K; Carson CA 90746. (213) 604-9702. *Akira* soundtrack CD $25 ppd.

KINGSLEY SOUND, 150 West 55th St, NYC NY 10019. Gershon Kingsley's *Anima* CD $20 ppd.

EDITION BLOCK, Schaperstrasse 11, D-1000 Berlin 15, Germany. *Music by Marcel Duchamp* CD $27 ppd.

ARF! ARF! Records, PO Box 465, Middleborough MA 02346. Eric Lindgren, (617) 876-1646. *Lucia Pamela* CD $20 ppd.

SORDIDE SENTIMENTAL, BP 534, Rouen Cedex, France 76005. Beautiful, limited edition CD/book/artwork packages. Send 6 International Reply Coupons for catalog.

Candi Strecker's *'70s* Magazine $6 ppd from 590 Lisbon, SF CA 94112. Back issues available.

DUPLEX PLANET magazines & recordings. Send SASE to David Greenberger, PO Box 1230, Saratoga Springs, NY 12866. Ask about "Picnic Ape" and the "Talent Show" cassette.

INTRADA, soundtrack source. 1488 Vallejo St, San Francisco CA 94109. Tel 415-776-1333. $2 for catalog.

SOUNDTRACK! 4-issue subscription $15 US cash to Luc Van de Ven, Astridlaan 171, 2800 Mechelen, Belgium.

FILM SCORE MONTHLY. $15/year to Lukas Kendall, Box 1554 Amherst College, Amherst MA 01002-5000.

VESTAL Press. $2 for catalog to 320 N. Jensen Rd, PO Box 97, Vestal NY 13851-0097.

RADIUM Records, Sodra Allegatan 3, 413 01 Gothenburg, Sweden. $2 for catalog. Tel 3113-0039.

DISCoveries magazine. To subscribe: 206-385-1200.

Goldmine magazine. To subscribe: 800-258-0929.

SHANACHIE Music Videos & Music. 1-800-497-1043.

Record Price Guides available from Collector's Clearinghouse, PO Box 135, North Syracuse NY 13212.

Small Planet Records, Box 3799, Beverly Hills CA 90212. *Forbidden Planet* soundtrack LP $15.

CARNAGE PRESS, PO Box 627, Northampton MA 01060. 413-549-2923. *Beat of the Traps* LP $13 ppd.

Cassette catalog (including William S. Burroughs) $1 from Sound Photosynthesis, PO Box 2111, Mill Valley CA 94942.

BINAURAL SOURCE for binaural headphone recordings (amazing sound for cheap). Catalog $1 from Box 1727, Ross CA 94957. 415-457-9052.

SOME VINYL RECORD SOURCES: Medium Rare 415-255-7273. Asta's 510-654-0335. Jack's 415-431-3047. Revolver 415-386-6128. Collector's 415-459-2870. Craig Moerer 503-232-1735. Get Hip 412-231-4766. Roundup Records 1-800-44-DISCS. Big Al's 408-241-7337. Jazz Quarter 415-661-2331. Mosaic Jazz Records, catalog 203-327-7111. Chuck Cleaver 513-734-2987 (PO Box 148, Bethel OH 45106).

GIORNO POETRY SYSTEMS. $1 for catalog from 222 Bowery, NY NY 10012.

Hillbilly Researcher. Sample issue $6 US cash from 20 Silkstream Rd, Burnt Oak, Edgware, Middlesex HA8 0DA, U.K.

78 Quarterly. Latest issue $10 US cash from PO Box 283, Key West FL 33041.

Musical Traditions. Sample issue $6 US cash from 98 Ashingdon Rd, Rochford, Essex SS4 1RE, U.K.

Cadence. Sample issue $5 US cash from The Cadence Building, Redwood NY 13679-9612. 315-287-2852.

3-D catalog $2 from Reel 3-D Enterprises, PO Box 35, Duarte CA 91010. 818-357-8345.

POCIAO, PO Box 190136, Bonn 1, D5300 Germany. Send $3 US cash for catalog. Source for W.S. Burroughs cassettes & books, etc.

Send 4 IRCs for catalog to Side Effects Records, BCM Mythos, London WC1N 3XX, U.K.

Send $1 for catalog to Charnel House, PO Box 170277, SF CA 94117-0277.

Steel Guitar Record Club, PO Box 931, Concord CA 94522. Send SASE.

Epitapes. Send $1 for catalog to Mike Tetrault, PO Box 458, Sunderland MA 01375.

SHAGGS CD $15 from Rounder Records, PO Box 154, N Cambridge MA 02140.

Catalog

RE/Search #14: Incredibly Strange Music Volume I

Enthusiastic, hilarious interviews illuminate the territory of neglected vinyl records (c.1950-1980) ignored by the music criticism establishment. Genres include: outer space exploration; abstract female vocals; tiki "exotica" (featuring bird calls and jungle sounds); motivational (*How to Overcome Discouragement* and *Music to Make Automobiles By*—made for factory workers); promotional (giveaways like *Rhapsody of Steel,* produced by U.S. Steel); lurid stripping and belly dancing (which often included instruction booklets); easy listening; and experimental instrumental (which used Theremin, Ondioline, Moog, whistling, harmonica, sitar, accordion and organ). Lavishly illustrated, with reference sections, quotations, sources and an index, this is a comprehensive guide to the last remaining "garage sale" records. Volume I (Volume 2 scheduled for Fall 1993): 8½x11", 208 pp, over 200 photos & illustrations.

$17.99

Featuring:

- ◆ **Eartha Kitt**
- ◆ **The Cramps**
- ◆ **Martin Denny**
- ◆ **Amok Books**
- ◆ **Norton Records**
- ◆ **Perrey & Kingsley**
- ◆ **Mickey McGowan (Unknown Museum)**
- ◆ **Phantom Surfers**
- ◆ **Lypsinka**
- ◆ **Mike Wilkins (author, *Roadside America*)**
- ◆ **and others . . .**

RE/Search #13: Angry Women

Featuring:

- Karen Finley
- Annie Sprinkle
- Diamanda Galás
- bell hooks
- Kathy Acker
- Avital Ronell
- Lydia Lunch
- Sapphire
- Susie Bright
- Valie Export
- Wanda Coleman
- Linda Montano
- Holly Hughes
- Suzy Kerr & Dianne Malley ◆ Carolee Schneemann

16 cutting-edge performance artists discuss critical questions such as: How can you have a revolutionary feminism that encompasses wild sex, humor, beauty and spirituality *plus* radical politics? How can you have a powerful movement for social change that's *inclusionary*—not exclusionary? A wide range of topics—from menstruation, masturbation, vibrators, S&M & spanking to racism, failed Utopias and the death of the Sixties—are discussed passionately. Armed with total contempt for dogma, stereotype and cliche, these creative visionaries probe deep into our social foundation of taboos, beliefs and totalitarian linguistic contradictions from whence spring (as well as thwart) our theories, imaginings, behavior and dreams. 8½x11", 240 pp, 135 photos & illustrations.

$18.99

"In this illustrated, interview-format volume, 16 women performance artists animatedly address the volatile issues of male domination, feminism, race and denial. Incendiary opinions of current issues such as the Gulf War and censorship and frequent allusions to empowering art and literature make this an excellent reference source. These informed discussions arm readers verbally, philosophically and behaviorally and provide uncompromising role models for women actively seeking change." —
PUBLISHER'S WEEKLY

"This is hardly the nurturing, Womanist vision espoused in the 1970s. For the most part, these artists have given up waiting for the train of sexual equality . . . The view here is largely prosex, proporn, and prochoice . . . Separatism is out, community in. Sexuality is fluid, spirituality ancient and animist. Art and activism are inseparable from life and being. The body is a creative field, the mind an exercise in liberation. This is the 13th step, beyond AA's 12: a healing rage."
—**THE VILLAGE VOICE**

RE/Search #12: Modern Primitives

An eye-opening, startling investigation of the undercover world of body modifications: tattooing, piercing and scarification. Amazing, explicit photos! *Fakir Musafar* (55-yr-old Silicon Valley ad executive who, since age 14, has practiced every body modification known to man); *Genesis & Paula P-Orridge* describing numerous ritual scarifications and personal, symbolic tattoos; *Ed Hardy* (editor of *Tattootime* and creator of over 10,000 tattoos); *Capt. Don Leslie* (sword-swallower); *Jim Ward* (editor, *Piercing Fans International*); *Anton LaVey* (founder of the Church of Satan); *Lyle Tuttle* (talking about getting tattooed in Samoa); *Raelyn Gallina* (women's piercer) & others talk about body practices that develop identity, sexual sensation and philosophic awareness. This issue spans the spectrum from S&M pain to New Age ecstasy. 22 interviews, 2 essays (including a treatise on Mayan body piercing based on recent findings), quotations, sources/bibliography & index. 8½ x 11", 212 pp, 279 photos & illustrations.

$17.99

"**MODERN PRIMITIVES** is not some shock rag parading crazies for your amusement. All of the people interviewed are looking for something very simple: a way of fighting back at a mass production consumer society that prizes standardization above all else. Through 'primitive' modifications, they are taking possession of the only thing that any of us will ever really own: our bodies."
—**WHOLE EARTH REVIEW**

"The photographs and illustrations are both explicit and astounding . . . This is the ideal biker coffee table book, a conversation piece that provides fascinating food for thought." —**IRON HORSE**

"**MODERN PRIMITIVES** approaches contemporary body adornment and ritual from the viewpoint that today's society suffers from an almost universal feeling of powerlessness to change the world, leaving the choice for exploration, individuation and primitive rite of passage to be fought out on the only ground readily available to us: our bodies."—**TIME OUT**

"In a world so badly made, as ours is, there is only one road—rebellion."
—Luis Bunuel

"Habit is probably the greatest block to seeing truth." —R.A. Schwaller de Lubicz

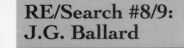

RE/Search #11: Pranks!

A prank is a "trick, a mischievous act, a ludicrous act." Although not regarded as poetic or artistic acts, pranks constitute an art form and genre in themselves. Here pranksters such as Timothy Leary, Abbie Hoffman, Paul Krassner, Mark Pauline, Monte Cazazza, Jello Biafra, Earth First!, Joe Coleman, Karen Finley, Frank Discussion, John Waters and Henry Rollins challenge the sovereign authority of words, images & behavioral convention. Some tales are bizarre, as when Boyd Rice presented the First Lady with a skinned sheep's head on a platter. This iconoclastic compendium will dazzle and delight all lovers of humor, satire and irony. 8½ x 11", 240 pp, 164 photos & illustrations.

$17.99

"The definitive treatment of the subject, offering extensive interviews with 36 contemporary tricksters. . . from the Underground's answer to Studs Terkel."
—**WASHINGTON POST**

RE/Search #8/9: J.G. Ballard

A comprehensive special on this supremely relevant writer, now famous for *Empire of the Sun* and *Day of Creation.* W.S. Burroughs described Ballard's novel *Love & Napalm: Export U.S.A.* (1972) as "profound and disquieting...This book stirs sexual depths untouched by the hardest-core illustrated porn." 3 interviews, biography by David Pringle, fiction and non-fiction excerpts, essays, quotations, bibliography, sources, & index. 8½ x 11", 176 pp. 76 photos & illustrations by Ana Barrado, Bobby Neel Adams, Ken Werner, Ed Ruscha, and others.

$14.99

"The RE/SEARCH to own if you must have just one . . . the most detailed, probing and comprehensive study of Ballard on the market."—**BOSTON PHOENIX**

"Highly recommended as both an introduction and a tribute to this remarkable writer."
—**WASHINGTON POST**

RE/Search #10: Incredibly Strange Films

A guide to important territory neglected by the film criticism establishment, spotlighting unhailed directors—*Herschell Gordon Lewis, Russ Meyer, Larry Cohen, Ray Dennis Steckler, Ted V. Mikels, Doris Wishman* and others—who have been critically consigned to the ghettos of gore and sexploitation films. In-depth interviews focus on philosophy, while anecdotes entertain as well as illuminate theory. 13 interviews, numerous essays, A-Z of film personalities, "Favorite Films" list, quotations, bibliography, filmography, film synopses, & index. 8½ x 11", 224 pp. 157 photos & illustrations.

$17.99

"Flicks like these are subversive alternatives to the mind control propagated by the mainstream media."
—**IRON HORSE**

"Whether discussing the ethics of sex and violence on the screen, film censorship, their personal motivations, or the nuts and bolts of filmmaking from financing through distribution, the interviews are intelligent, enthusiastic and articulate."—**SMALL PRESS**

RE/Search #4/5: W. S. Burroughs, Brion Gysin, Throbbing Gristle

Interviews, scarce fiction, essays: this is a manual of ideas and insights. Strikingly designed, with rare photos, bibliographies, discographies, chronologies & illustrations. 7 interviews, essays, chronologies, bibliographies, discographies, sources. 8½ x 11", 100 pp. 58 photos & illustrations.

$12.99

"Interviews with pioneering cut-up artists William S. Burroughs, Brion Gysin and Throbbing Gristle . . . proposes a ground-breaking, radical cultural agenda for the '80s and '90s."—Jon Savage, **LONDON OBSERVER**

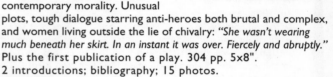

The Confessions of Wanda von Sacher-Masoch

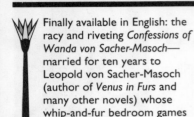

Finally available in English: the racy and riveting *Confessions of Wanda von Sacher-Masoch*—married for ten years to Leopold von Sacher-Masoch (author of *Venus in Furs* and many other novels) whose whip-and-fur bedroom games spawned the term "masoch-ism." In this feminist classic from 100 years ago, Wanda was forced to play "sadistic" roles in Leopold's fantasies to ensure the survival of herself and her 3 children—games which called into question who was the Master and who the Slave. Besides being a compelling study of a woman's search for her own identity, strength and ultimately—complete independence—this is a true-life adventure story—an odyssey through many lands peopled by amazing characters. Underneath its unforgettable poetic imagery and almost unbearable emotional cataclysms reigns a woman's consistent unblinking investigation of the limits of morality and the deepest meanings of love. Translated by Marian Phillips, Caroline Hébert & V. Vale. 8½ x 11", 136 pages, illustrations.

$13.99

"As with all RE/Search editions, *The Confessions of Wanda von Sacher-Masoch* is extravagantly designed, in an illustrated, oversized edition that is a pleasure to hold. It is also exquisitely written, engaging and literary and turns our preconceptions upside down."—LA READER

Freaks: We Who Are Not As Others by Daniel P. Mannix

Another long out-of-print classic book based on Mannix's personal acquaintance with sideshow stars such as the Alligator Man and the Monkey Woman, etc. Read all about the notorious love affairs of midgets; the amazing story of the elephant boy; the unusual amours of Jolly Daisy, the fat woman; the famous pinhead who inspired Verdi's *Rigoletto;* the tragedy of Betty Lou Williams and her parasitic twin; the black midget, only 34 inches tall, who was happily married to a 264-pound wife; the human torso who could sew, crochet and type; and bizarre accounts of normal humans turned into freaks—either voluntarily or by evil design! 88 astounding photographs and additional material from the author's personal collection. 8½ x 11", 124pp.

$13.99

SIGNED HARDBOUND: Limited edition of 300 signed by the author on acid-free paper **$50.00**

"RE/Search has provided us with a moving glimpse at the rarified world of physical deformity; a glimpse that ultimately succeeds in its goal of humanizing the inhuman, revealing the beauty that often lies behind the grotesque and in dramatically illustrating the triumph of the human spirit in the face of overwhelming debility."
—SPECTRUM WEEKLY

The Torture Garden by Octave Mirbeau

This book was once described as the "most sickening work of art of the nineteenth century!" Long out of print, Octave Mirbeau's macabre classic (1899) features a corrupt Frenchman and an insatiably cruel Englishwoman who meet and then frequent a fantastic 19th century Chinese garden where torture is practiced as an art form. The fascinating, horrific narrative slithers deep into the human spirit, uncovering murderous proclivities and demented desires. Lavish, loving detail of description. Illustrated with evocative, dream-like photos. Introduction, biography & bibliography. 8½ x 11", 120 pp, 21 photos. **$13.99**
HARDBOUND: Limited edition of 200 hardbacks on acid-free paper **$29.00**

". . . sadistic spectacle as apocalyptic celebration of human potential . . . A work as chilling as it is seductive."
—THE DAILY CALIFORNIAN

The Atrocity Exhibition by J.G. Ballard

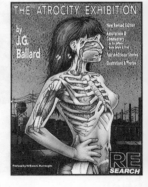

A large-format, illustrated edition of this long out-of-print classic, widely regarded as Ballard's finest, most complex work. Withdrawn by E.P. Dutton after having been shredded by Doubleday, this outrageous work was finally printed in a small edition by Grove before lapsing out of print 15 years ago. With 4 additional fiction pieces, extensive annotations (a book in themselves), disturbing photographs by Ana Barrado and dazzling, anatomically explicit medical illustrations by Phoebe Gloeckner. 8½ x 11", 136pp.

$13.99

SIGNED HARDBOUND: Limited Edition of 300 signed by the author on acid-free paper **$50.00**

"*The Atrocity Exhibition* is remarkably fresh. One does not read these narratives as one does other fiction . . . one enters into them as a kind of ritual . . ."
—SAN FRANCISCO CHRONICLE

RE/Search #1-2-3

Deep into the heart of the Control Process. Preoccupation: Creativity & Survival, past, present & future. These are the early tabloid issues, 11x17", full of photos & innovative graphics.

◆ **#1** J.G. Ballard, Cabaret Voltaire, Julio Cortazar, Octavio Paz, Sun Ra, *The Slits*, Robert K. Brown (editor, *Soldier of Fortune*), *Non*, Conspiracy Theory Guide, Punk Prostitutes, and more.

◆ **#2** *DNA*, James Blood Ulmer, *Z'ev*, Aboriginal Music, West African Music Guide, Surveillance Technology, Monte Cazazza on poisons, Diane Di Prima, Seda, German Electronic Music Chart, Isabelle Eberhardt, and more.

◆ **#3** Fela, New Brain Research, The Rattlesnake Man, Sordide Sentimental, New Guinea, Kathy Acker, Sado-Masochism (interview with Pat Califia); Joe Dante, Johanna Went, *SPK, Flipper*, Physical Modification of Women, and more.

$8.00 each.

SET OF RE/SEARCH 1-2-3: $17.99

> **"Who wishes to be creative, must first destroy and smash accepted values."**
> **— Nietzsche**

Search & Destroy:

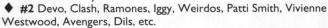

Incendiary interviews, passionate photographs, art brutal. Corrosive minimalist documentation of the only youth rebellion of the seventies: punk rock (1977-78). The philosophy and culture, BEFORE the mass media takeover and inevitable cloning.

◆ **#1** Premiere issue. Crime, Nuns, Global Punk Survey.

◆ **#2** Devo, Clash, Ramones, Iggy, Weirdos, Patti Smith, Vivienne Westwood, Avengers, Dils, etc.

◆ **#3** Devo, Damned, Patti Smith, Avengers, Tom Verlaine, Capt. Beefheart, Blondie, Residents, Alternative TV, Throbbing Gristle.

◆ **#4** Iggy, Dead Boys, Bobby Death, Jordan & the Ants, Mumps, Metal Urbain, Helen Wheels, Sham 69, Patti Smith.

◆ **#5** Sex Pistols, Nico, Crisis, Screamers, Suicide, Crime, Talking Heads, Anarchy, Surrealism & New Wave essay.

◆ **#6** Throbbing Gristle, Clash, Nico, Talking Heads, Pere Ubu, Nuns, UXA, Negative Trend, Mutants, Sleepers, Buzzcocks.

◆ **#7** John Waters, Devo, DNA, Cabaret Voltaire, Roky Erickson, Clash, Amos Poe, Mick Farren, Offs, Vermilion & more.

◆ **#8** Mutants, Dils, Cramps, Devo, Siouxsie, Chrome, Pere Ubu, Judy Nylon & Patti Palladin, Flesheaters, Offs, Weirdos, etc.

◆ **#9** Dead Kennedys, Rockabilly Rebels, X, Winston Tong, David Lynch, Television, Pere Ubu, DOA, etc.

◆ **#10** J.G. Ballard, William S. Burroughs, Feederz, Plugz, X, Russ Meyer, Steve Jones, etc. Reprinted by Demand!

◆ **#11** The all photo supplement. Black and White.

$4.00 each.

SEARCH & DESTROY: COMPLETE SET ISSUES #1-11 for only $39.00.

BOOKS DISTRIBUTED BY RE/SEARCH

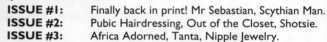

Body Art

From England, a glossy 8½ x 11" magazine devoted to tattoo, piercing, body painting, tribal influences, pubic hairdressing, *et al.* Outstanding explicit Color/B&W photographs, instructive text—a beautiful production. Approx. 48 pgs.

$17.00 EACH

ISSUE #1:	Finally back in print! Mr Sebastian, Scythian Man.
ISSUE #2:	Pubic Hairdressing, Out of the Closet, Shotsie.
ISSUE #3:	Africa Adorned, Tanta, Nipple Jewelry.
ISSUE #4:	Tattoo Expo '88, Tribal Influence, Male Piercings.
ISSUE #5:	Female Piercings, The Year of the Snake.
ISSUE #6:	Body Painting, Celtic Tattoos.
ISSUE #7:	Female Nipple Development, Plastic Bodies.
ISSUE #8:	Tattoo Symbolism, Piercing Enlargement.
ISSUE #9:	Tattoos, Nipple Piercing, The Perfect Body.
ISSUE #10:	Amsterdam Tattoo Convention, Cliff Raven.
ISSUE #11:	Ed Hardy, Fred Corbin, Beyond The Pain Barrier.
ISSUE #12:	Tattoo Expo '90, Genital Modifications.
ISSUE #13:	New Orleans Tattoo Convention 1990.
ISSUE #14:	Krystyne Kolorful, Paris Tattoo Convention.
ISSUE #15:	The Stainless Steel Ball, Bodyshots: Richard Todd
ISSUE #16:	Tattoo Expo '91, Indian Hand Painting, Nail Tattoos.

Please list an alternate title for all Body Art selections.

PopVoid #1: '60s Culture.
edited by Jim Morton

Edited by Jim Morton (who guest-edited *Incredibly Strange Films*). Fantastic anthology of neglected pop culture: Lawrence Welk, Rod McKuen, Paper Dresses, Nudist Colonies, Goofy Grape, etc. 8½ x 11", 100 pp.
$9.95

TattooTime
edited by Don Ed Hardy

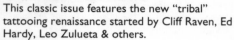

◆ **#1: NEW TRIBALISM.**
This classic issue features the new "tribal" tattooing renaissance started by Cliff Raven, Ed Hardy, Leo Zulueta & others.
$10.00

◆ **#2: TATTOO MAGIC.**
This issue examines all facets of Magic & the Occult.
$10.00

◆ **#3: MUSIC & SEA TATTOOS.**
Deluxe double book issue with over 300 photos.
$15.00

◆ **#4: LIFE & DEATH.**
Deluxe double book issue with fantastic photos, examining trademarks, architectural and mechanical tattoos, the Eternal Spiral, a Tattoo Museum, plus the gamut of Death imagery.
$15.00

◆ **#5: ART FROM THE HEART.**
All *NEW* issue that's bigger than ever before (128 pgs) with hundreds of color photographs. Featuring in-depth articles on tattooers, contemporary tattooing in Samoa, a survey of the new weirdo monster tattoos and much more!
$20.00

Halloween by Ken Werner

A classic photo book. Startling photographs from the "Mardi Gras of the West," San Francisco's *adult* Halloween festivities in the Castro district. Limited supply. Beautiful 9x12" hardback bound in black boards. 72 pgs. Black glossy paper.
$11.00

SPECIAL DISCOUNTS

Special Deluxe Offer (Save $80!)
Complete set of RE/Search serials plus reprints and complete set of Search & Destroy.

Offer includes Re/Search #1-2-3 tabloids, #4/5 Burroughs/Gysin/Throbbing Gristle, #6/7 Industrial Culture Handbook, #8/9 J.G. Ballard, #10 Incredibly Strange Films, #11 Pranks!, #12 Modern Primitives, #13: Angry Women, Search & Destroy Issues #1-11, The Confessions of Wanda von Sacher-Masoch, Freaks: We Who Are Not As Others, The Atrocity Exhibition, Torture Garden, the Willeford Trilogy and Me & Big Joe.
Special Discount Offer: $200 ppd. Seamail/Canada: $220. AIR Europe: $307. AIR Austr./Japan: $346.
FOR *RE/Search #14: Incredibly Strange Music* ADD ONLY $10.

PRICES FOR THE SPECIAL DISCOUNT OFFERS INCLUDE SHIPPING & HANDLING!

Special Discount Offer (Save $45!)
Complete set of all RE/Search serials

Offer includes the Re/Search #1-2-3 tabloids, #4/5 Burroughs/Gysin/Throbbing Gristle, #6/7 Industrial Culture Handbook, #8/9 J.G. Ballard, #10 Incredibly Strange Films, #11 Pranks!, #12 Modern Primitives, and #13 Angry Women.
Special Discount Offer Only: $110 ppd. Seamail/Canada: $120. AIR Europe: $176. AIR Austr/Japan: $200.
FOR *RE/Search #14: Incredibly Strange Music* ADD ONLY $10.

Special Reprints Offer (Save $20!)
Complete set of all RE/Search Classics

Offer includes the Willeford Trilogy, Freaks: We Who Are Not As Others, The Torture Garden, The Atrocity Exhibition, and The Confessions of Wanda von Sacher-Masoch.
Special Discount Offer: $58 ppd. Seamail/Canada: $60. AIR Europe: $85. AIR Austr/Japan $96.

Subscribe to RE/Search:

REGULAR SUBSCRIPTION:
You will receive the next three books published by RE/Search which will include either our numbered interview format serials or Re/Search classics. **$40.**
INSTITUTION SUBSCRIPTION:
Sorry no library or university subscriptions. Please place individual orders from this catalog.
SUBSCRIPTIONS SENT SURFACE MAIL ONLY!
NO AIRMAIL.

Do you know someone who would like our catalog? Write name & address below.

NAME _____

ADDRESS _____

CITY, STATE, ZIP _____

PLEASE SEE PREVIOUS PAGE FOR SPECIAL DISCOUNTS

◆ ◆ ◆ ORDER FORM ◆ ◆ ◆

HAVE YOU ORDERED FROM US BEFORE? circle one **YES NO**

NAME _____

ADDRESS _____

CITY, STATE, ZIP

> **Order by mail or phone:** Phone orders may be placed Monday through Friday, from 10 a.m. to 6 p.m. Pacific Standard Time.
> **Phone #415-362-1465**

Check or Money Order Enclosed (Payable to RE/Search Publications) or

VISA/MasterCard # _____

Exp. Date [____] Signature: _____

MAIL TO: RE/SEARCH PUBLICATIONS
20 ROMOLO ST., #B
SAN FRANCISCO, CA 94133

TITLE	QUANTITY	TOTAL

Subtotal	
CA Residents (add 8½% Sales Tax)	
Shipping/Handling (except Special Discounts)	
Add $3 UPS (Continental U.S. only)	
TOTAL DUE	

SHIPPING & HANDLING CHARGES
First item $4. Add $1 per each additional item.
For UPS add $3 (flat rate per order). You must give a street address—no PO Box addresses.

INTERNATIONAL CUSTOMERS. For SEAMAIL: first item $6; add $2 per each additional item. **For AIRMAIL:** first item $15; add $12 per each additonal item.

ATTENTION CANADIAN CUSTOMERS: WE DO NOT ACCEPT PERSONAL CHECKS EVEN IF IT IS FROM A U.S. DOLLAR ACCOUNT. SEND INTERNATIONAL MONEY ORDERS ONLY! (available from the post office.)

SEND SASE FOR CATALOG (or 4 IRCs for OVERSEAS)
FOR INFORMATION CALL: (415) 362-1465

PAYMENT IN U.S. DOLLARS
ALLOW 6-8 WEEKS FOR DELIVERY

DEC, 1992

Norrie Paramor's *The Zodiac Suite*, Capitol Records.

Ruth Welcome's *Zither Magic*, Capitol Records.
Album cover credits: cover model: Dolores Greer.